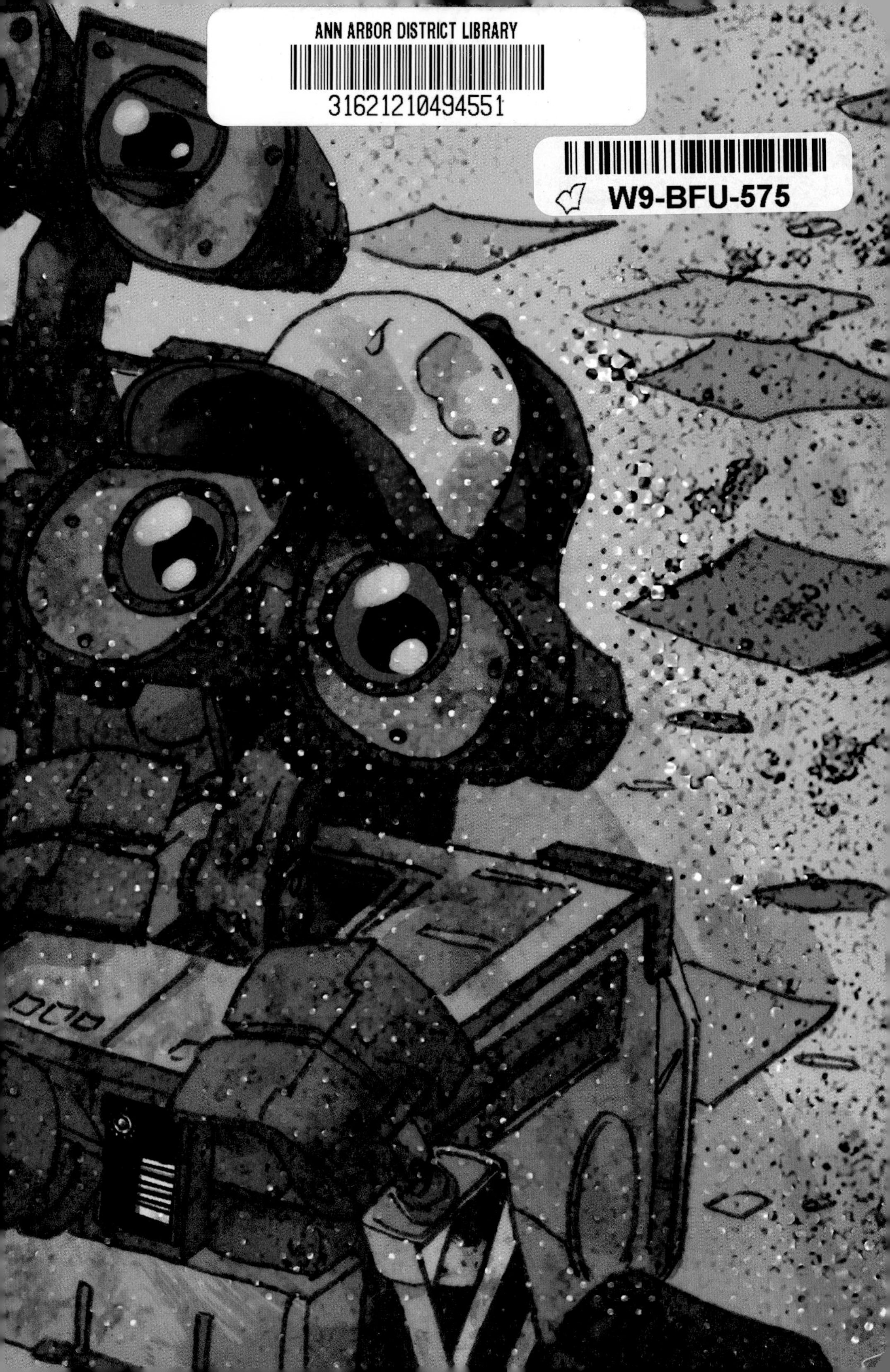

DISNEY · PIXAR
WALL·E
OUT THERE

ROSS RICHIE
chief executive officer

MARK WAID
chief creative officer

MATT GAGNON
editor-in-chief

ADAM FORTIER
vice president,
new business

WES HARRIS
vice president,
publishing

LANCE KREITER
vice president,
licensing & merchandising

CHIP MOSHER
marketing director

FIRST EDITION: JULY 2010

10 9 8 7 6 5 4 3 2 1
FOR INFORMATION REGARDING THE CPSIA ON THIS PRINTED MATERIAL
CALL: 203-595-3636 AND PROVIDE REFERENCE # EAST – 67006

Office of publication: 6310 San Vicente Blvd Ste 404, Los Angeles, CA 90048-5457.

A catalog record for this book is available from OCLC and on our website www.boom-kids.com on the
Librarians page.

WRITER:
BRYCE CARLSON

ARTIST:
MORGAN LUTHI

COLORS:
DIGIKORE STUDIOS

LETTERS:
JOSE MACASOCOL, JR.

DESIGNER:
ERIKA TERRIQUEZ

ASSISTANT EDITOR:
JASON LONG

EDITOR:
AARON SPARROW

COVER:
MORGAN LUTHI

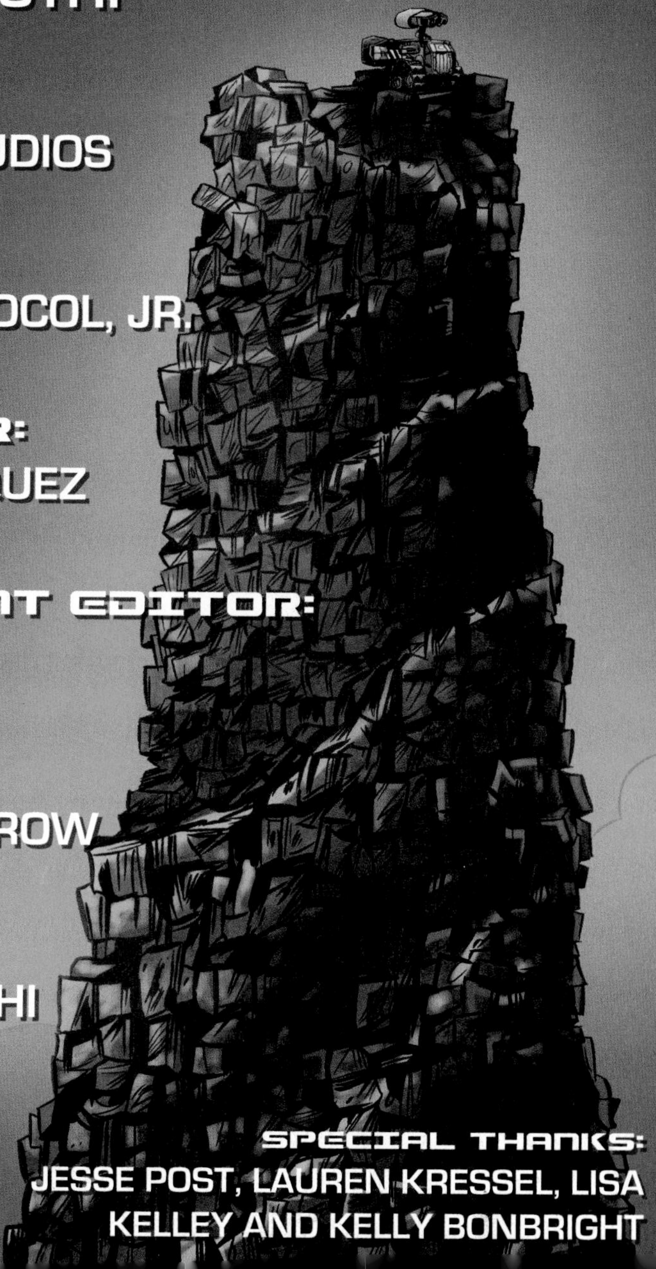

SPECIAL THANKS:
JESSE POST, LAUREN KRESSEL, LISA KELLEY AND KELLY BONBRIGHT

OUT THERE

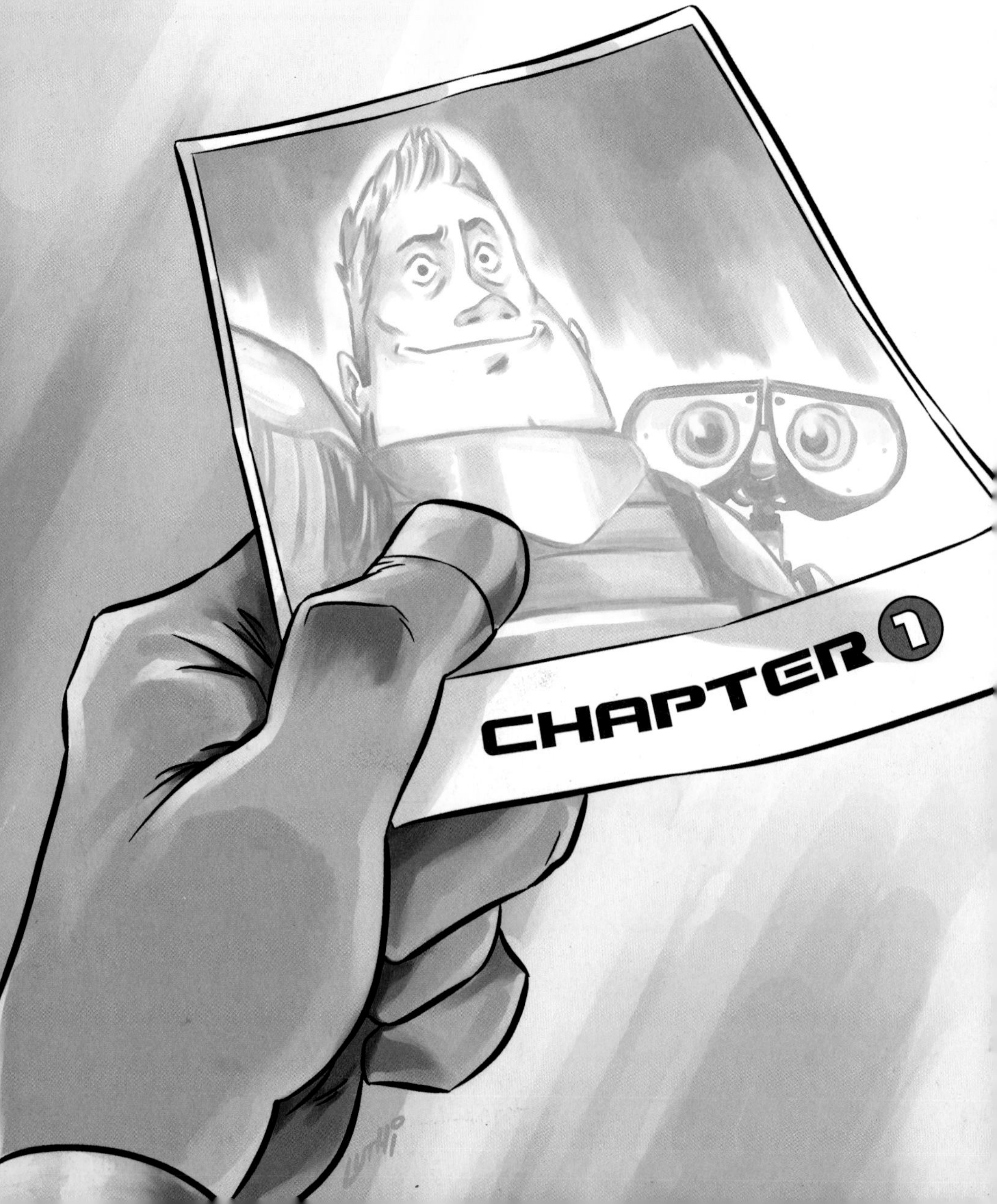
CHAPTER 1

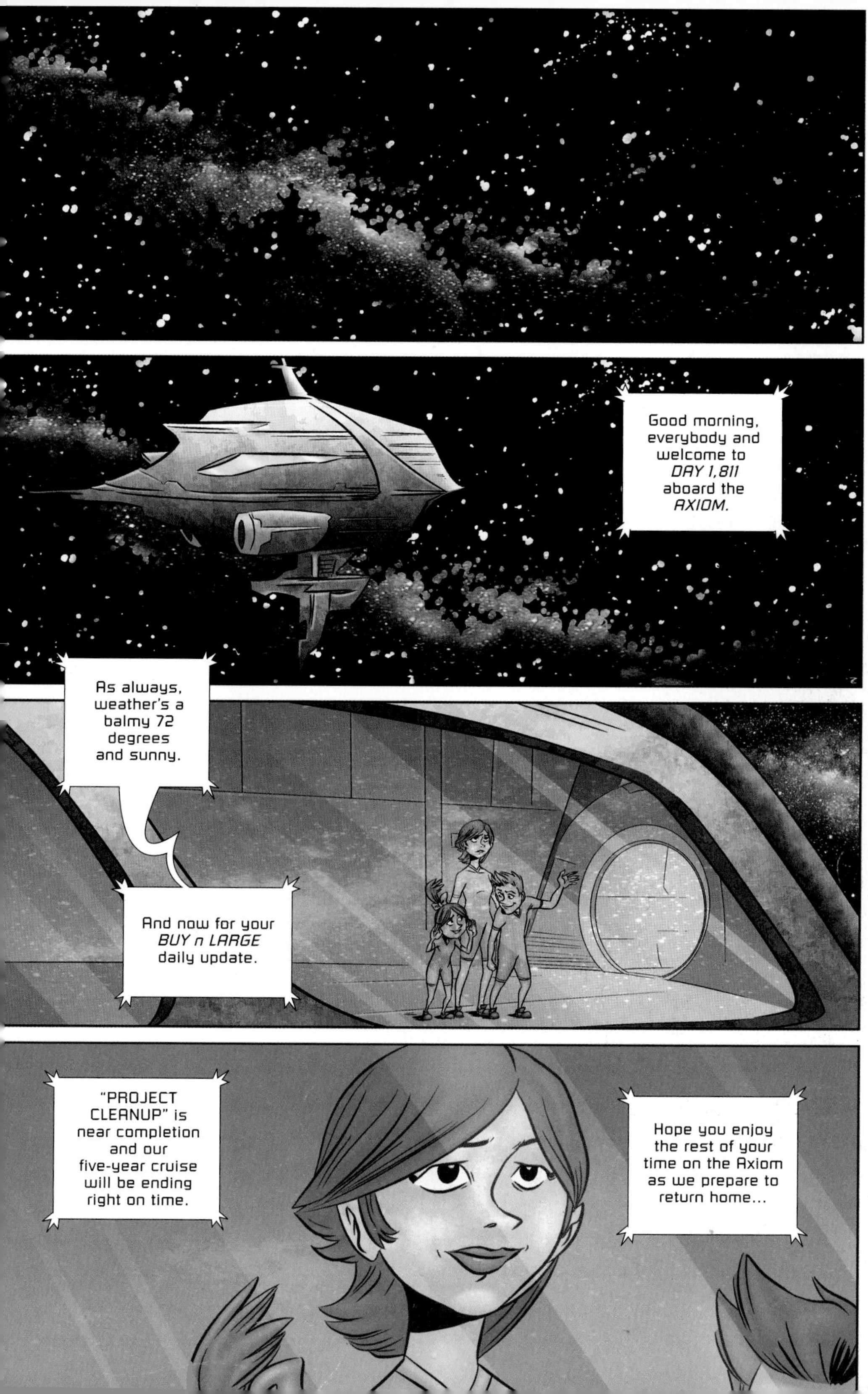

Good morning, everybody and welcome to *DAY 1,811* aboard the *AXIOM.*
As always, weather's a balmy 72 degrees and sunny.
And now for your *BUY n LARGE* daily update.
"PROJECT CLEANUP" is near completion and our five-year cruise will be ending right on time.
Hope you enjoy the rest of your time on the Axiom as we prepare to return home...

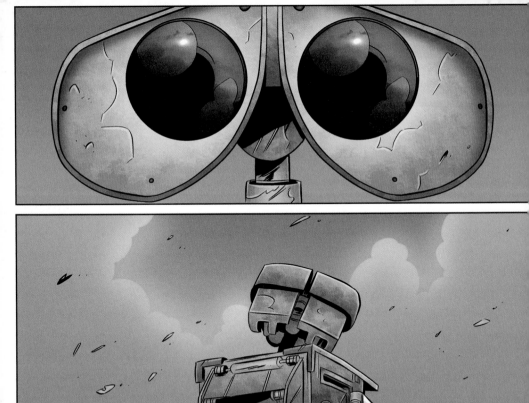

BZZEEEN

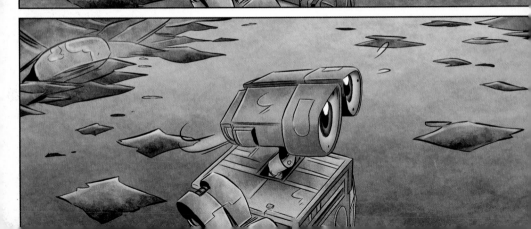

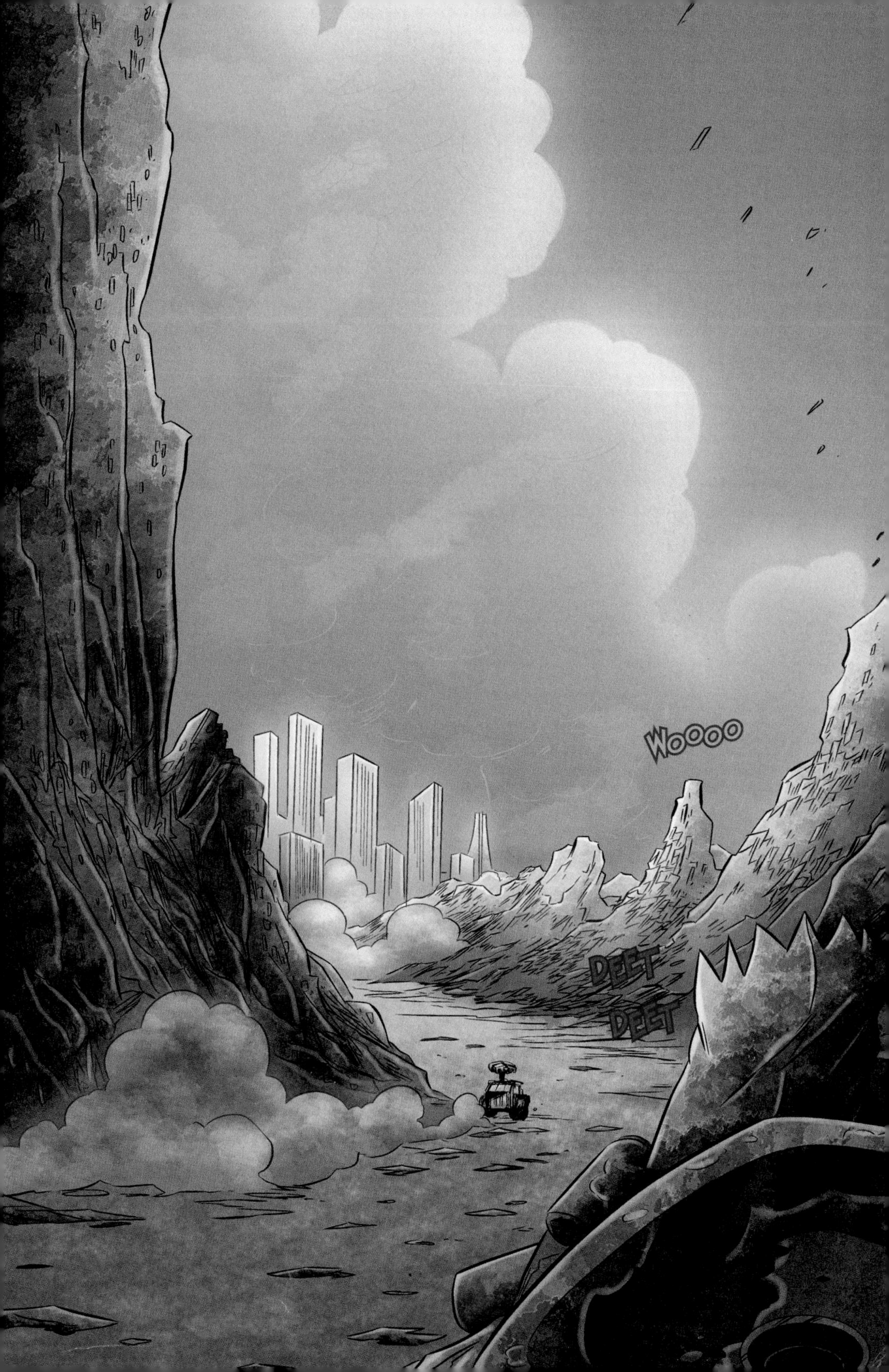
WOOOO
DEET
DEET

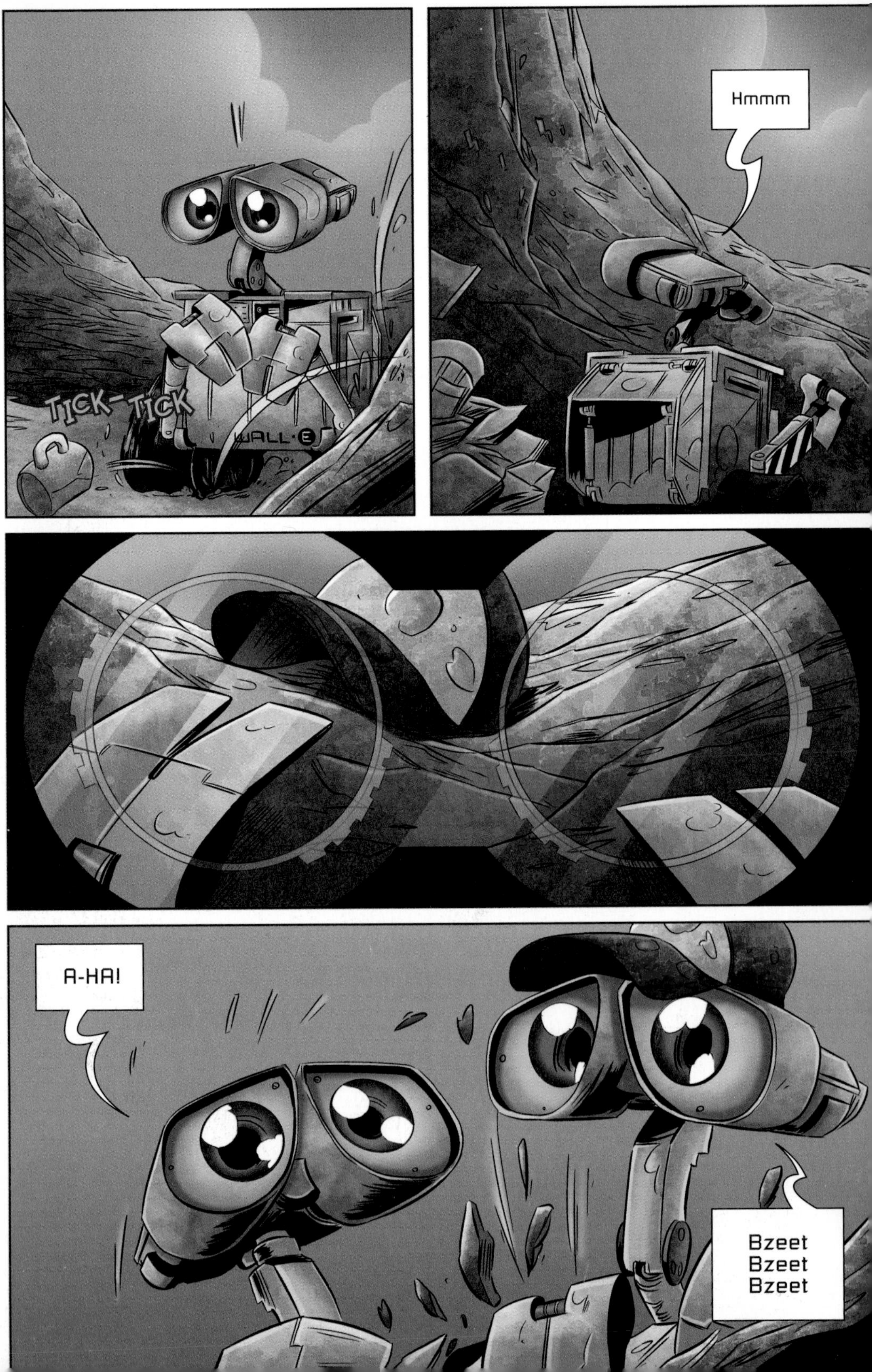
TICK-TICK
WALL·E
Hmmm
A-HA!
Bzeet
Bzeet
Bzeet

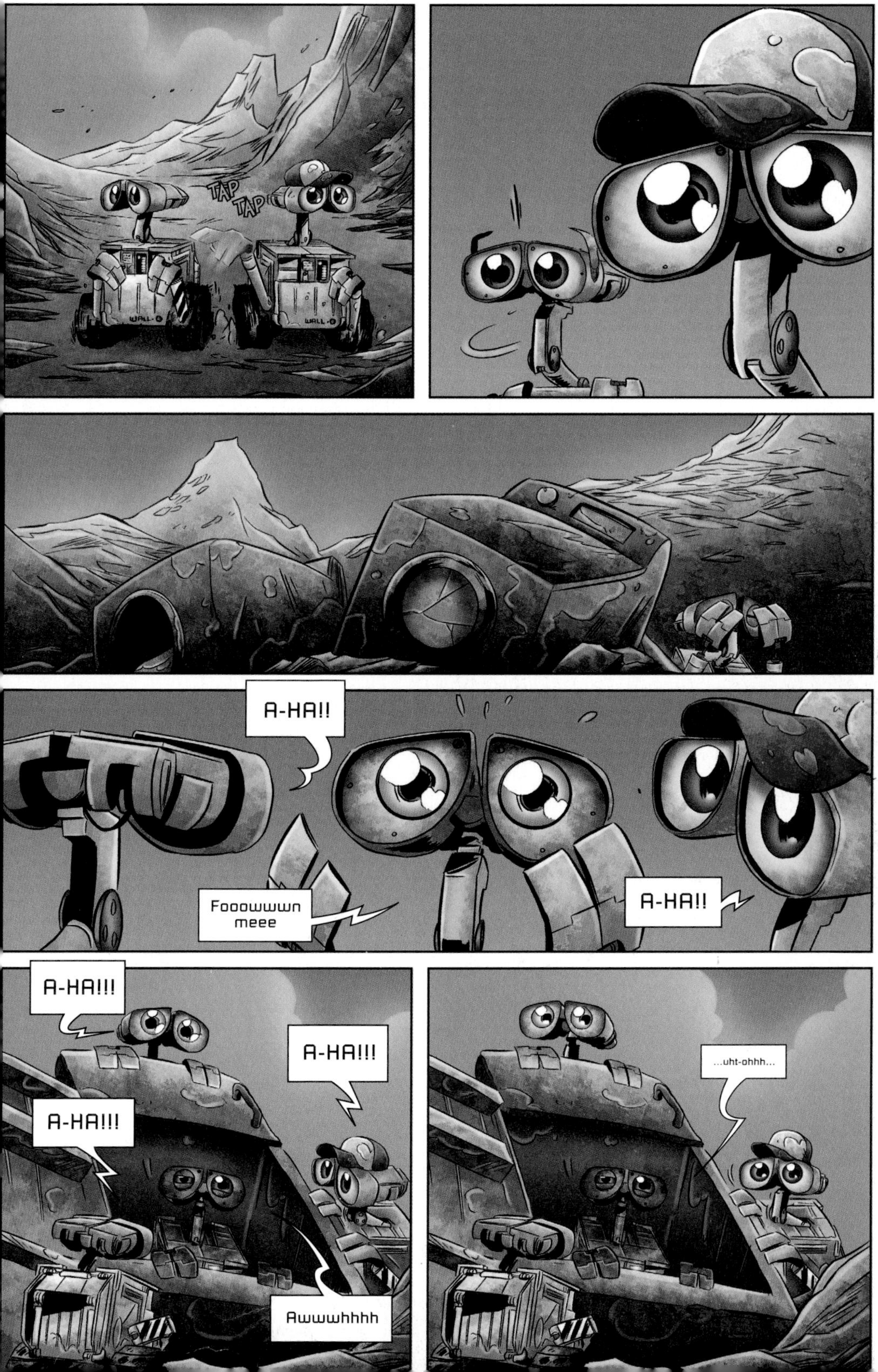
TAP
TAP
A-HA!!
Fooowwwn meee
A-HA!!
A-HA!!!
A-HA!!!
A-HA!!!
Awwwhhhh
...uht-ohhh...

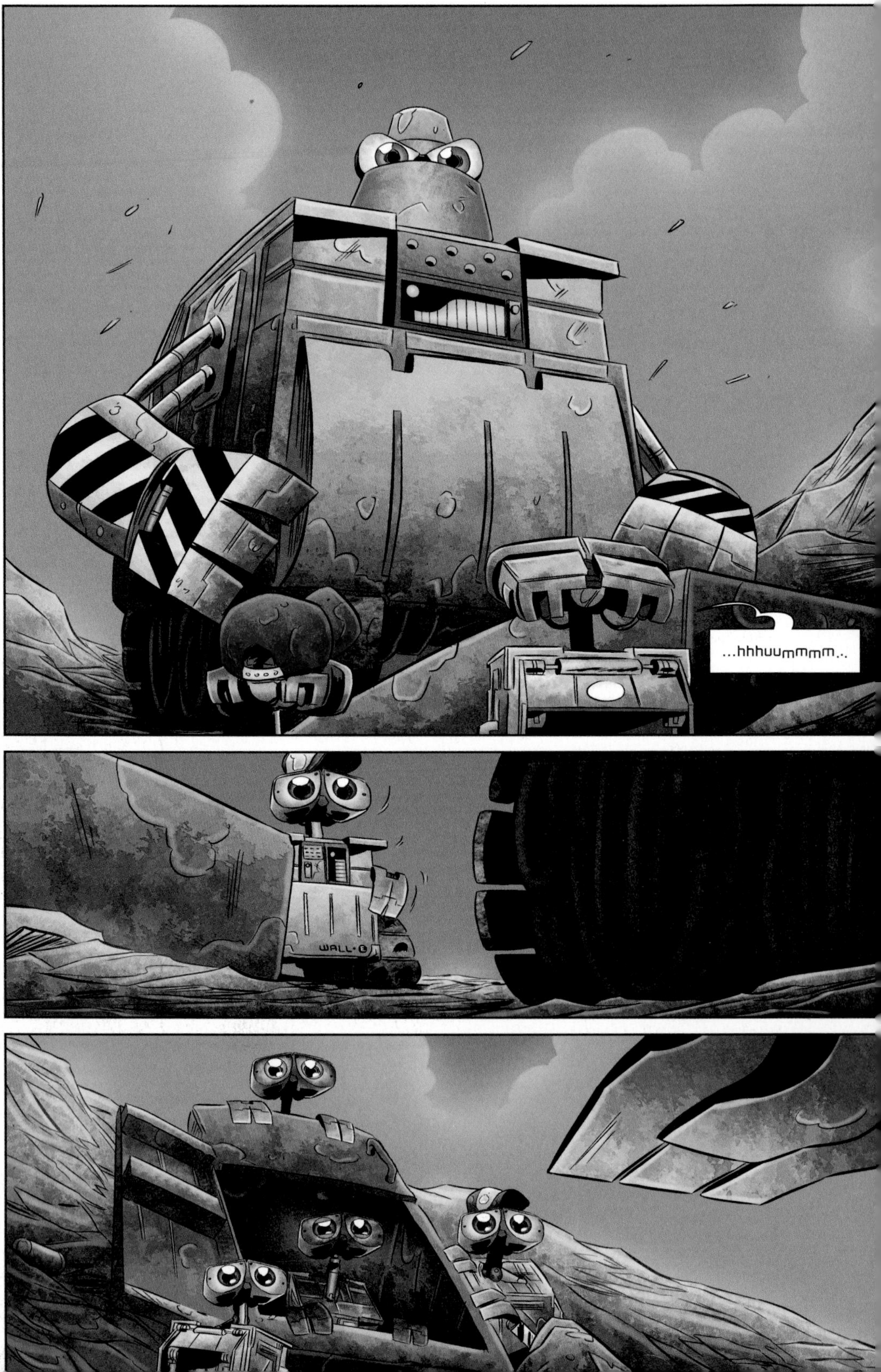
...hhhuummmm...
WALL-E

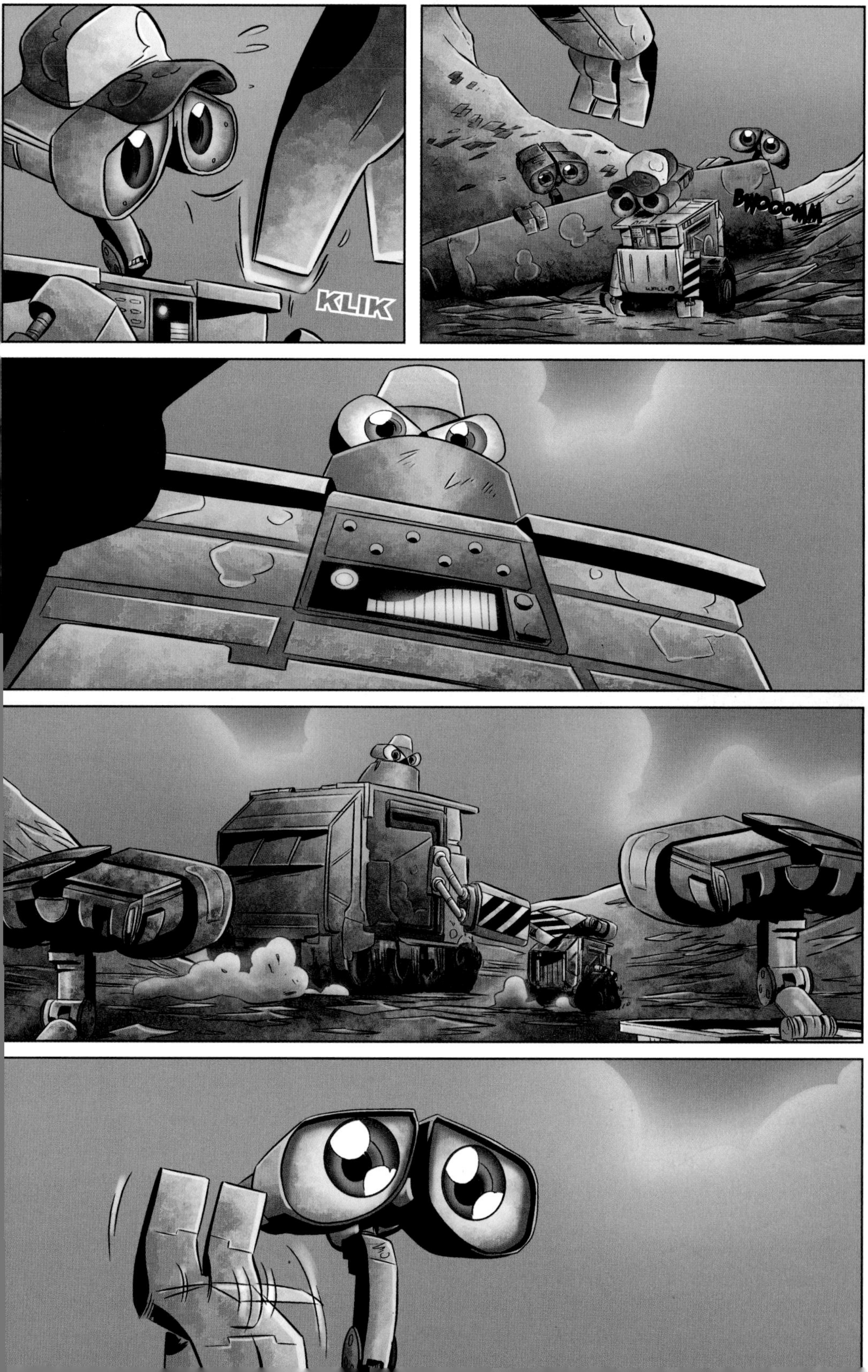
KLIK
BWOOOMM
WALL•E

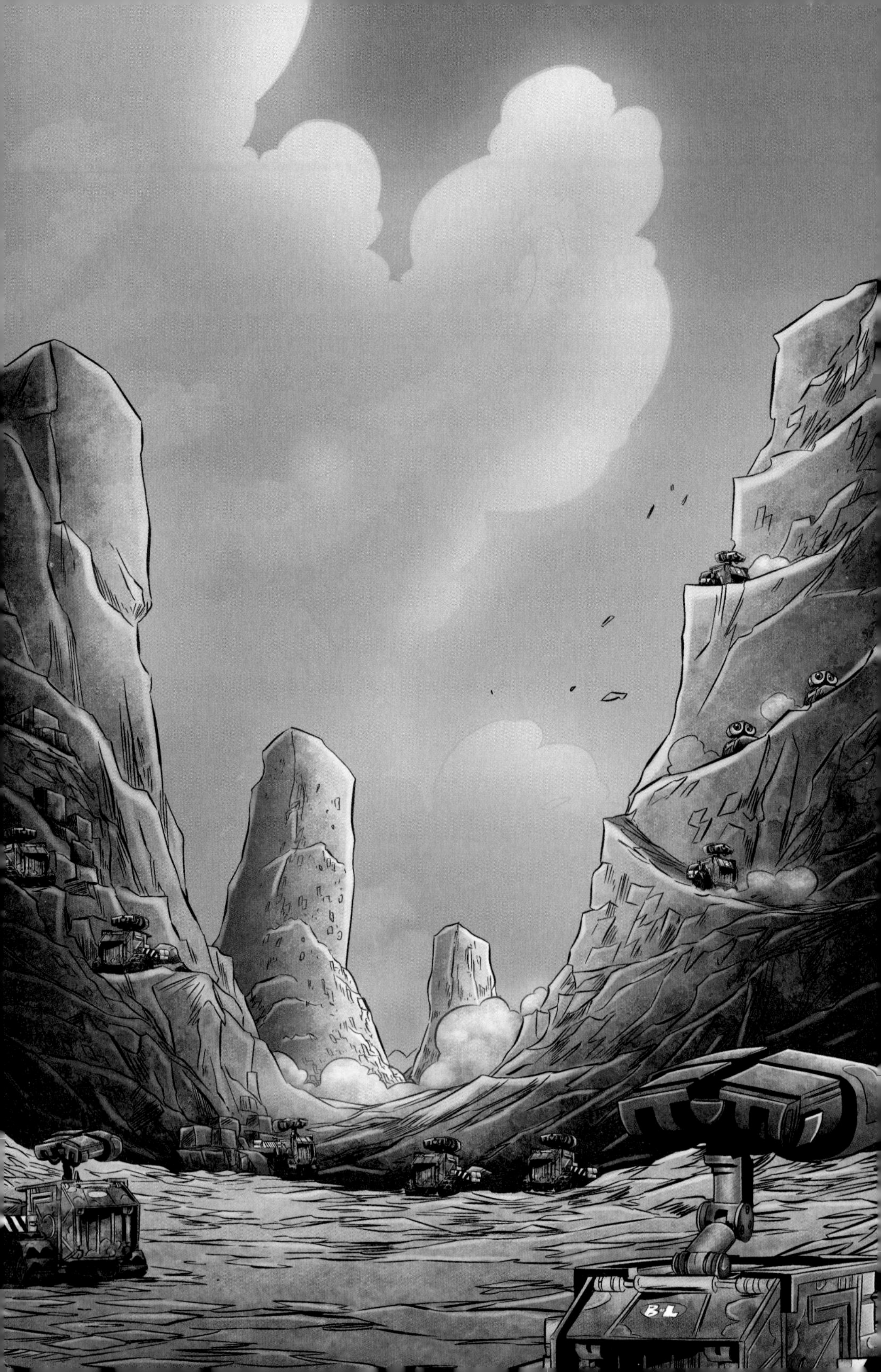
B·L

♪
TIK
TIK

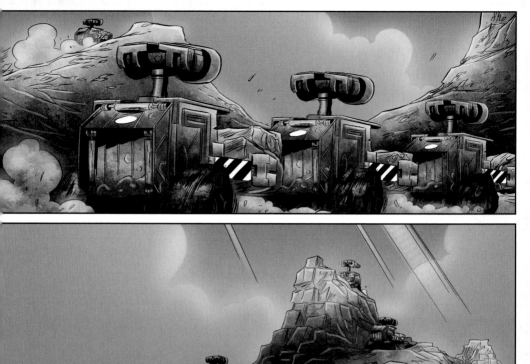

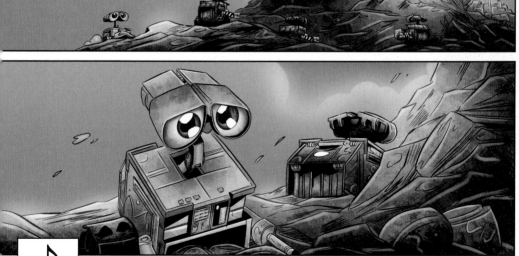

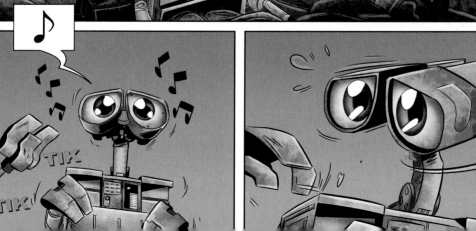

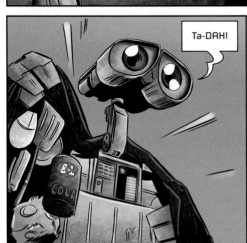

Ta-DAH!

hHMmmm

fiSsSsSs

whoa...

♪♪♪

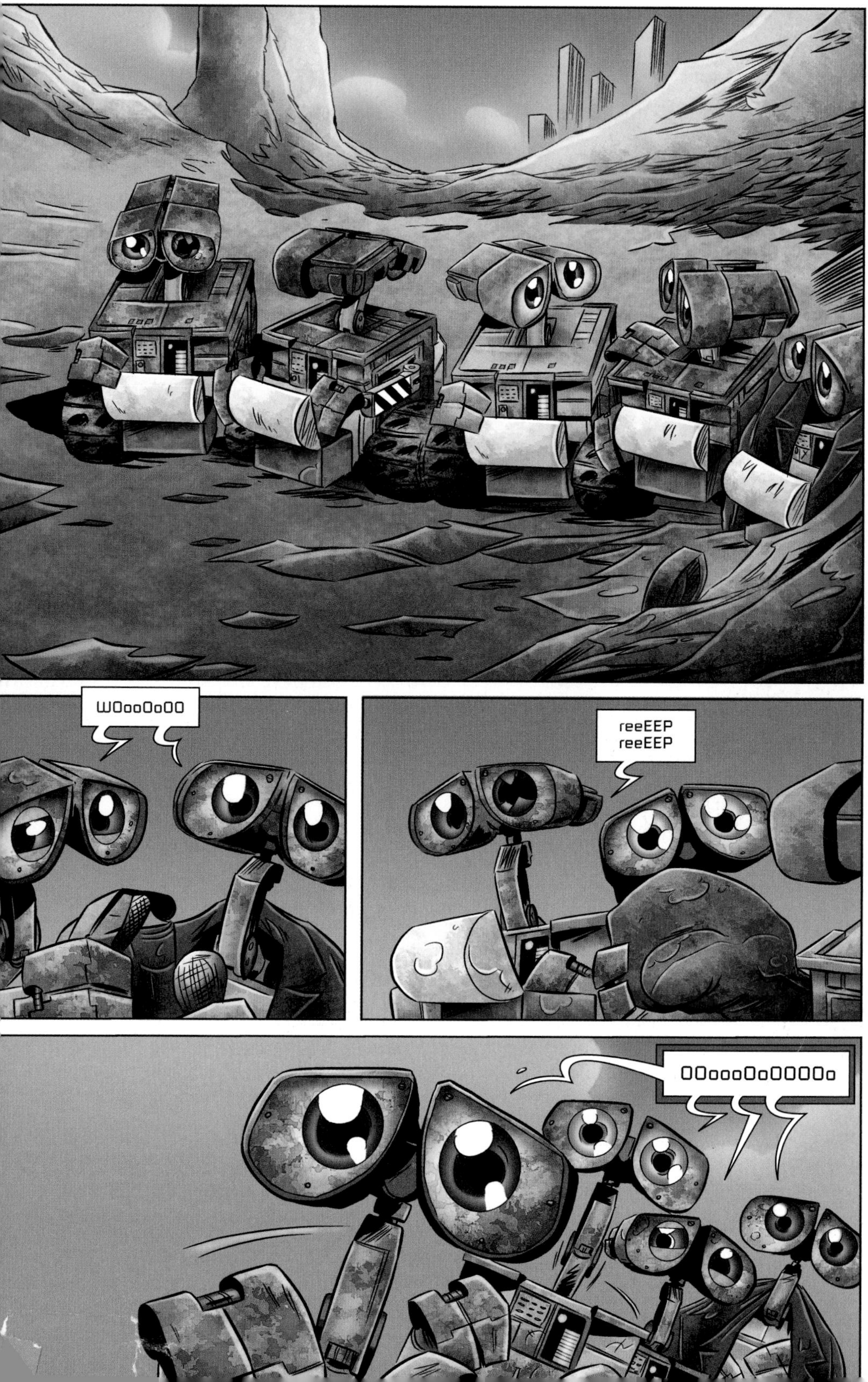
WOooOoOO
reeEEP reeEEP
OOoooOoOOOOo

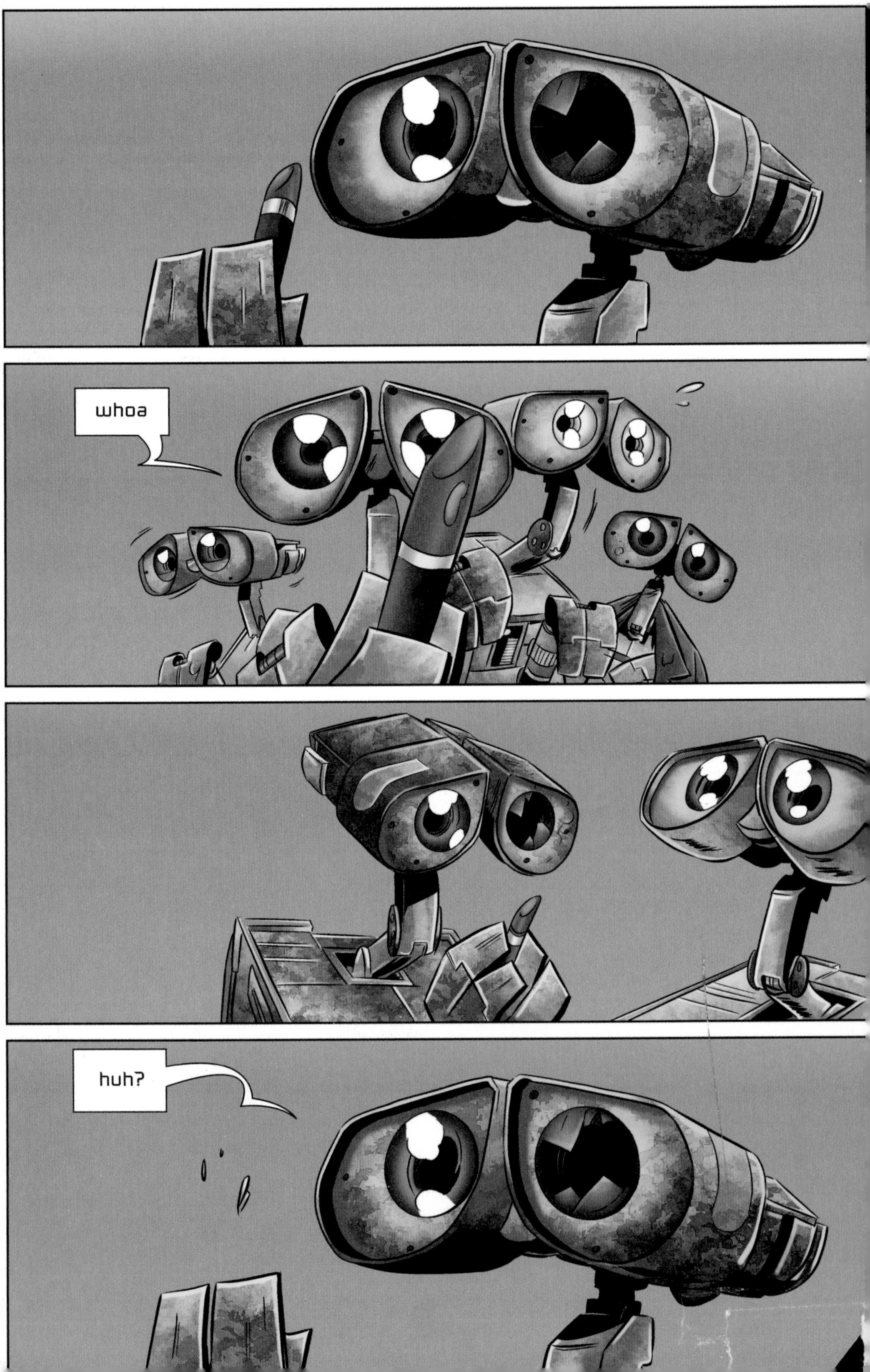
whoa
huh?

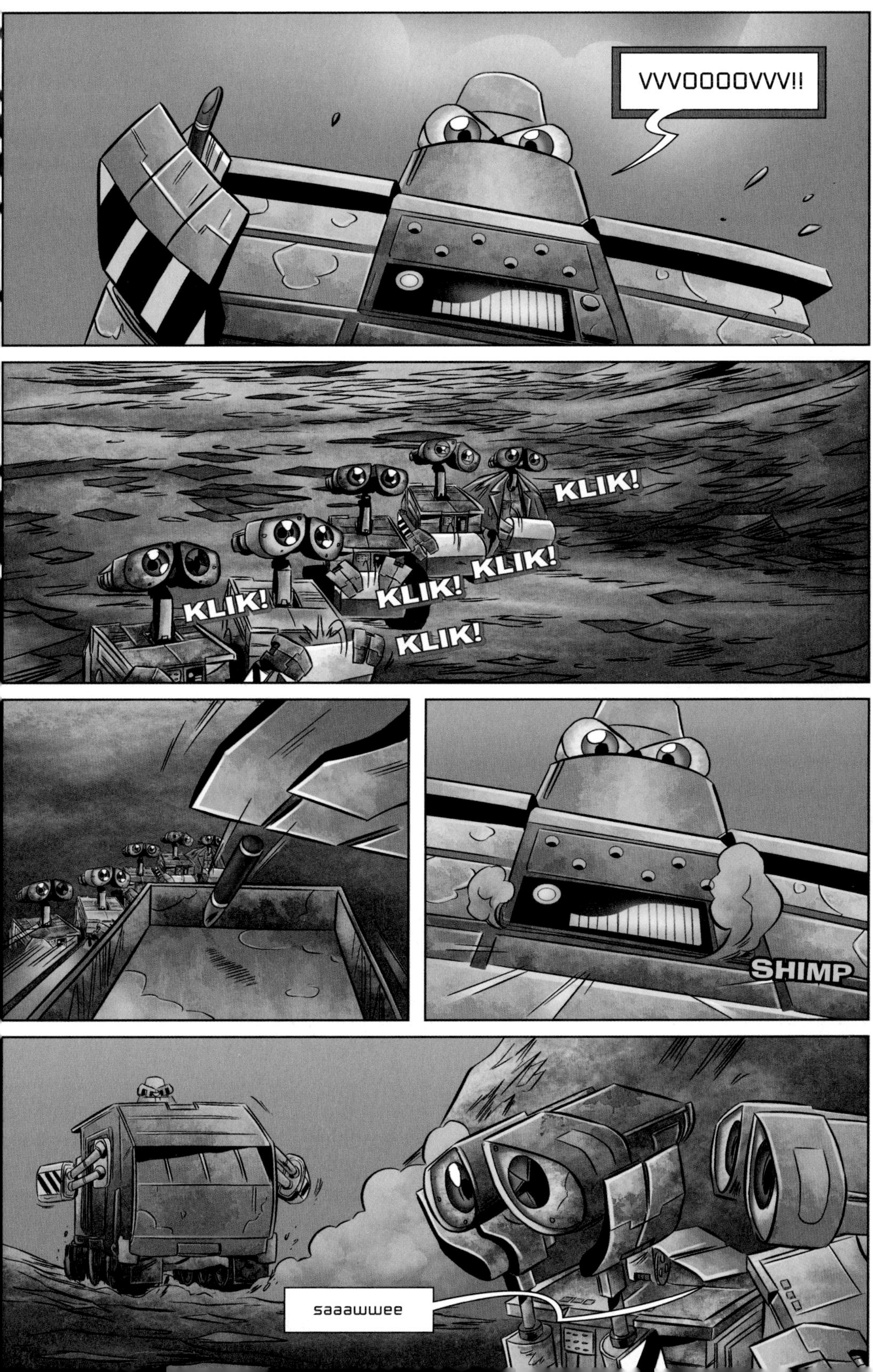
VVVOOOOVVV!!
KLIK!
KLIK!
KLIK!
KLIK!
KLIK!
SHIMP
saaawwee

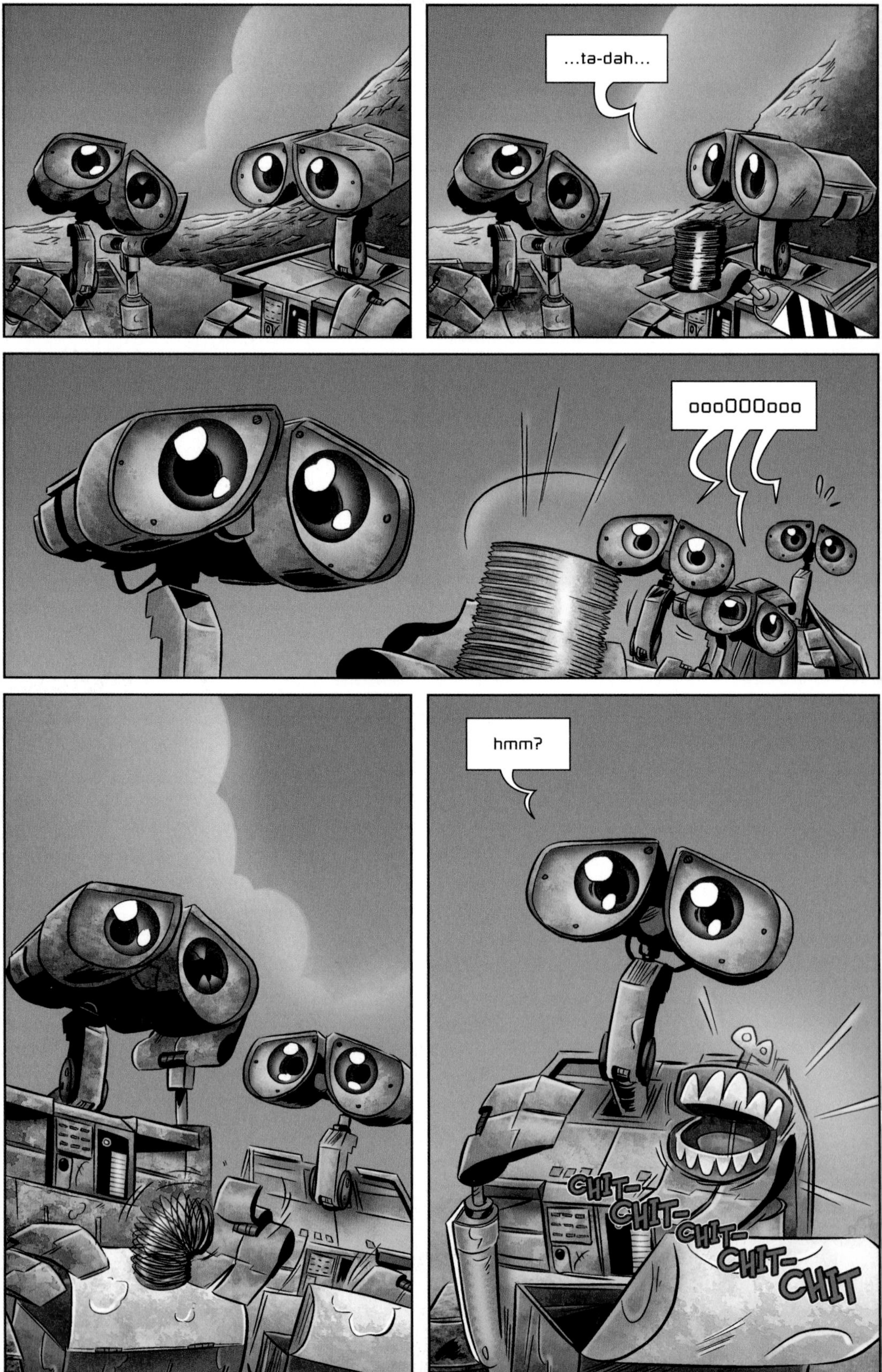
...ta-dah...
oooOOOooo
hmm?
CHIT-
CHIT-
CHIT-
CHIT-
CHIT

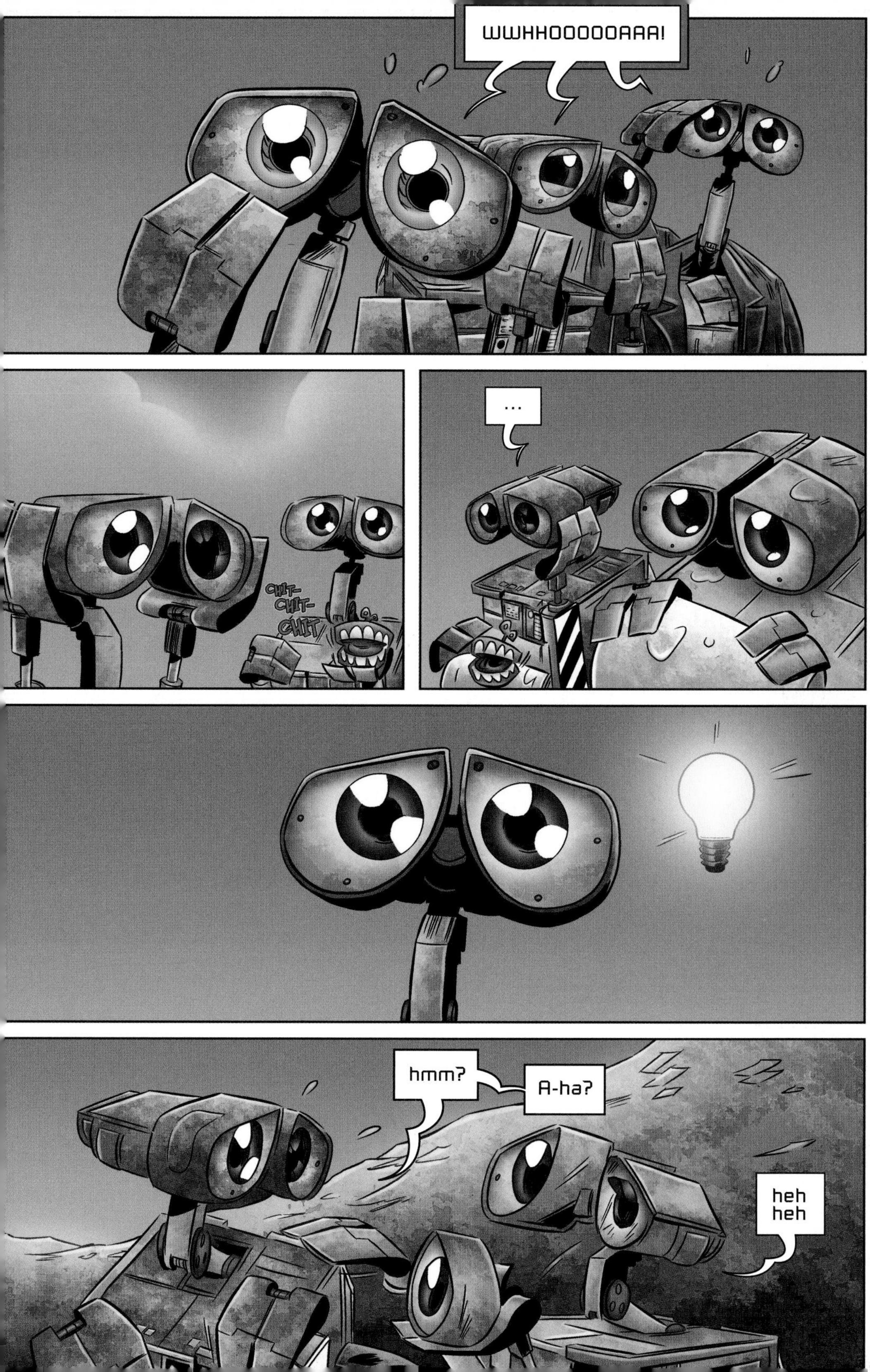
WWHHOOOOOAAA!
CHIT-
CHIT-
CHIT
...
hmm?
A-ha?
heh
heh

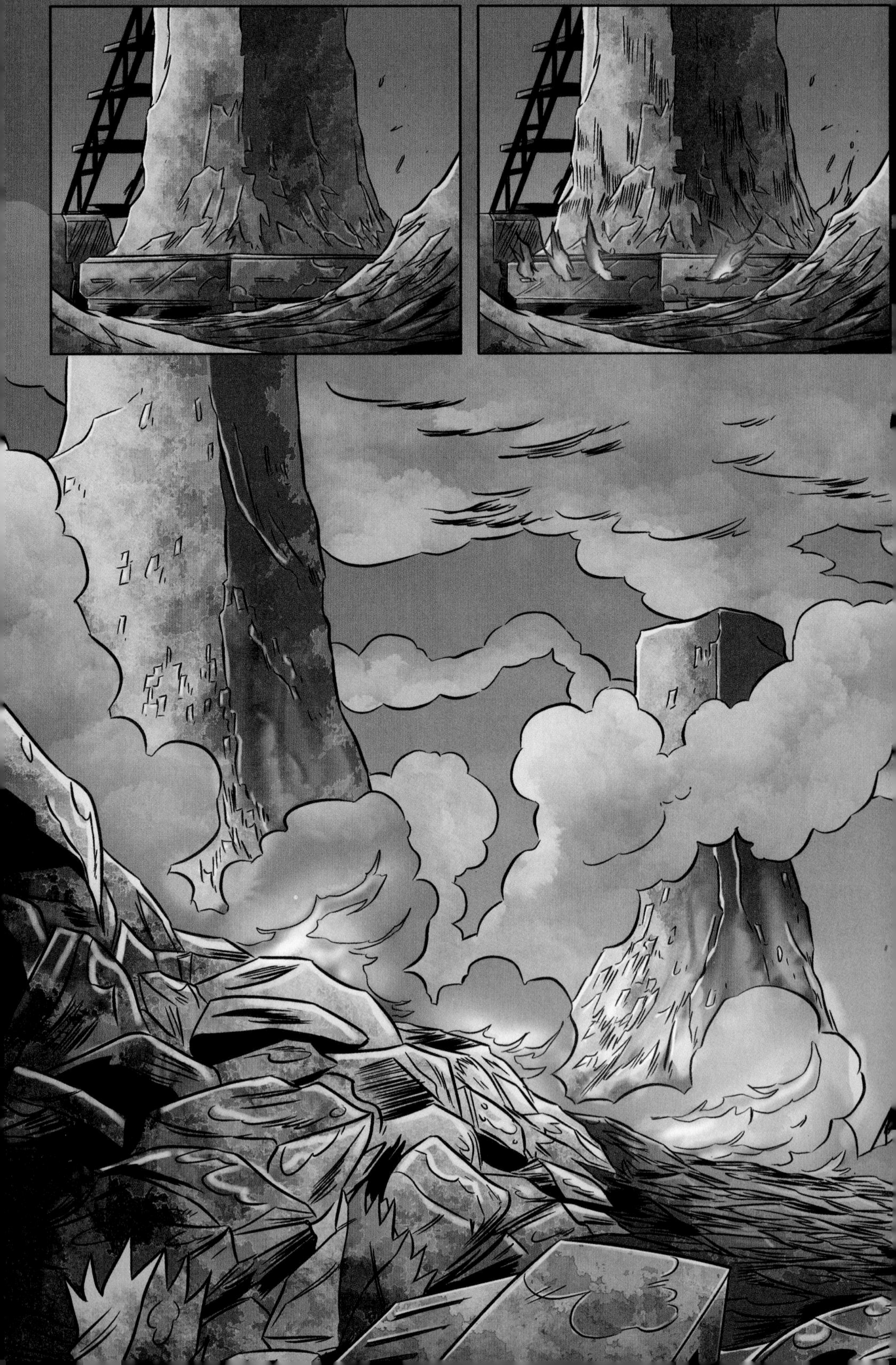

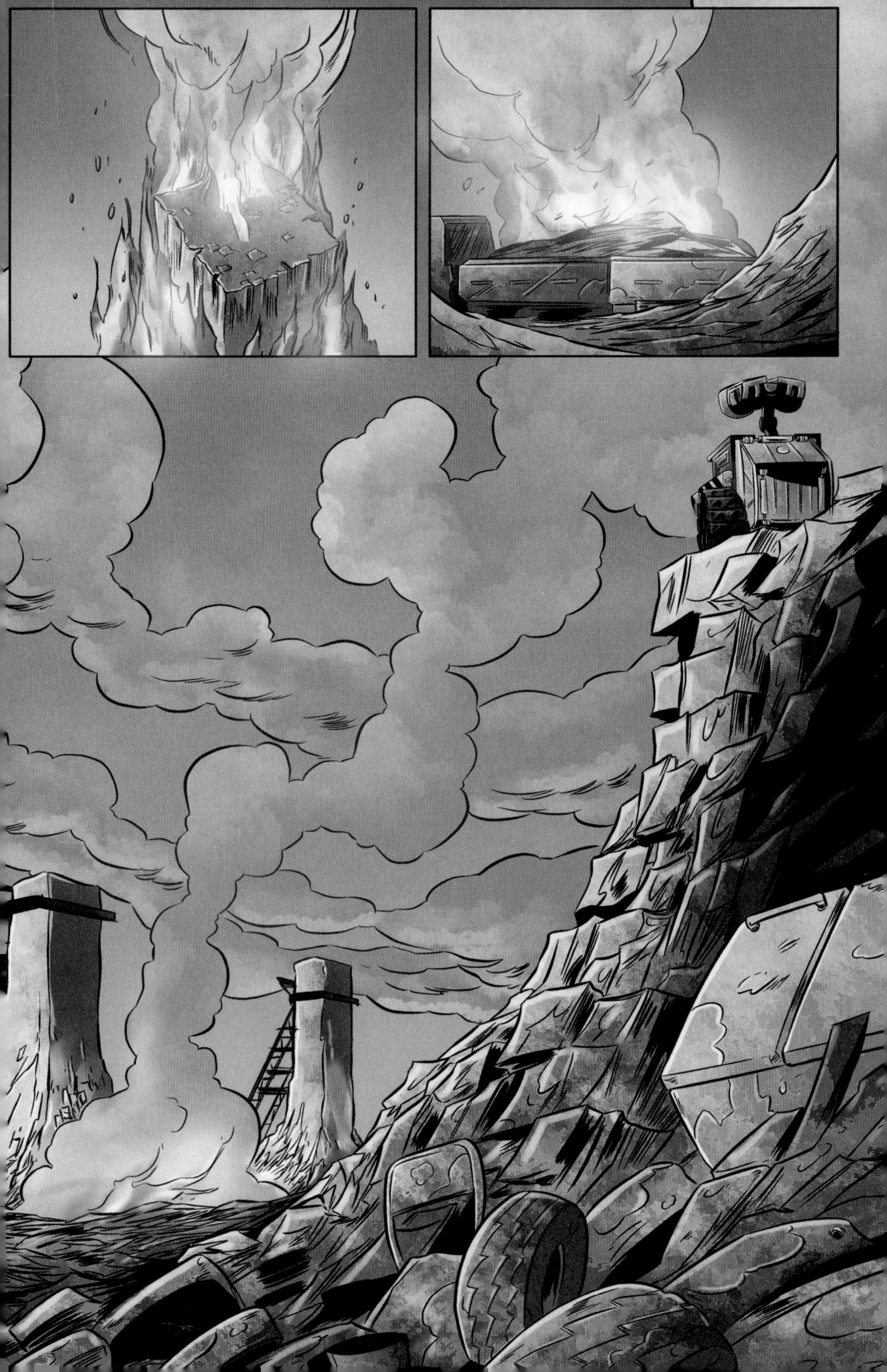

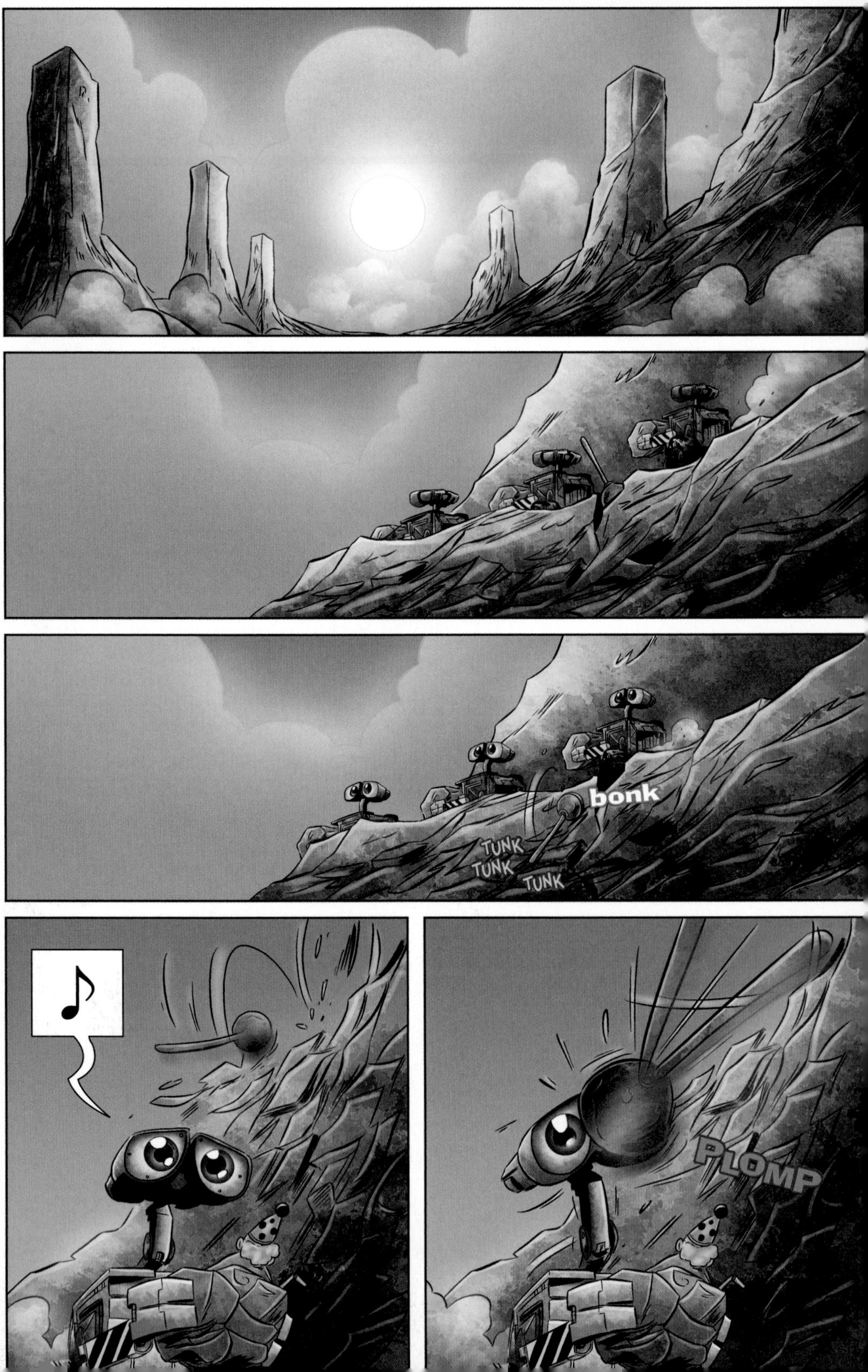
bonk
TUNK
TUNK
TUNK
♪
PLOMP

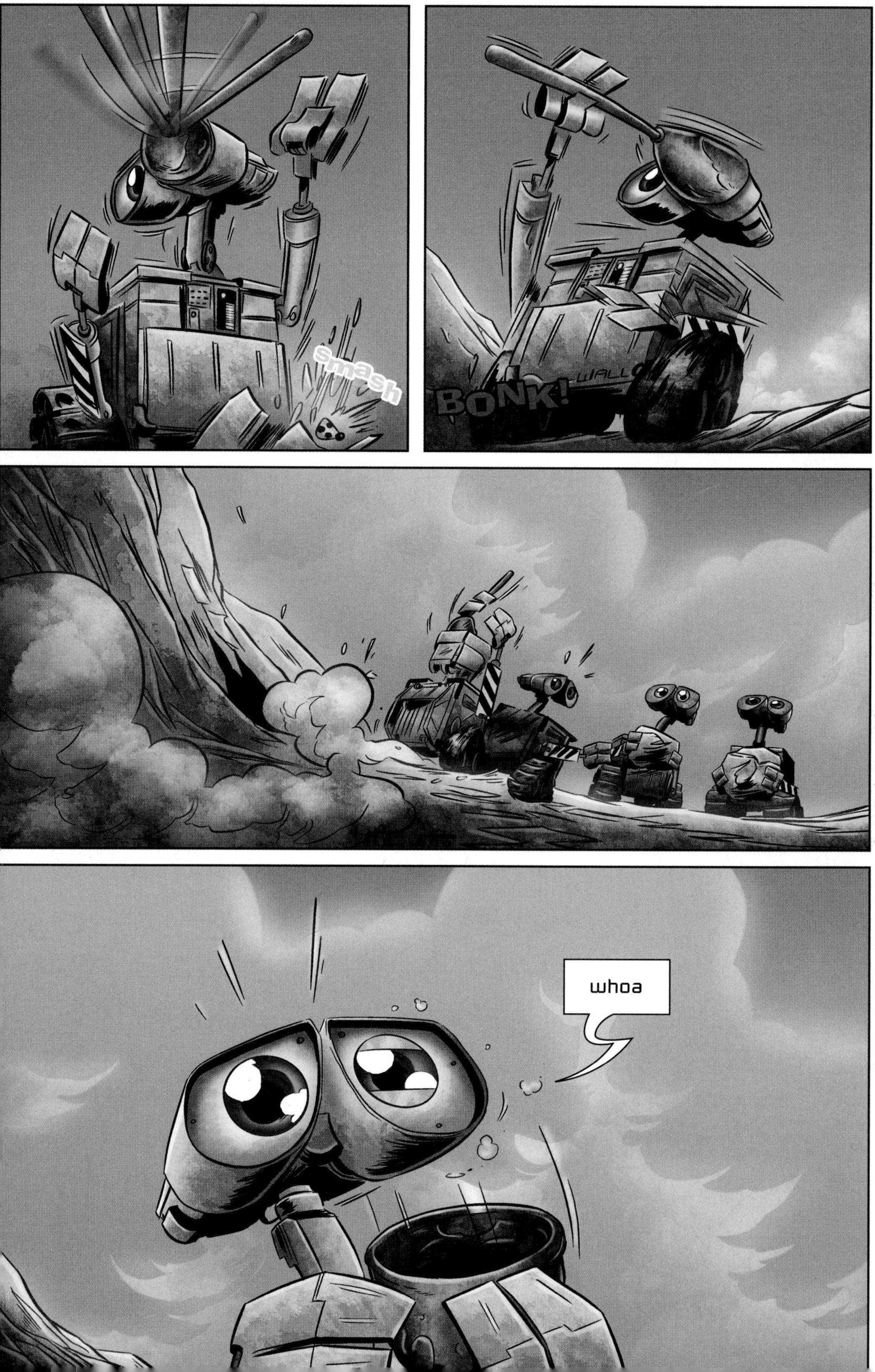
smash
BONK!
WALL
whoa

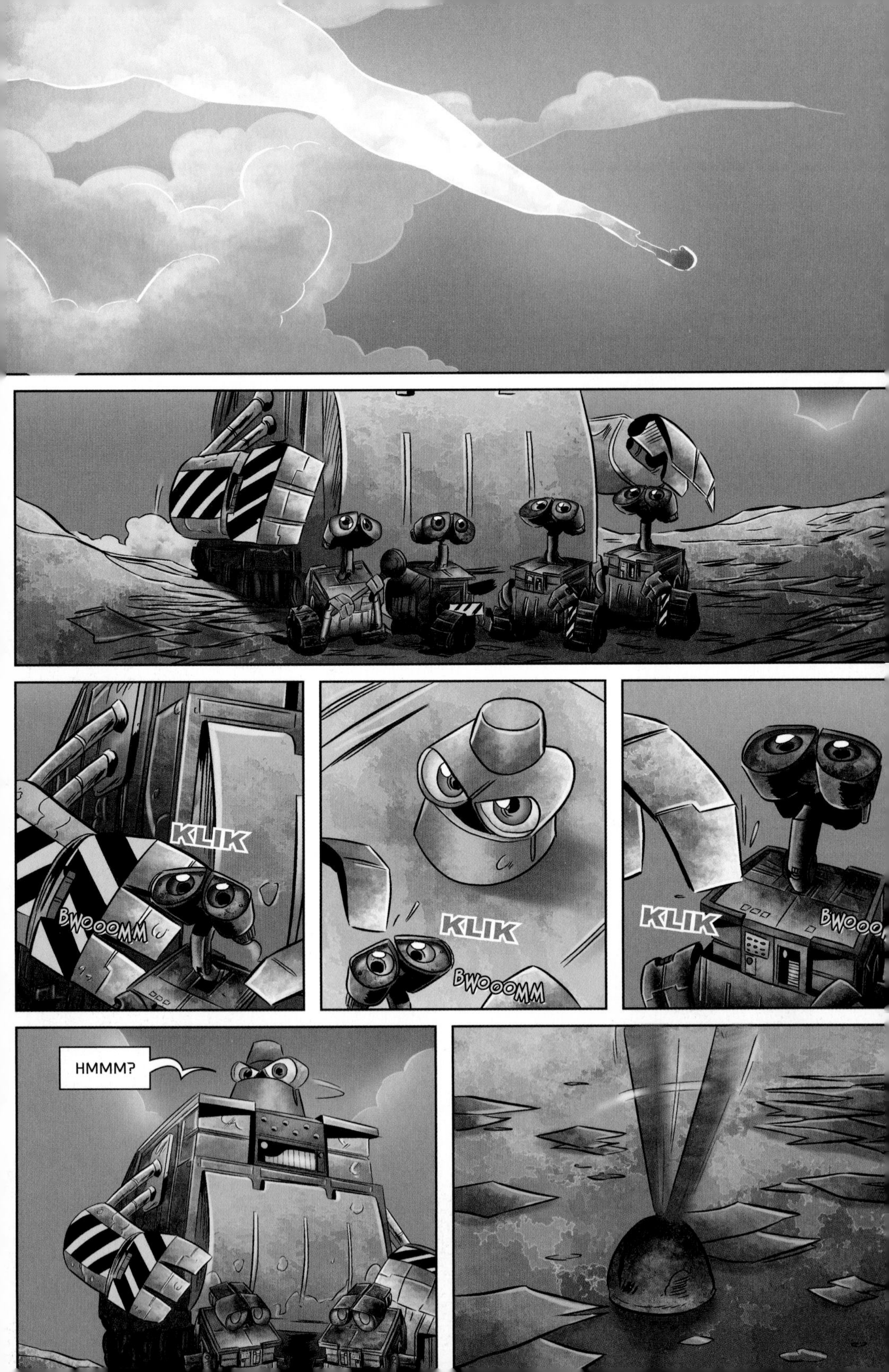
KLIK
BWOOOMM
KLIK
BWOOOMM
KLIK
BWOOO
HMMM?

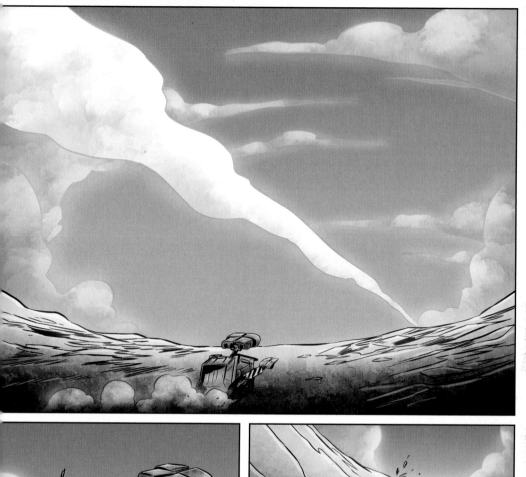

SLAM

D-DUH

D-DUH
D-DUH

...

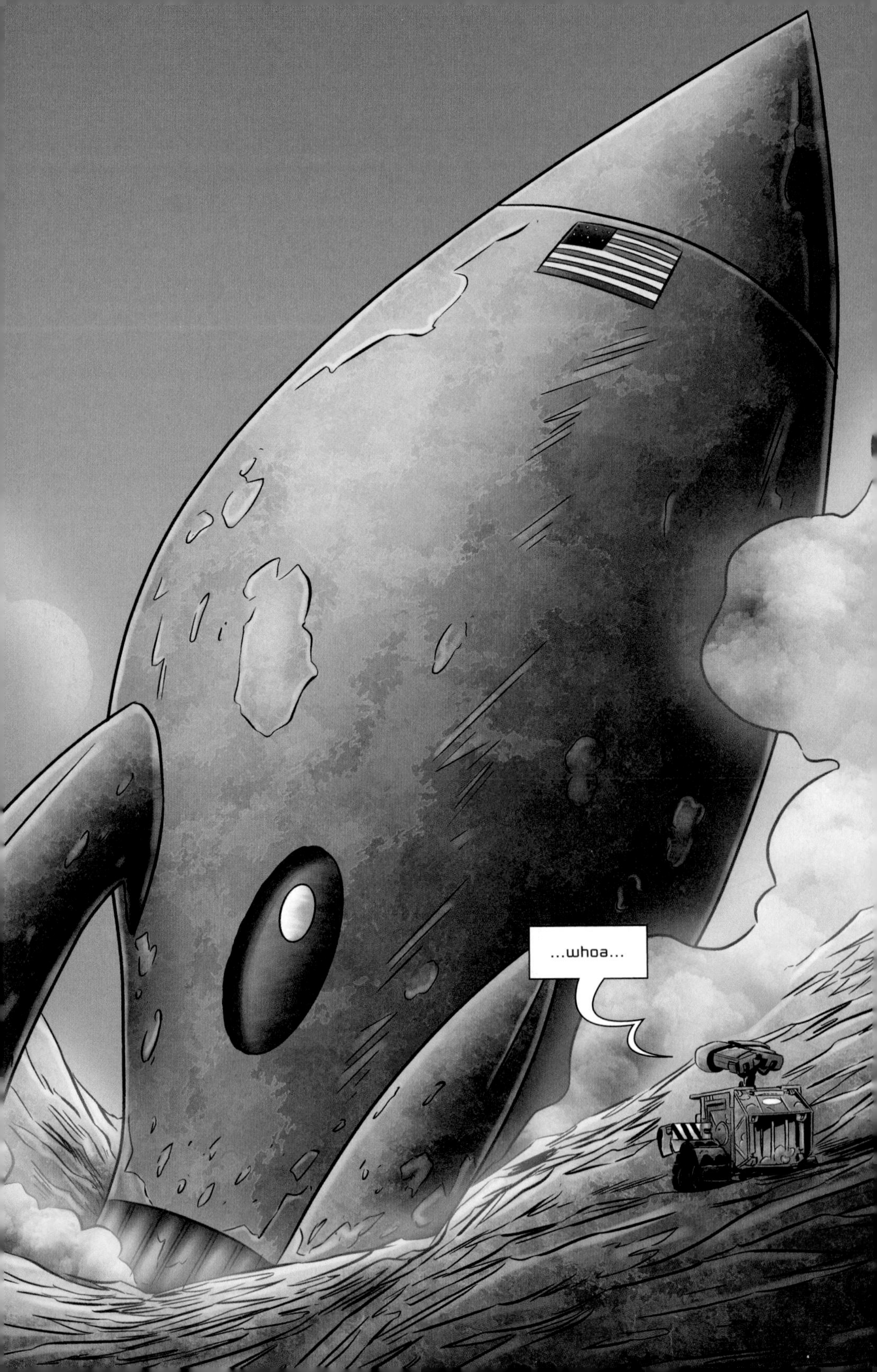
...whoa...

CHAPTER 2

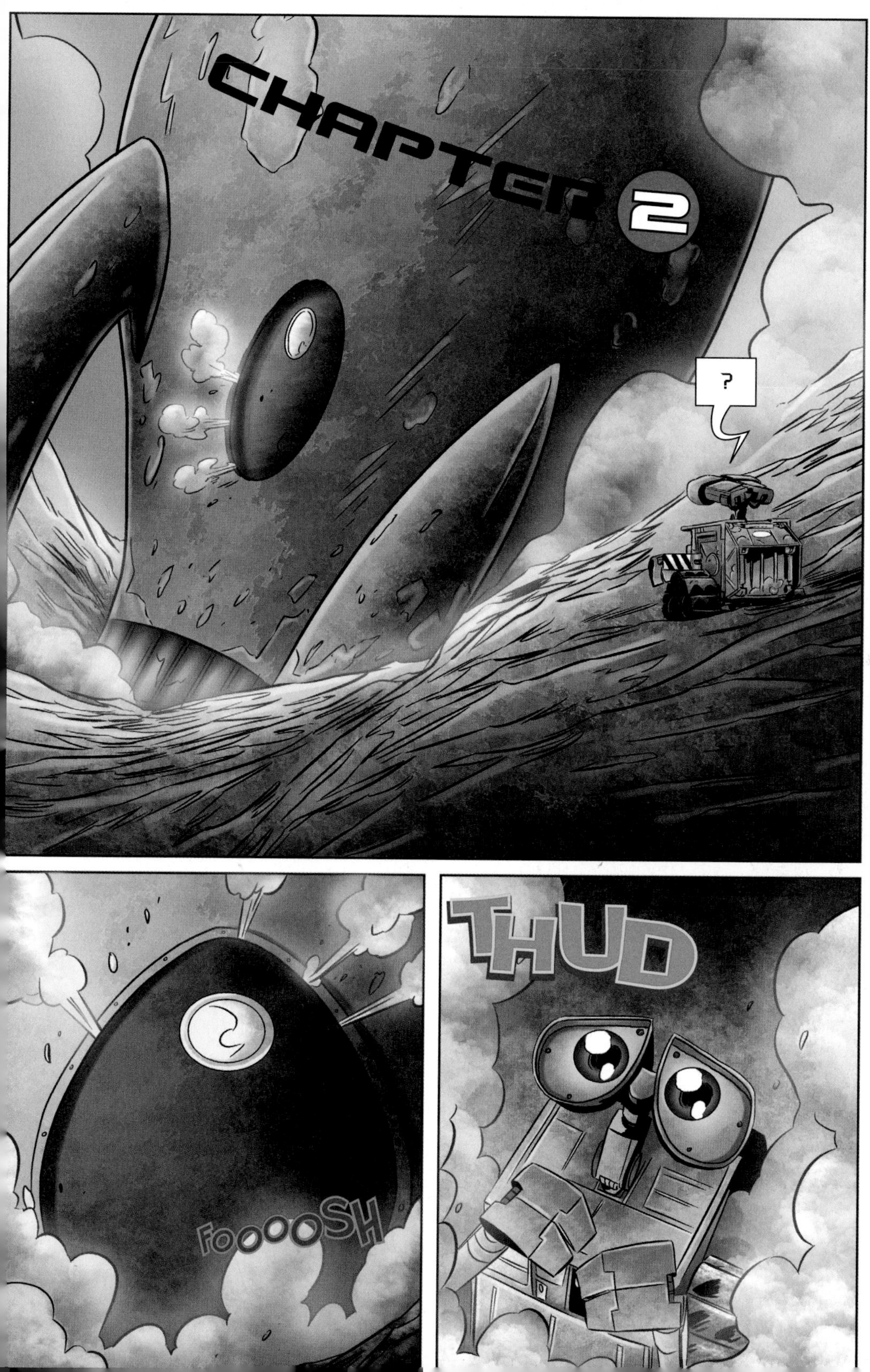
?
FOOOOOSH
THUD

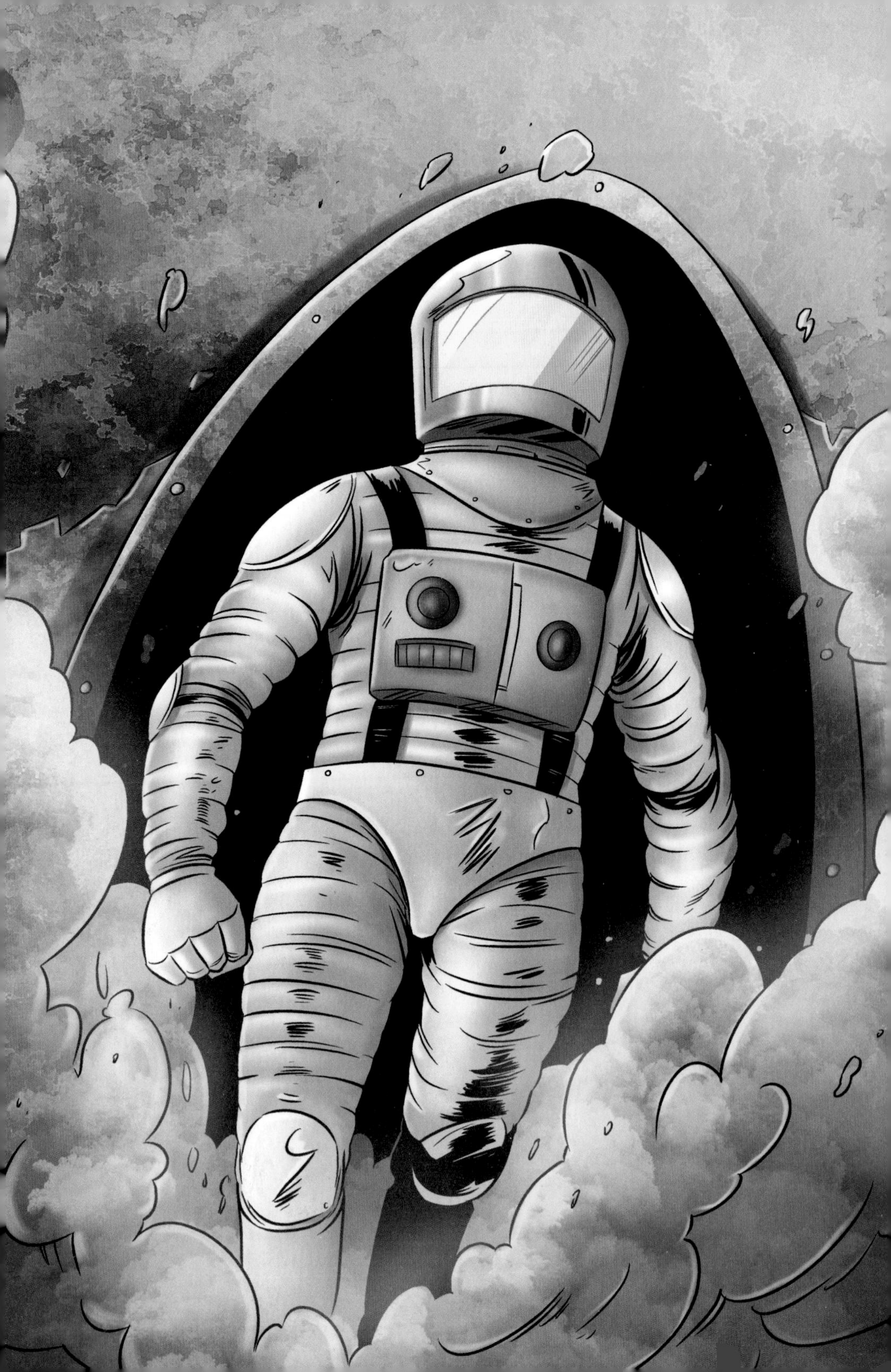

HEY THERE, LITTLE BUDDY.
HmMmm?
HEHEH.
HEYA.
OH,
E MY
UEST.
SO WHAT DO THEY CALL YOU, LITTLE BUDDY?
WAAALLeeee.

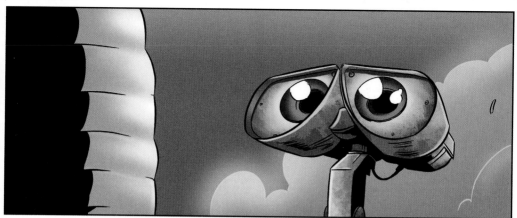

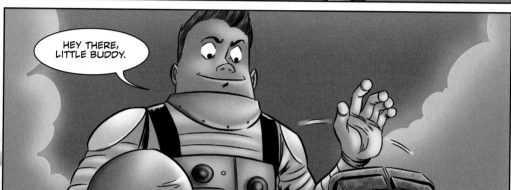

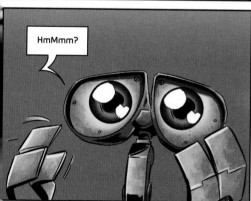

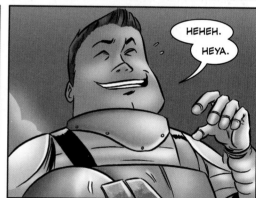

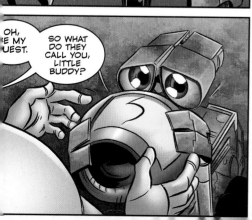

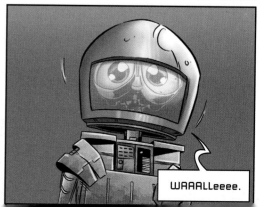

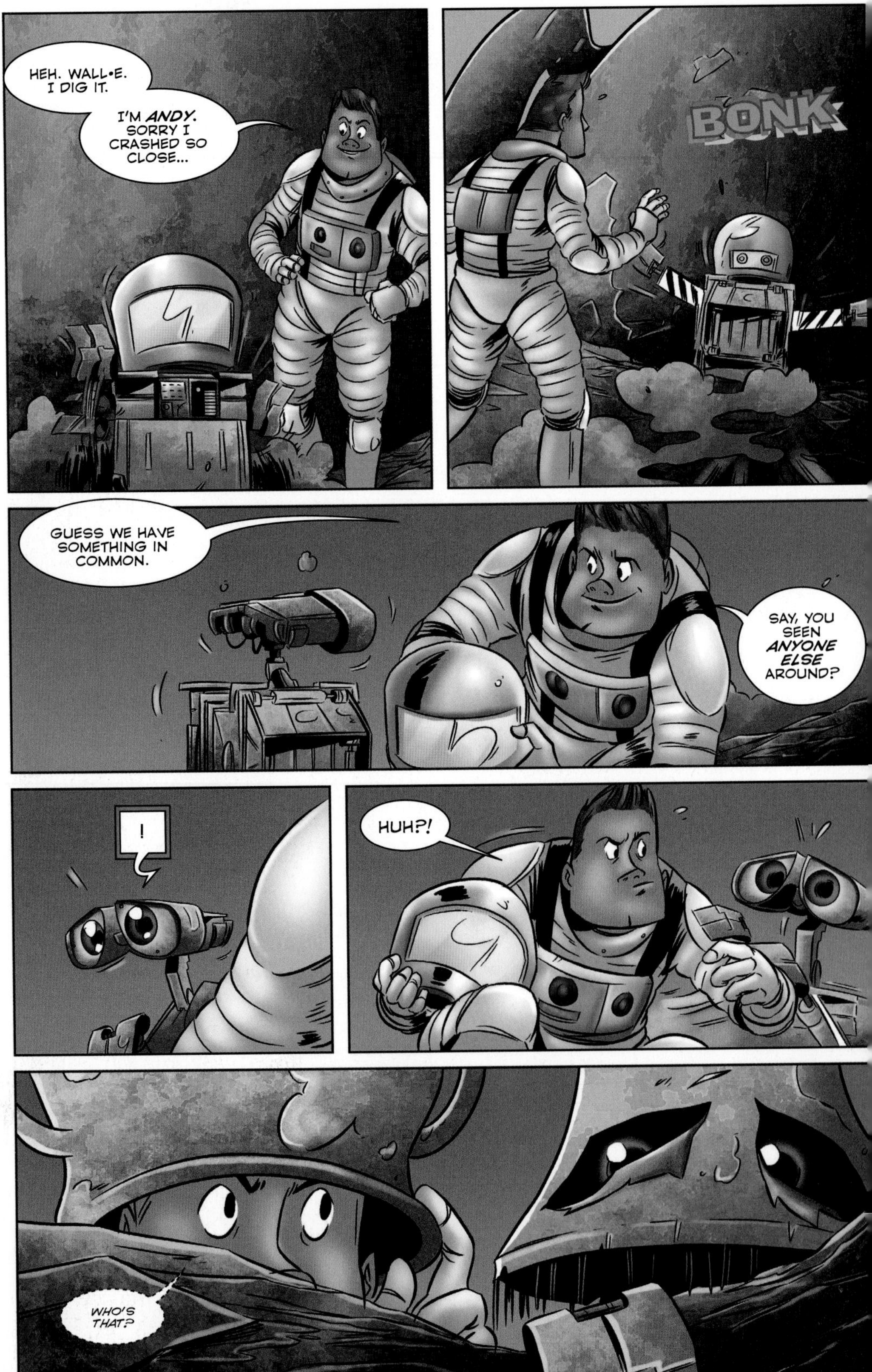
HEH. WALL•E. I DIG IT.
I'M ANDY. SORRY I CRASHED SO CLOSE...
BONK
GUESS WE HAVE SOMETHING IN COMMON.
SAY, YOU SEEN ANYONE ELSE AROUND?
!
HUH?!
WHO'S THAT?

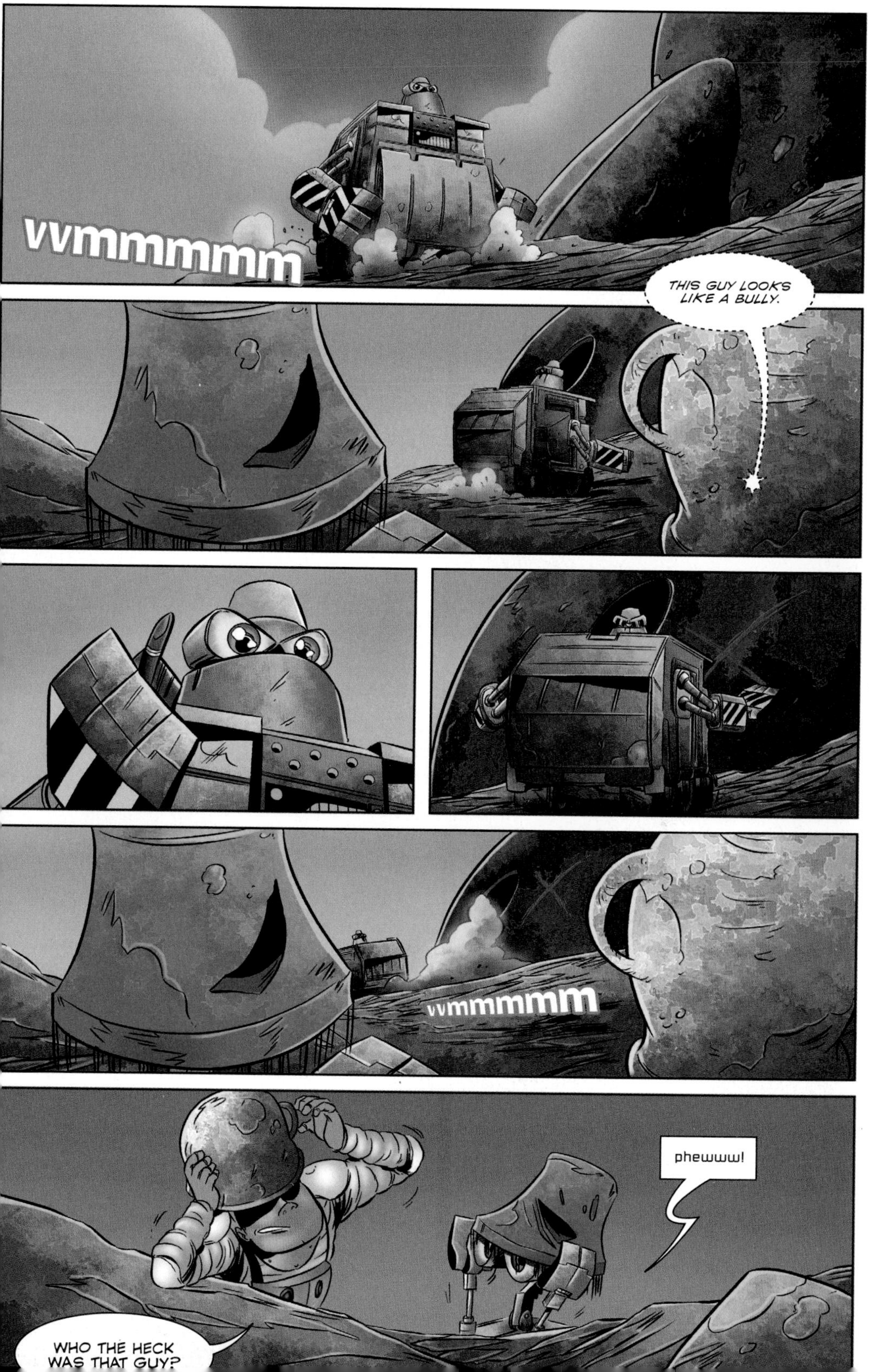
vvmmmmmm
THIS GUY LOOKS LIKE A BULLY.
vvmmmmmm
phewww!
WHO THE HECK WAS THAT GUY?

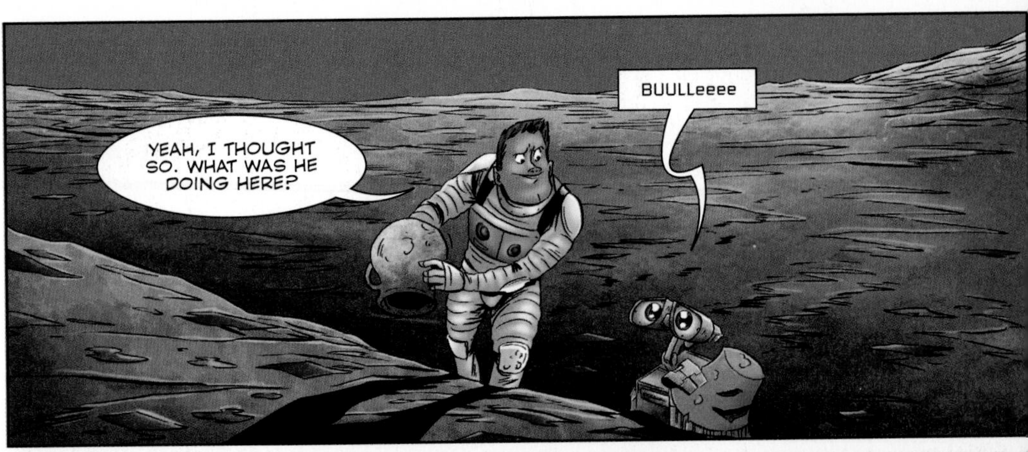
YEAH, I THOUGHT SO. WHAT WAS HE DOING HERE?
BUULLeeee
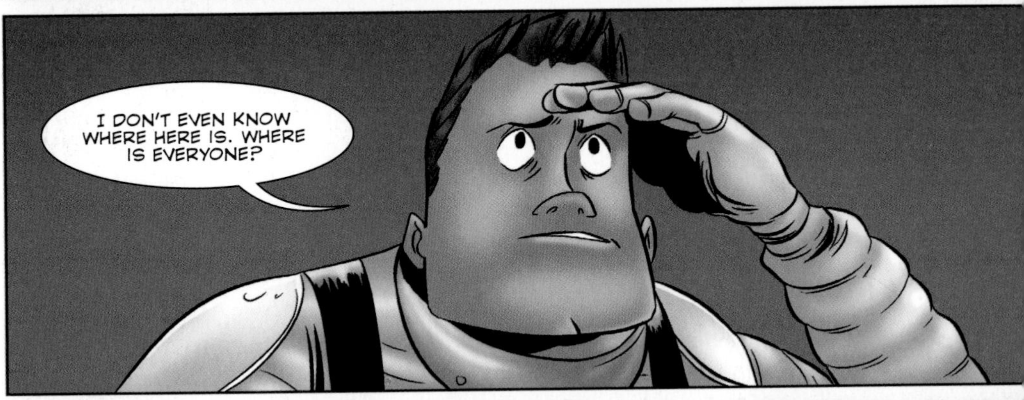
I DON'T EVEN KNOW WHERE HERE IS. WHERE IS EVERYONE?
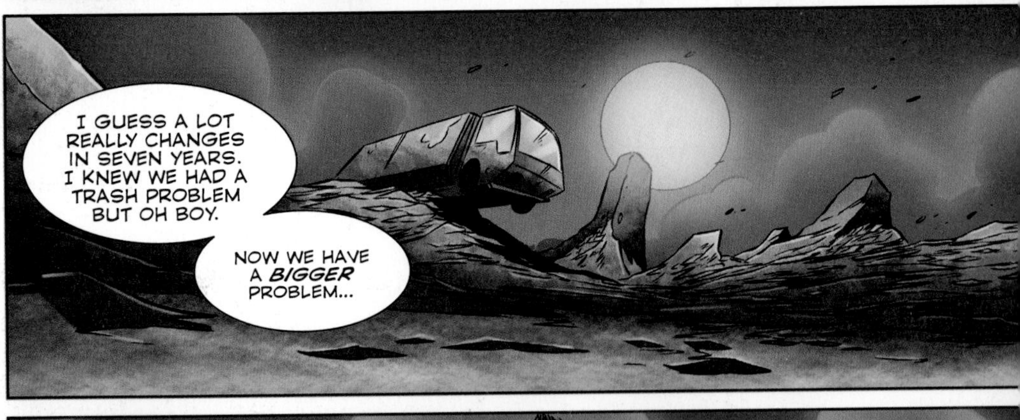
I GUESS A LOT REALLY CHANGES IN SEVEN YEARS. I KNEW WE HAD A TRASH PROBLEM BUT OH BOY.
NOW WE HAVE A *BIGGER* PROBLEM...
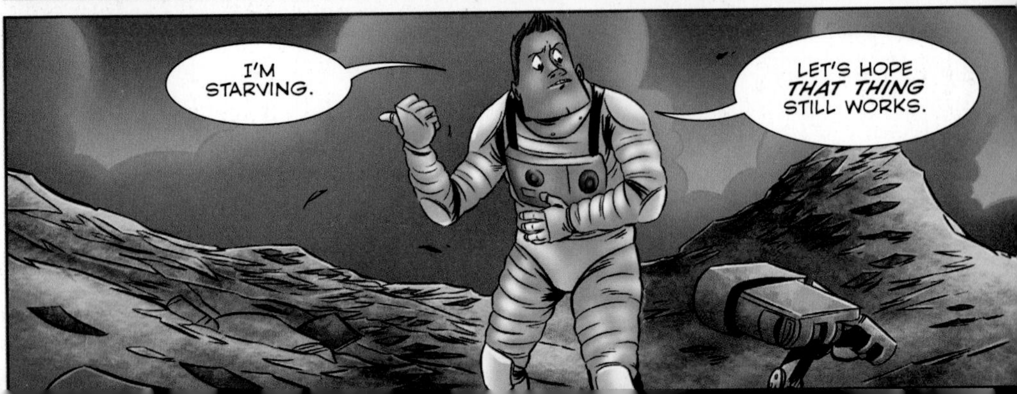
I'M STARVING.
LET'S HOPE *THAT THING* STILL WORKS.

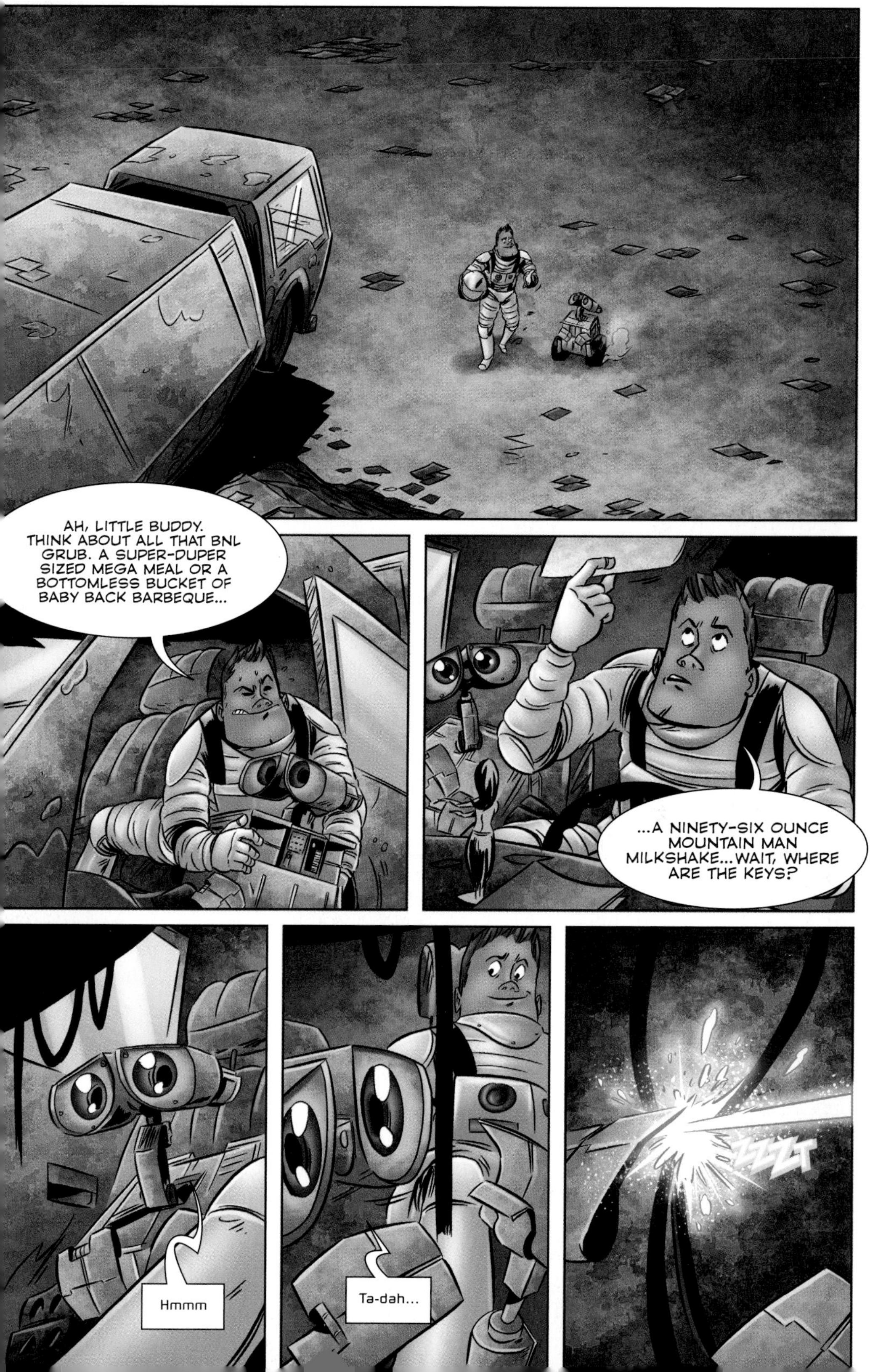
AH, LITTLE BUDDY. THINK ABOUT ALL THAT BNL GRUB. A SUPER-DUPER SIZED MEGA MEAL OR A BOTTOMLESS BUCKET OF BABY BACK BARBEQUE...
...A NINETY-SIX OUNCE MOUNTAIN MAN MILKSHAKE...WAIT, WHERE ARE THE KEYS?
Hmmm
Ta-dah...
ZZZZT

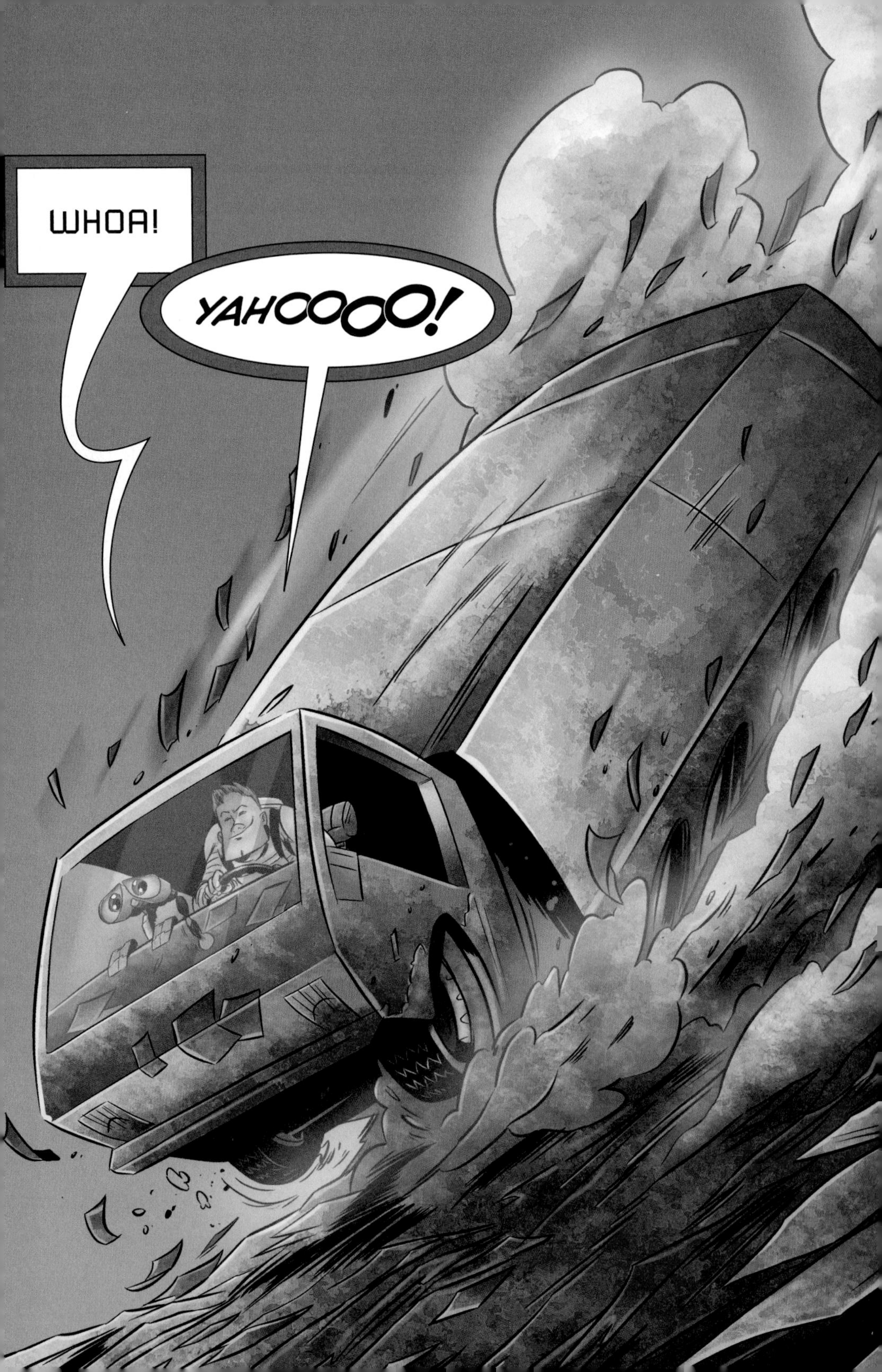
WHOA!
YAHOOOOO!

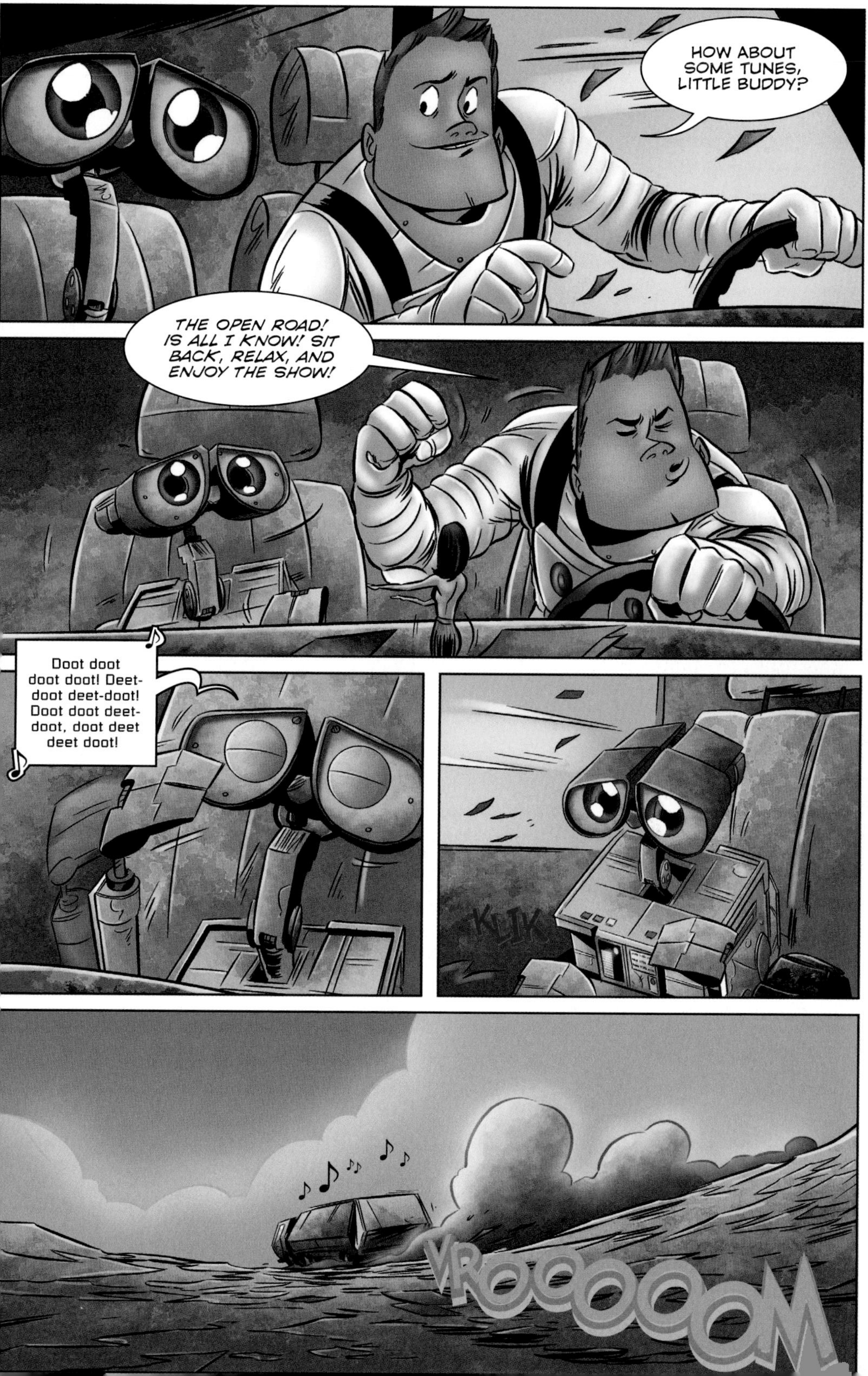
HOW ABOUT SOME TUNES, LITTLE BUDDY?
THE OPEN ROAD! IS ALL I KNOW! SIT BACK, RELAX, AND ENJOY THE SHOW!
Doot doot doot doot! Deet-doot deet-doot! Doot doot deet-doot, doot deet deet doot!
KLIK
VROOOOOOM

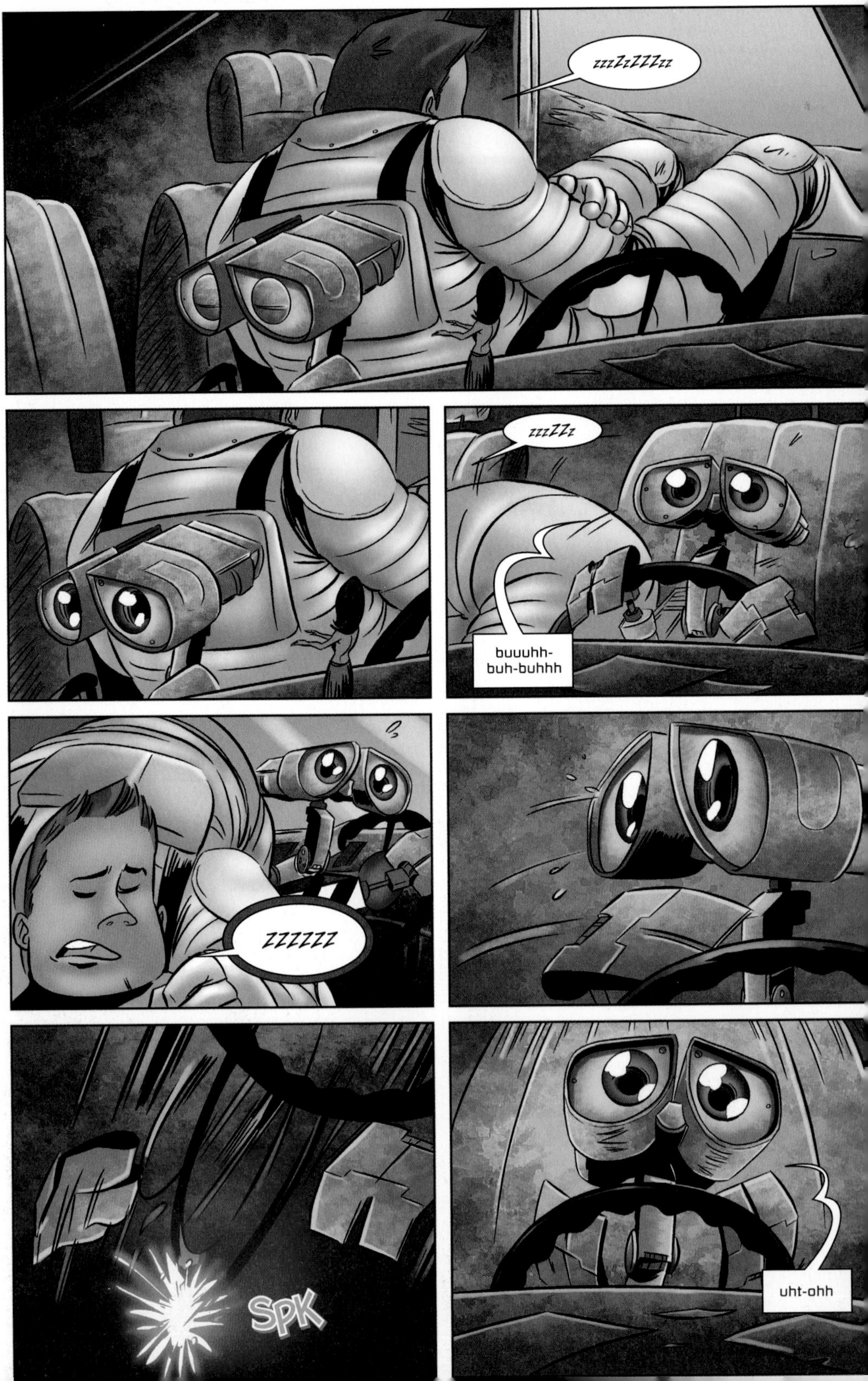
zzzZzZZZzz
zzzZZz
buuuhh-
buh-buhhh
ZZZZZZ
SPK
uht-ohh

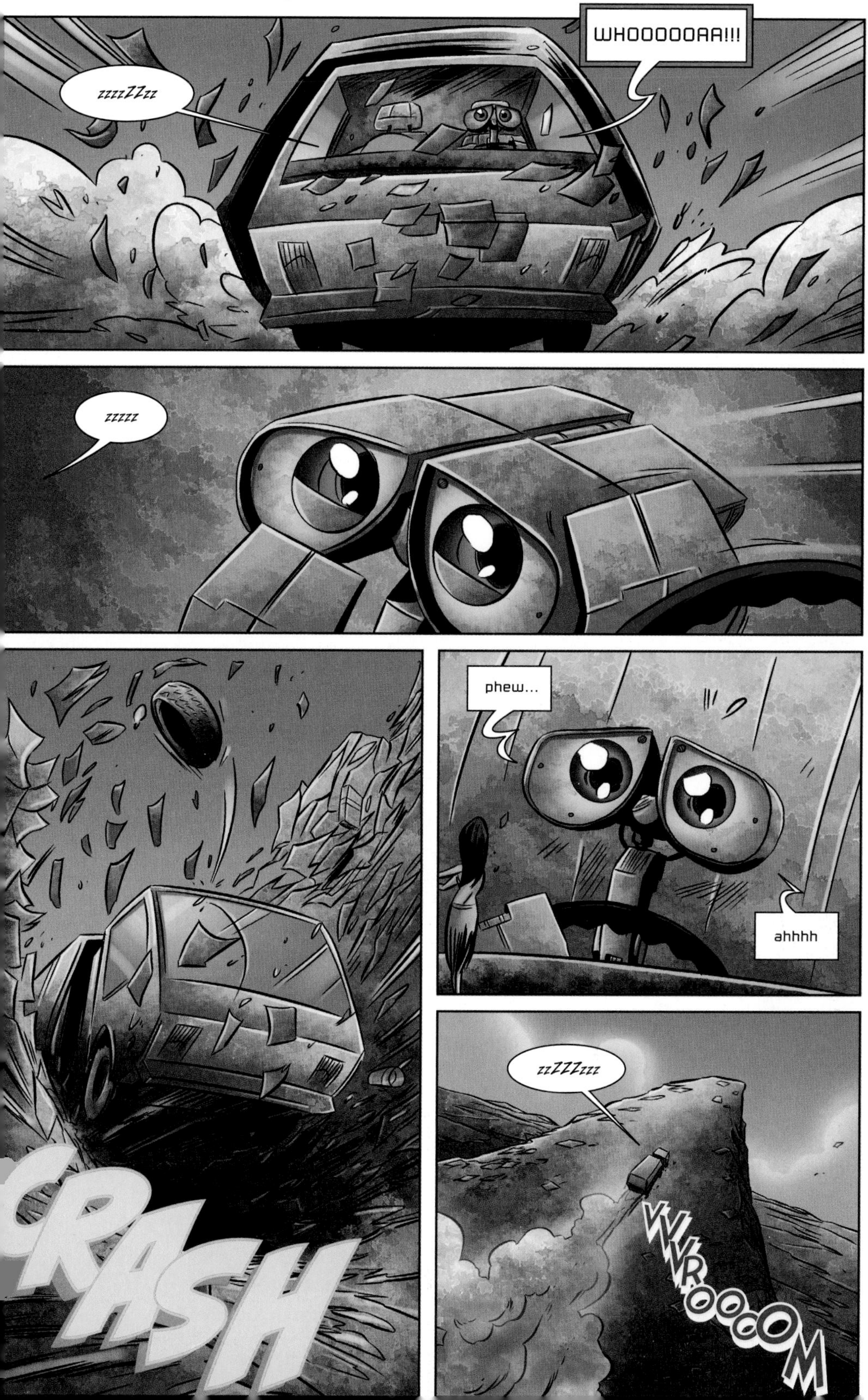
zzzzZZzz
WHOOOOOAA!!!
zzzzz
CRASH
phew...
ahhhh
zzZZZzzz
VVVROOOOOM

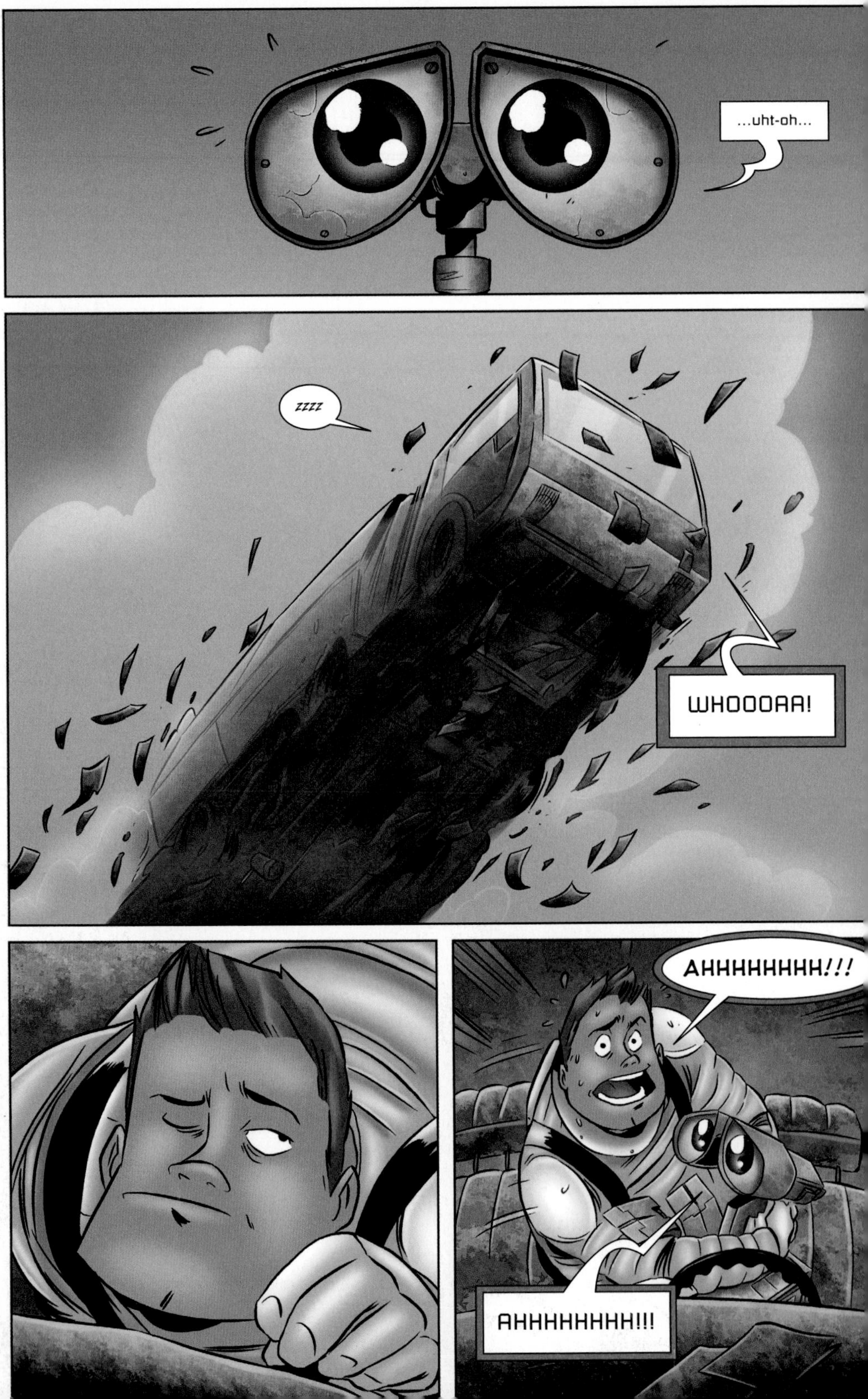
...uht-oh...
zzzz
WHOOOAA!
AHHHHHHHH!!!
AHHHHHHHH!!!

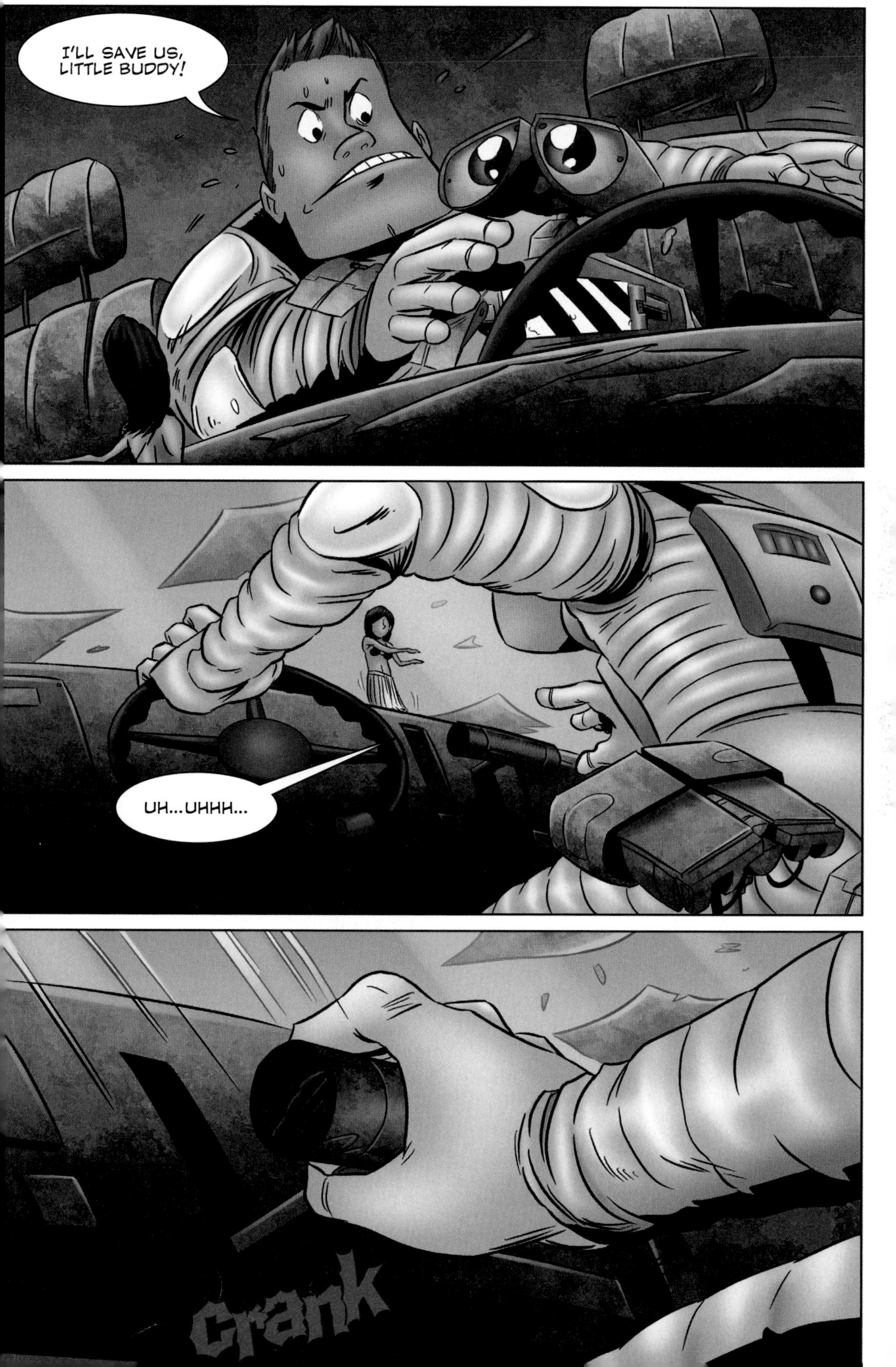
I'LL SAVE US, LITTLE BUDDY!
UH...UHHH...
crank

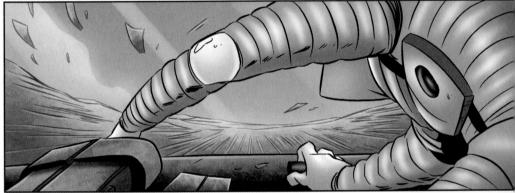

BAHAHAHAHAHA!!!

hehehehehe!

WAIT, WHAT'S THAT?

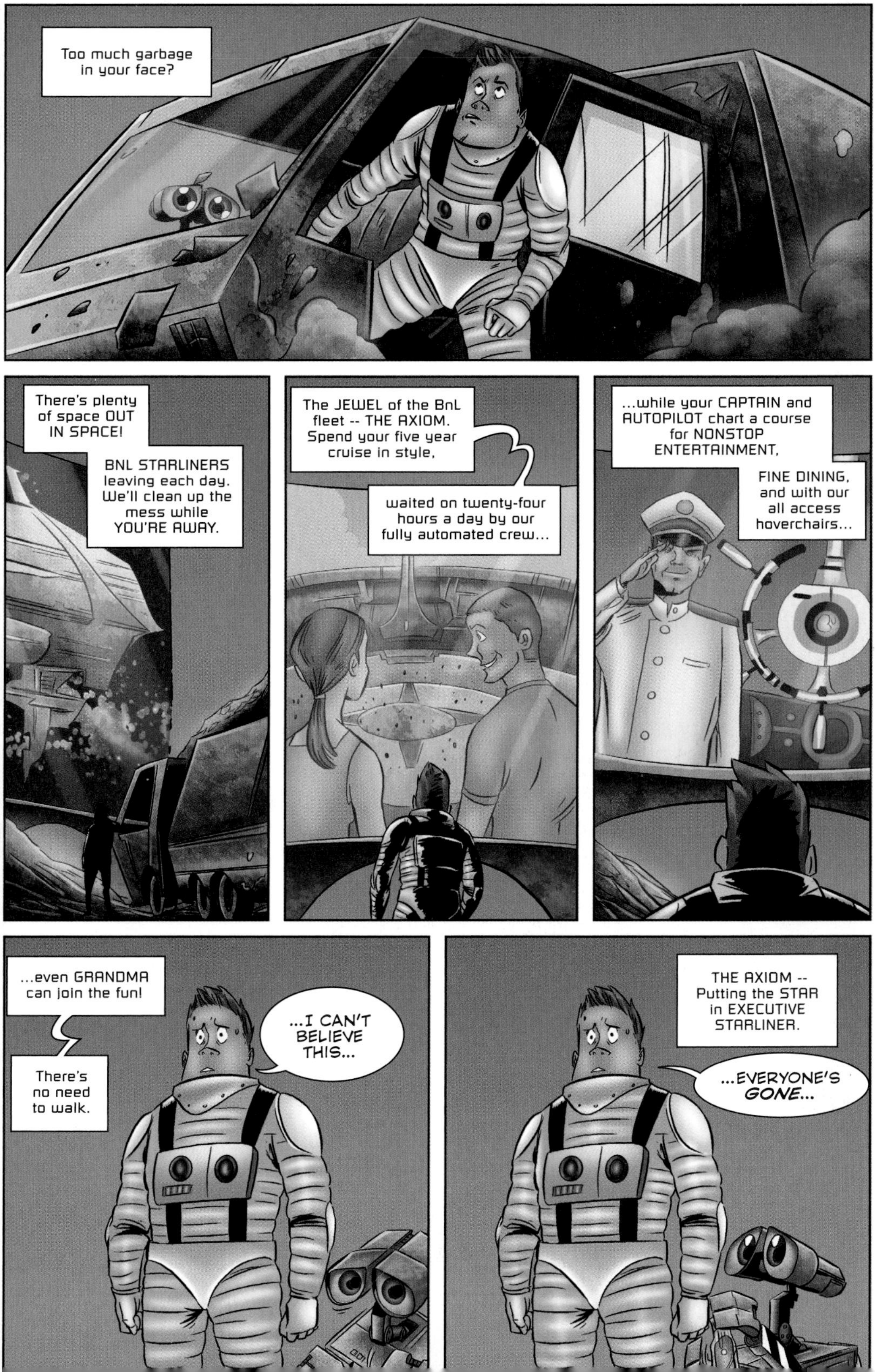
Too much garbage in your face?
There's plenty of space OUT IN SPACE!
BNL STARLINERS leaving each day. We'll clean up the mess while YOU'RE AWAY.
The JEWEL of the BnL fleet -- THE AXIOM. Spend your five year cruise in style,
waited on twenty-four hours a day by our fully automated crew...
...while your CAPTAIN and AUTOPILOT chart a course for NONSTOP ENTERTAINMENT,
FINE DINING, and with our all access hoverchairs...
...even GRANDMA can join the fun!
There's no need to walk.
...I CAN'T BELIEVE THIS...
THE AXIOM -- Putting the STAR in EXECUTIVE STARLINER.
...EVERYONE'S *GONE*...

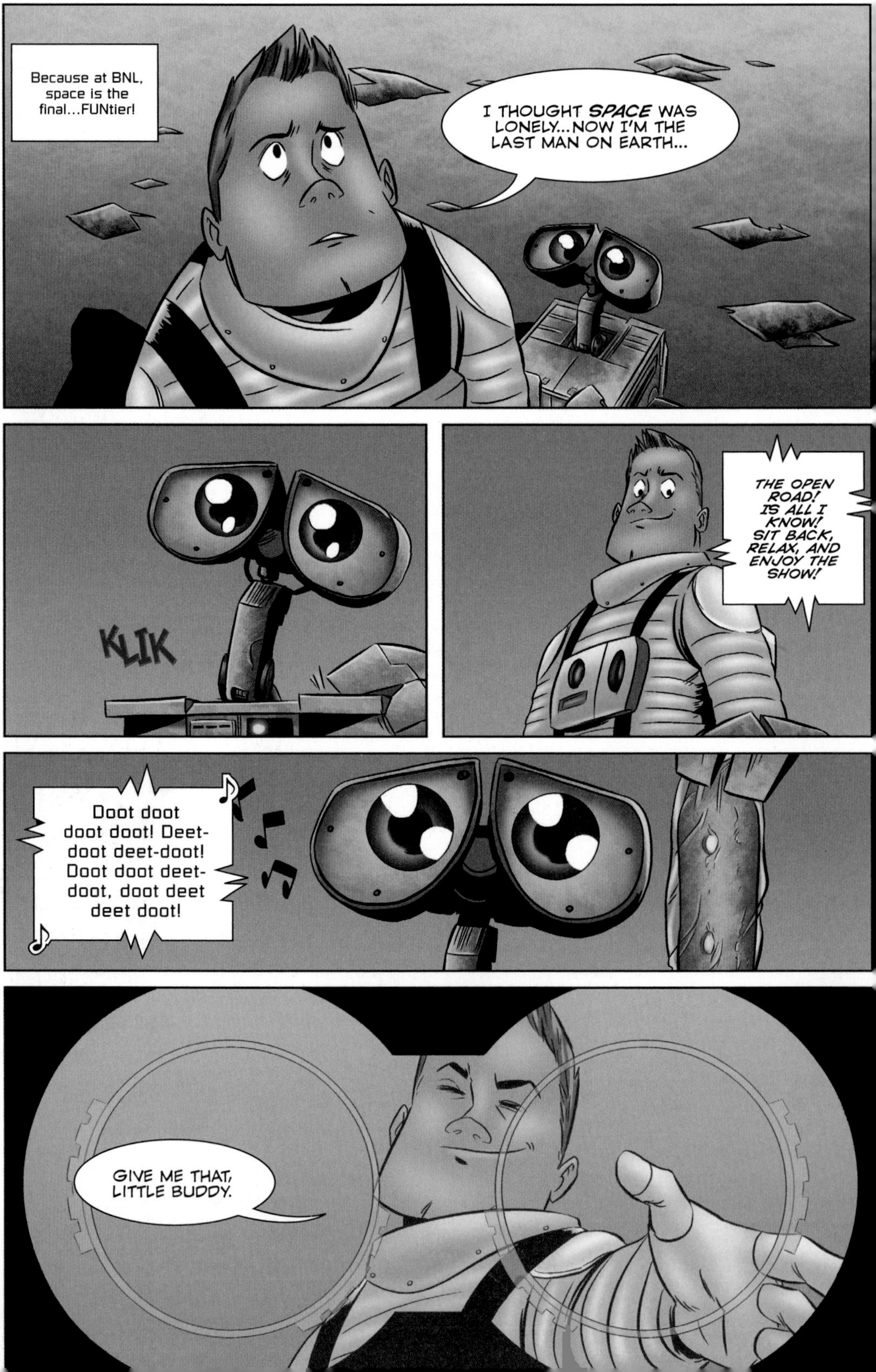

Because at BNL, space is the final...FUNtier!
I THOUGHT SPACE WAS LONELY...NOW I'M THE LAST MAN ON EARTH...
KLIK
THE OPEN ROAD! IS ALL I KNOW! SIT BACK, RELAX, AND ENJOY THE SHOW!
Doot doot doot doot! Deet-doot deet-doot! Doot doot deet-doot, doot deet deet doot!
GIVE ME THAT, LITTLE BUDDY.

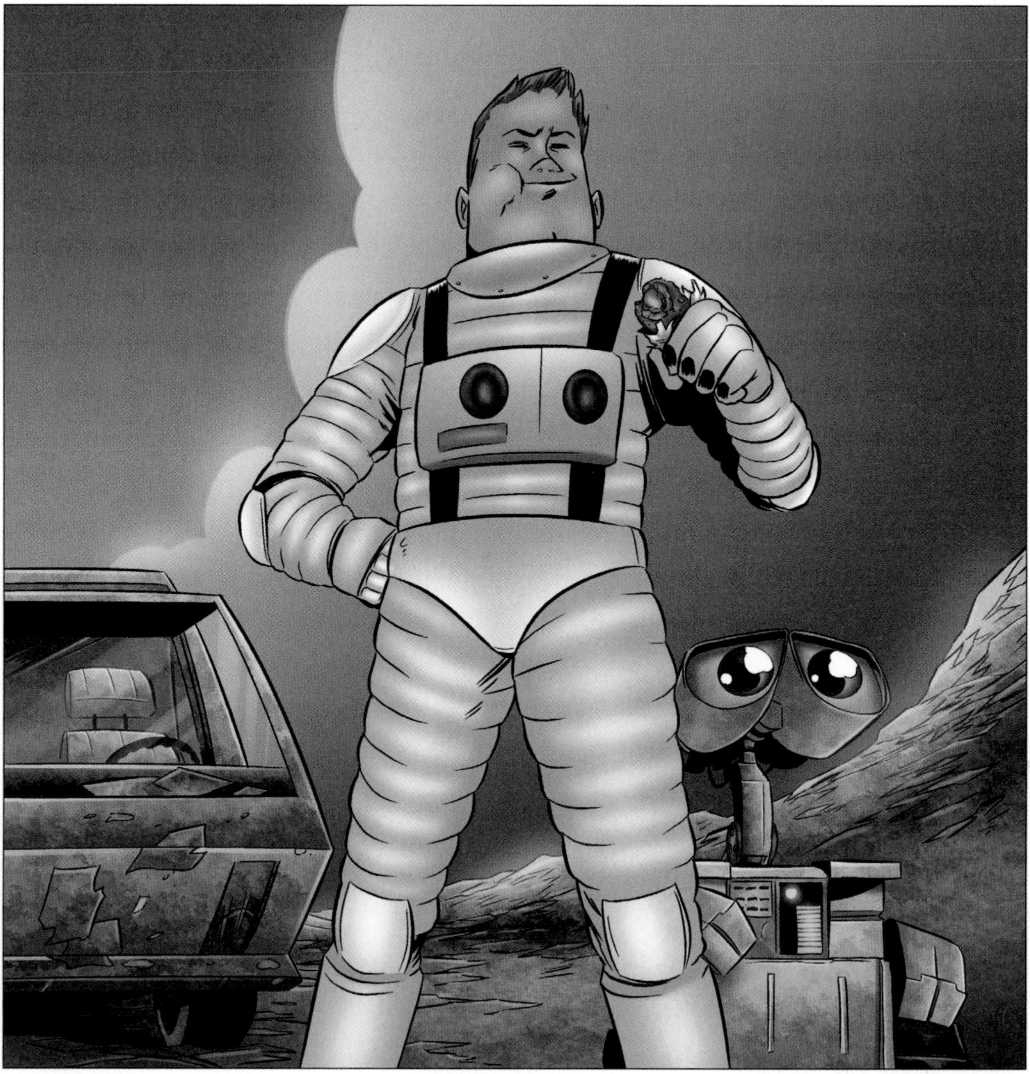

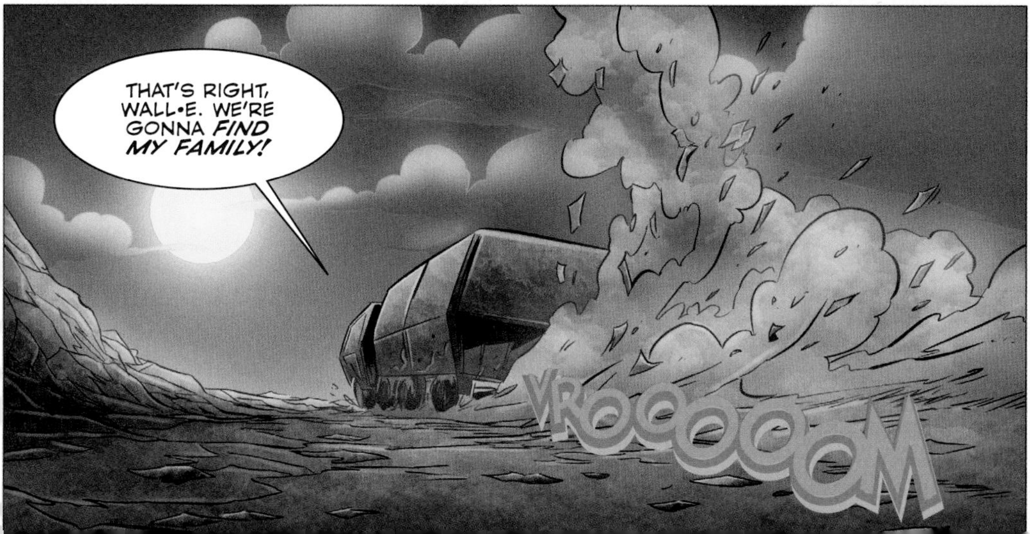
THAT'S RIGHT, WALL•E. WE'RE GONNA *FIND MY FAMILY!*
VROOOOOOM

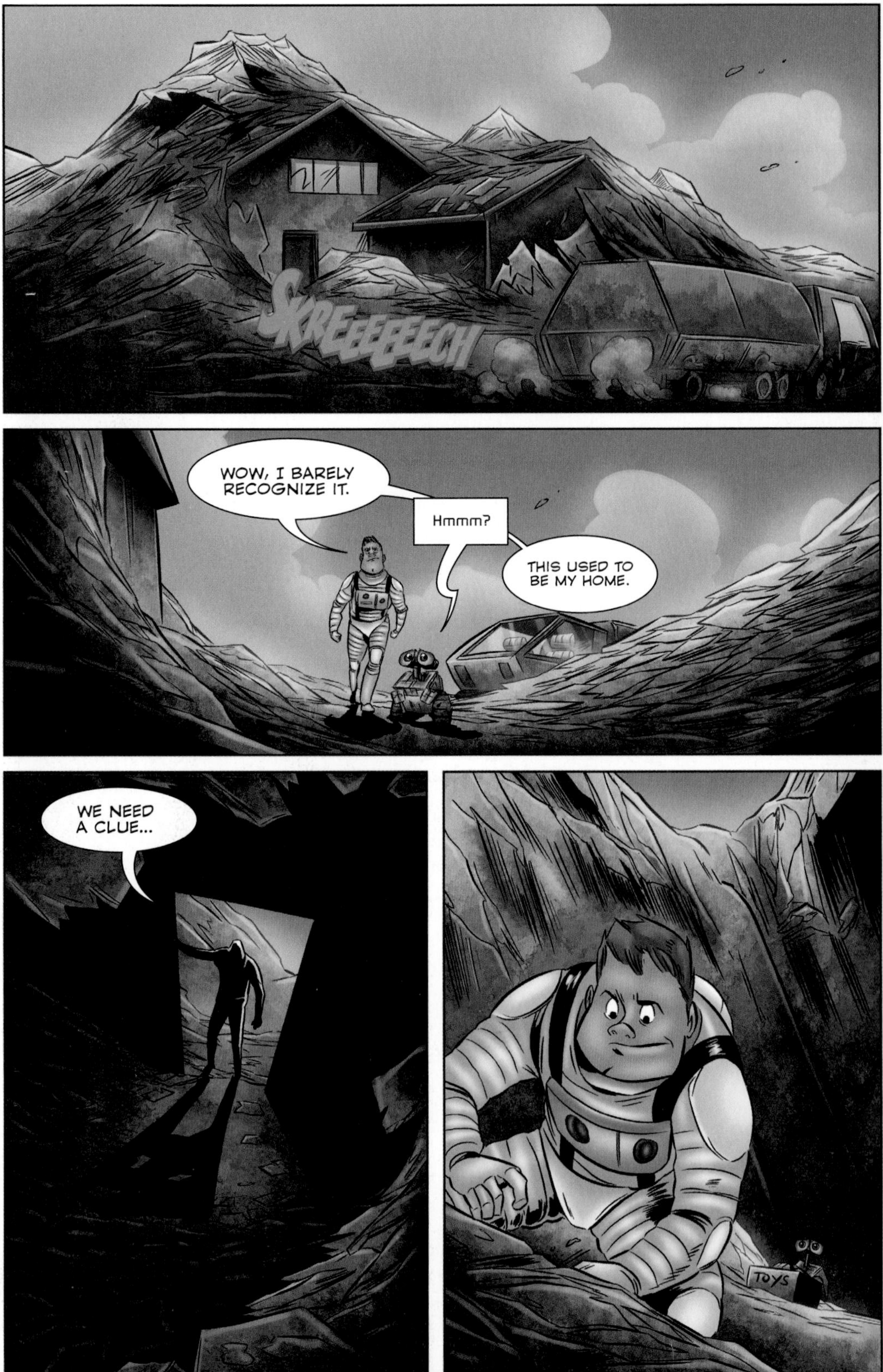
SKREEEEEEECH
WOW, I BARELY RECOGNIZE IT.
Hmmm?
THIS USED TO BE MY HOME.
WE NEED A CLUE...
TOYS

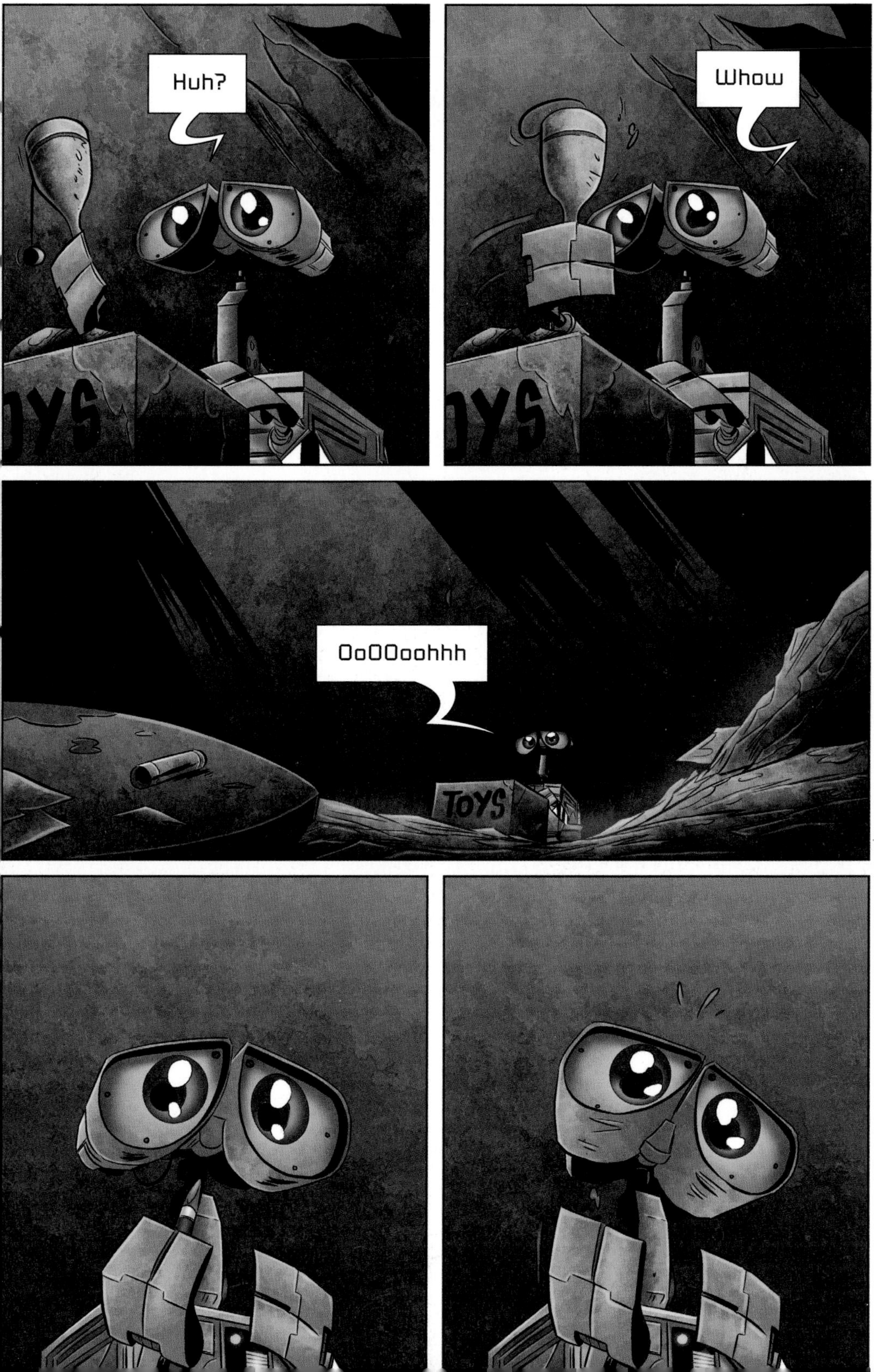
Huh?
Whow
TOYS
OoOOoohhh

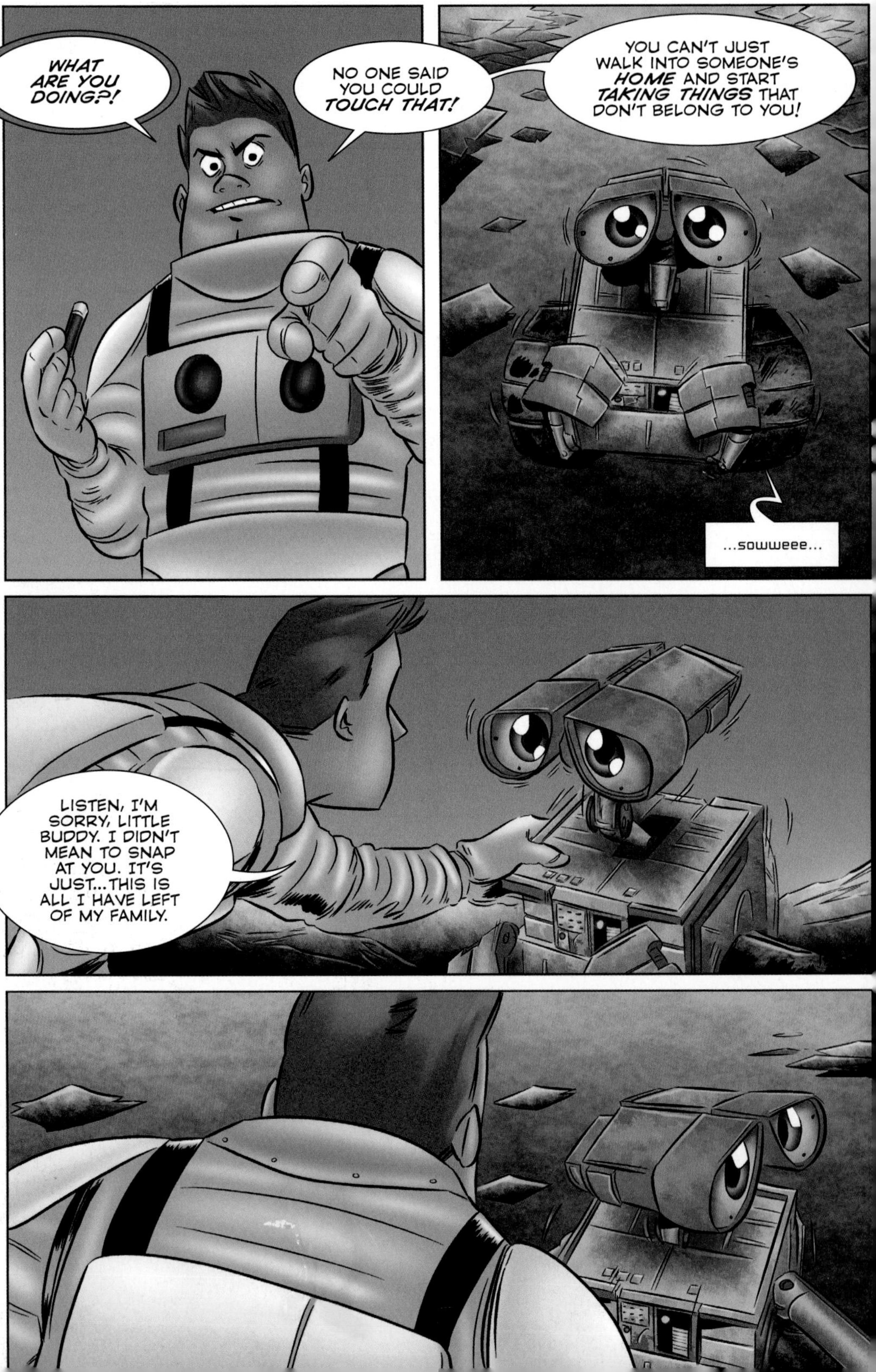
WHAT ARE YOU DOING?!
NO ONE SAID YOU COULD TOUCH THAT!
YOU CAN'T JUST WALK INTO SOMEONE'S HOME AND START TAKING THINGS THAT DON'T BELONG TO YOU!
...sowweee...
LISTEN, I'M SORRY, LITTLE BUDDY. I DIDN'T MEAN TO SNAP AT YOU. IT'S JUST...THIS IS ALL I HAVE LEFT OF MY FAMILY.

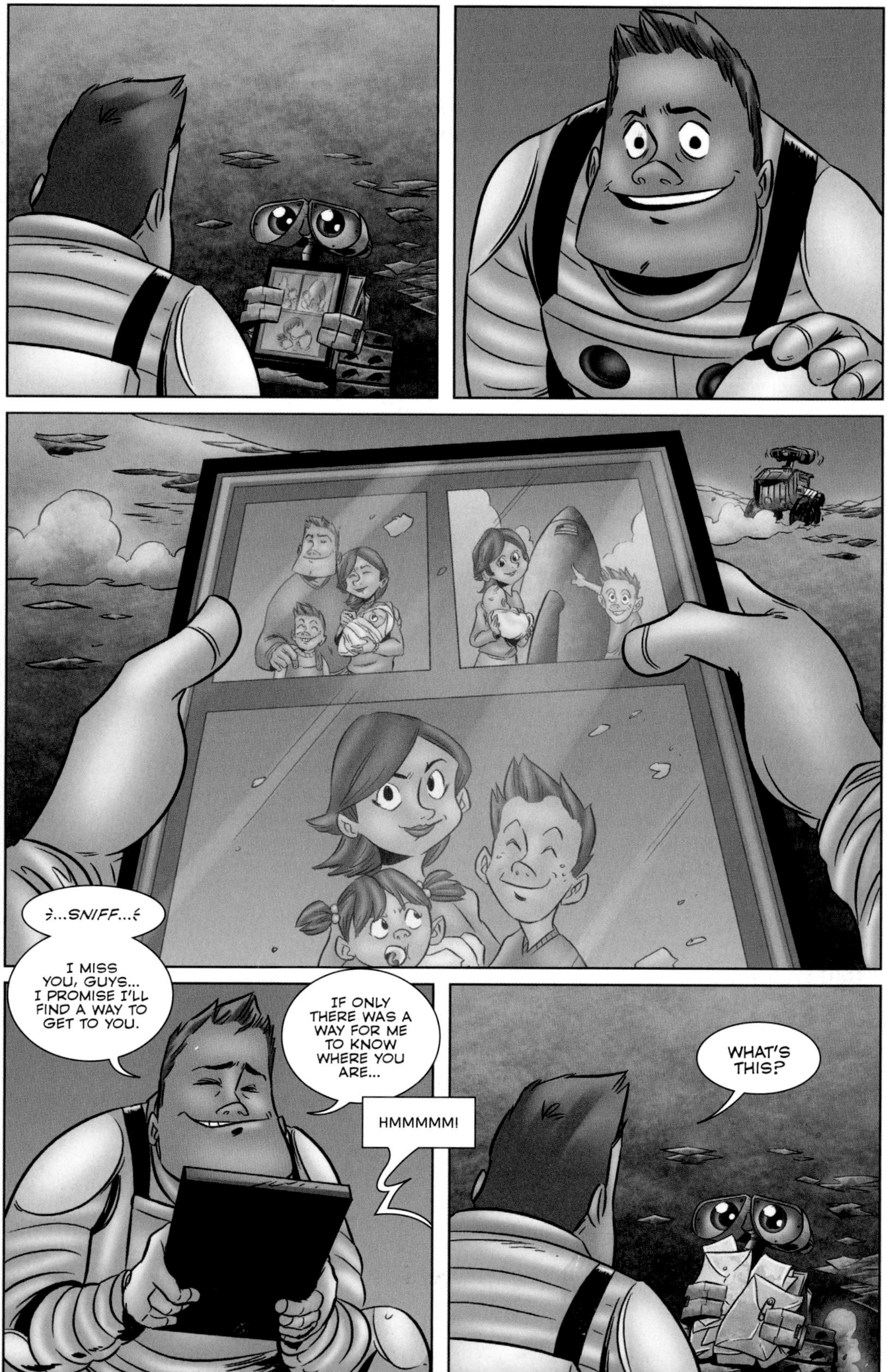
...SNIFF...
I MISS YOU, GUYS... I PROMISE I'LL FIND A WAY TO GET TO YOU.
IF ONLY THERE WAS A WAY FOR ME TO KNOW WHERE YOU ARE...
HMMMMM!
WHAT'S THIS?

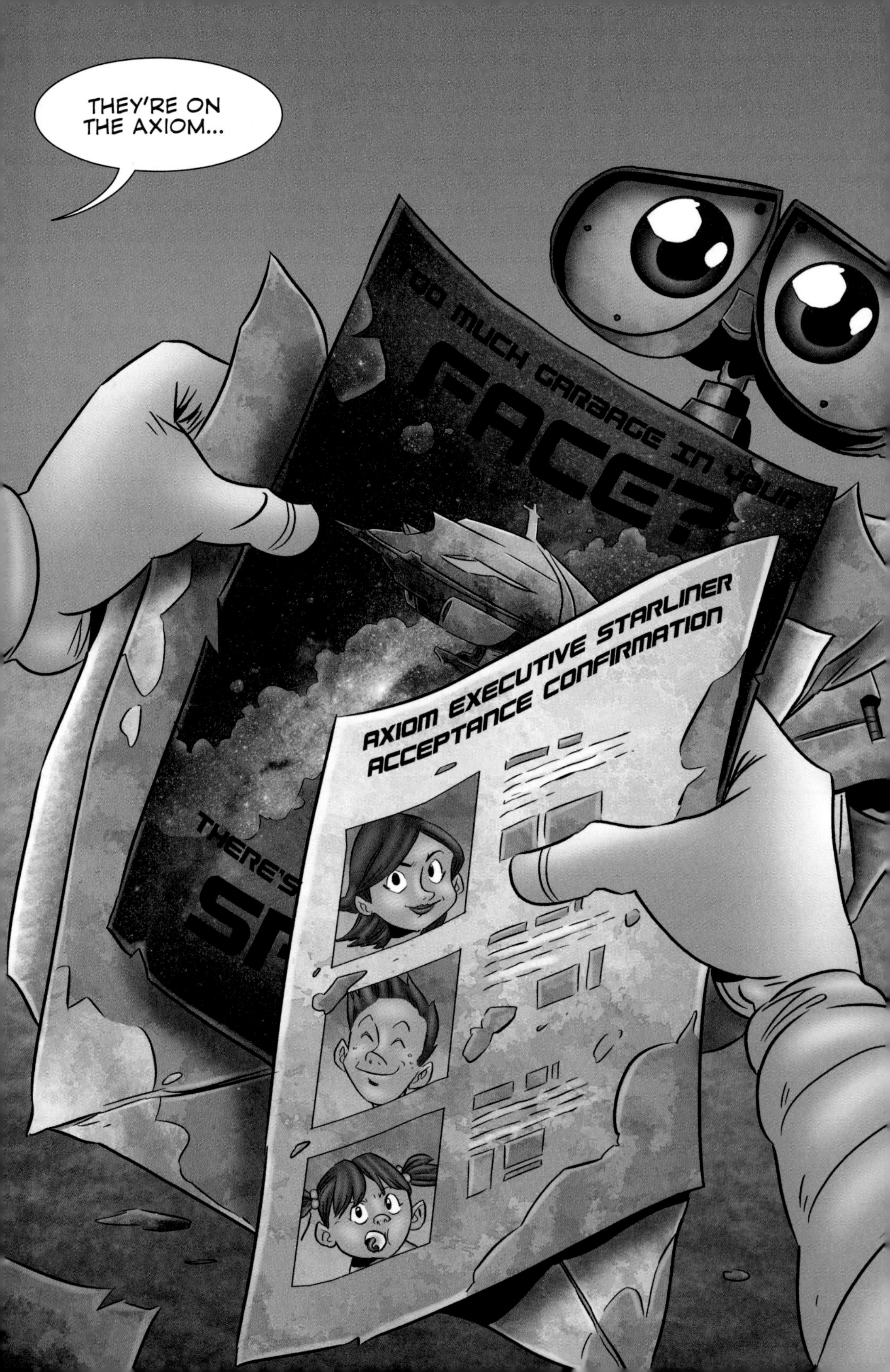
THEY'RE ON THE AXIOM...
TOO MUCH GARBAGE IN YOUR
FACE?
THERE'S
AXIOM EXECUTIVE STARLINER
ACCEPTANCE CONFIRMATION

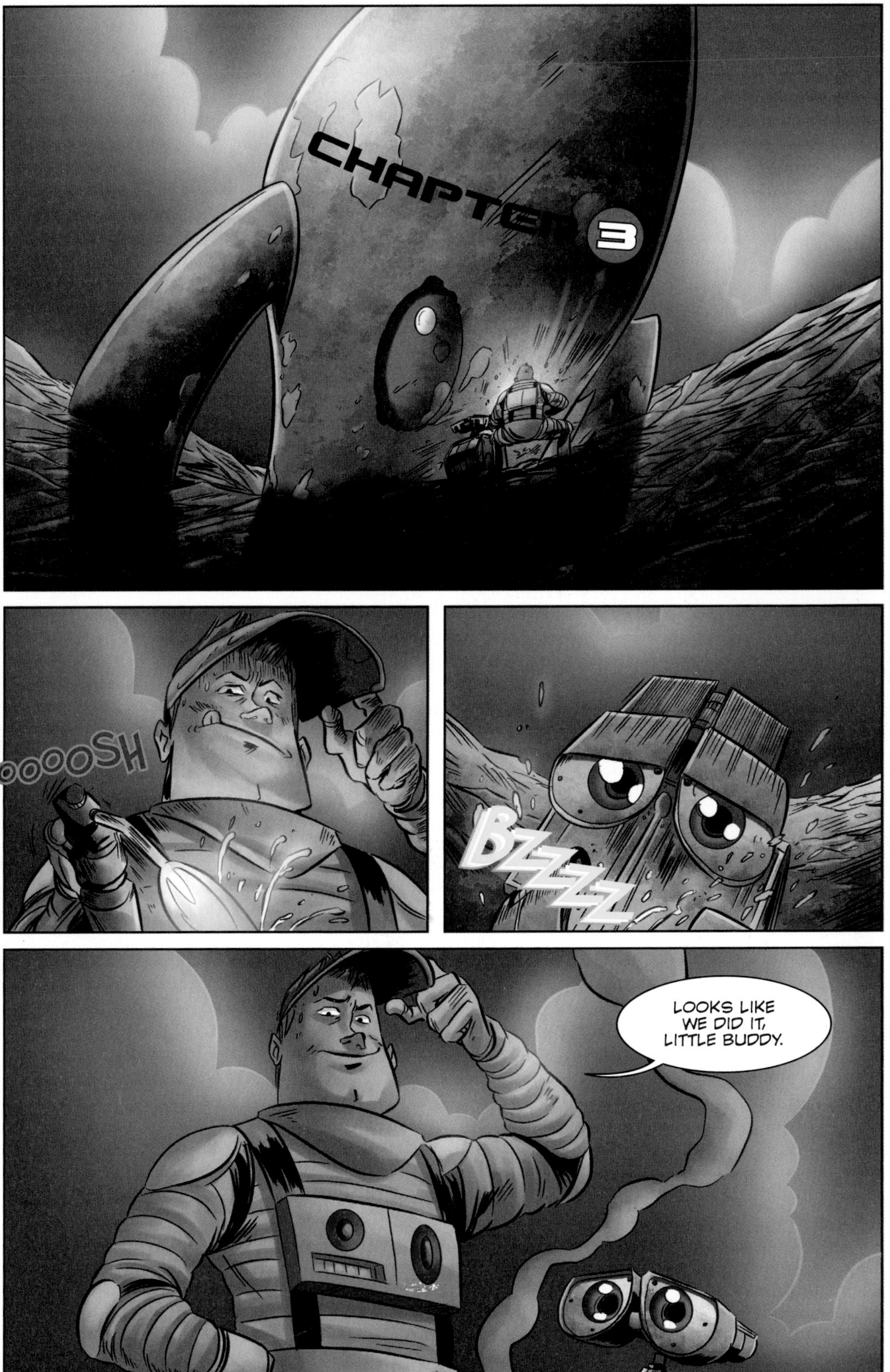
CHAPTER 3
OOOOOSH
BZZZZ
LOOKS LIKE WE DID IT, LITTLE BUDDY.

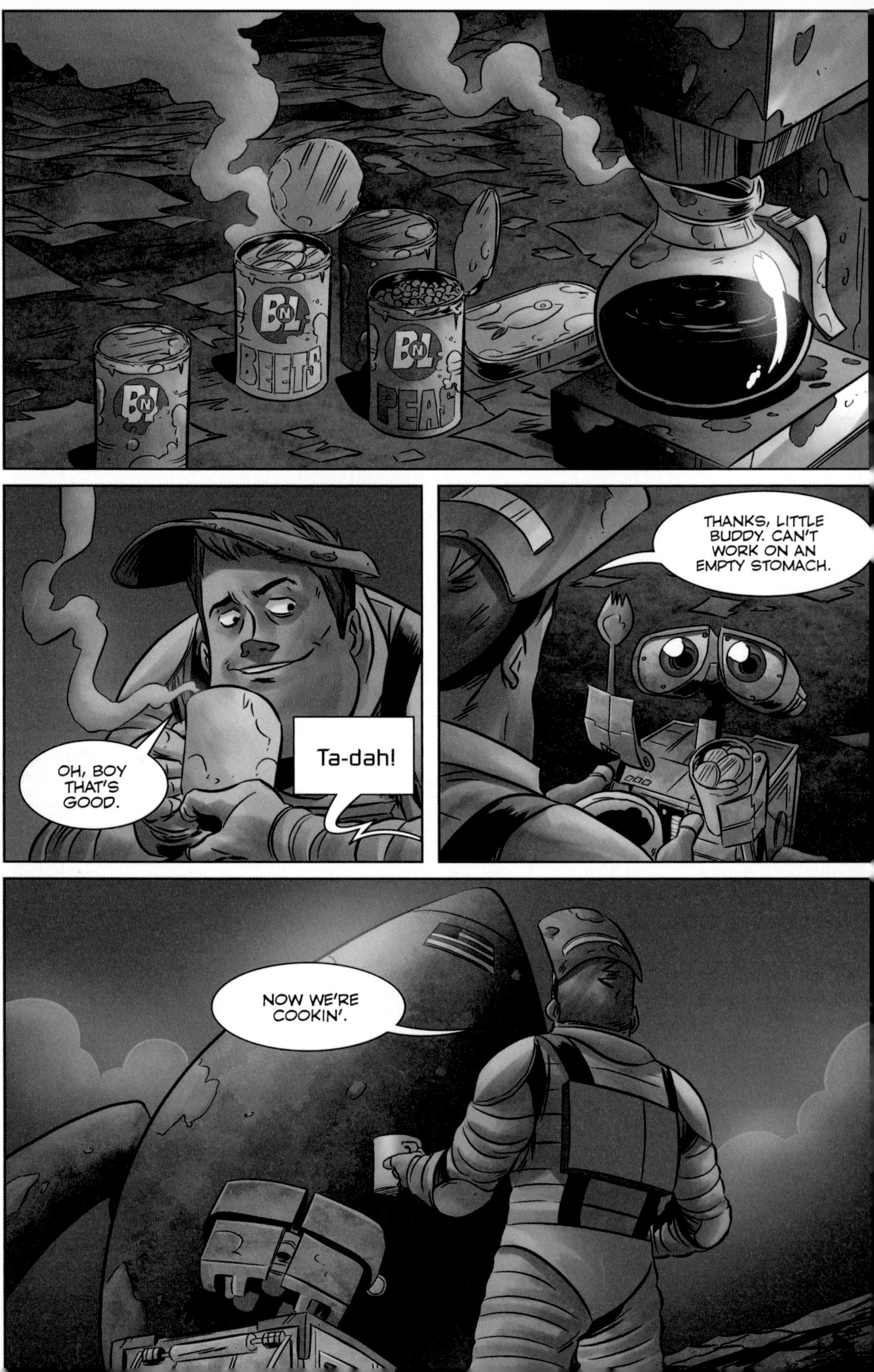
BnL
BEETS
BnL
PEAS
BnL
OH, BOY THAT'S GOOD.
Ta-dah!
THANKS, LITTLE BUDDY. CAN'T WORK ON AN EMPTY STOMACH.
NOW WE'RE COOKIN'.

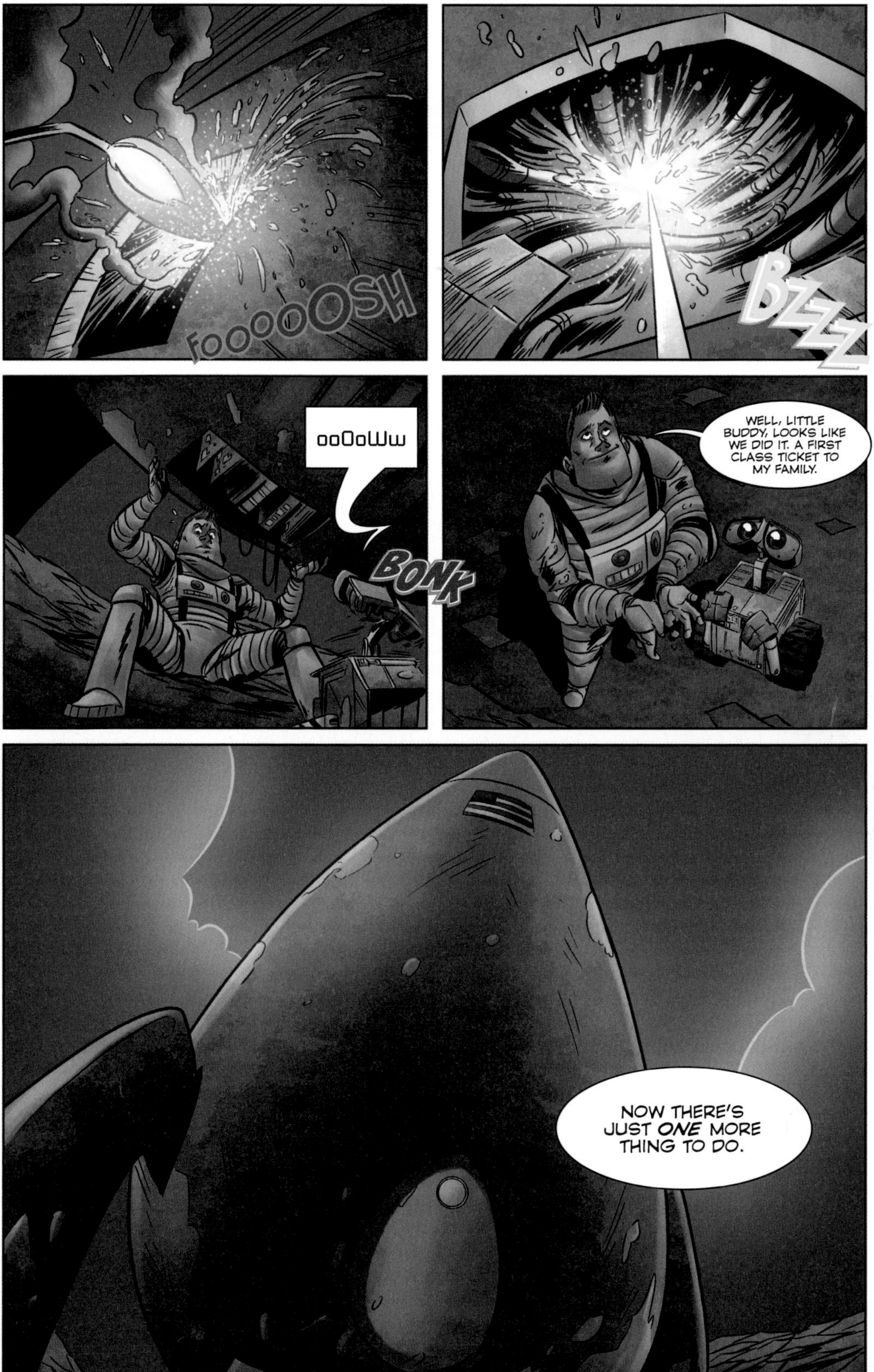
FOOOOOOSH
BZZZ
ooOoWw
BONK
WELL, LITTLE BUDDY, LOOKS LIKE WE DID IT. A FIRST CLASS TICKET TO MY FAMILY.
NOW THERE'S JUST *ONE* MORE THING TO DO.

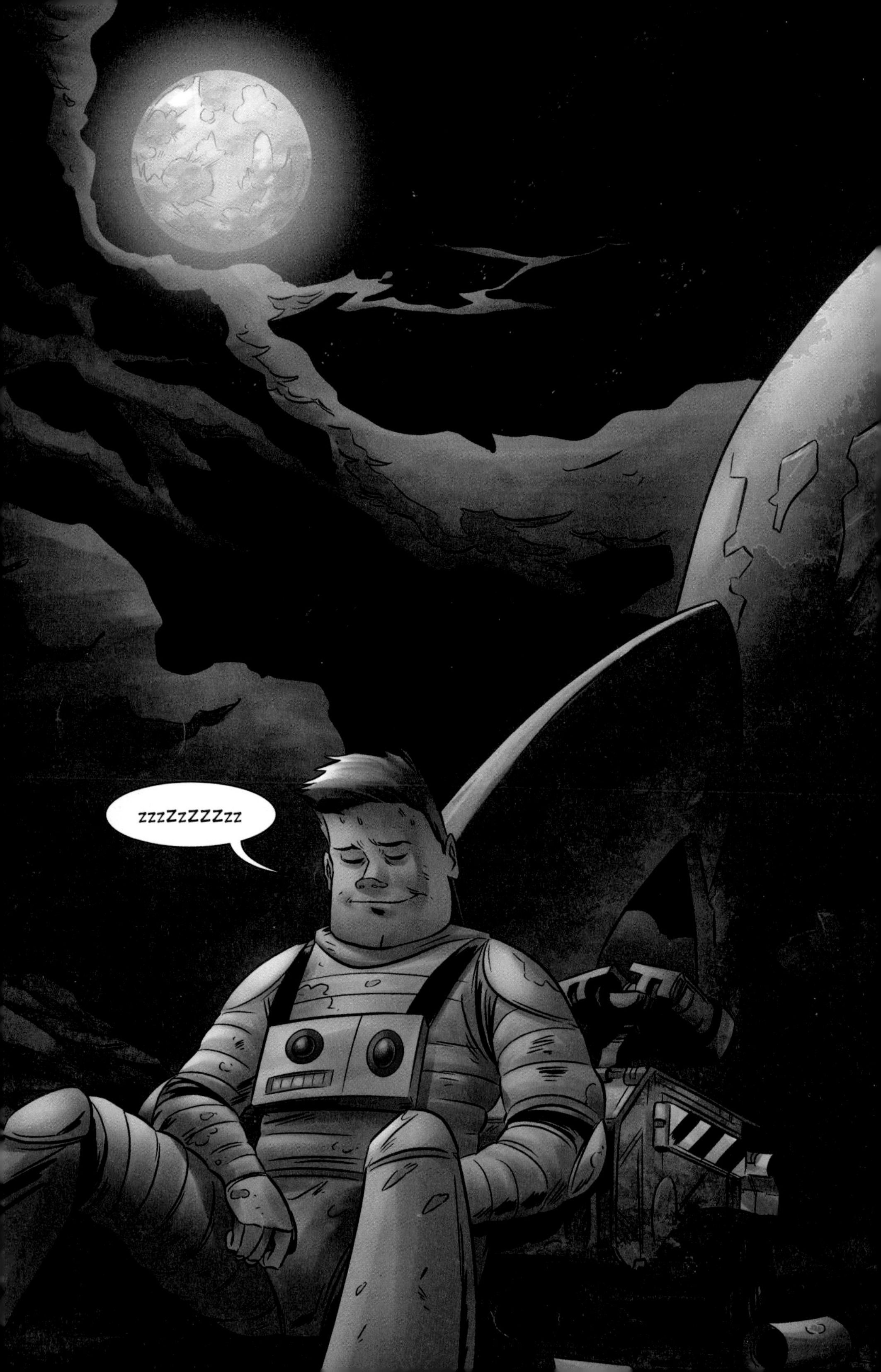
zzzZzZZZzz

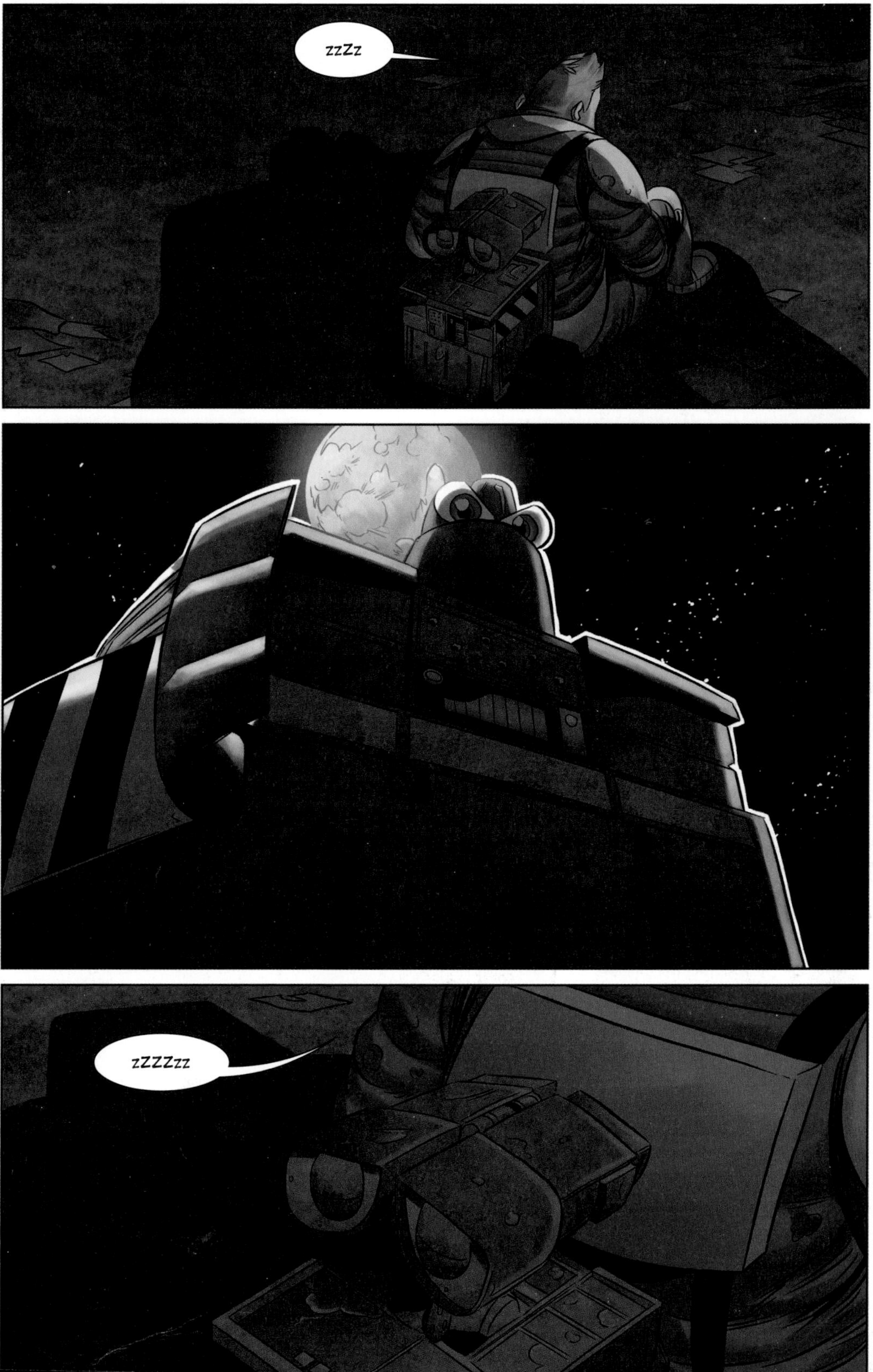
zzZz
zZZZzz

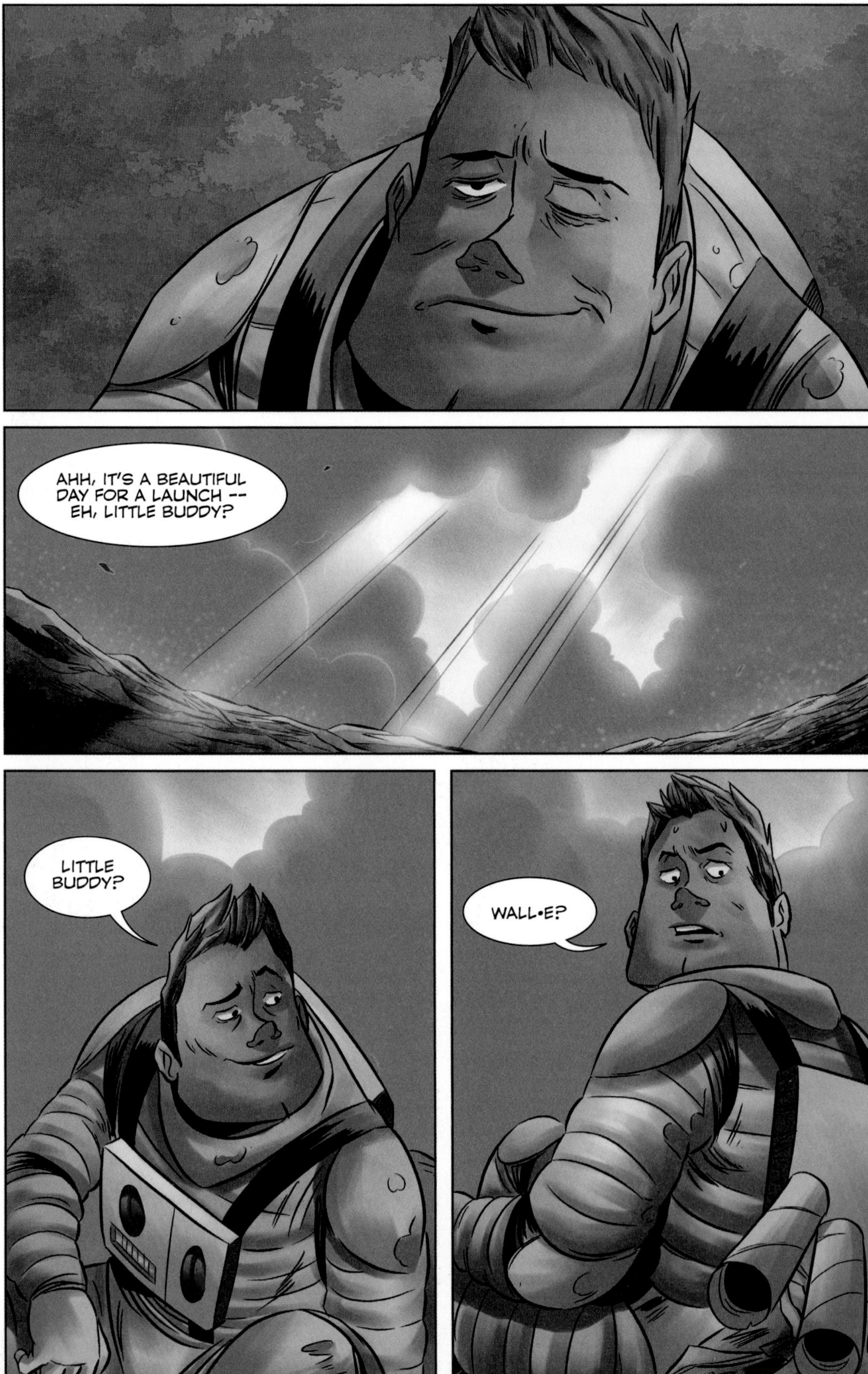
AHH, IT'S A BEAUTIFUL DAY FOR A LAUNCH -- EH, LITTLE BUDDY?
LITTLE BUDDY?
WALL•E?

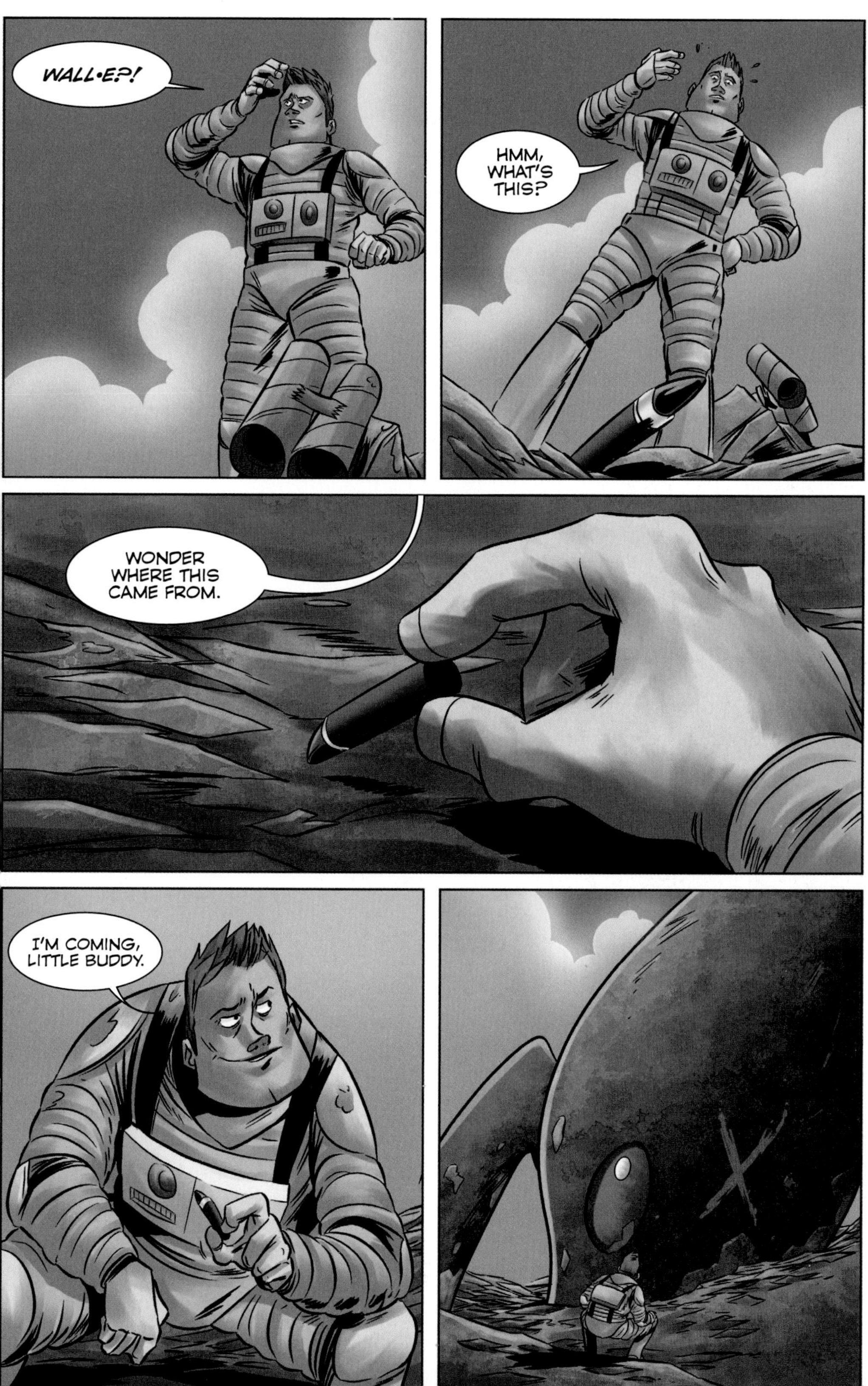
WALL•E?!
HMM, WHAT'S THIS?
WONDER WHERE THIS CAME FROM.
I'M COMING, LITTLE BUDDY.

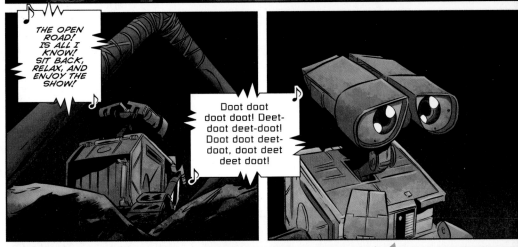

THE OPEN ROAD! IS ALL I KNOW! SIT BACK, RELAX, AND ENJOY THE SHOW!

Doot doot doot doot! Deet-doot deet-doot! Doot doot deet-doot, doot deet deet doot!

ahhh

FoOOOSHHH

BEET BEET

REEEEP

ZZT ZZT

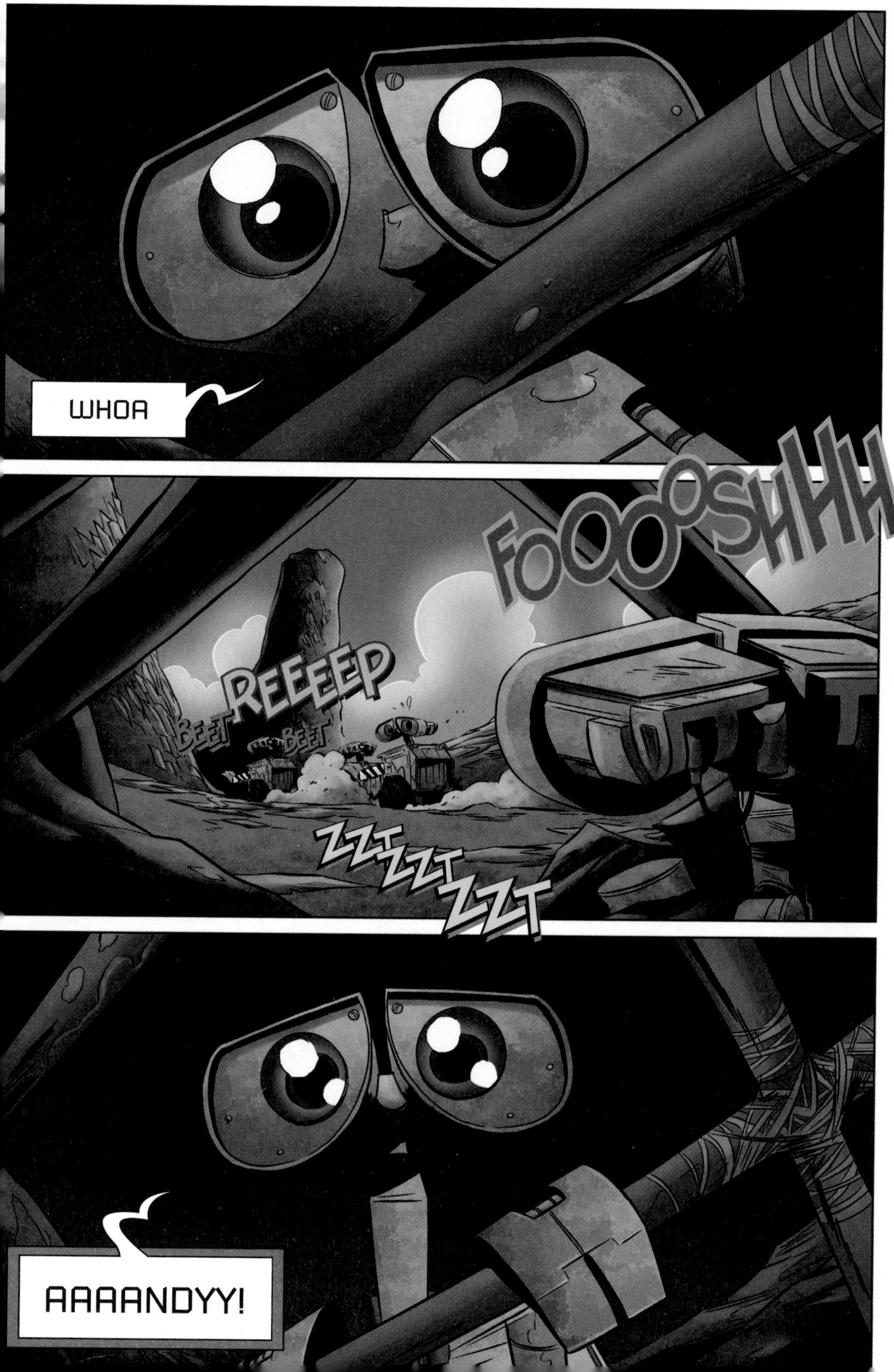
WHOA
FOOOOSHHH
BEET REEEEP
BEET
ZZT ZZT ZZT
AAAANDYY!

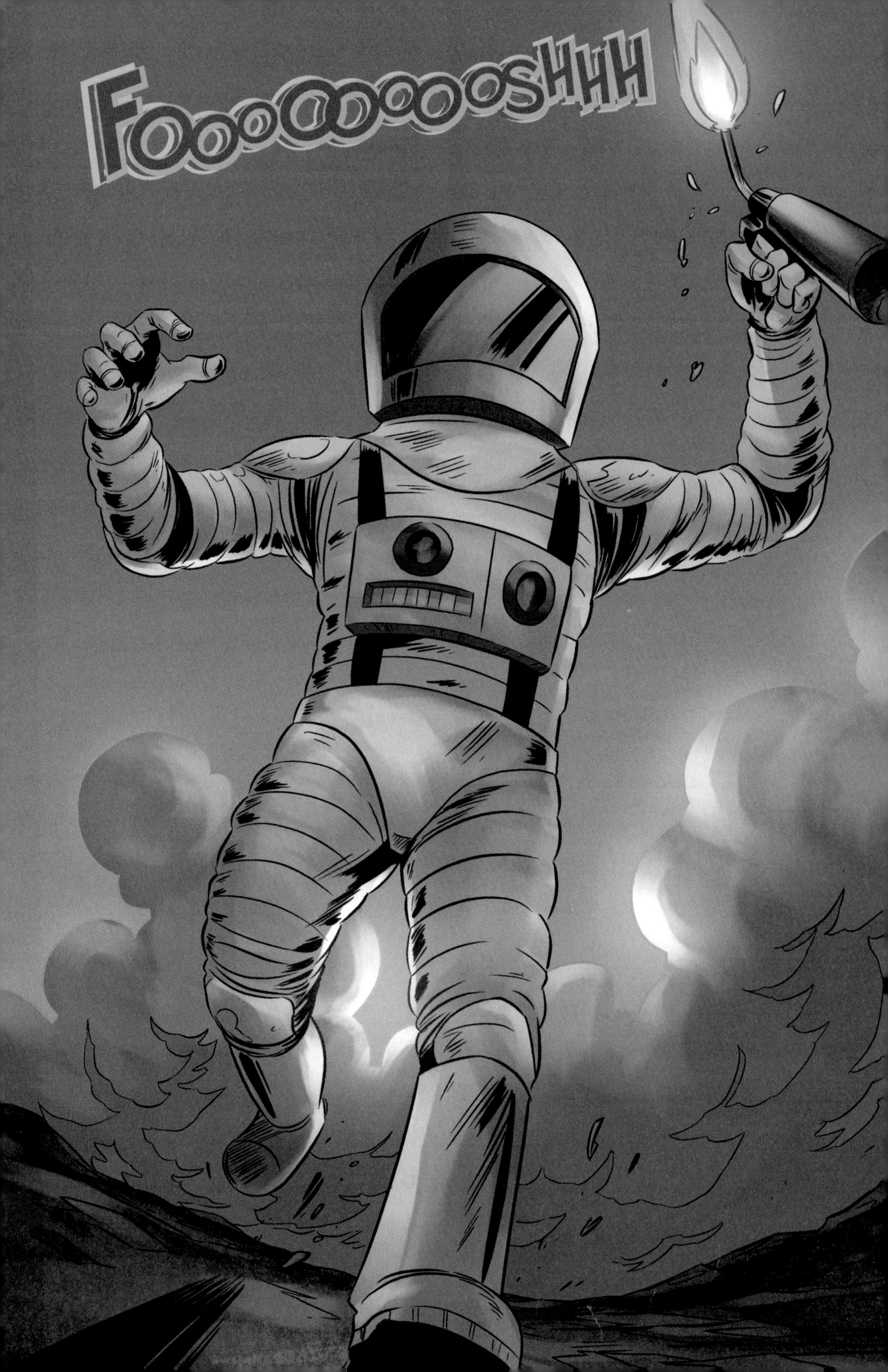
FOOOOOOOOOOSHHH

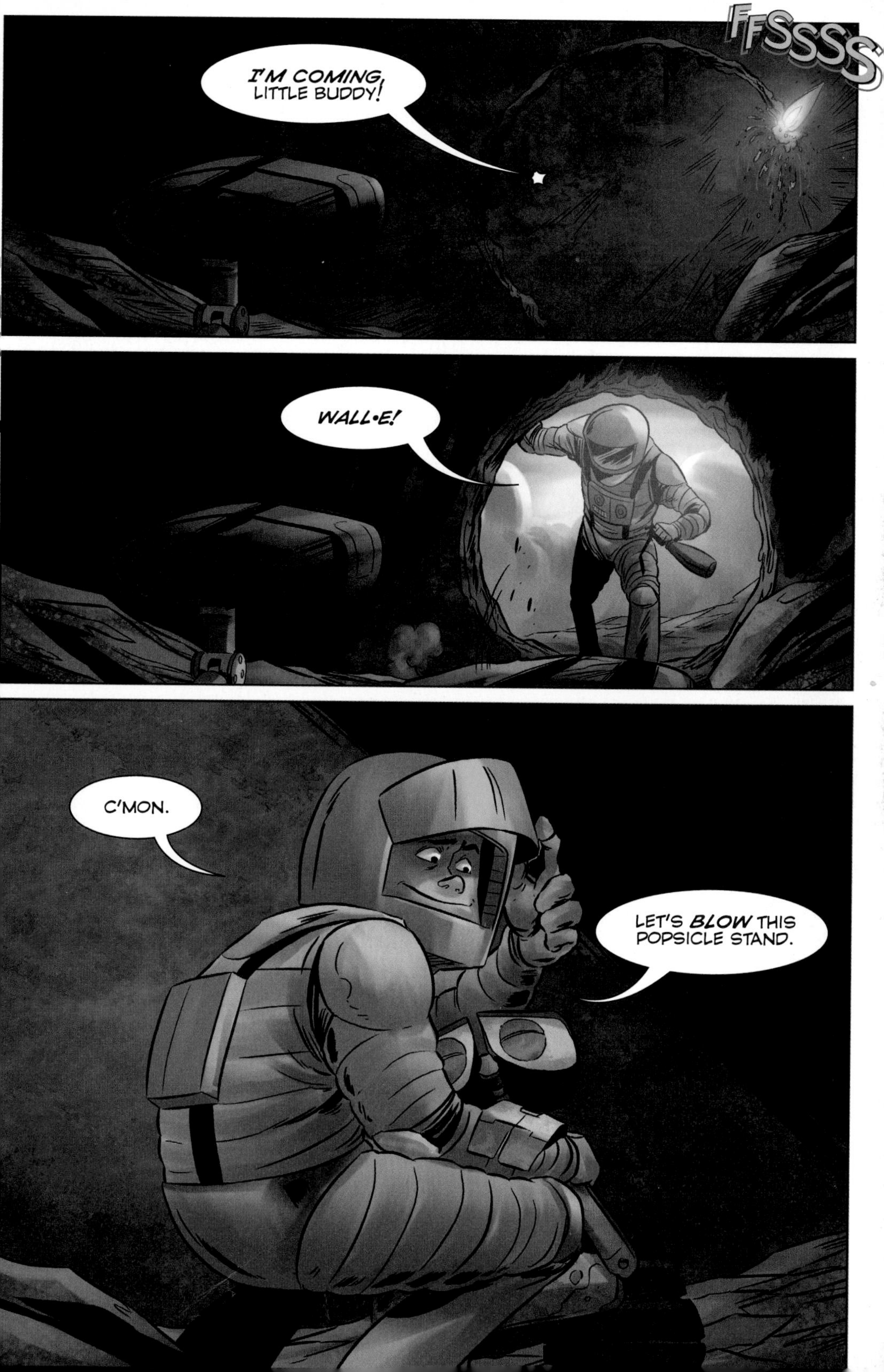
FFSSSS
I'M COMING, LITTLE BUDDY!
WALL•E!
C'MON.
LET'S BLOW THIS POPSICLE STAND.

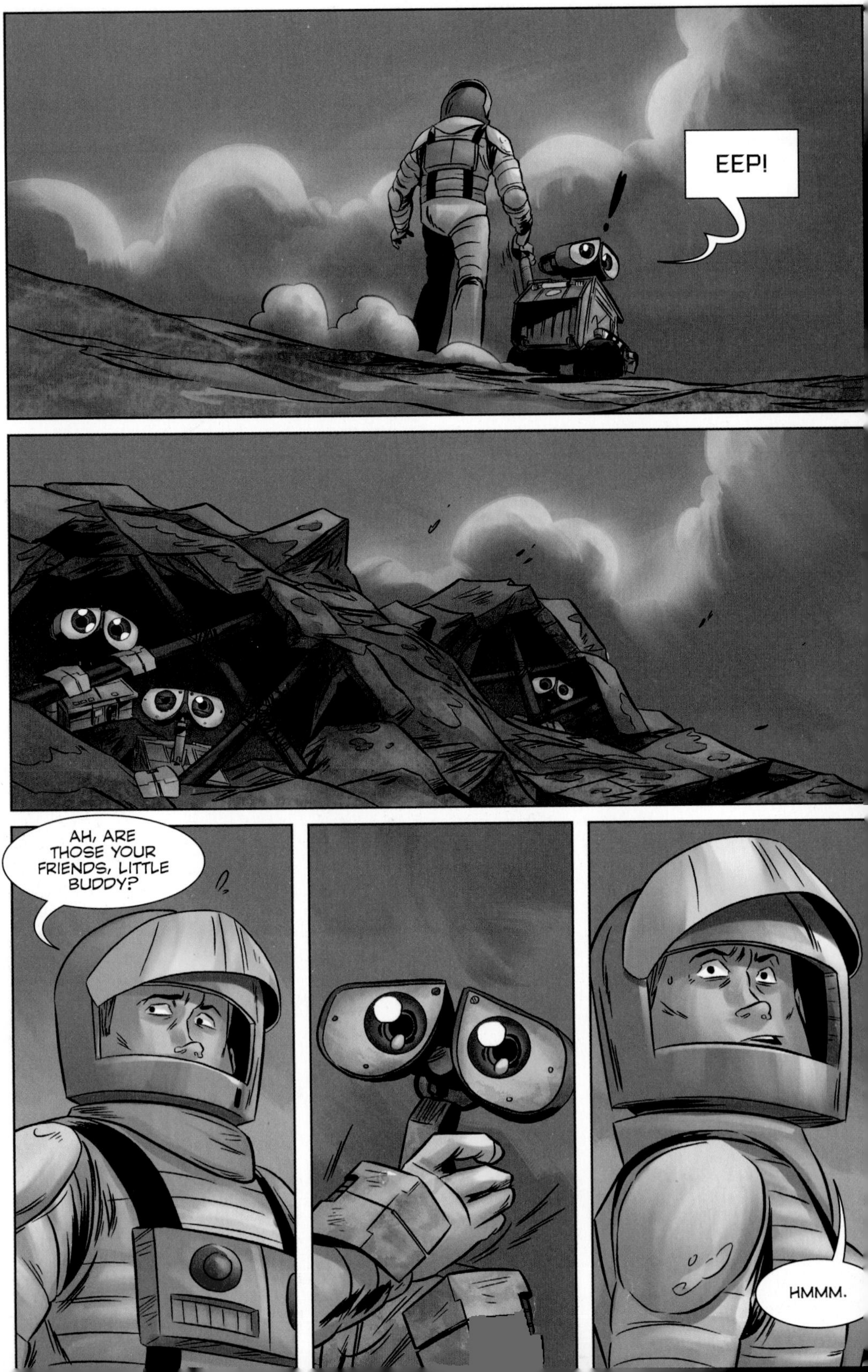
EEP!
AH, ARE THOSE YOUR FRIENDS, LITTLE BUDDY?
HMMM.

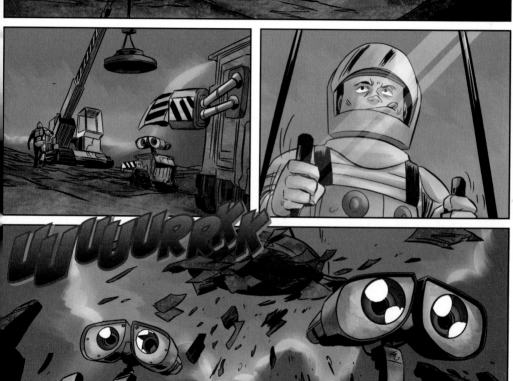

WWUUURRKK

AAANDYYYY!!!

...OH NO YOU DON'T...

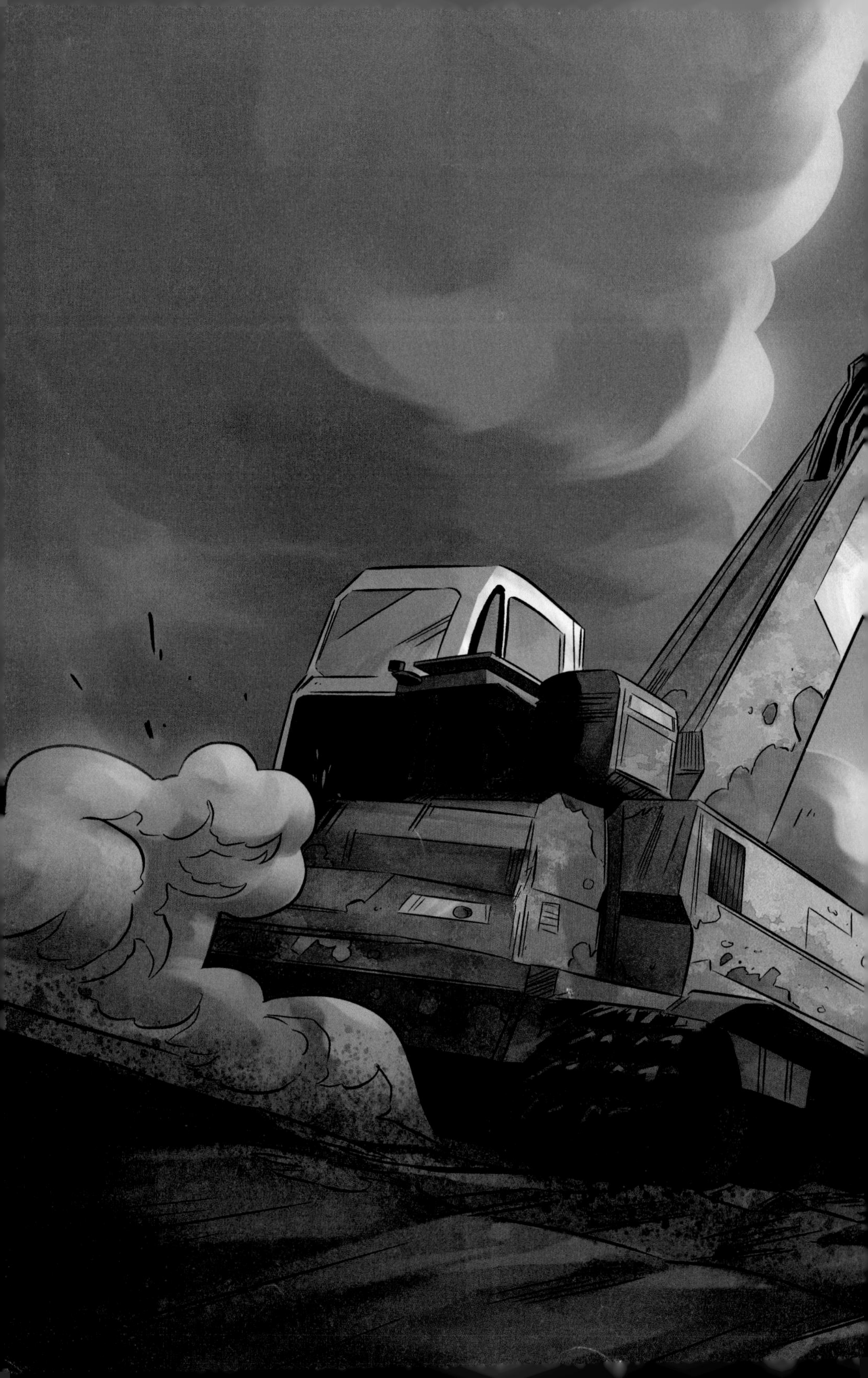

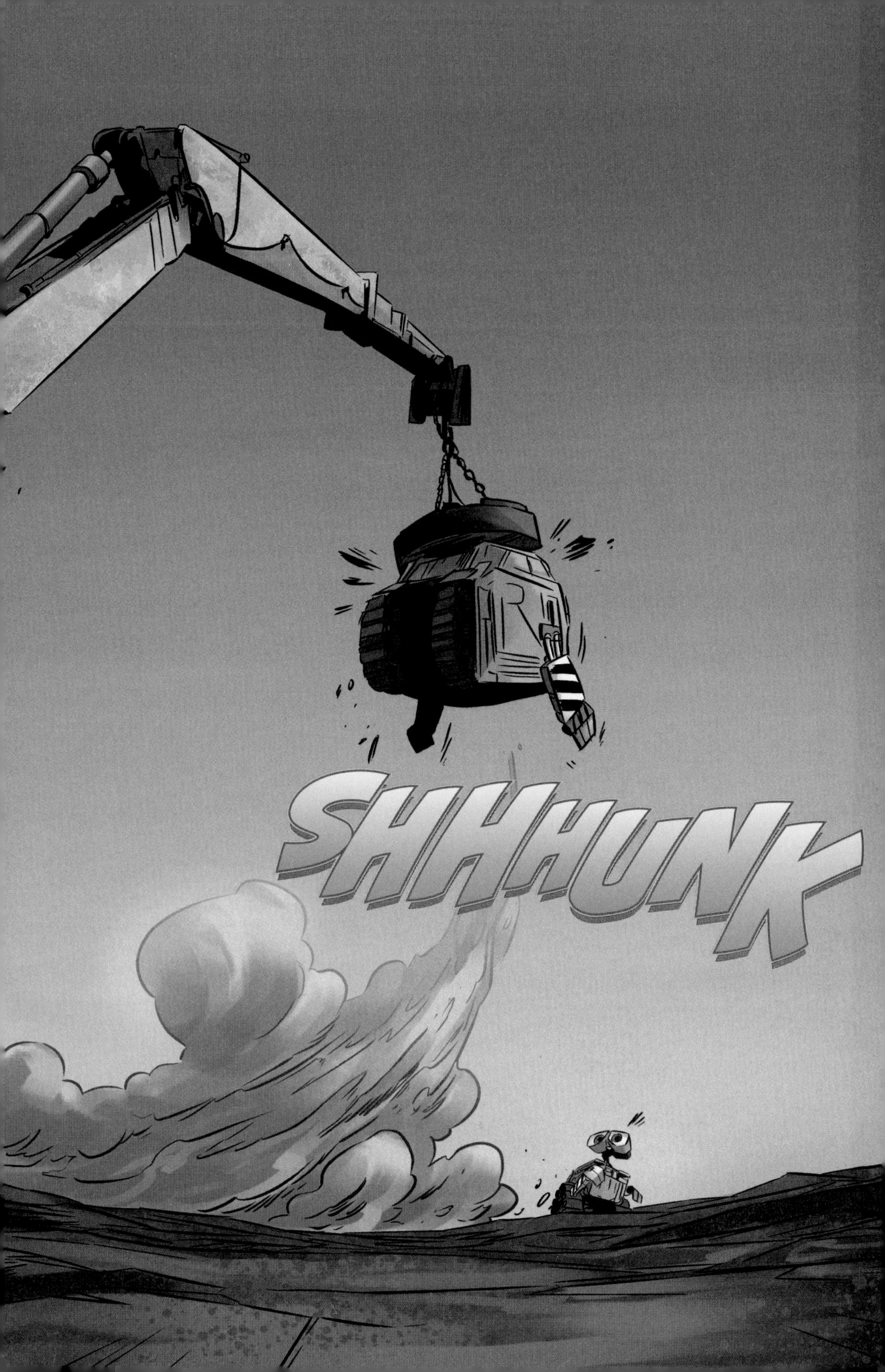
SHHHUNK

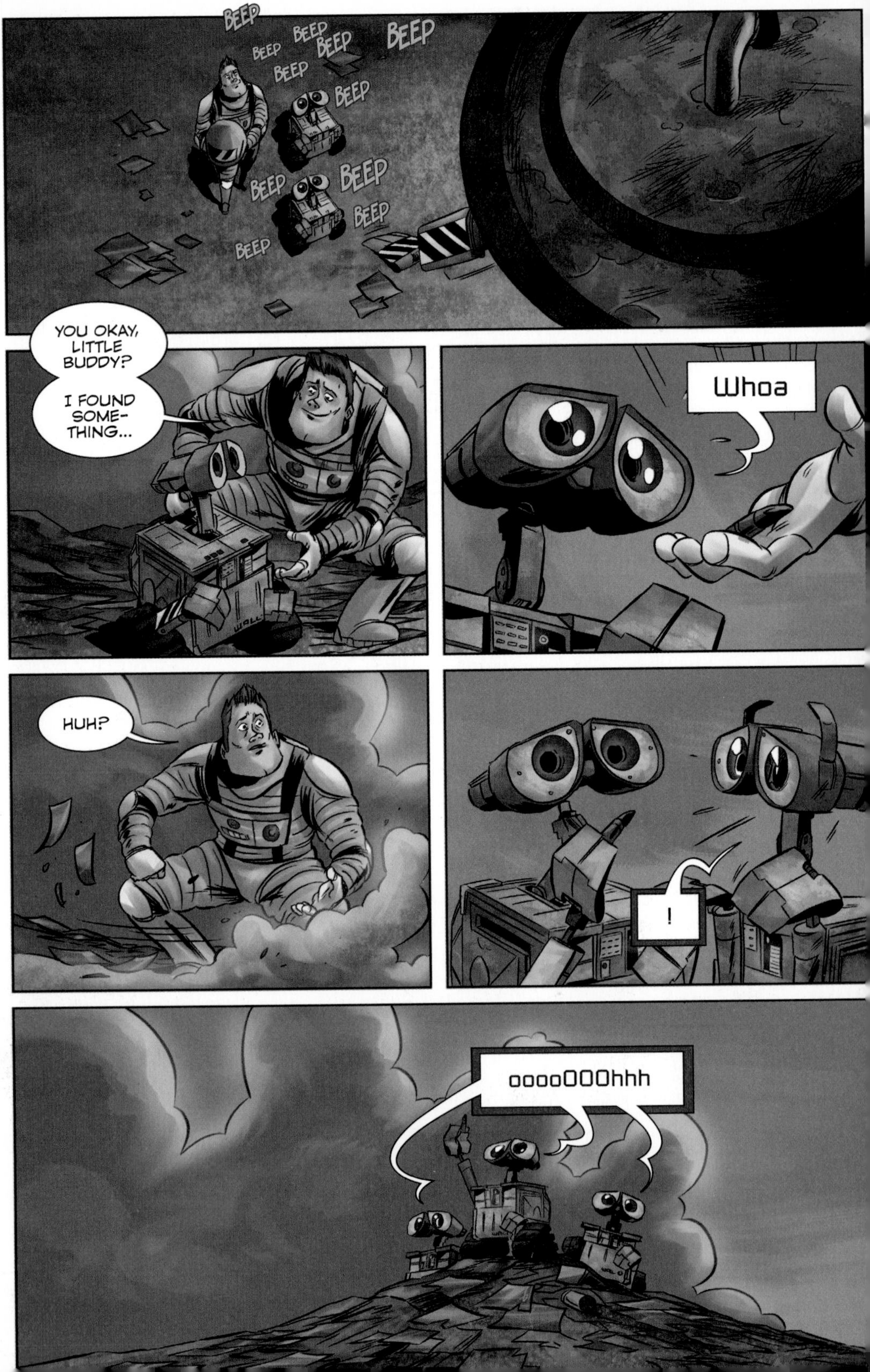

BEEP
BEEP
BEEP
BEEP
BEEP
BEEP
BEEP
BEEP
BEEP
BEEP
BEEP
YOU OKAY, LITTLE BUDDY?
I FOUND SOME-THING...
Whoa
HUH?
!
ooooOOOhhh

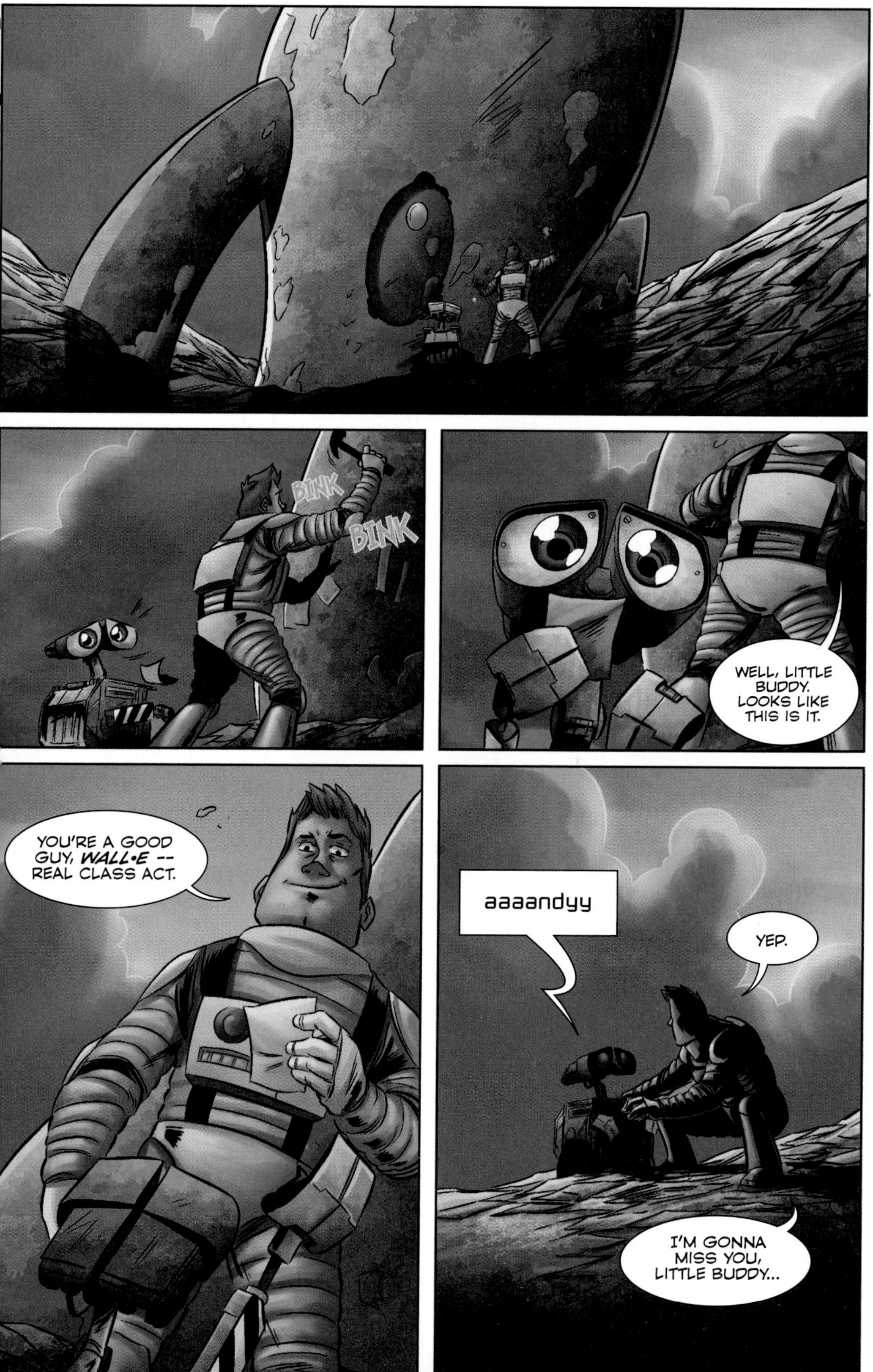
BINK
BINK
WELL, LITTLE BUDDY. LOOKS LIKE THIS IS IT.
YOU'RE A GOOD GUY, *WALL•E* -- REAL CLASS ACT.
aaaandyy
YEP.
I'M GONNA MISS YOU, LITTLE BUDDY...

fudd

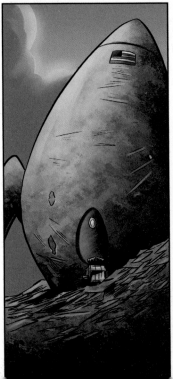

PISSHHHH

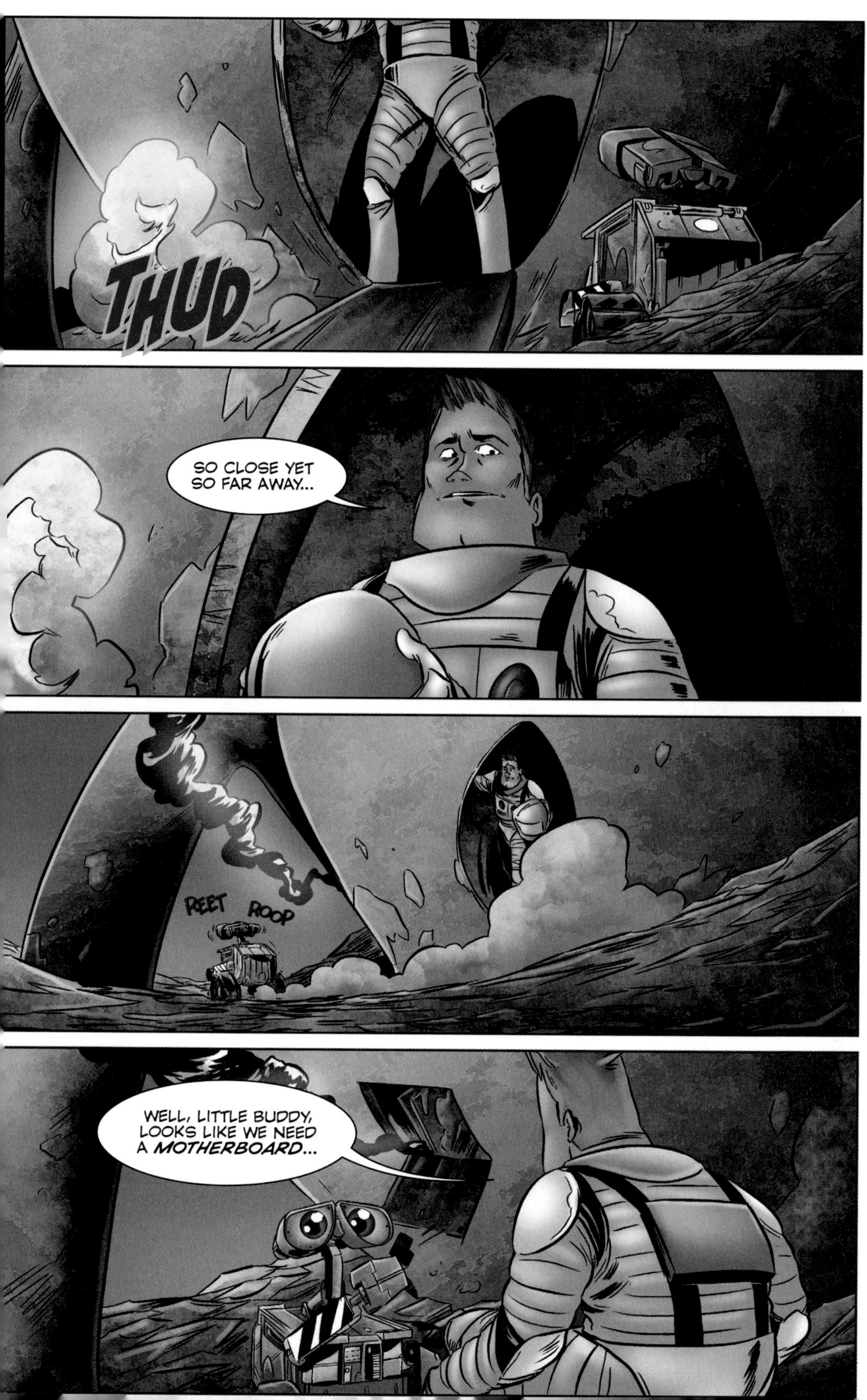
THUD
SO CLOSE YET SO FAR AWAY...
REET
ROOP
WELL, LITTLE BUDDY, LOOKS LIKE WE NEED A *MOTHERBOARD*...

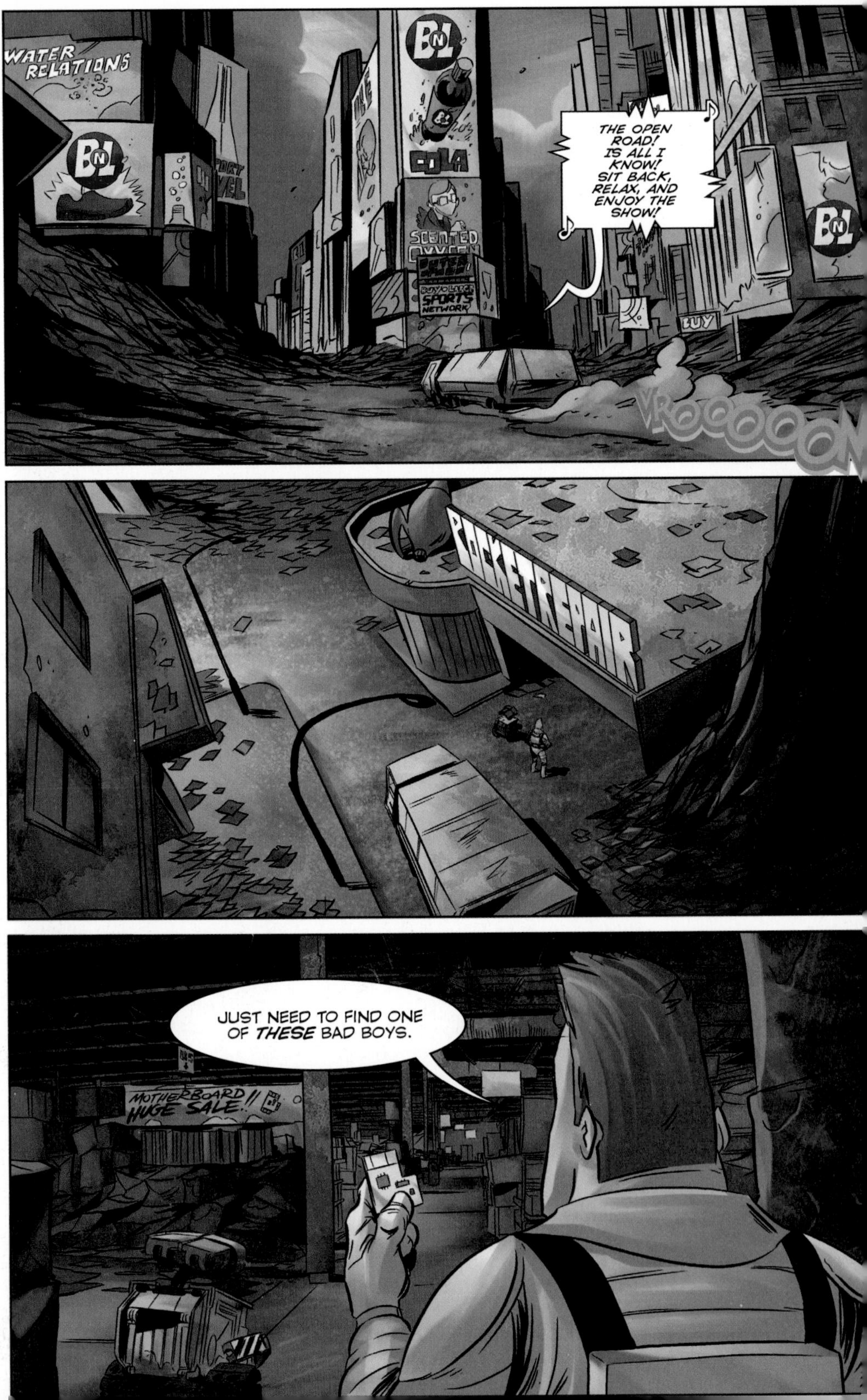

WATER RELATIONS
BnL
BnL
COLA
SCENTED OXYGEN
SPORTS NETWORK
THE OPEN ROAD! IS ALL I KNOW! SIT BACK, RELAX, AND ENJOY THE SHOW!
BnL
BUY
VROOOOOOM
ROCKET REPAIR
JUST NEED TO FIND ONE OF *THESE* BAD BOYS.
MOTHERBOARD HUGE SALE!!

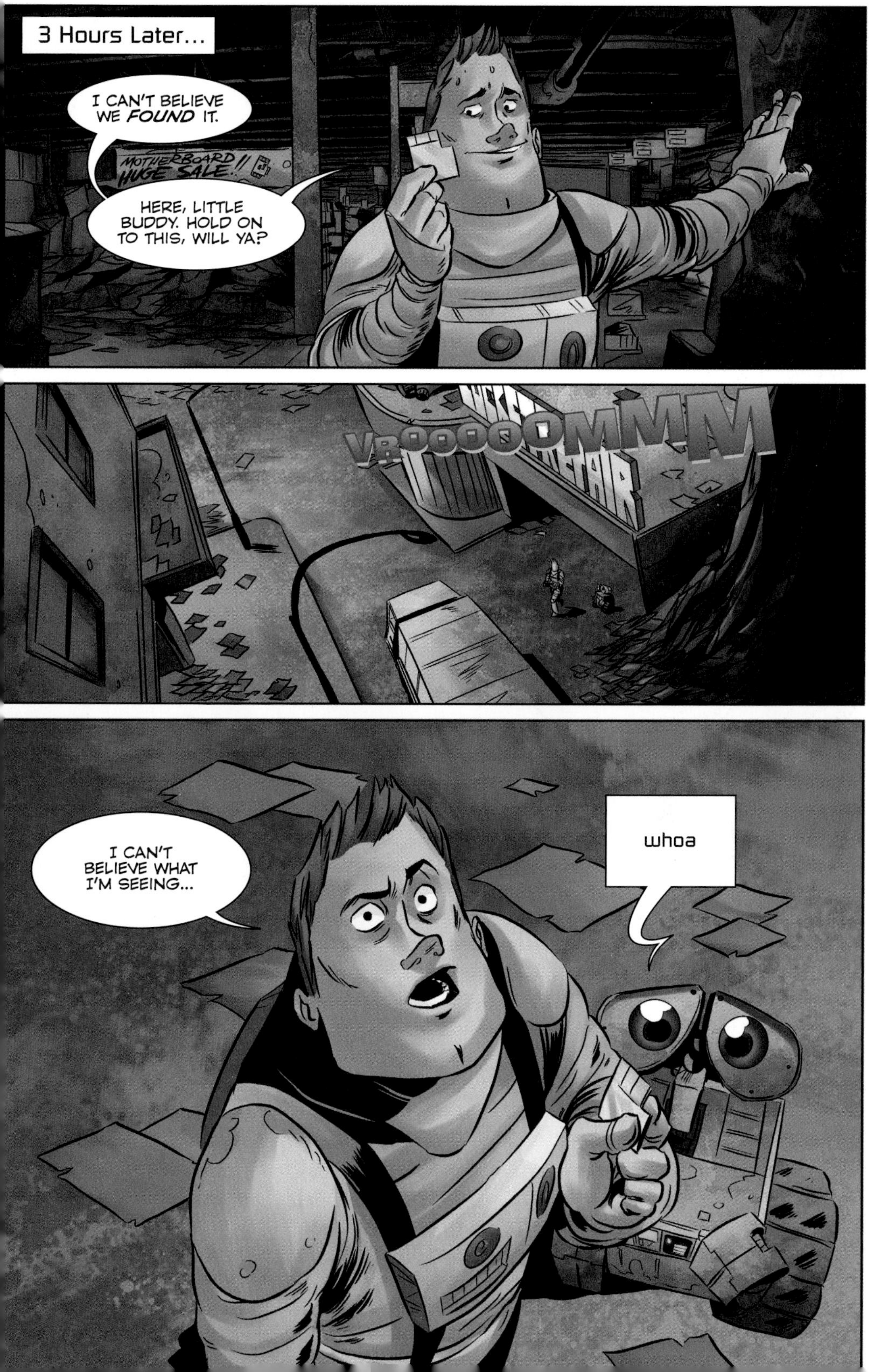
3 Hours Later...
I CAN'T BELIEVE WE *FOUND* IT.
MOTHERBOARD HUGE SALE!!
HERE, LITTLE BUDDY. HOLD ON TO THIS, WILL YA?
VROOOOOMMM
I CAN'T BELIEVE WHAT I'M SEEING...
whoa

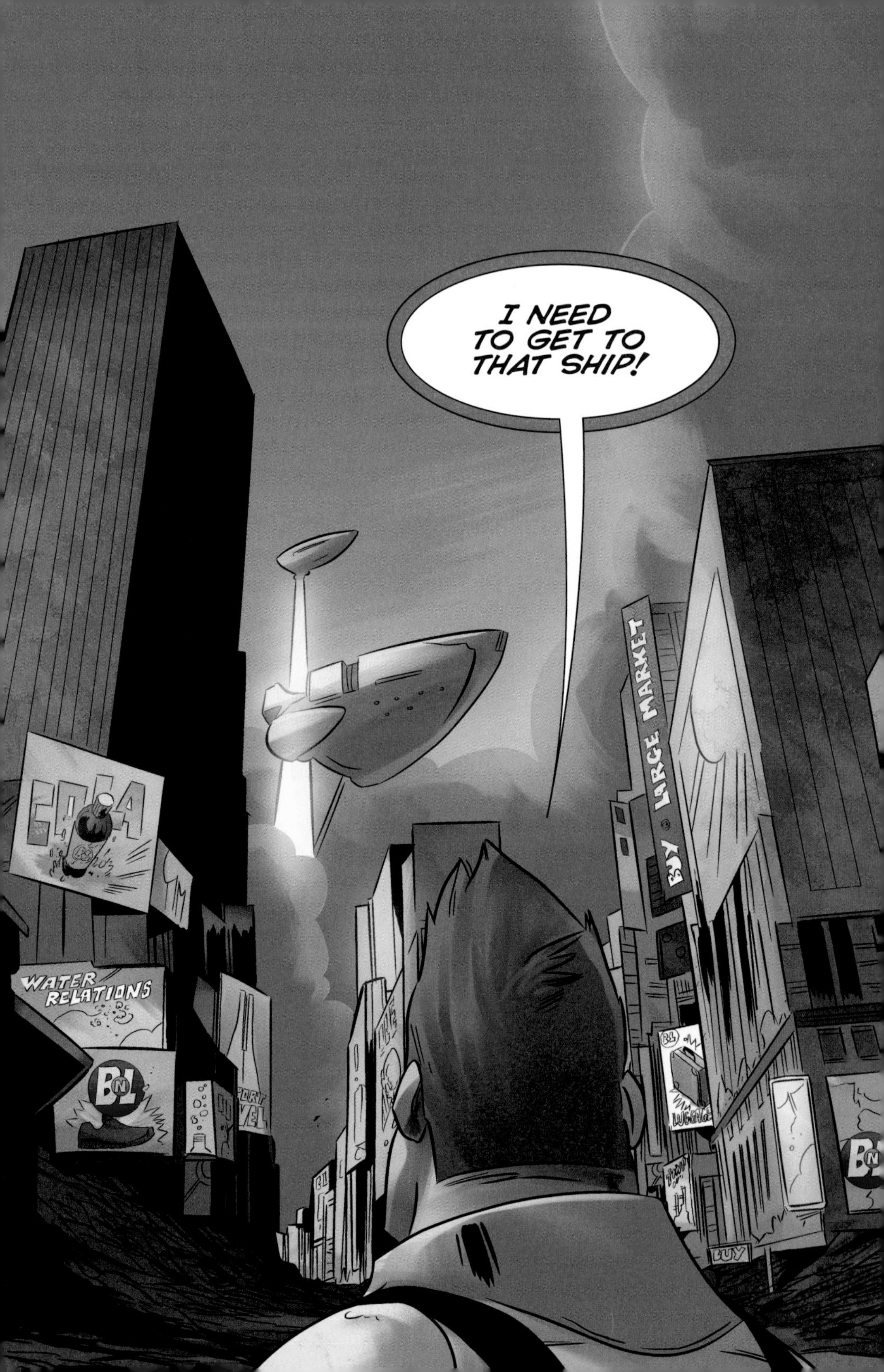
I NEED TO GET TO THAT SHIP!
BUY LARGE MARKET
WATER RELATIONS
BUY

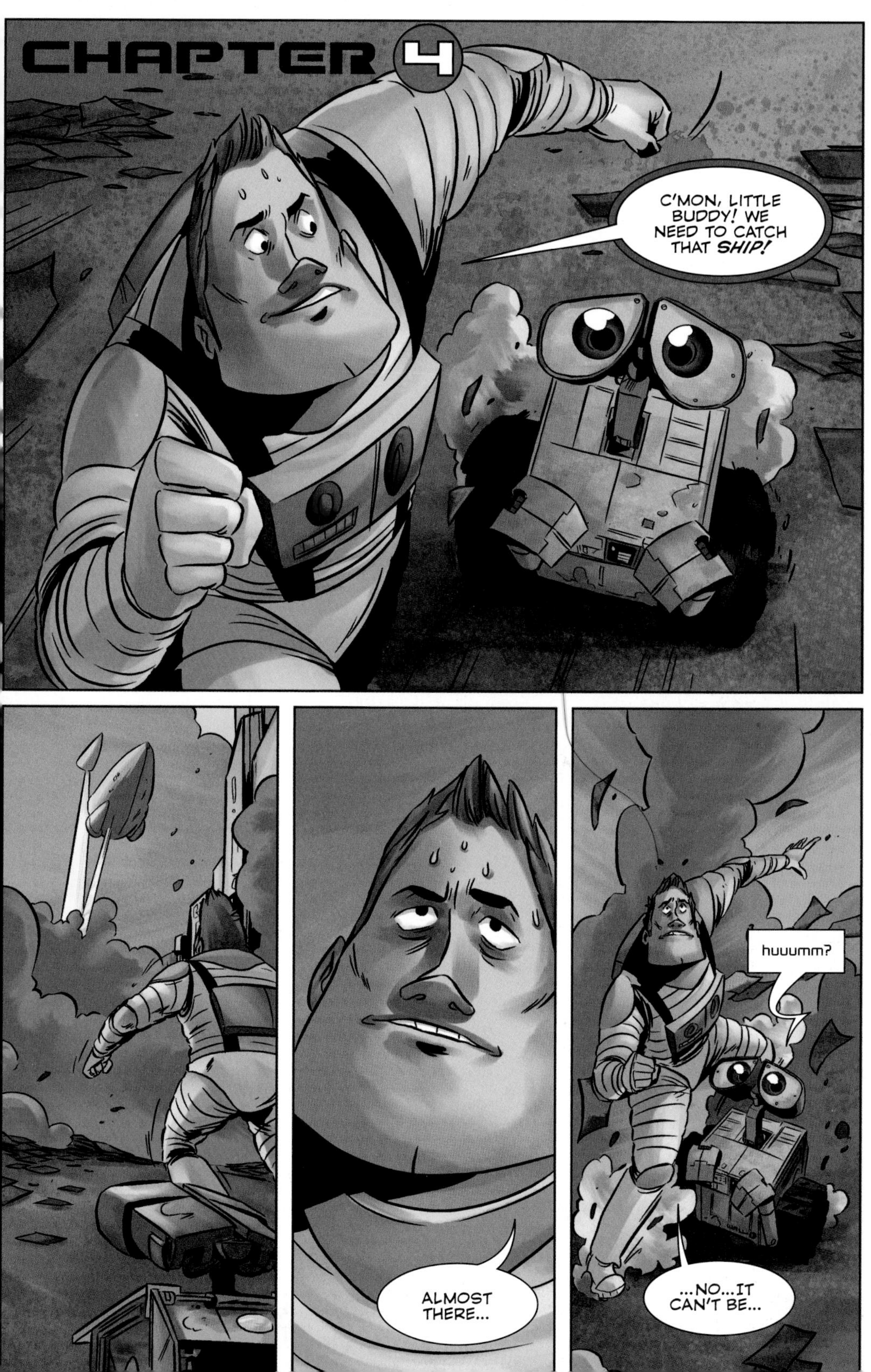
CHAPTER 4
C'MON, LITTLE BUDDY! WE NEED TO CATCH THAT *SHIP!*
ALMOST THERE...
huuumm?
...NO...IT CAN'T BE...

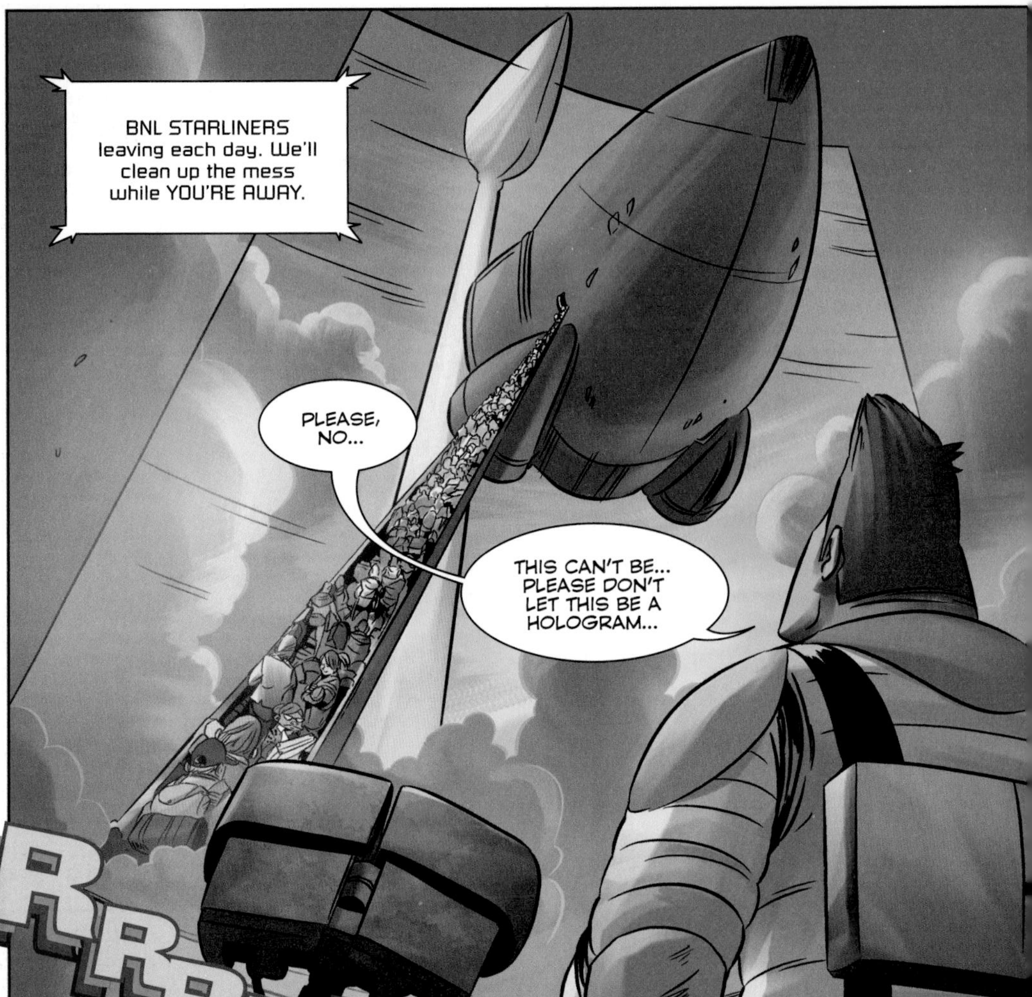
BNL STARLINERS leaving each day. We'll clean up the mess while YOU'RE AWAY.
PLEASE, NO...
THIS CAN'T BE... PLEASE DON'T LET THIS BE A HOLOGRAM...
RRRRUMMMMBBLE

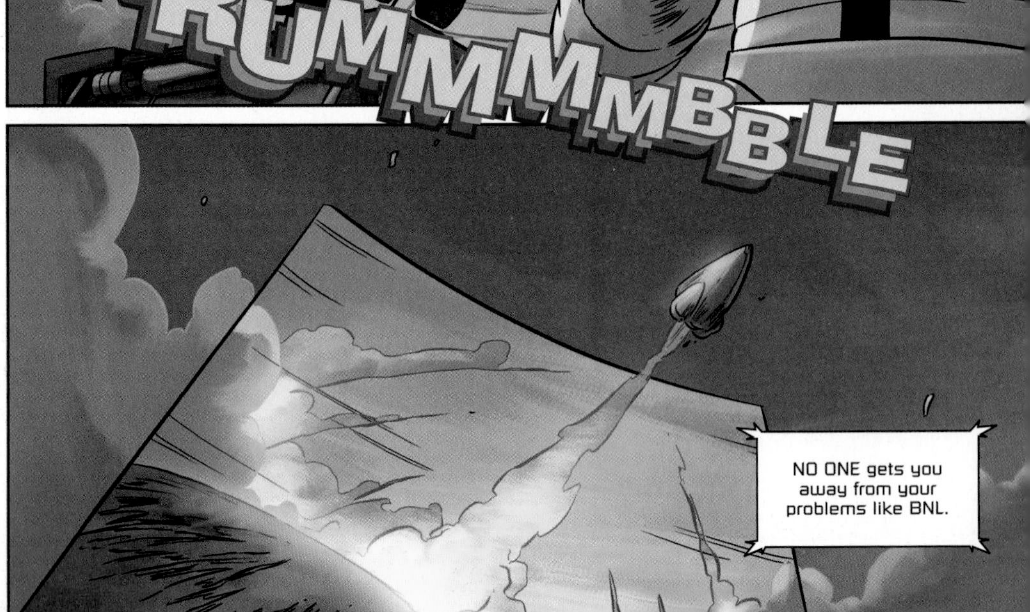
NO ONE gets you away from your problems like BNL.

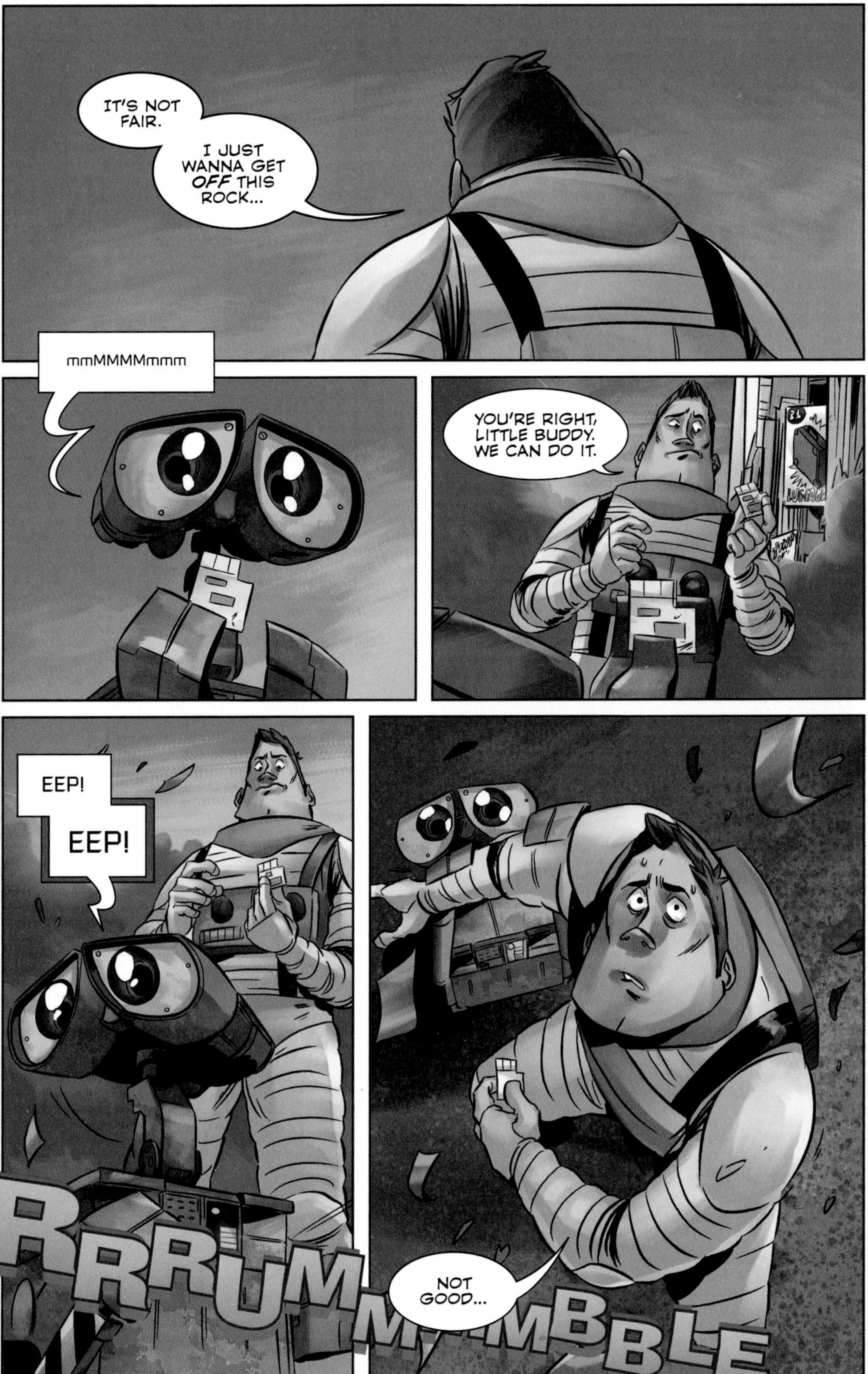
IT'S NOT FAIR.
I JUST WANNA GET *OFF* THIS ROCK...
mmMMMMmmm
YOU'RE RIGHT, LITTLE BUDDY. WE CAN DO IT.
LUGGAGE
EEP!
EEP!
RRRUMMMMMBBLE
NOT GOOD...

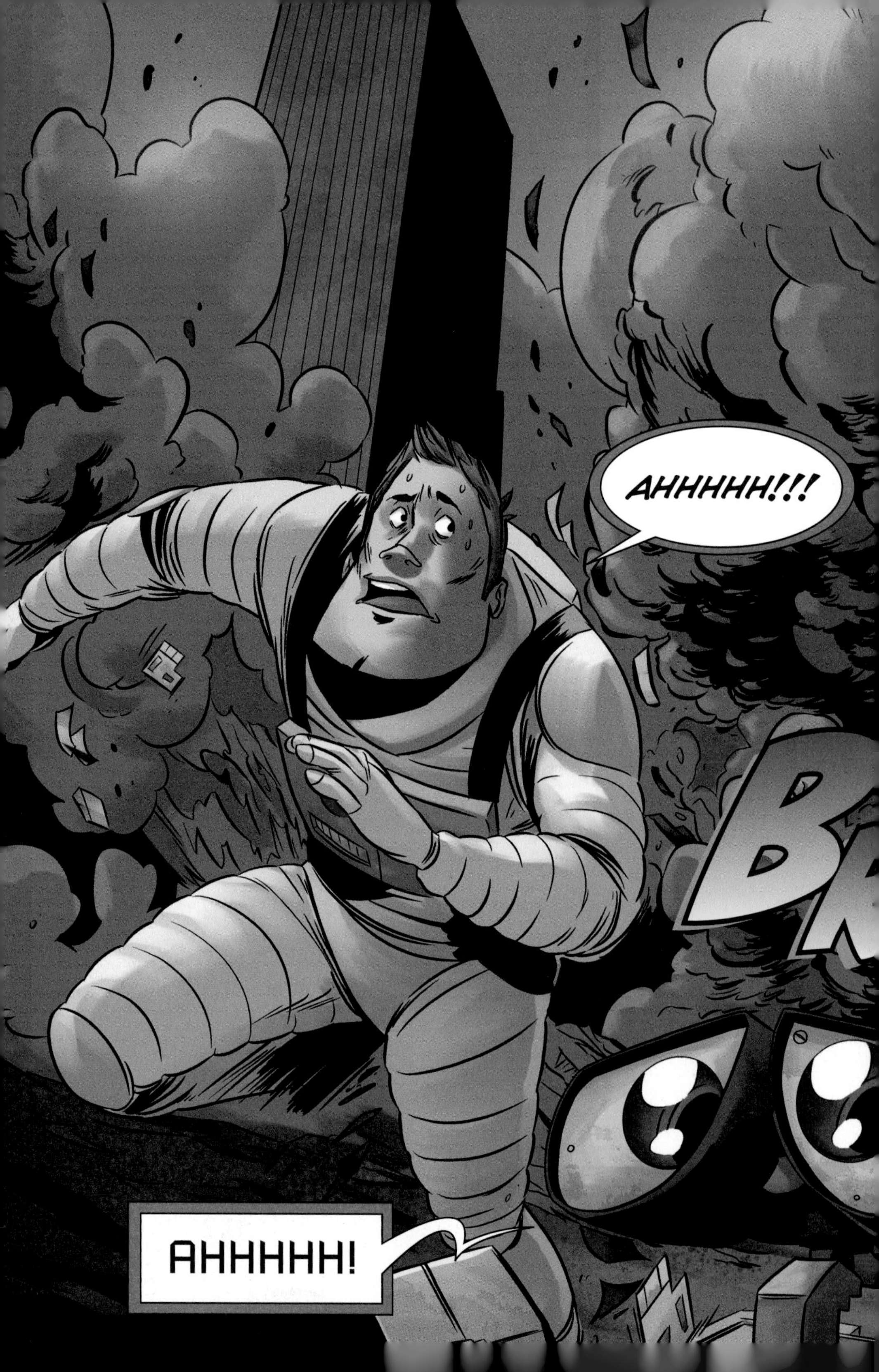
AHHHHH!!!
AHHHHH!

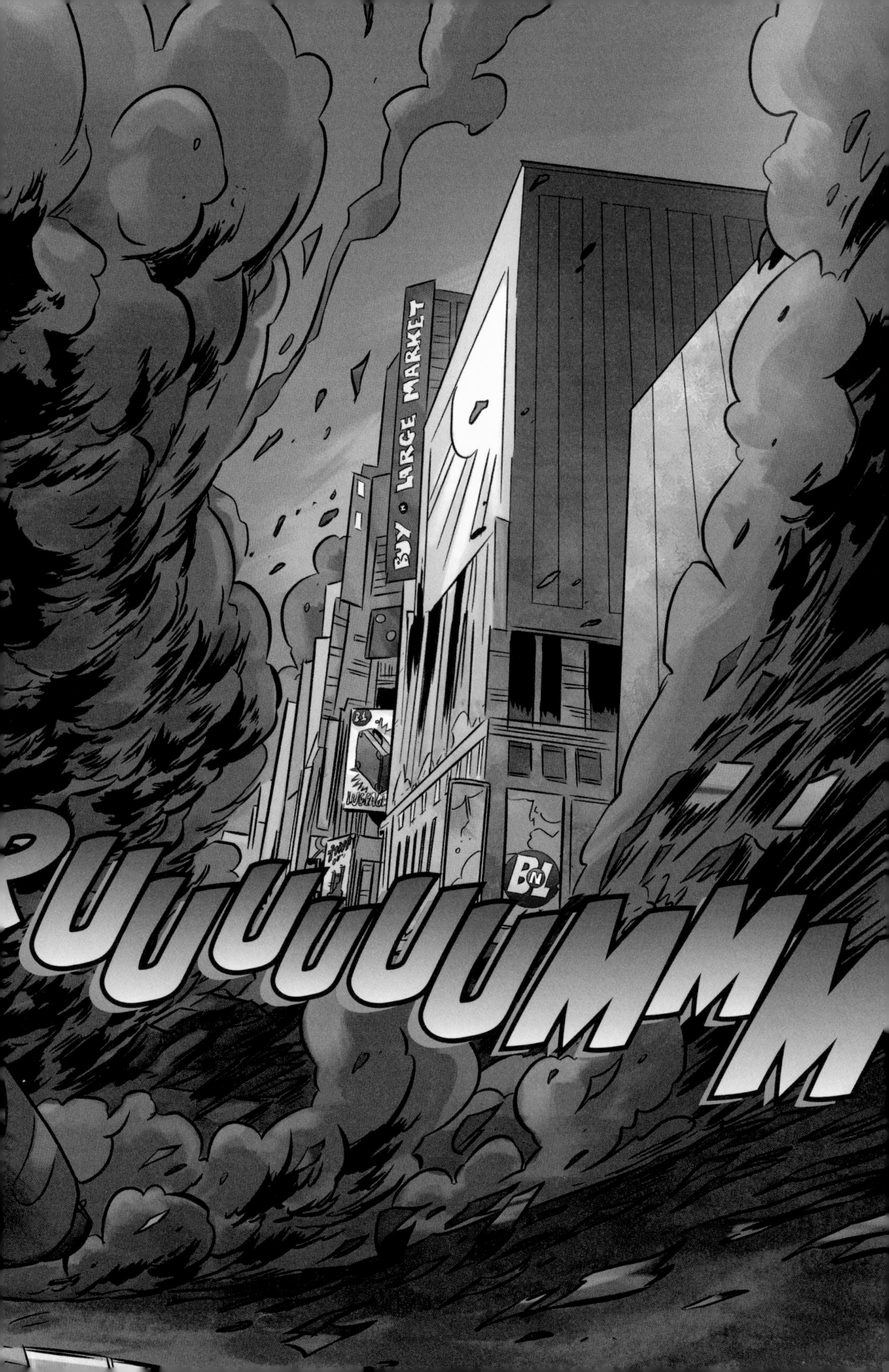
BUY N LARGE MARKET
LUGGAGE
RUUUUUUMMM

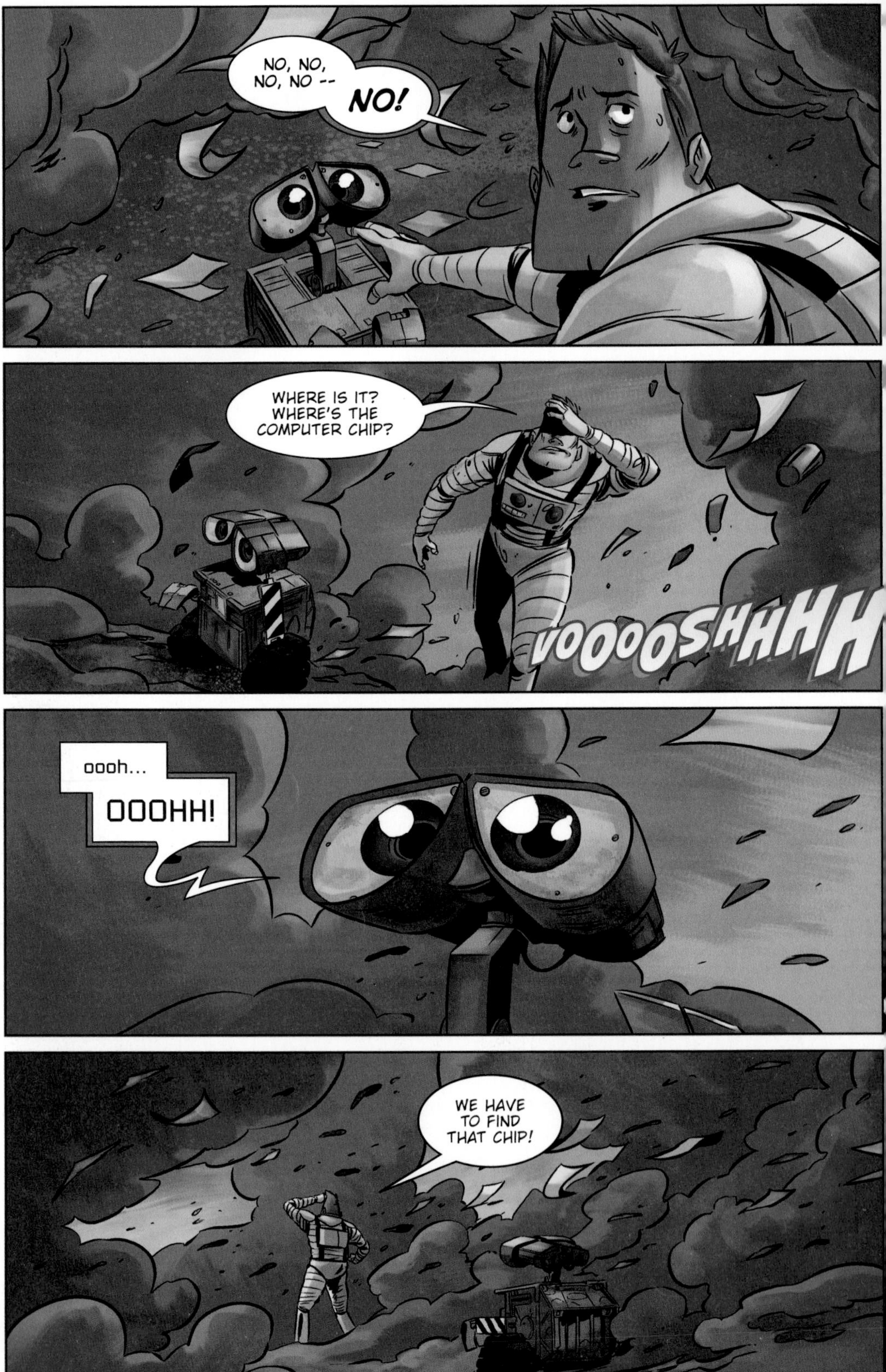
NO, NO,
NO, NO --
NO!
WHERE IS IT?
WHERE'S THE
COMPUTER CHIP?
VOOOOSHHHH
oooh...
OOOHH!
WE HAVE
TO FIND
THAT CHIP!

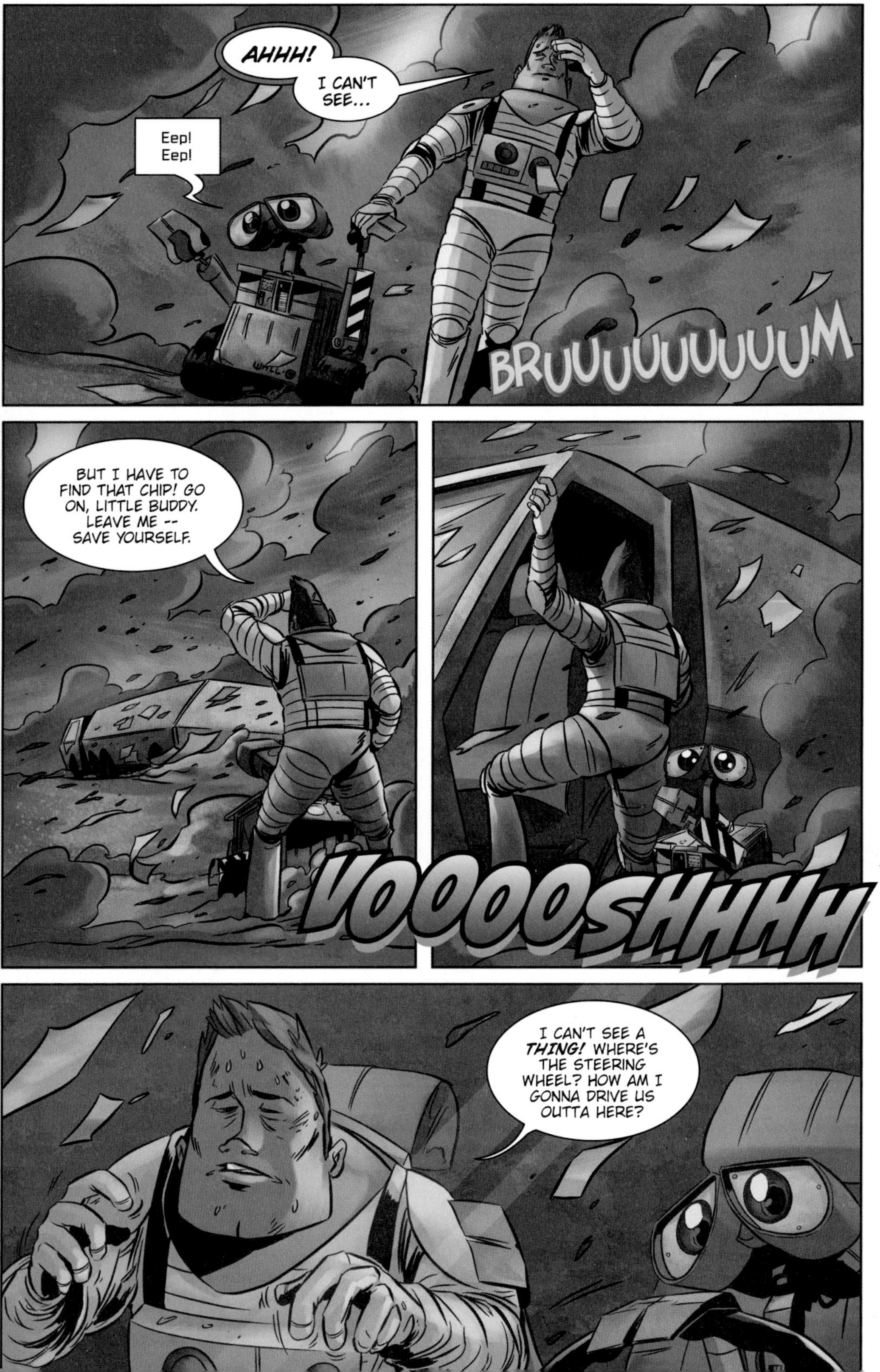
AHHH!
I CAN'T SEE...
Eep! Eep!
BRUUUUUUUUUM
BUT I HAVE TO FIND THAT CHIP! GO ON, LITTLE BUDDY. LEAVE ME -- SAVE YOURSELF.
VOOOOOSHHHH
I CAN'T SEE A THING! WHERE'S THE STEERING WHEEL? HOW AM I GONNA DRIVE US OUTTA HERE?

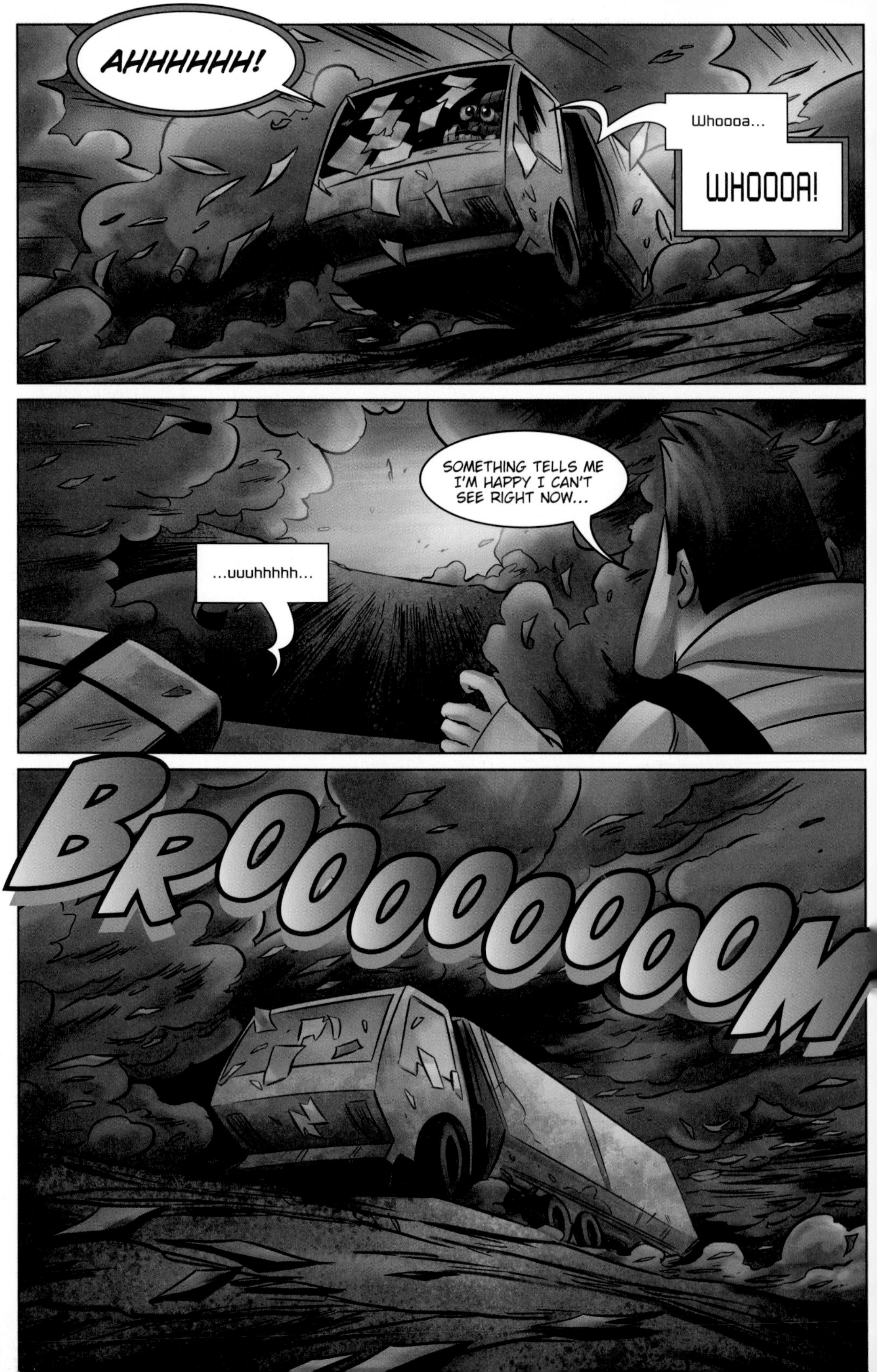
AHHHHHH!
Whoooa...
WHOOOA!
SOMETHING TELLS ME I'M HAPPY I CAN'T SEE RIGHT NOW...
...uuuhhhhh...
BROOOOOOOOM

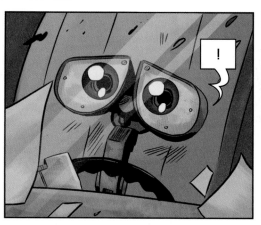

!

...LITTLE BUDDY...

‡gulp‡

...

WOOOOOO!

I *REALLY* HOPE THAT'S A GOOD "WOO"...

FOoOOOSH

WHERE ARE WE GOING?

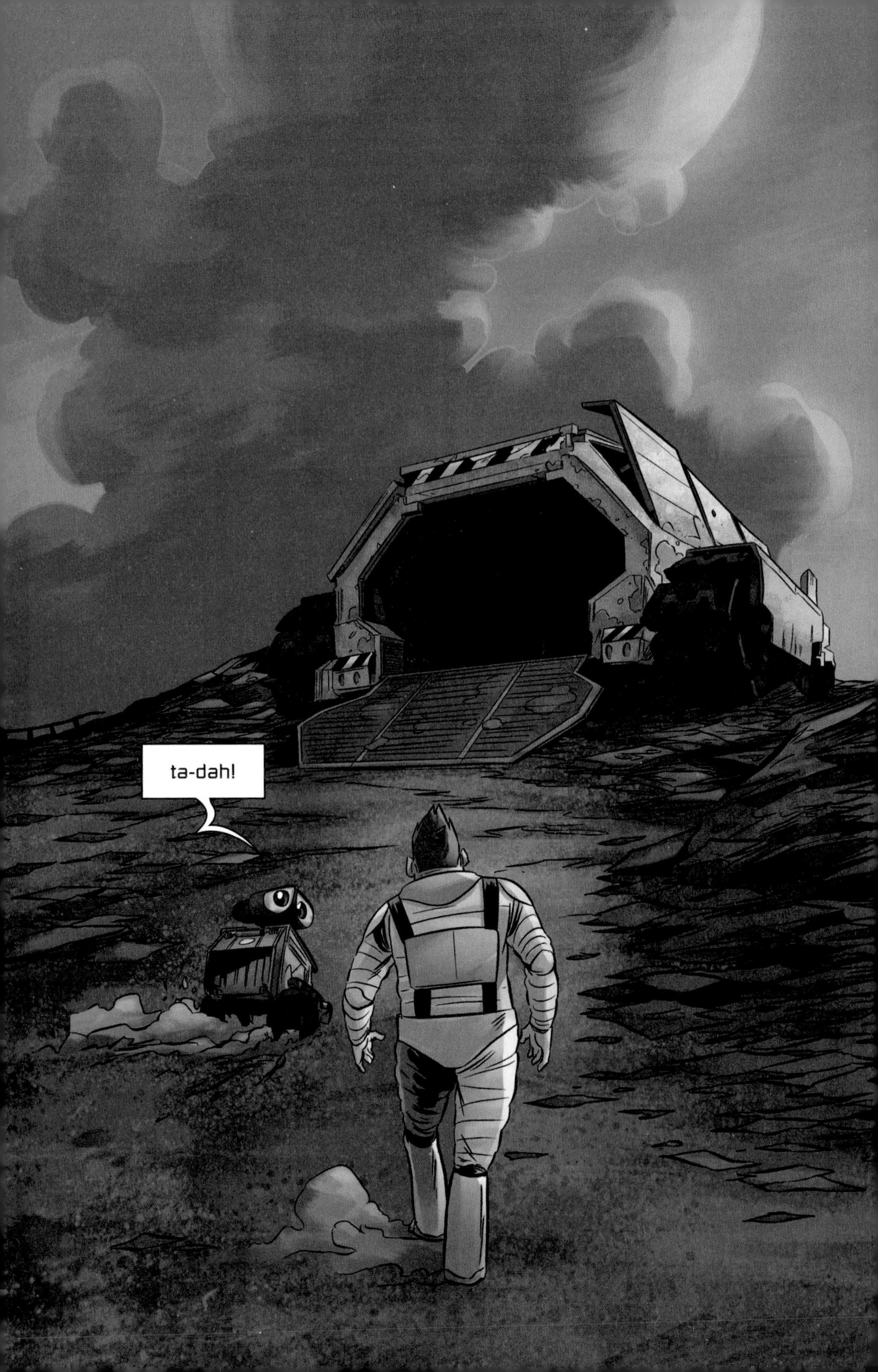
ta-dah!

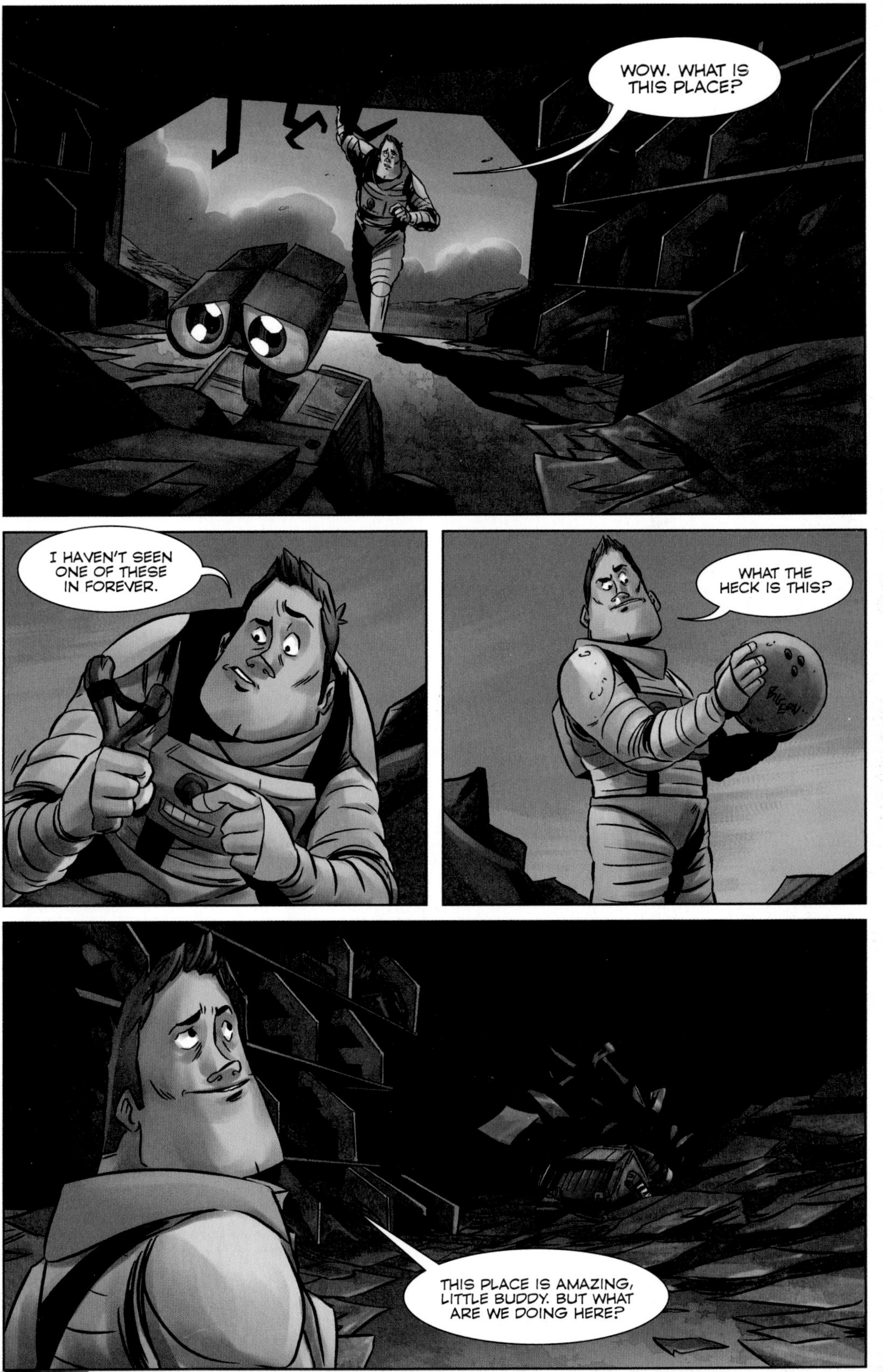
WOW. WHAT IS THIS PLACE?
I HAVEN'T SEEN ONE OF THESE IN FOREVER.
WHAT THE HECK IS THIS?
THIS PLACE IS AMAZING, LITTLE BUDDY. BUT WHAT ARE WE DOING HERE?

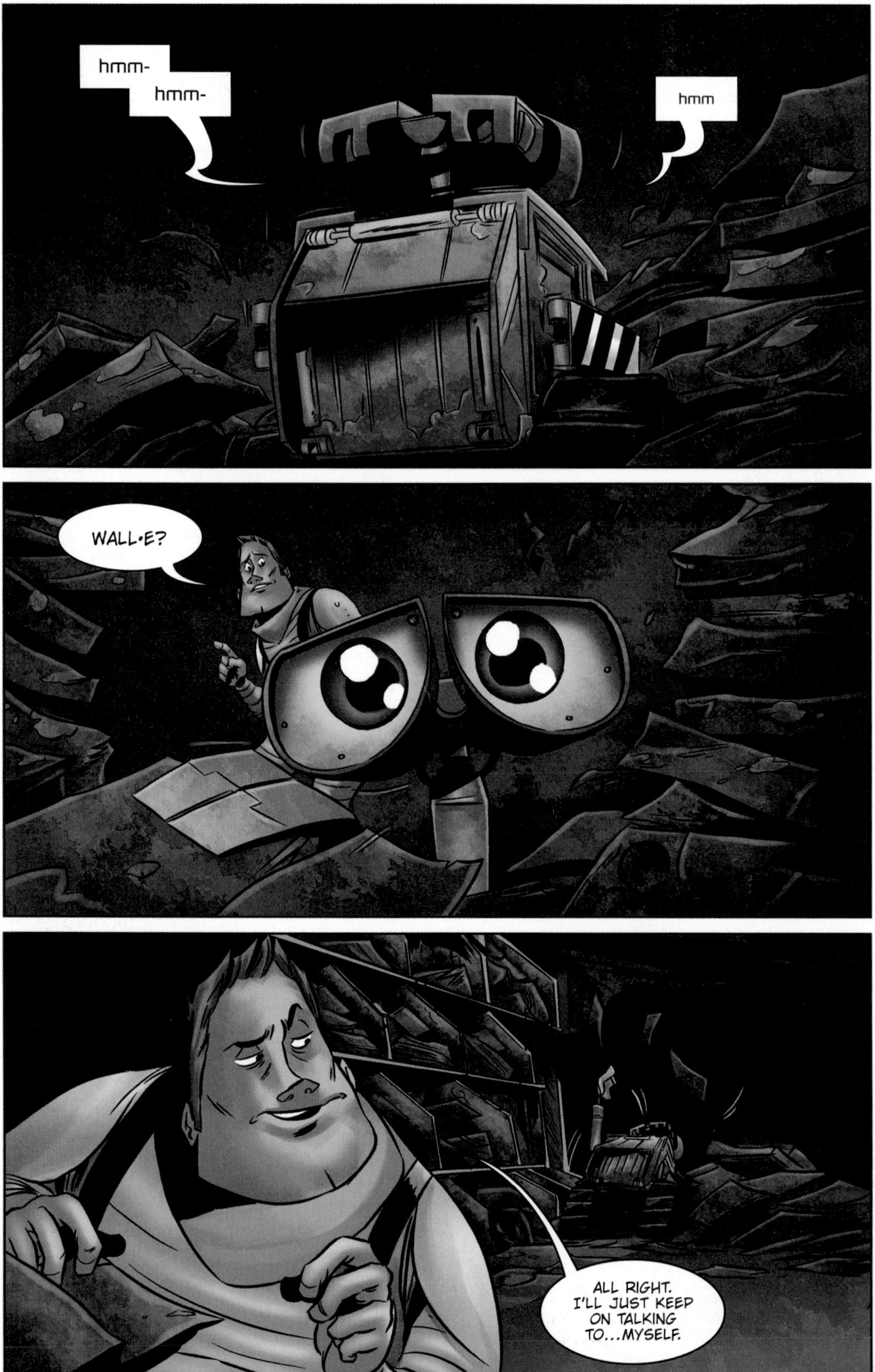
hmm-
hmm-
hmm
WALL•E?
ALL RIGHT. I'LL JUST KEEP ON TALKING TO...MYSELF.

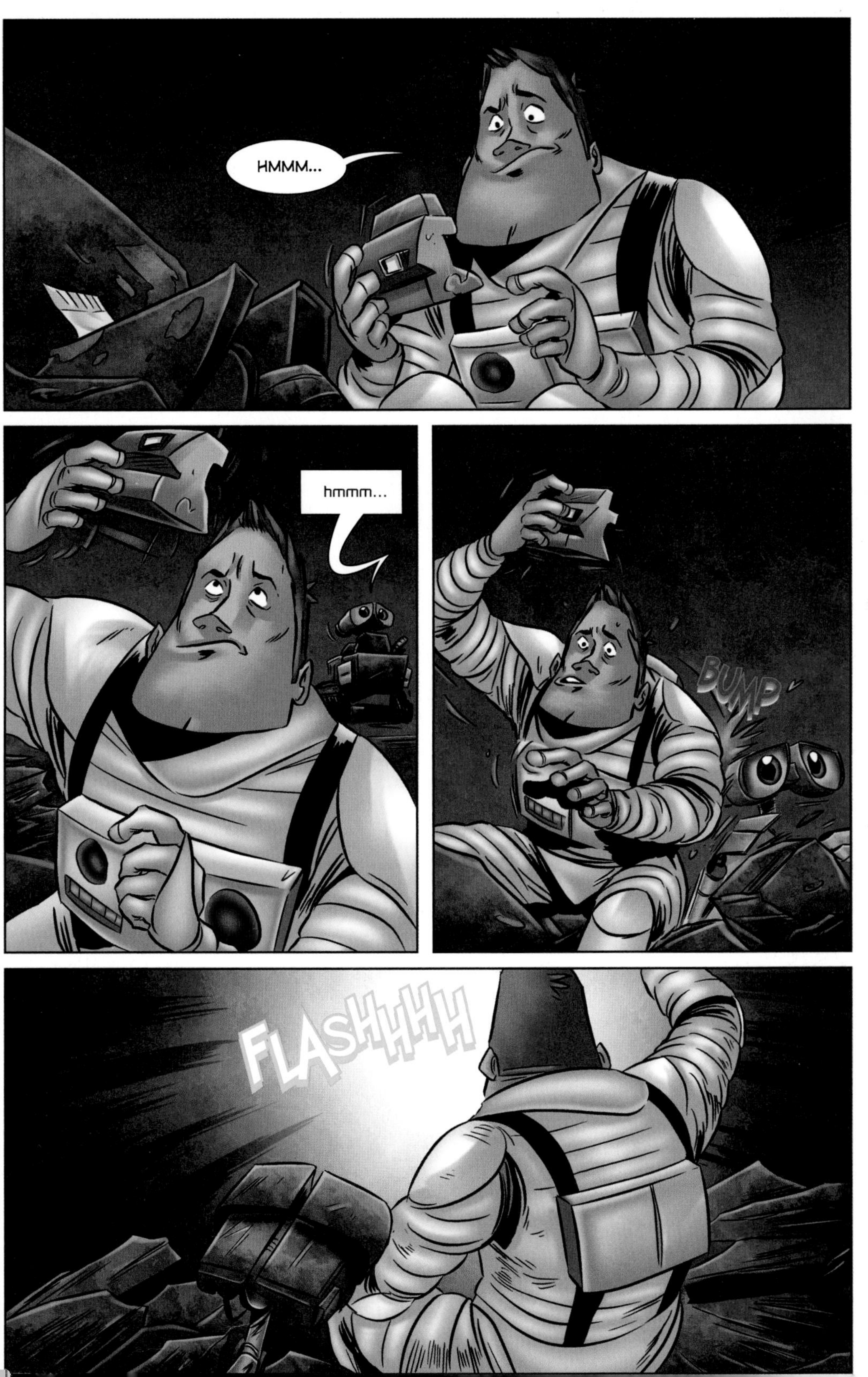
HMMM...
hmmm...
BUMP
FLASHHHH

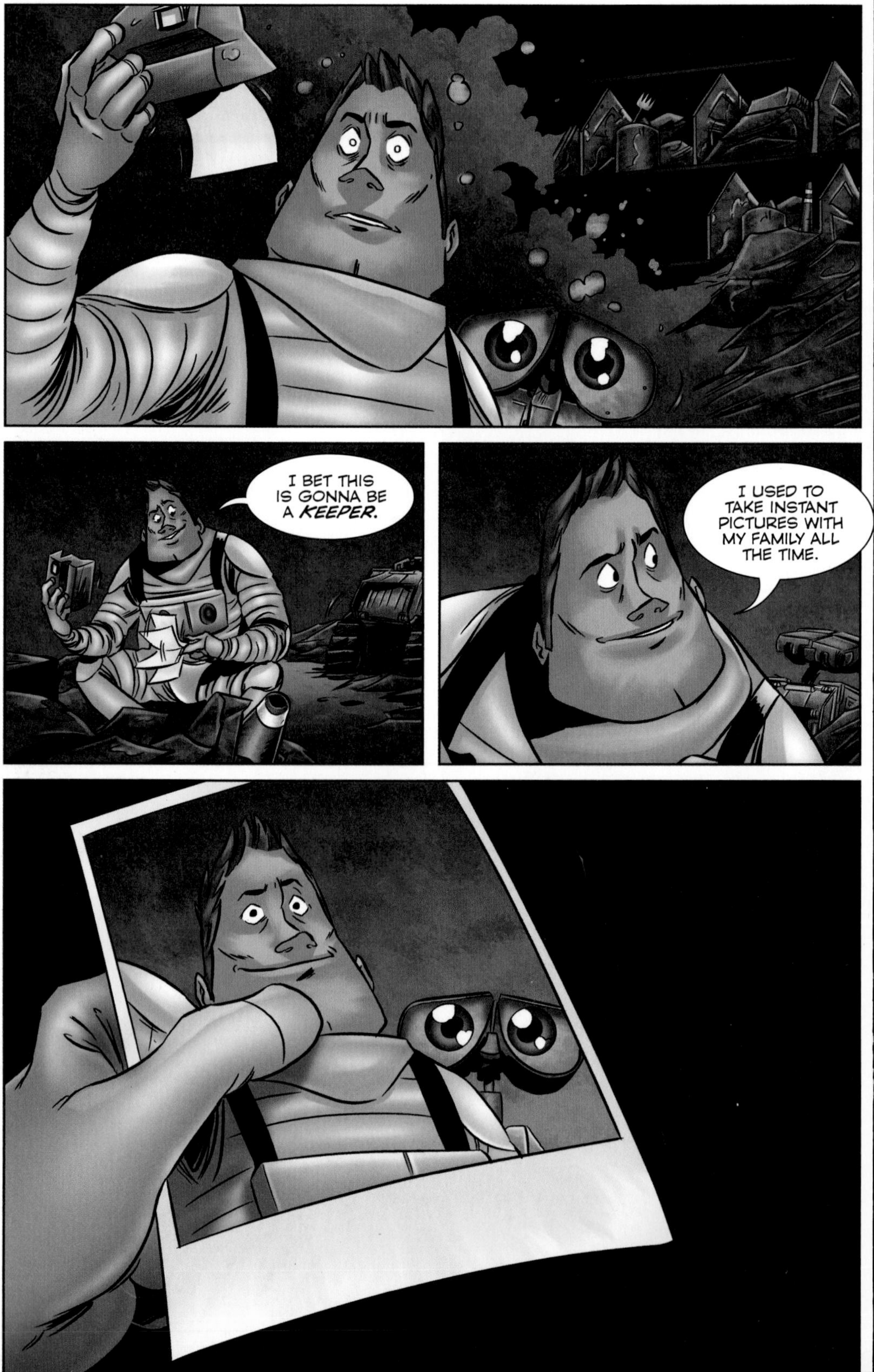
I BET THIS IS GONNA BE A *KEEPER*.
I USED TO TAKE INSTANT PICTURES WITH MY FAMILY ALL THE TIME.

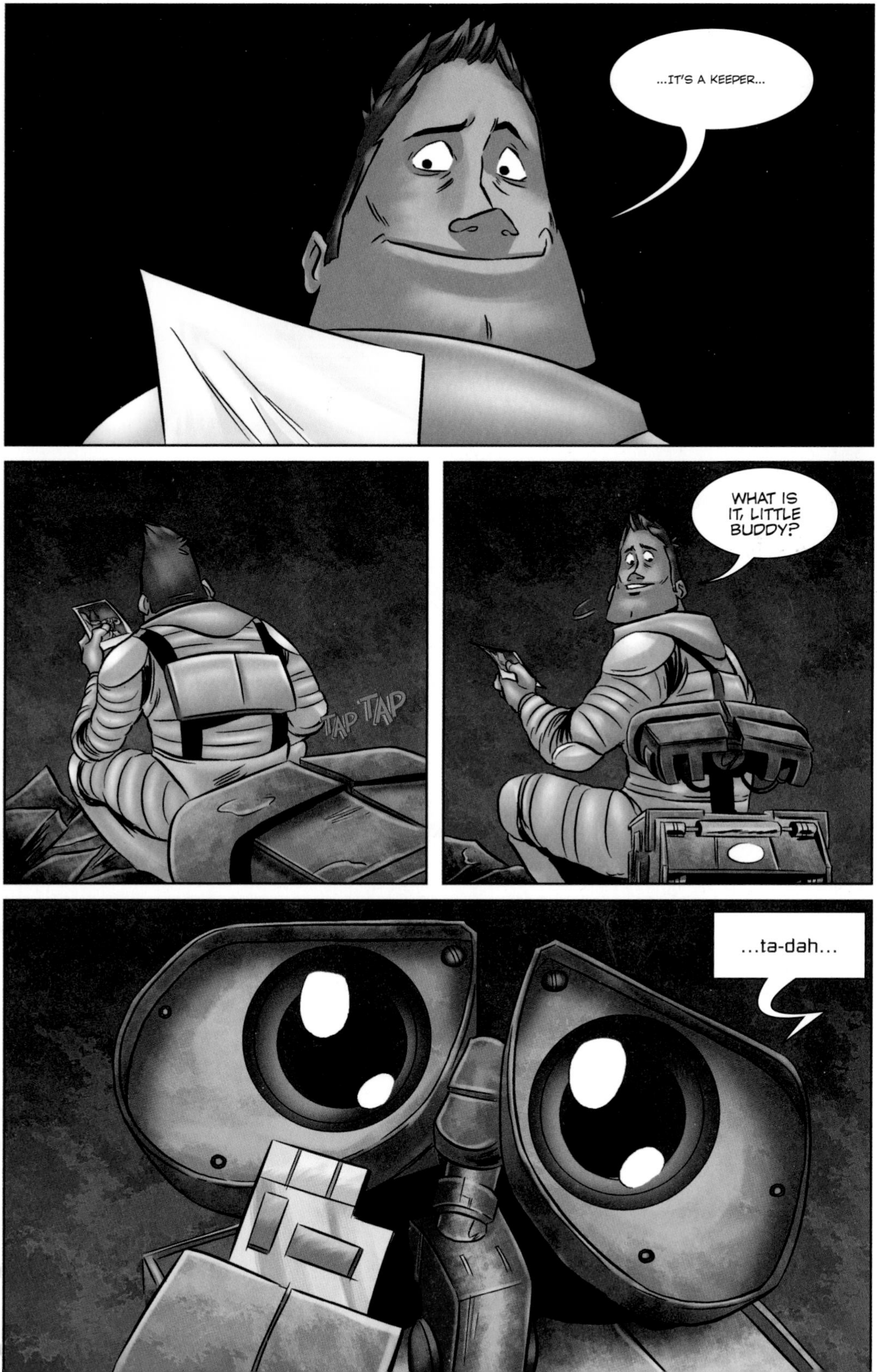
...IT'S A KEEPER...
TAP TAP
WHAT IS IT, LITTLE BUDDY?
...ta-dah...

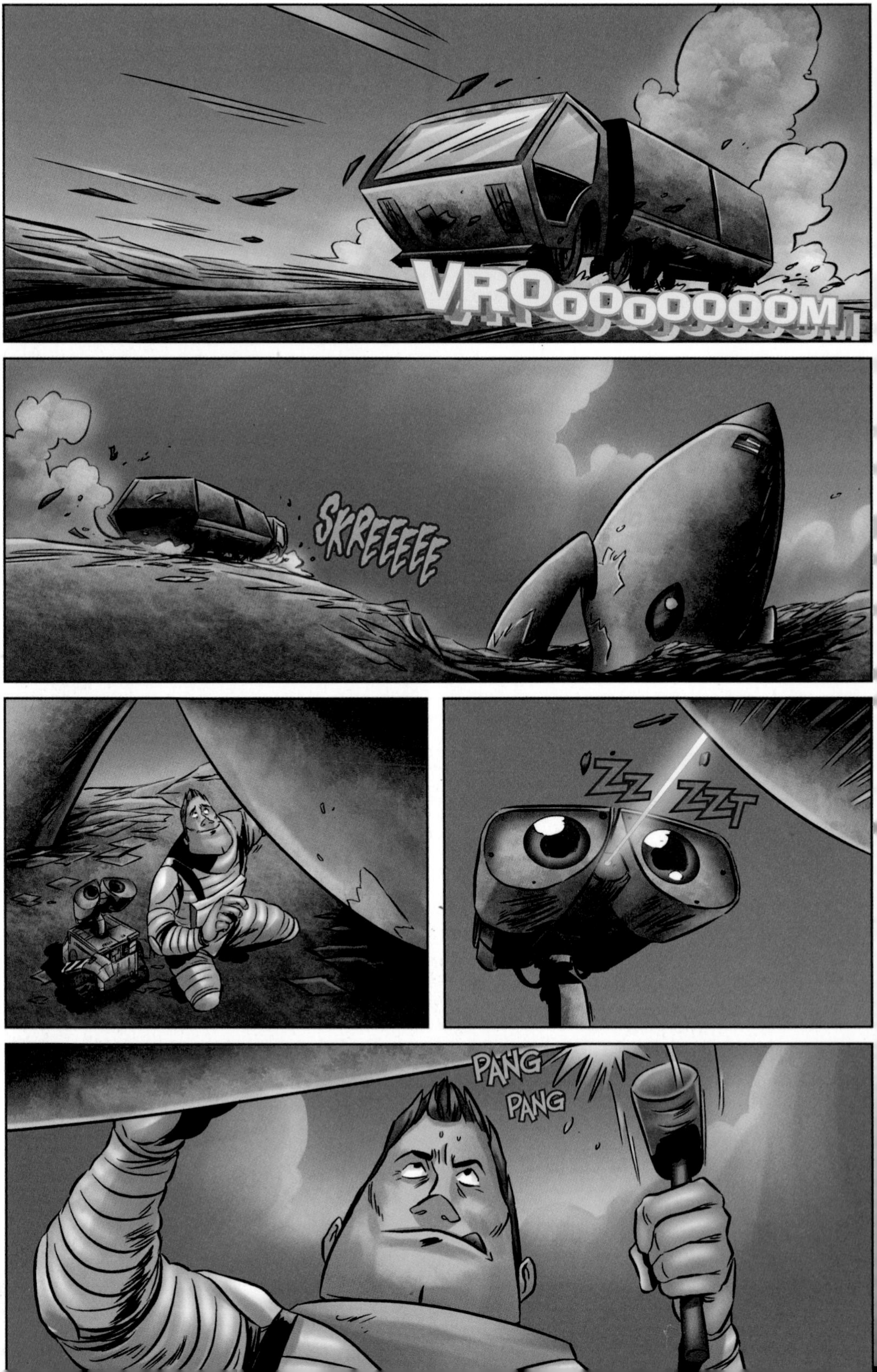
VROOOOOOOOOOM
SKREEEEE
ZZ ZZZT
PANG
PANG

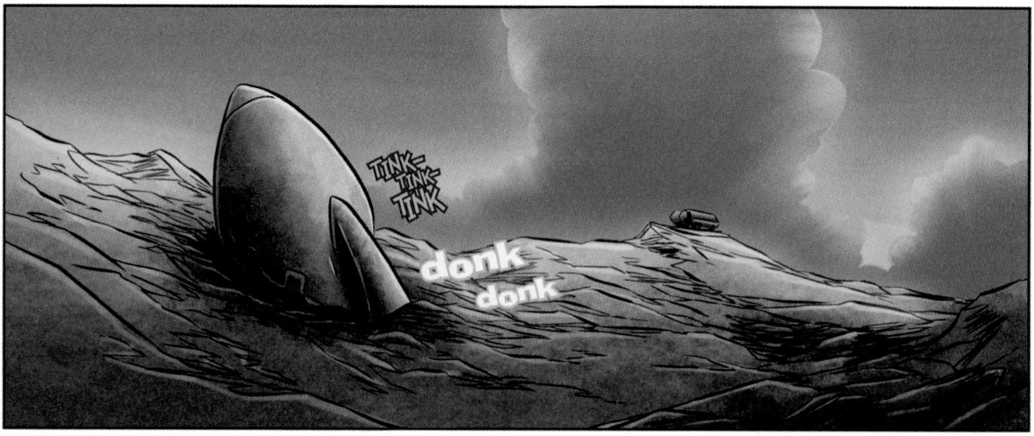
TINK-
TINK-
TINK
donk
donk

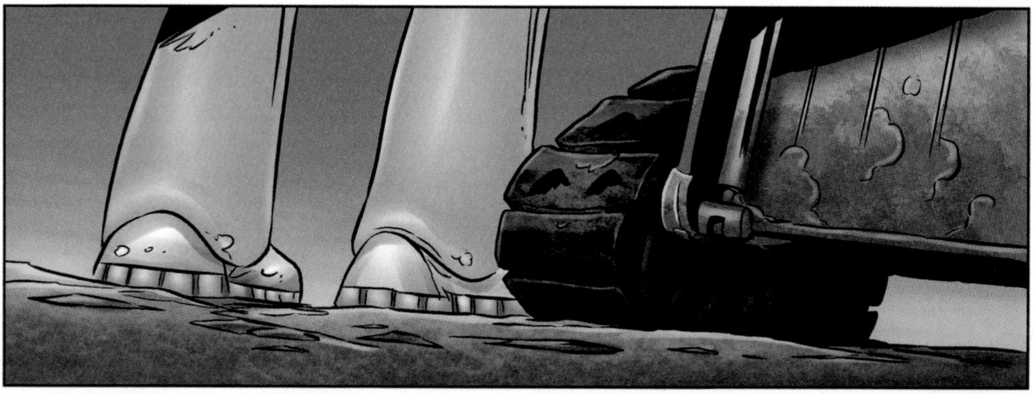

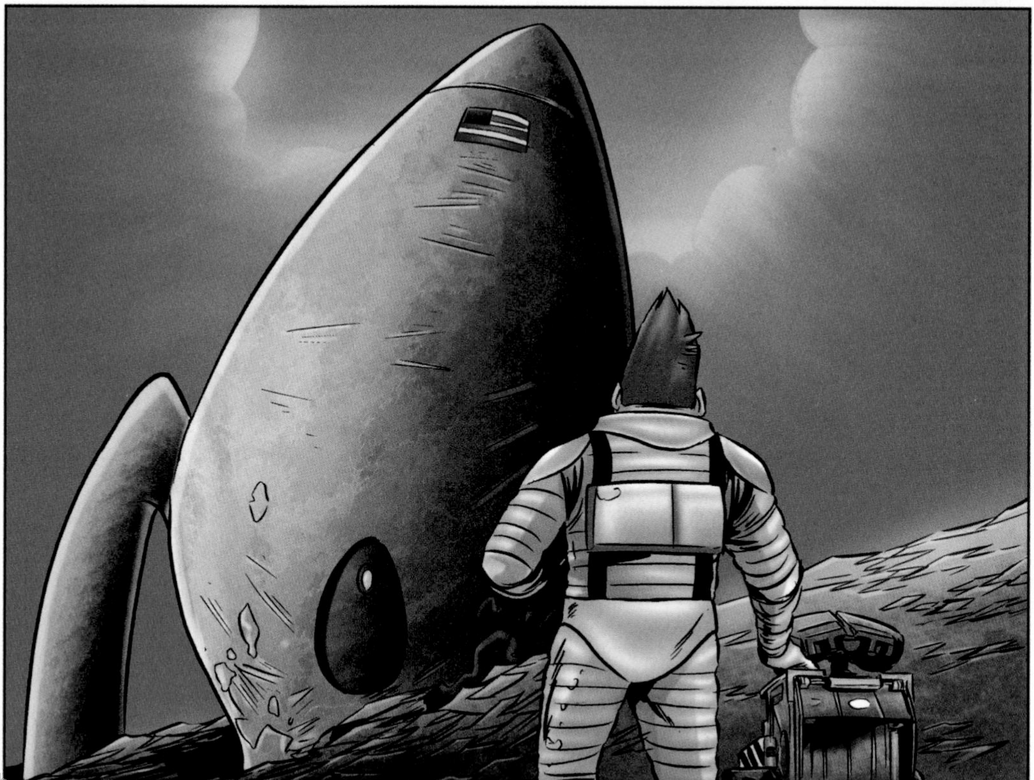

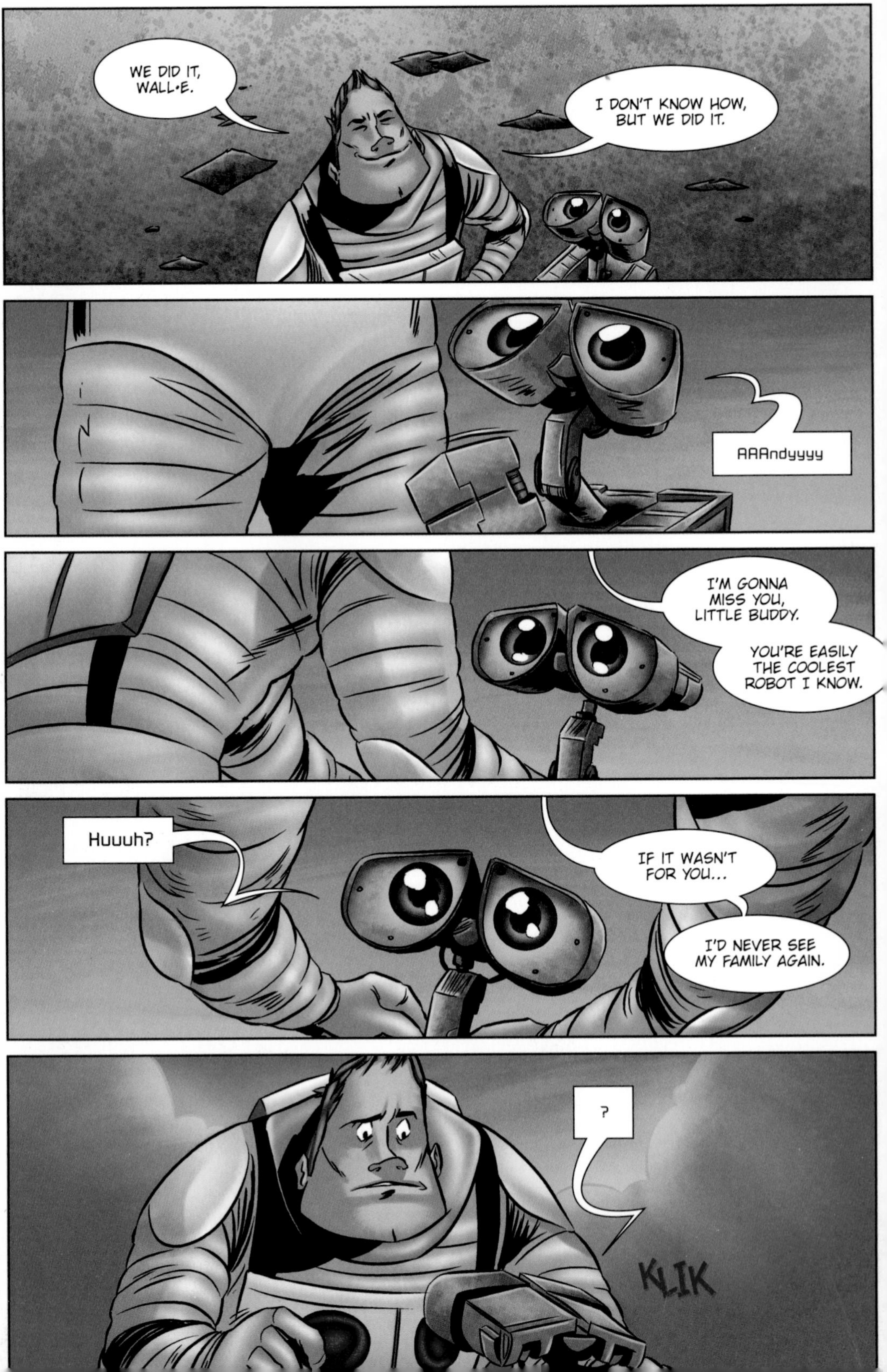

WE DID IT, WALL•E.
I DON'T KNOW HOW, BUT WE DID IT.
AAAndyyyy
I'M GONNA MISS YOU, LITTLE BUDDY.
YOU'RE EASILY THE COOLEST ROBOT I KNOW.
Huuuh?
IF IT WASN'T FOR YOU...
I'D NEVER SEE MY FAMILY AGAIN.
?
KLIK

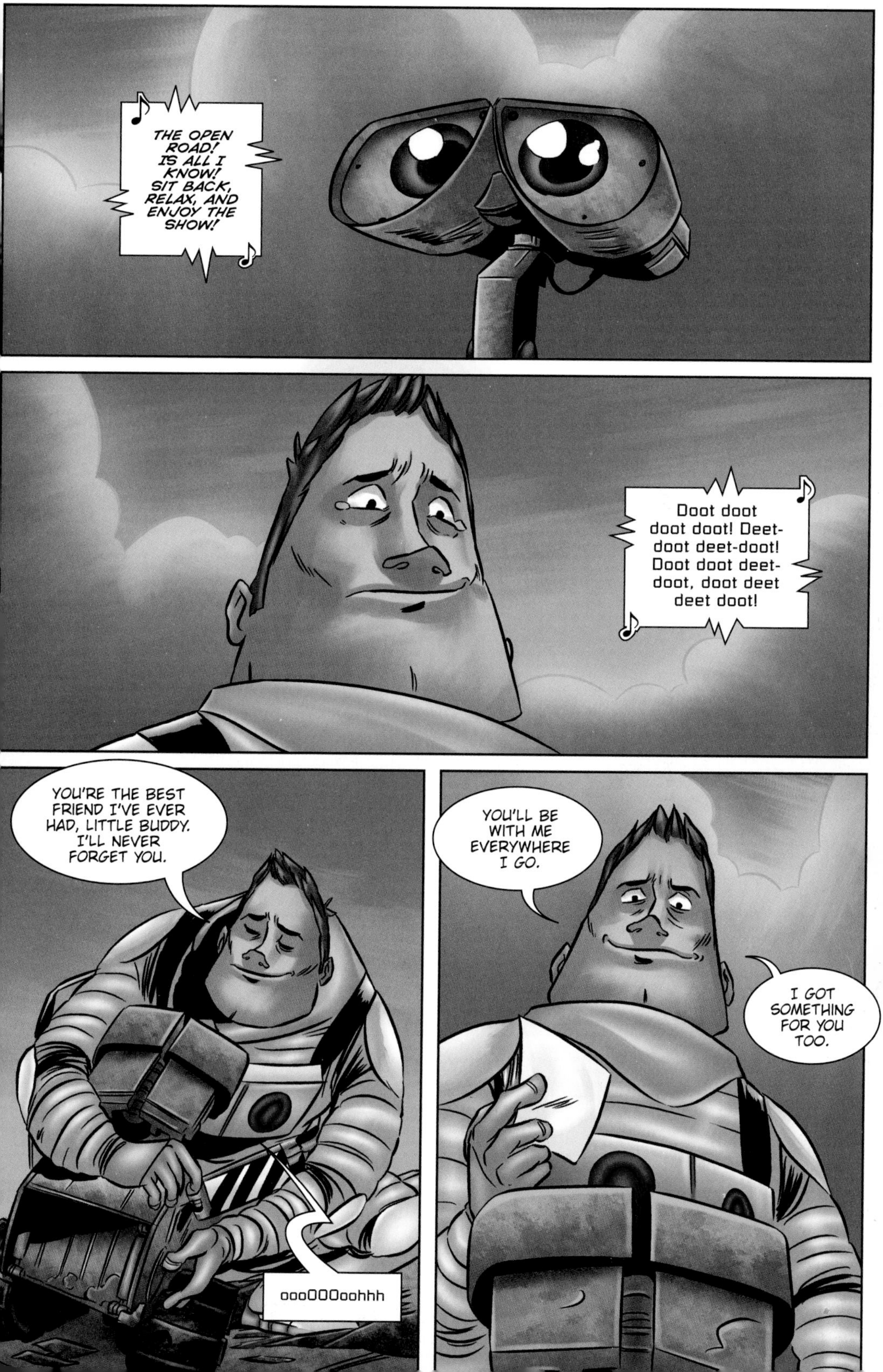

THE OPEN ROAD! IS ALL I KNOW! SIT BACK, RELAX, AND ENJOY THE SHOW!
Doot doot doot doot! Deet-doot deet-doot! Doot doot deet-doot, doot deet deet doot!
YOU'RE THE BEST FRIEND I'VE EVER HAD, LITTLE BUDDY. I'LL NEVER FORGET YOU.
oooOOOoohhh
YOU'LL BE WITH ME EVERYWHERE I GO.
I GOT SOMETHING FOR YOU TOO.

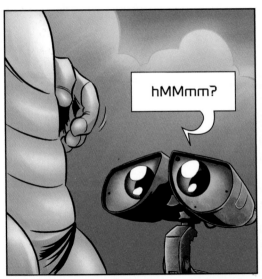

hMMmm?

I WANT YOU TO HAVE THIS, LITTLE BUDDY.

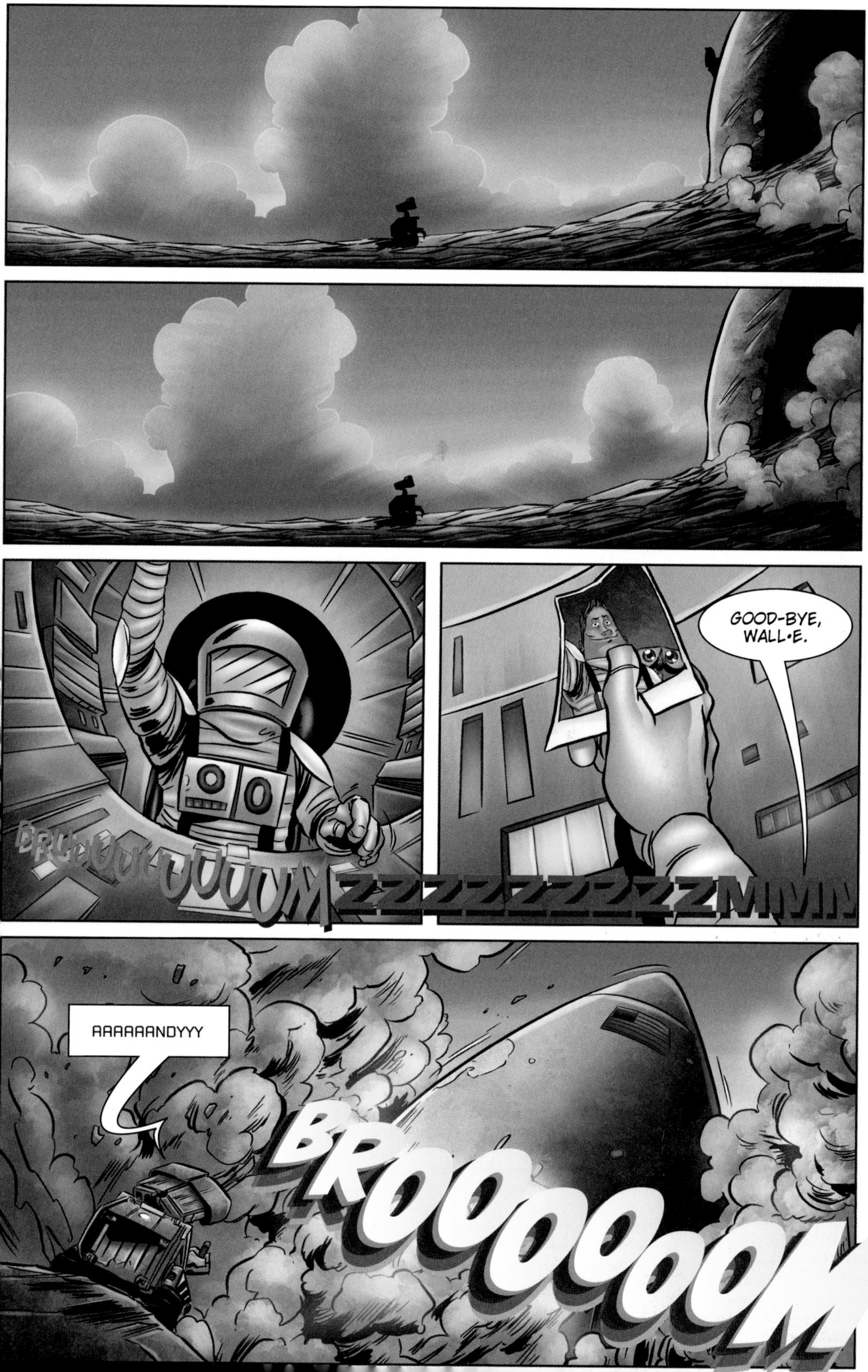
GOOD-BYE, WALL•E.
AAAAAANDYYY
BROOOOOOOM

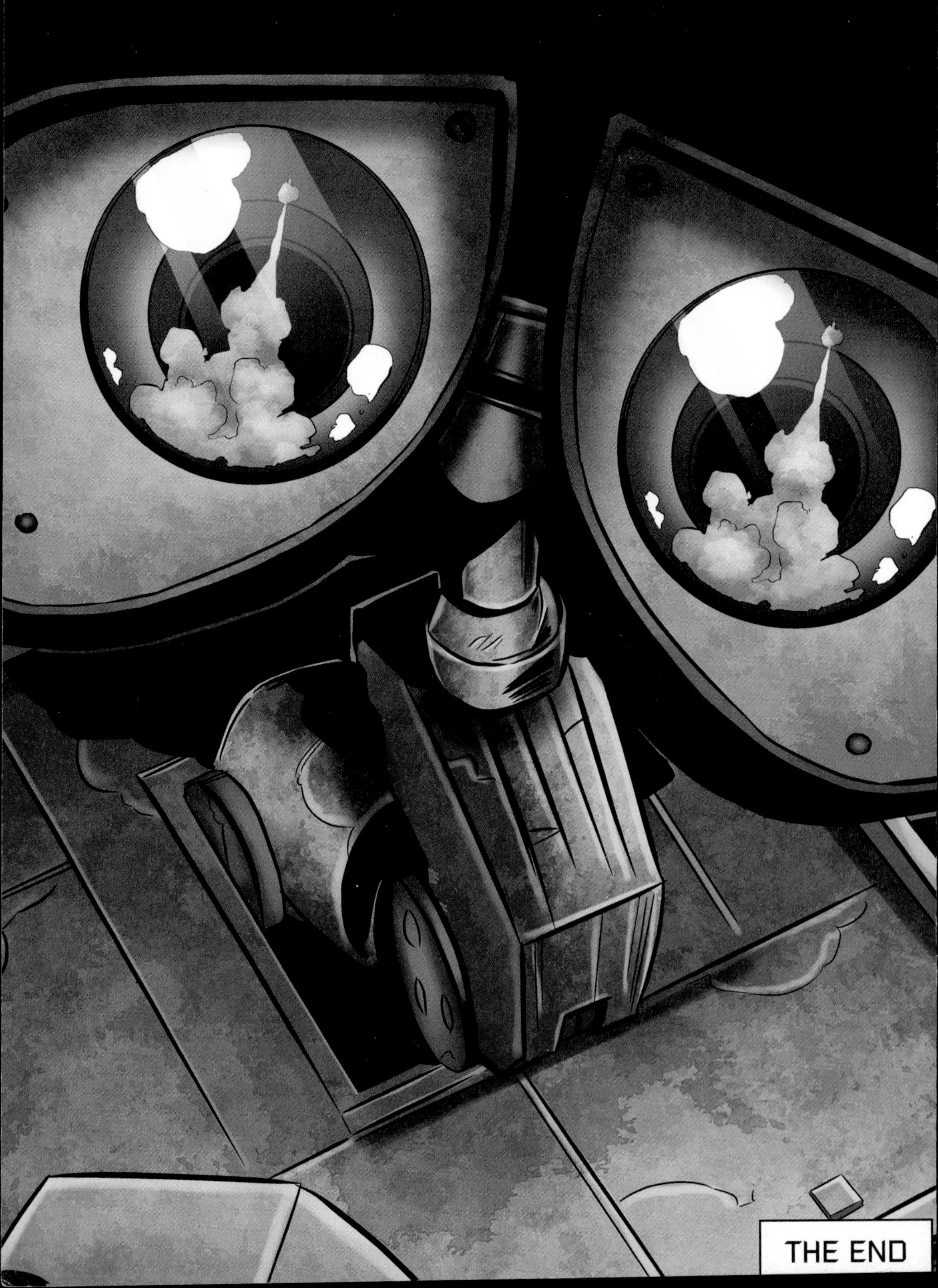
THE END

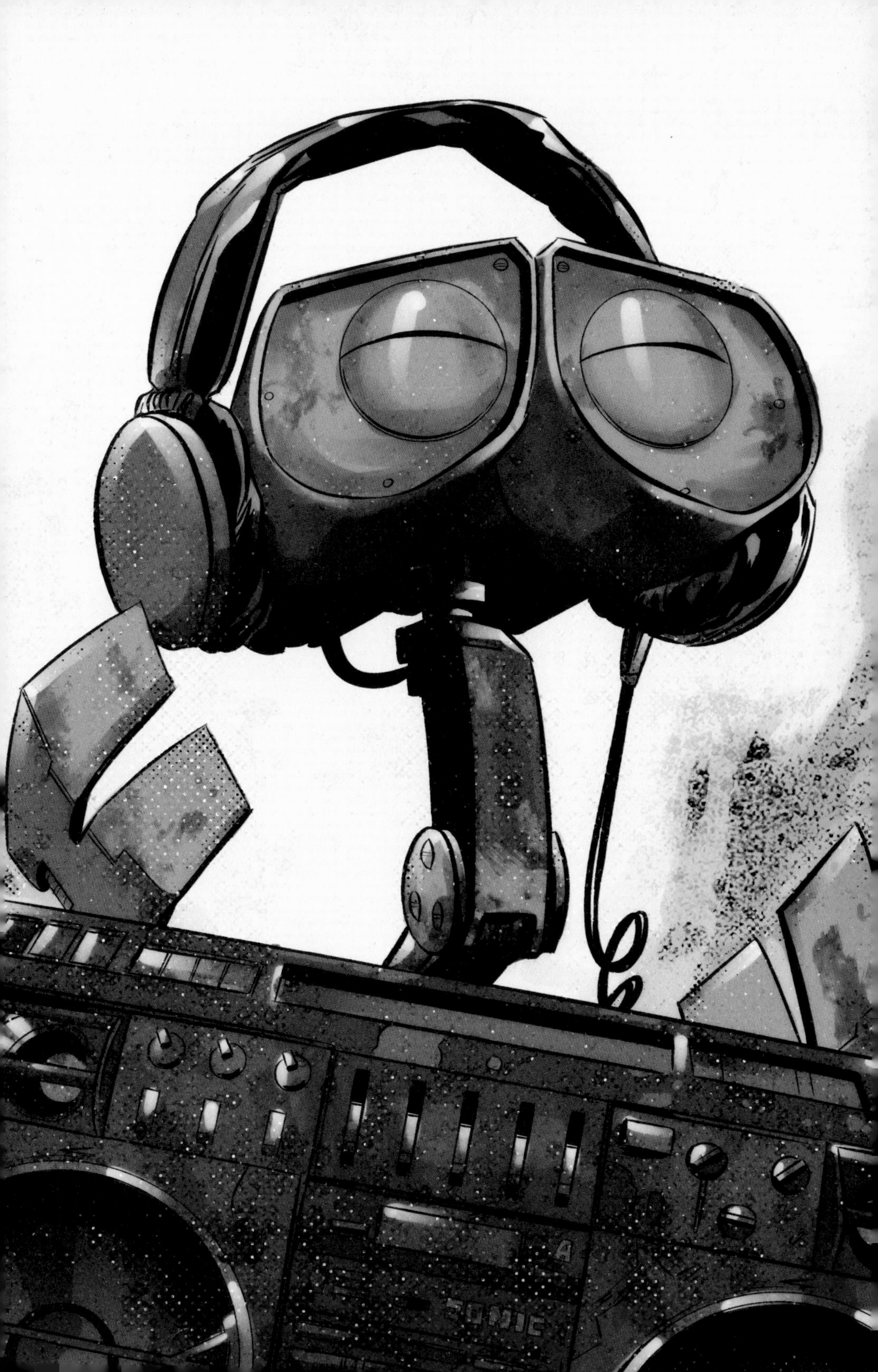
A
SONIC

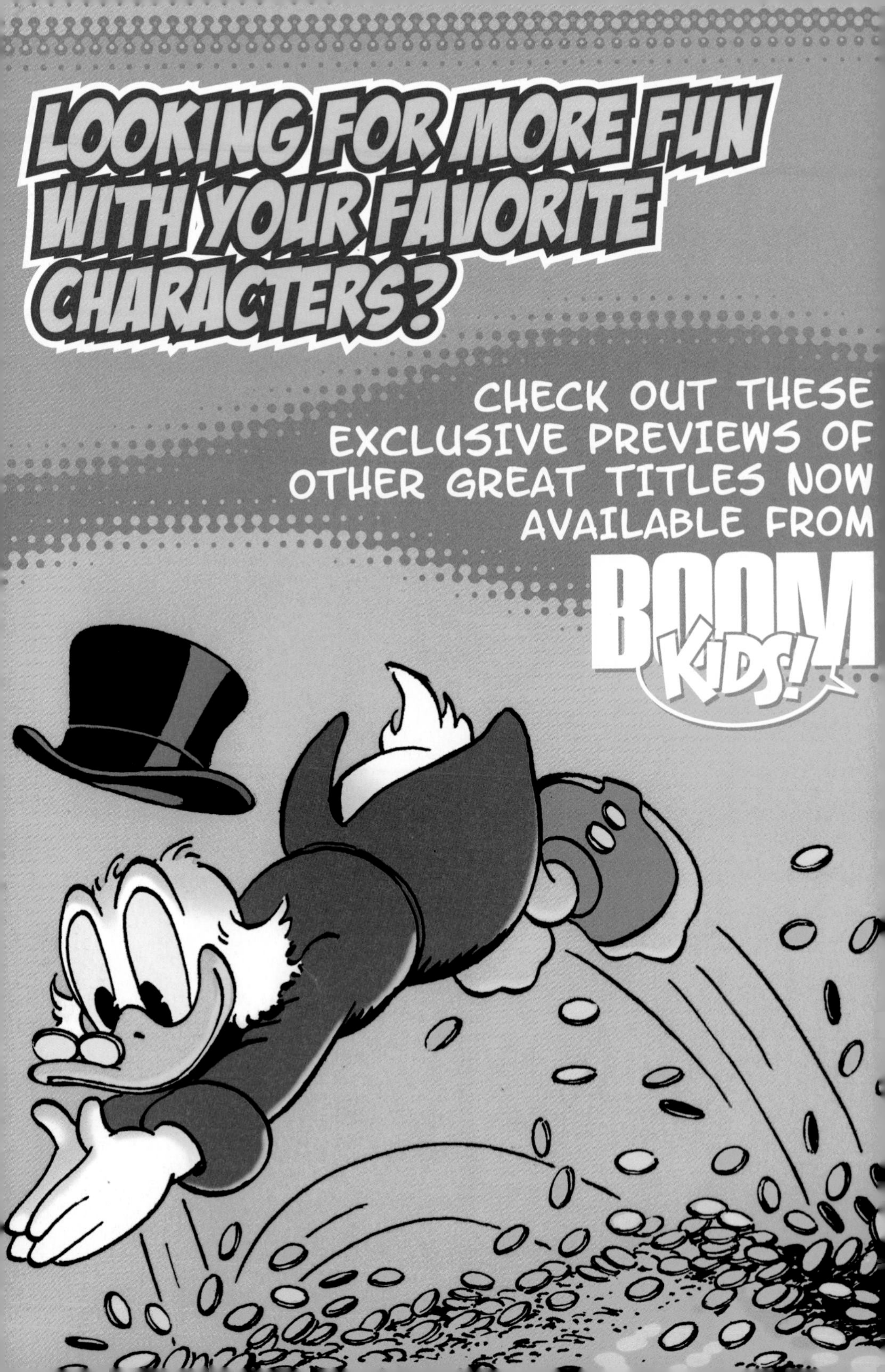
LOOKING FOR MORE FUN WITH YOUR FAVORITE CHARACTERS?
CHECK OUT THESE EXCLUSIVE PREVIEWS OF OTHER GREAT TITLES NOW AVAILABLE FROM
BOOM KIDS!

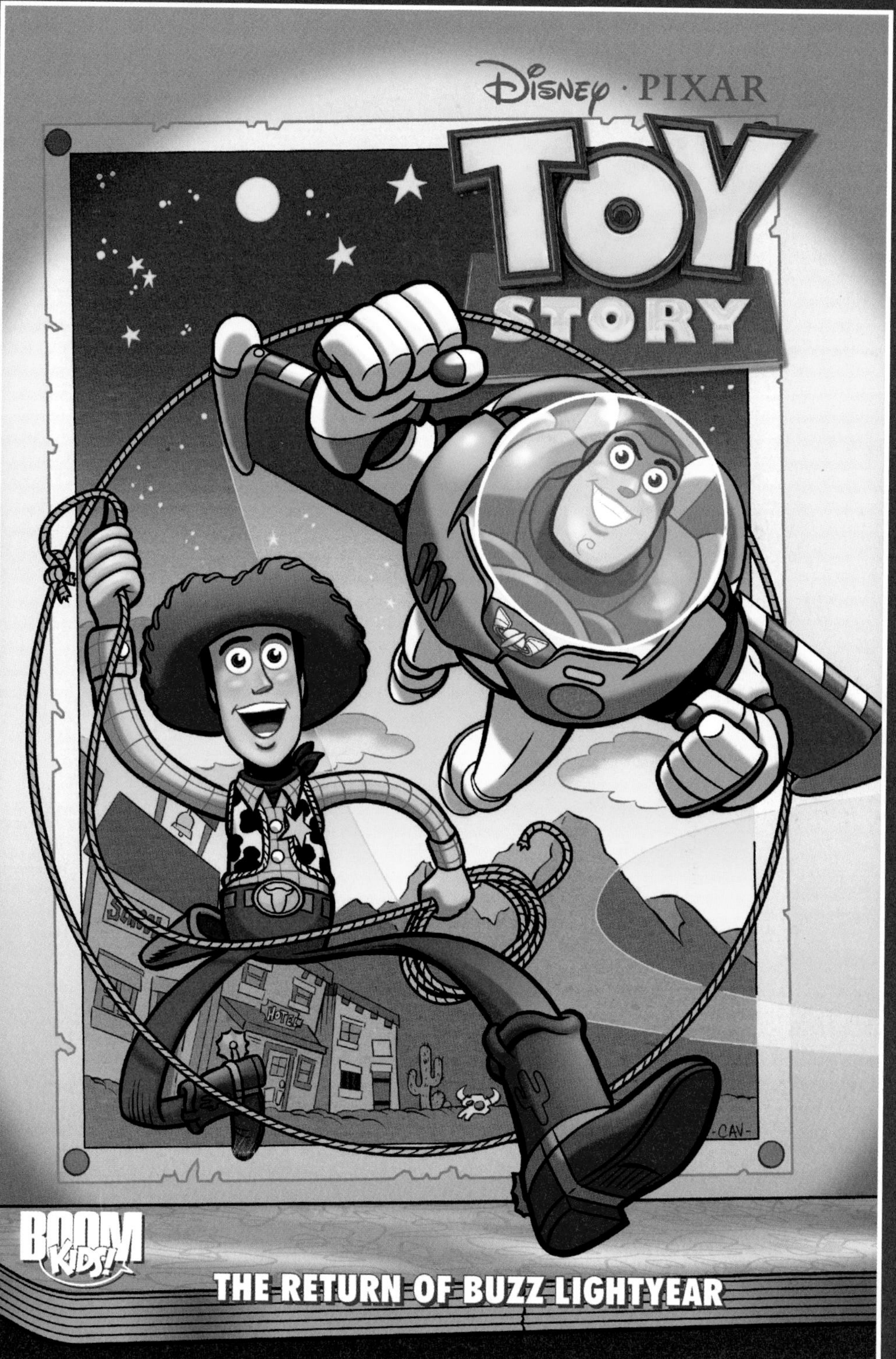
DISNEY · PIXAR
TOY STORY
HOTEL
-CAV-
BOOM KIDS!
THE RETURN OF BUZZ LIGHTYEAR

ANDY, HOW MANY TIMES HAVE I TOLD YOU NOT TO RUN DOWN THE STAIRS?!

SORRY, MOM.

WHAT'S A *"GIFT RECEIPT"*? AND WHAT DOES SHE MEAN *"RETURN IT AND GET SOMETHING NEW?"* YOU CAN DO THAT?!

YEAH, BUZZ...YOU CAN.

THAT JUST SEEMS... *WRONG.*

IT'S LIKE THE POOR TOY NEVER EVEN HAD A CHANCE...

TRUST ME BUZZ...IT'S FOR THE BEST.

"FOR THE BEST?" I THOUGHT YOU'D BE ON MY SIDE.

I *AM* ON YOUR SIDE.

OBVIOUSLY *NOT*, WOODY.

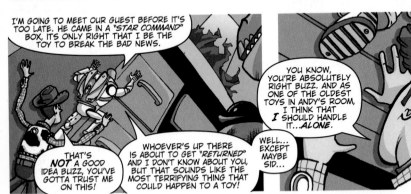

I'M GOING TO MEET OUR GUEST BEFORE IT'S TOO LATE. HE CAME IN A *"STAR COMMAND"* BOX, IT'S ONLY RIGHT THAT I BE THE TOY TO BREAK THE BAD NEWS.

THAT'S *NOT* A GOOD IDEA BUZZ, YOU'VE GOTTA TRUST ME ON THIS!

WHOEVER'S UP THERE IS ABOUT TO GET *"RETURNED"* AND I DON'T KNOW ABOUT YOU, BUT THAT SOUNDS LIKE THE MOST TERRIFYING THING THAT COULD HAPPEN TO A TOY!

YOU KNOW, YOU'RE ABSOLUTELY RIGHT BUZZ. AND AS ONE OF THE OLDEST TOYS IN ANDY'S ROOM, I THINK THAT *I* SHOULD HANDLE IT...*ALONE.*

WELL... EXCEPT MAYBE SID...

COME ON WOODY STILL SCARED I'M GOING TO STEAL YOUR THUNDER?

OF COURSE NOT, IT'S JUST.. WELL, YOU DON' KNOW WHAT'S UP THERE!

YOU'RE RIGHT. THAT'S WHY I'M GOING UP THERE TO FIND OUT!

OH...

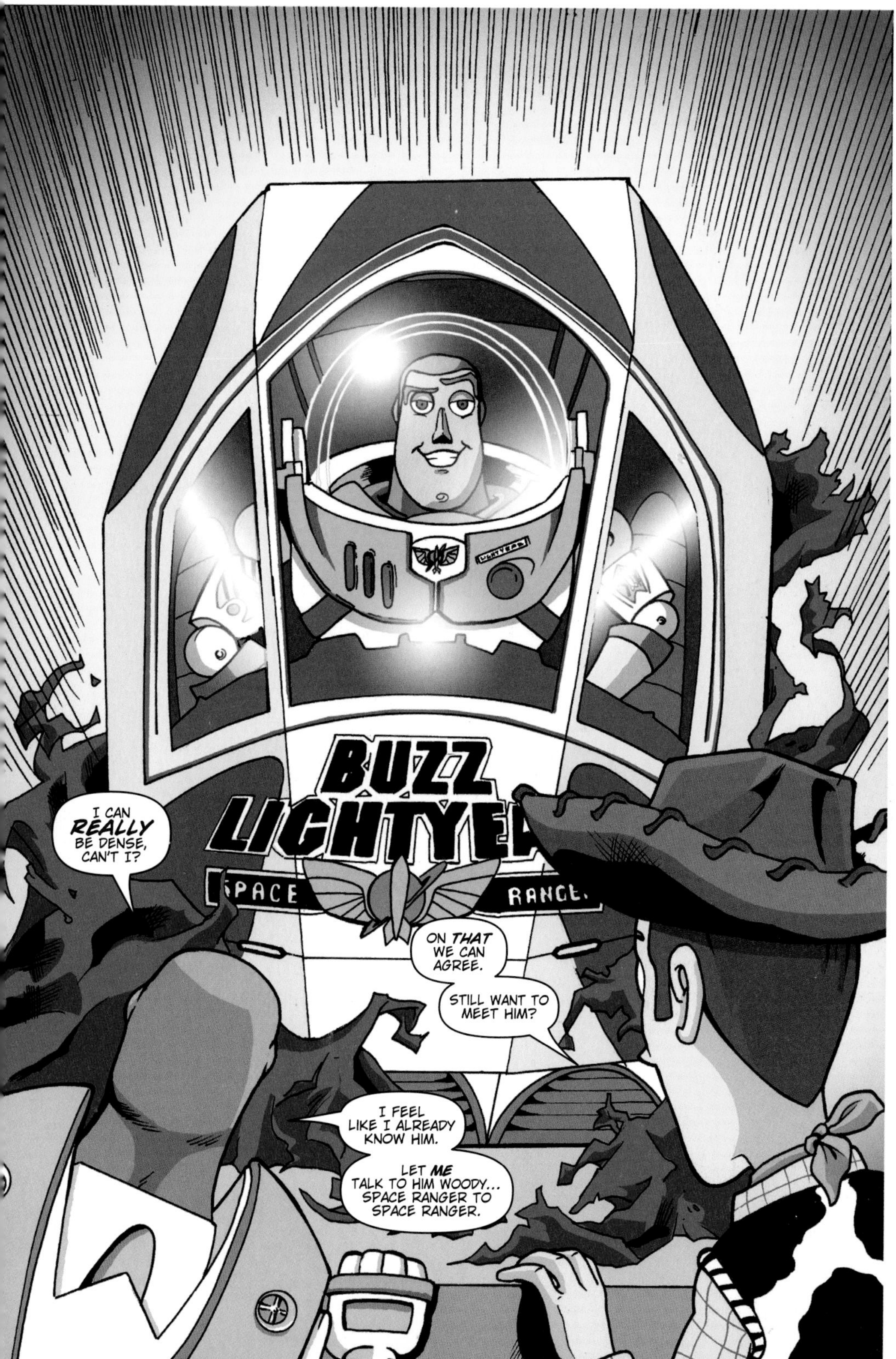
BUZZ LIGHTYEA
SPACE RANGE
I CAN REALLY BE DENSE, CAN'T I?
ON THAT WE CAN AGREE.
STILL WANT TO MEET HIM?
I FEEL LIKE I ALREADY KNOW HIM.
LET ME TALK TO HIM WOODY... SPACE RANGER TO SPACE RANGER.

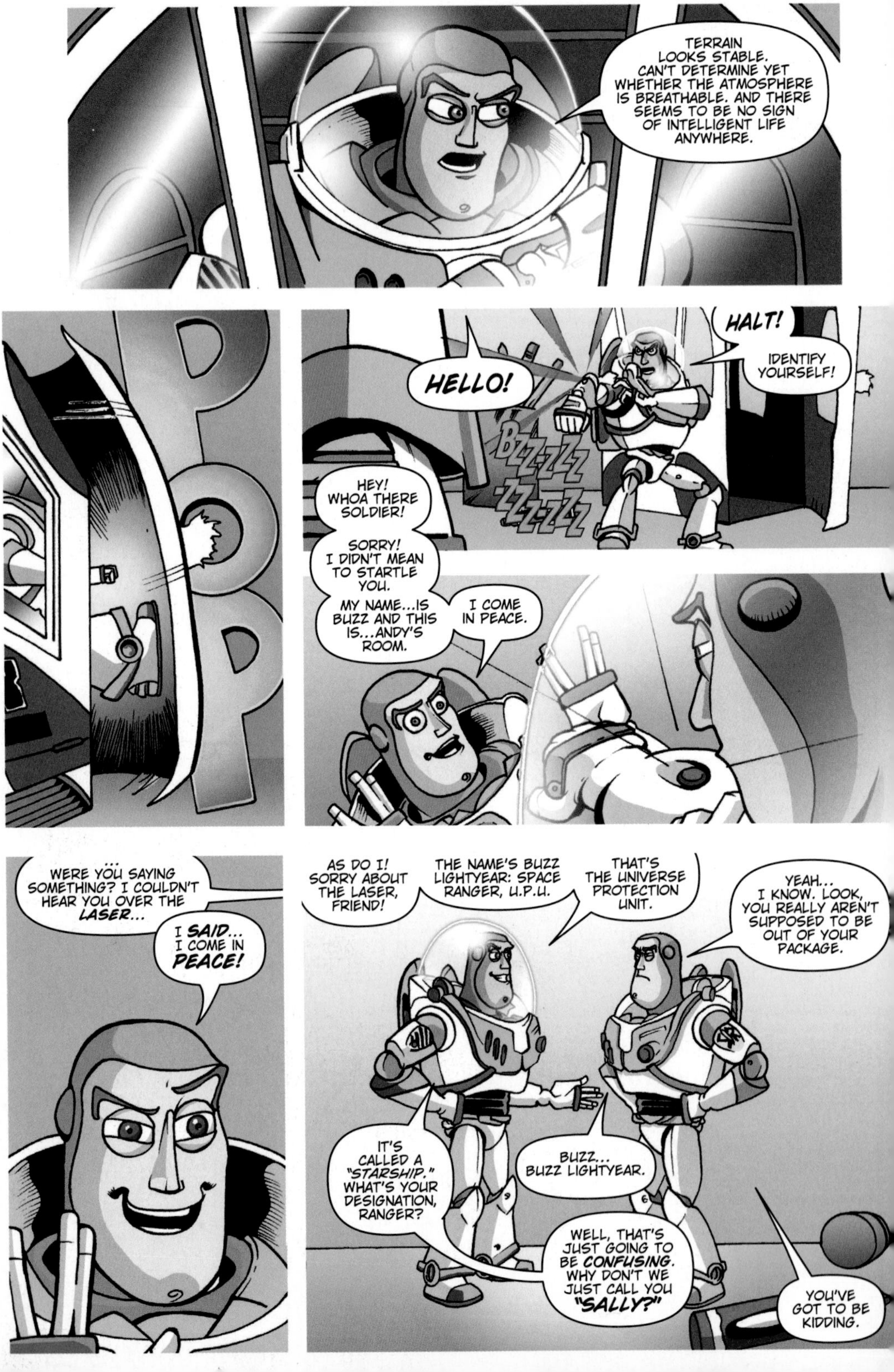
TERRAIN LOOKS STABLE. CAN'T DETERMINE YET WHETHER THE ATMOSPHERE IS BREATHABLE. AND THERE SEEMS TO BE NO SIGN OF INTELLIGENT LIFE ANYWHERE.
POP
HALT!
IDENTIFY YOURSELF!
HELLO!
BZZZZZ ZZZZZZ
HEY! WHOA THERE SOLDIER!
SORRY! I DIDN'T MEAN TO STARTLE YOU.
MY NAME...IS BUZZ AND THIS IS...ANDY'S ROOM.
I COME IN PEACE.
...WERE YOU SAYING SOMETHING? I COULDN'T HEAR YOU OVER THE LASER...
I SAID... I COME IN PEACE!
AS DO I! SORRY ABOUT THE LASER, FRIEND!
THE NAME'S BUZZ LIGHTYEAR: SPACE RANGER, U.P.U.
THAT'S THE UNIVERSE PROTECTION UNIT.
YEAH... I KNOW. LOOK, YOU REALLY AREN'T SUPPOSED TO BE OUT OF YOUR PACKAGE.
IT'S CALLED A "STARSHIP." WHAT'S YOUR DESIGNATION, RANGER?
BUZZ... BUZZ LIGHTYEAR.
WELL, THAT'S JUST GOING TO BE CONFUSING. WHY DON'T WE JUST CALL YOU "SALLY?"
YOU'VE GOT TO BE KIDDING.

It's time to meet the Muppets once again! Join Kermit, Fozzie, Gonzo, Miss Piggy and the rest of the gang for a hilarious collection of madcap skits and gags perfect for new and old fans alike!

THE MUPPET SHOW: MEET THE MUPPETS
DIAMOND CODE: MAY090750
SC $9.99 ISBN 9781934506851
HC $24.99 ISBN 9781608865277

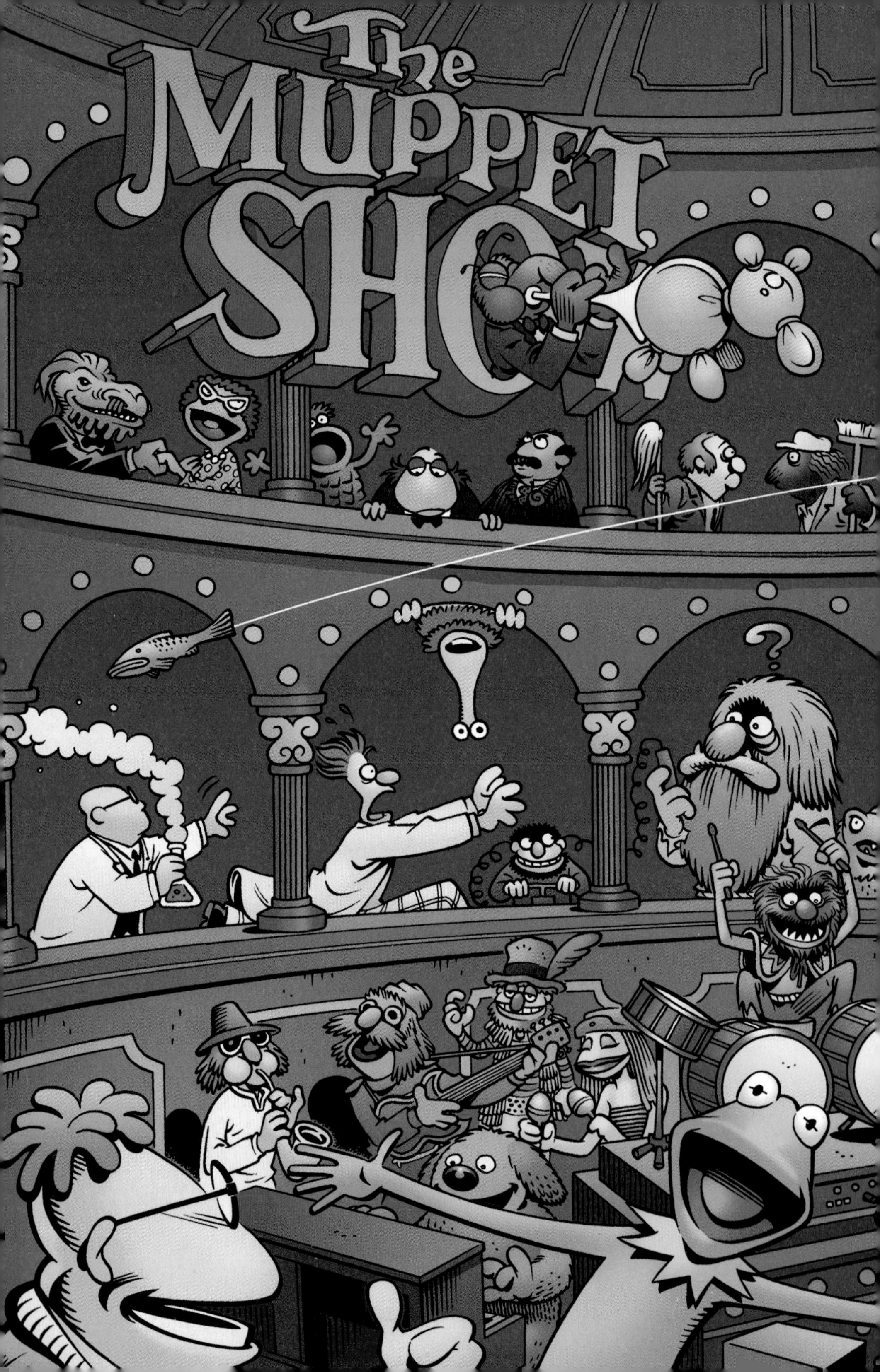
The MUPPET SHO

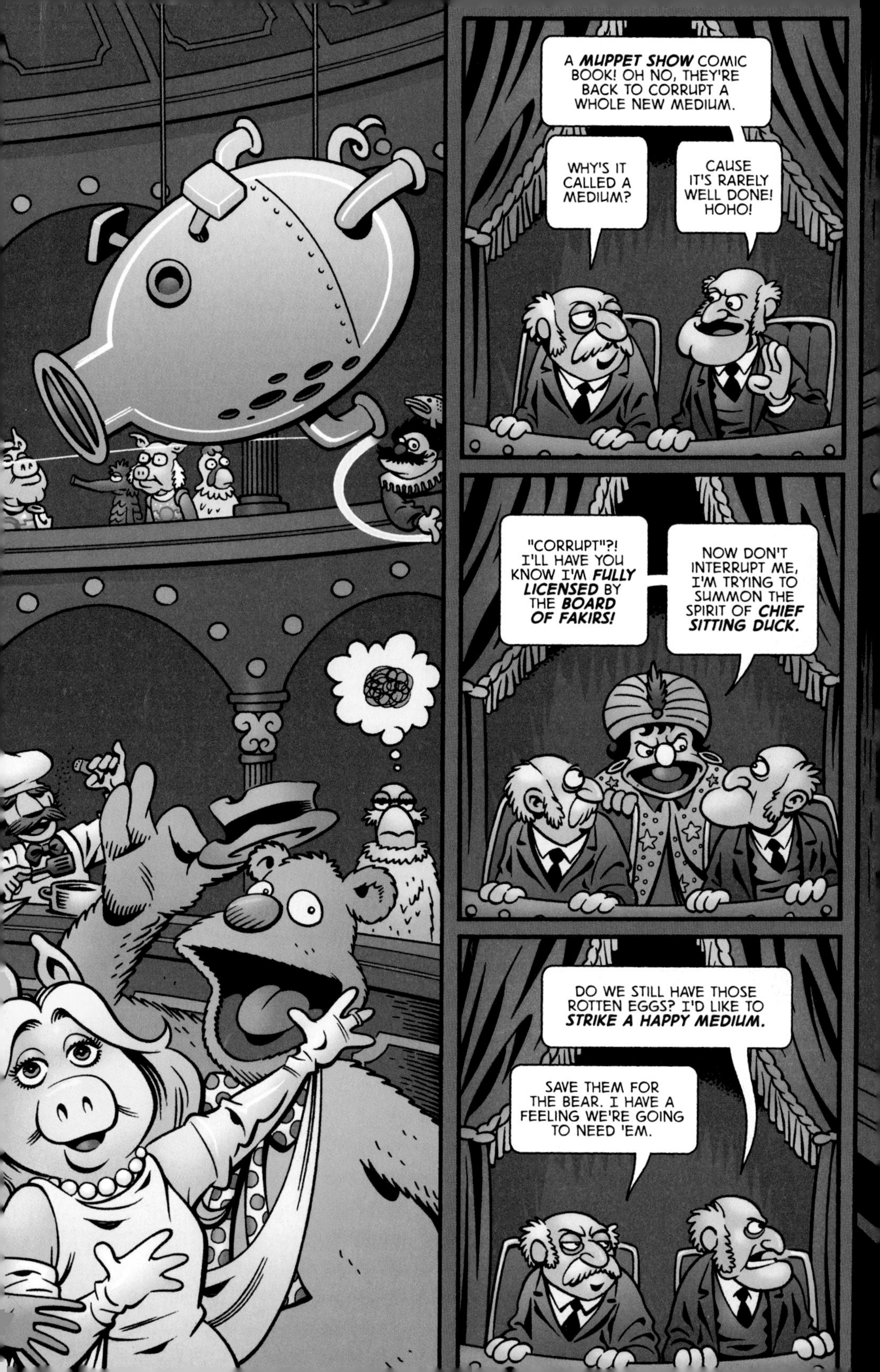
A MUPPET SHOW COMIC BOOK! OH NO, THEY'RE BACK TO CORRUPT A WHOLE NEW MEDIUM.
WHY'S IT CALLED A MEDIUM?
CAUSE IT'S RARELY WELL DONE! HOHO!
"CORRUPT"?! I'LL HAVE YOU KNOW I'M FULLY LICENSED BY THE BOARD OF FAKIRS!
NOW DON'T INTERRUPT ME, I'M TRYING TO SUMMON THE SPIRIT OF CHIEF SITTING DUCK.
DO WE STILL HAVE THOSE ROTTEN EGGS? I'D LIKE TO STRIKE A HAPPY MEDIUM.
SAVE THEM FOR THE BEAR. I HAVE A FEELING WE'RE GOING TO NEED 'EM.

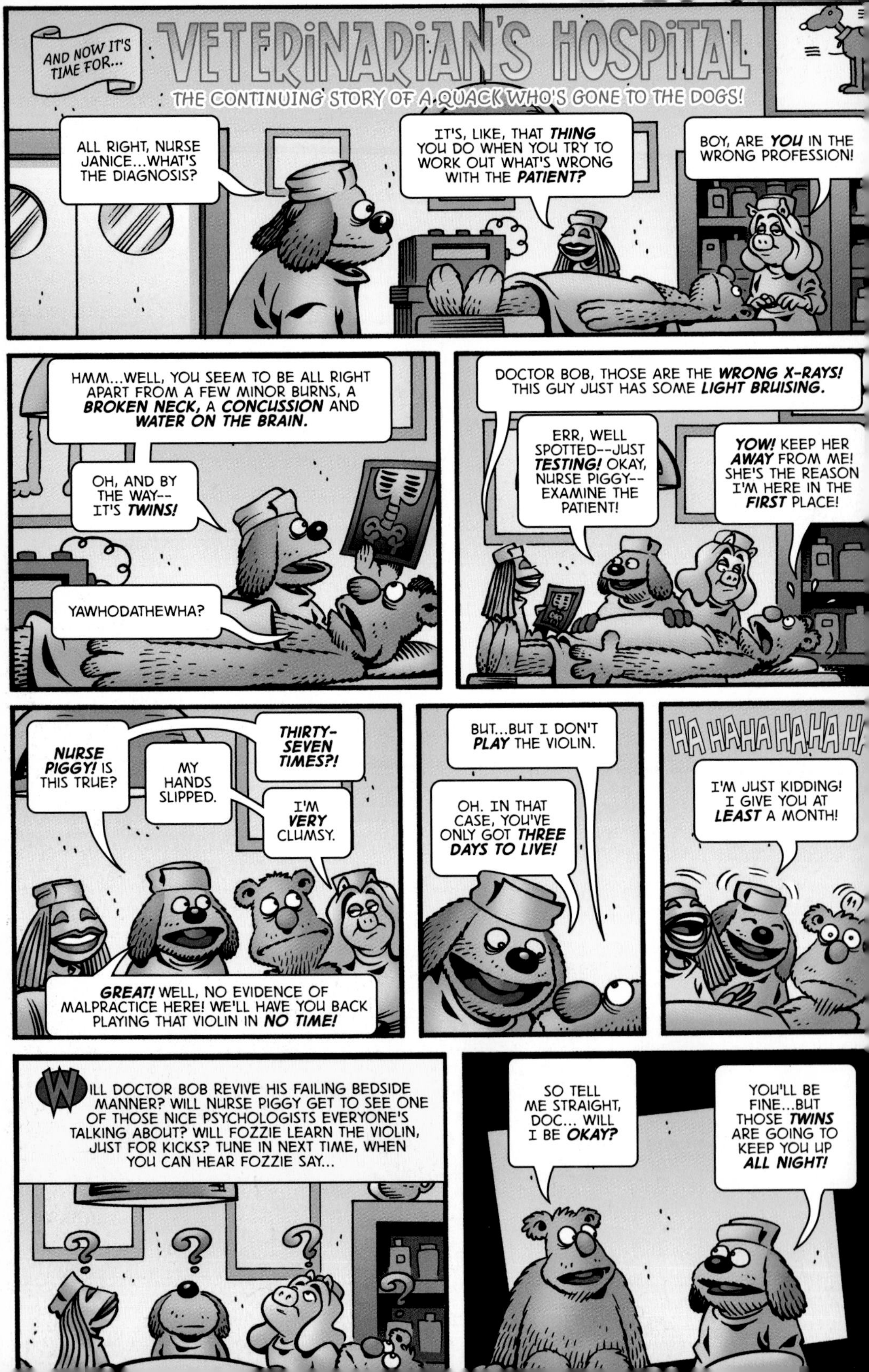
AND NOW IT'S TIME FOR...
VETERINARIAN'S HOSPITAL
THE CONTINUING STORY OF A QUACK WHO'S GONE TO THE DOGS!
ALL RIGHT, NURSE JANICE...WHAT'S THE DIAGNOSIS?
IT'S, LIKE, THAT THING YOU DO WHEN YOU TRY TO WORK OUT WHAT'S WRONG WITH THE PATIENT?
BOY, ARE YOU IN THE WRONG PROFESSION!
HMM...WELL, YOU SEEM TO BE ALL RIGHT APART FROM A FEW MINOR BURNS, A BROKEN NECK, A CONCUSSION AND WATER ON THE BRAIN.
OH, AND BY THE WAY-- IT'S TWINS!
YAWHODATHEWHA?
DOCTOR BOB, THOSE ARE THE WRONG X-RAYS! THIS GUY JUST HAS SOME LIGHT BRUISING.
ERR, WELL SPOTTED--JUST TESTING! OKAY, NURSE PIGGY-- EXAMINE THE PATIENT!
YOW! KEEP HER AWAY FROM ME! SHE'S THE REASON I'M HERE IN THE FIRST PLACE!
NURSE PIGGY! IS THIS TRUE?
MY HANDS SLIPPED.
THIRTY-SEVEN TIMES?!
I'M VERY CLUMSY.
GREAT! WELL, NO EVIDENCE OF MALPRACTICE HERE! WE'LL HAVE YOU BACK PLAYING THAT VIOLIN IN NO TIME!
BUT...BUT I DON'T PLAY THE VIOLIN.
OH. IN THAT CASE, YOU'VE ONLY GOT THREE DAYS TO LIVE!
HA HAHAHA HAHAH
I'M JUST KIDDING! I GIVE YOU AT LEAST A MONTH!
WILL DOCTOR BOB REVIVE HIS FAILING BEDSIDE MANNER? WILL NURSE PIGGY GET TO SEE ONE OF THOSE NICE PSYCHOLOGISTS EVERYONE'S TALKING ABOUT? WILL FOZZIE LEARN THE VIOLIN, JUST FOR KICKS? TUNE IN NEXT TIME, WHEN YOU CAN HEAR FOZZIE SAY...
SO TELL ME STRAIGHT, DOC... WILL I BE OKAY?
YOU'LL BE FINE...BUT THOSE TWINS ARE GOING TO KEEP YOU UP ALL NIGHT!

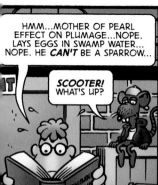

HMM...MOTHER OF PEARL EFFECT ON PLUMAGE...NOPE. LAYS EGGS IN SWAMP WATER... NOPE. HE *CAN'T* BE A SPARROW...

SCOOTER! WHAT'S UP?

RIZZO! TELL ME...DO YOU KNOW GONZO'S *SPECIES?* IT'S REALLY, REALLY IMPORTANT!

CAN'T SAY AS I DO, SPORT. I *CAN* TELL YOU HE'S DEFINITELY NOT A *COW.*

NOT A C-O... *AARGH!* WHAT AM I *DOING?!*

MAYBE YOU SHOULD JUST, LIKE, *OBSERVE FROM A DISTANCE.* HE'S BOUND TO DO SOMETHING *SPECIES-SPECIFIC* SOONER OR LATER...

AND SO...

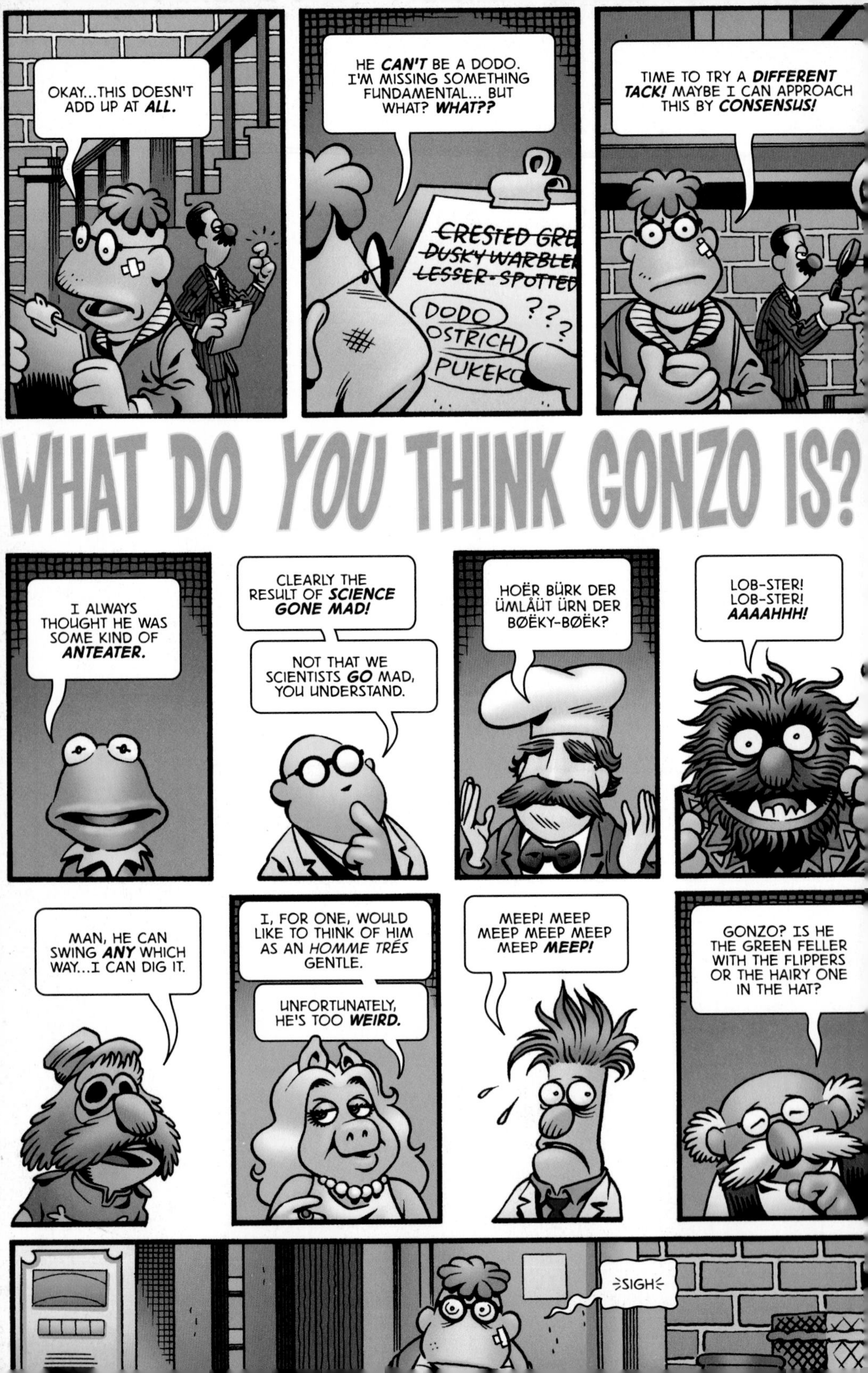

OKAY...THIS DOESN'T ADD UP AT ***ALL.***
HE ***CAN'T*** BE A DODO. I'M MISSING SOMETHING FUNDAMENTAL... BUT WHAT? ***WHAT??***
~~CRESTED GRE~~
~~DUSKY WARBLER~~
~~LESSER-SPOTTED~~
DODO
OSTRICH
PUKEKO
???
TIME TO TRY A ***DIFFERENT TACK!*** MAYBE I CAN APPROACH THIS BY ***CONSENSUS!***
WHAT DO *YOU* THINK GONZO IS?
I ALWAYS THOUGHT HE WAS SOME KIND OF ***ANTEATER.***
CLEARLY THE RESULT OF ***SCIENCE GONE MAD!***
NOT THAT WE SCIENTISTS ***GO*** MAD, YOU UNDERSTAND.
HOËR BÜRK DER ÜMLÅÜT ÜRN DER BØËKY-BØËK?
LOB-STER! LOB-STER! ***AAAAHHH!***
MAN, HE CAN SWING ***ANY*** WHICH WAY...I CAN DIG IT.
I, FOR ONE, WOULD LIKE TO THINK OF HIM AS AN *HOMME TRÉS* GENTLE.
UNFORTUNATELY, HE'S TOO ***WEIRD.***
MEEP! MEEP MEEP MEEP MEEP MEEP ***MEEP!***
GONZO? IS HE THE GREEN FELLER WITH THE FLIPPERS OR THE HAIRY ONE IN THE HAT?
SIGH

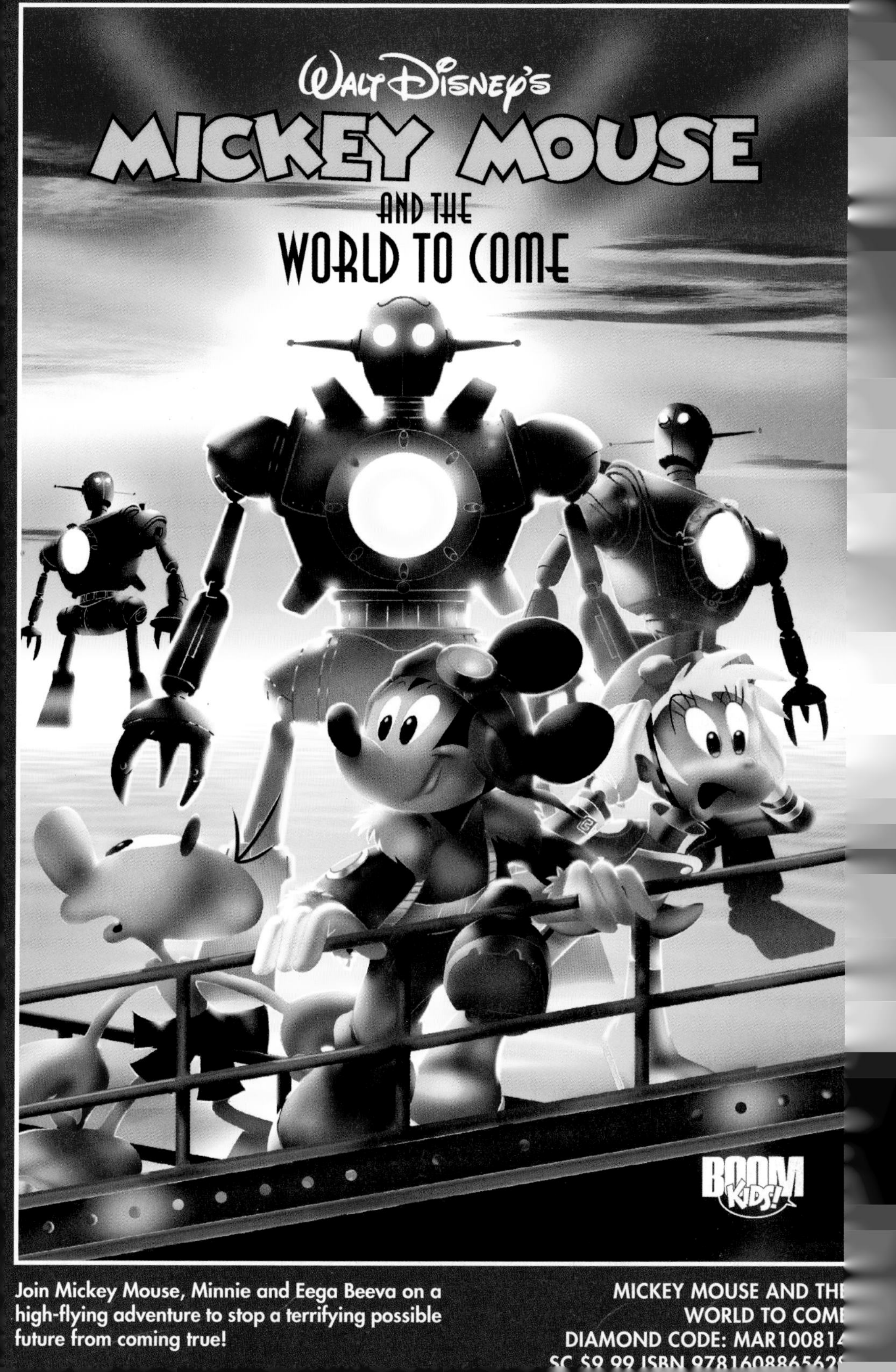
WALT DISNEY'S
MICKEY MOUSE
AND THE
WORLD TO COME
BOOM KIDS!

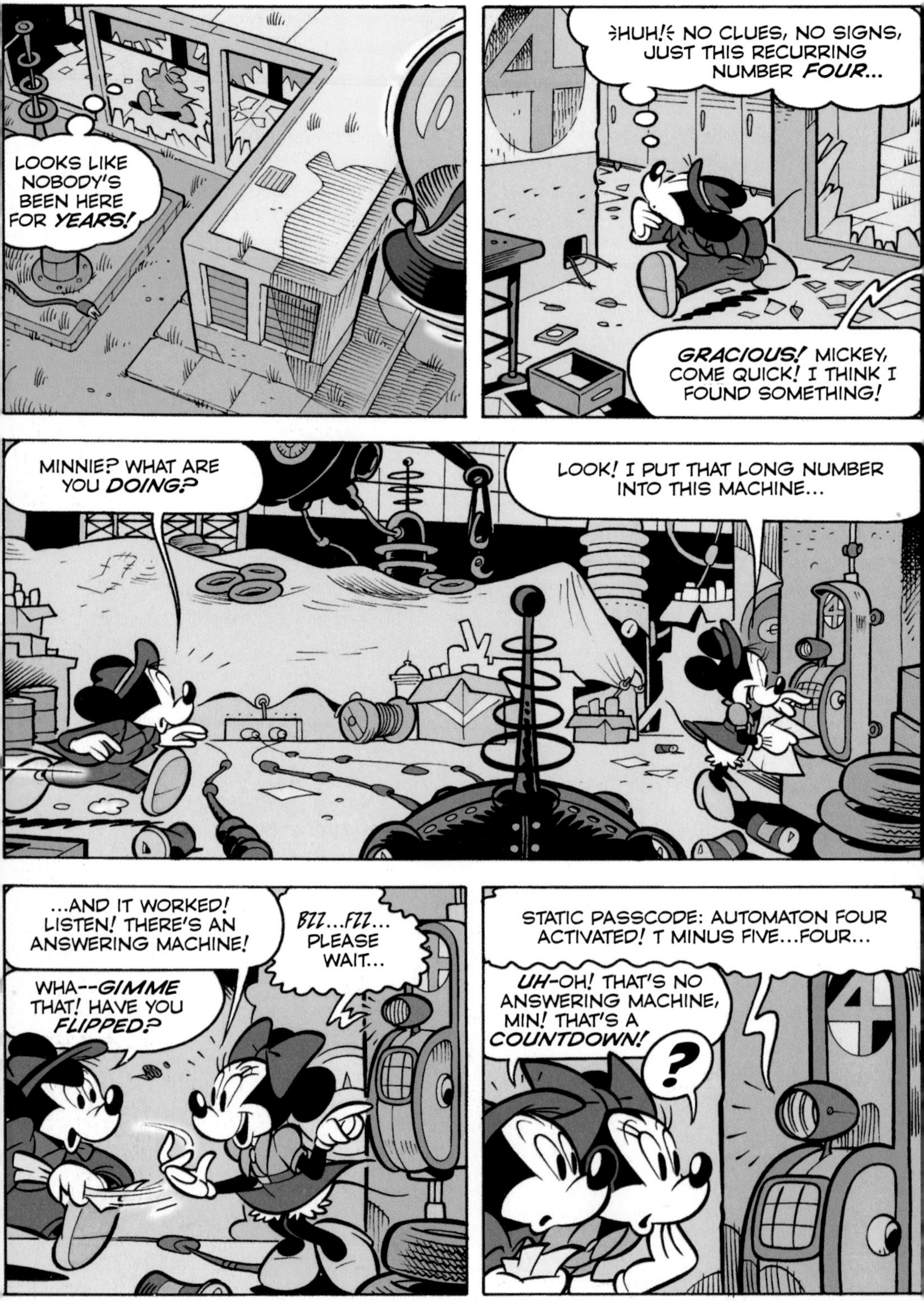

LOOKS LIKE NOBODY'S BEEN HERE FOR YEARS!
HUH! NO CLUES, NO SIGNS, JUST THIS RECURRING NUMBER FOUR...
GRACIOUS! MICKEY, COME QUICK! I THINK I FOUND SOMETHING!
MINNIE? WHAT ARE YOU DOING?
LOOK! I PUT THAT LONG NUMBER INTO THIS MACHINE...
...AND IT WORKED! LISTEN! THERE'S AN ANSWERING MACHINE!
BZZ...FZZ... PLEASE WAIT...
WHA--GIMME THAT! HAVE YOU FLIPPED?
STATIC PASSCODE: AUTOMATON FOUR ACTIVATED! T MINUS FIVE...FOUR...
UH-OH! THAT'S NO ANSWERING MACHINE, MIN! THAT'S A COUNTDOWN!
?

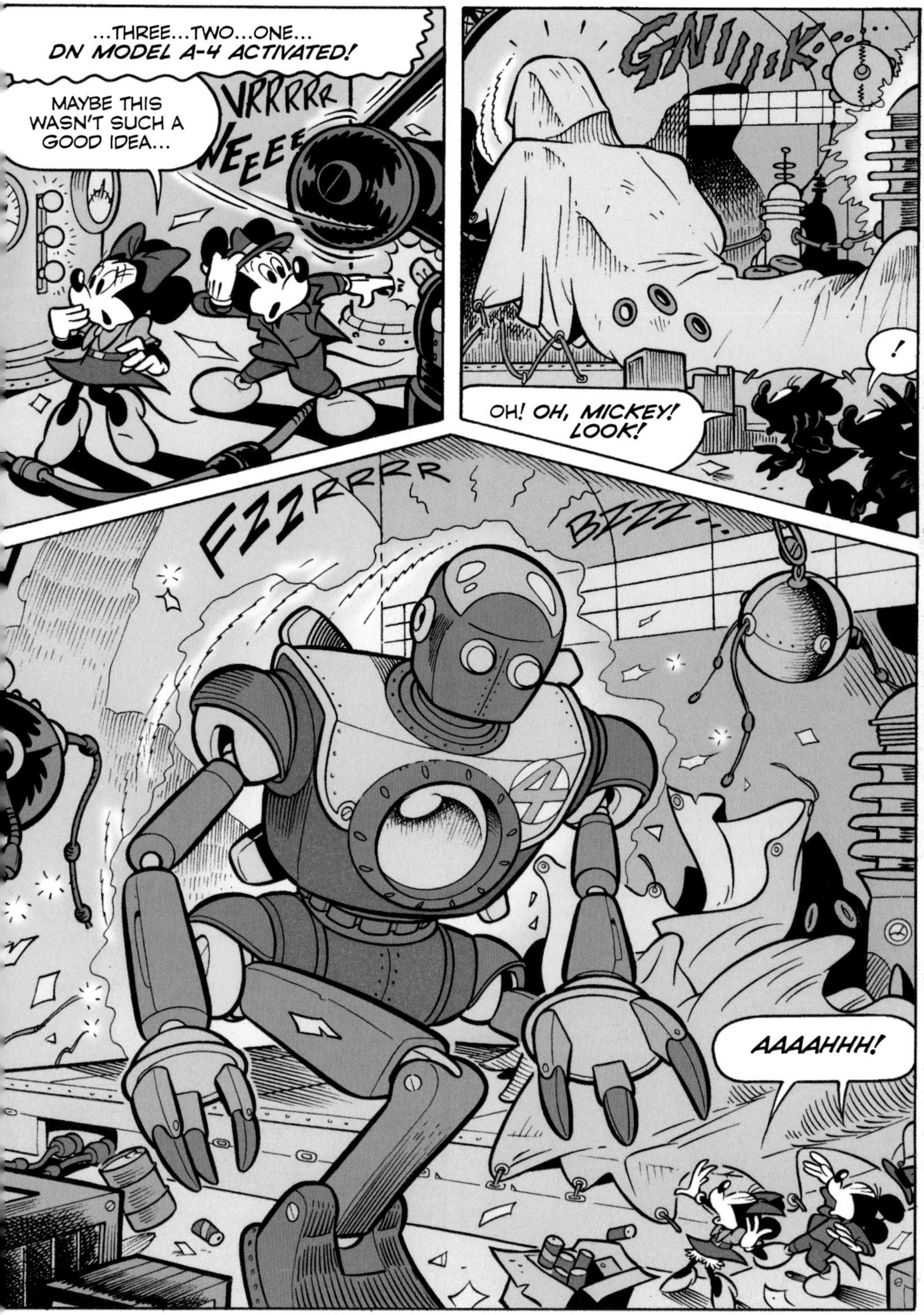
...THREE...TWO...ONE...
DN MODEL A-4 ACTIVATED!
MAYBE THIS WASN'T SUCH A GOOD IDEA...
VRRRRR
WEEEE
GNIIIIK
!
OH! OH, MICKEY! LOOK!
FZZRRRRR
BZZZ
AAAAHHH!

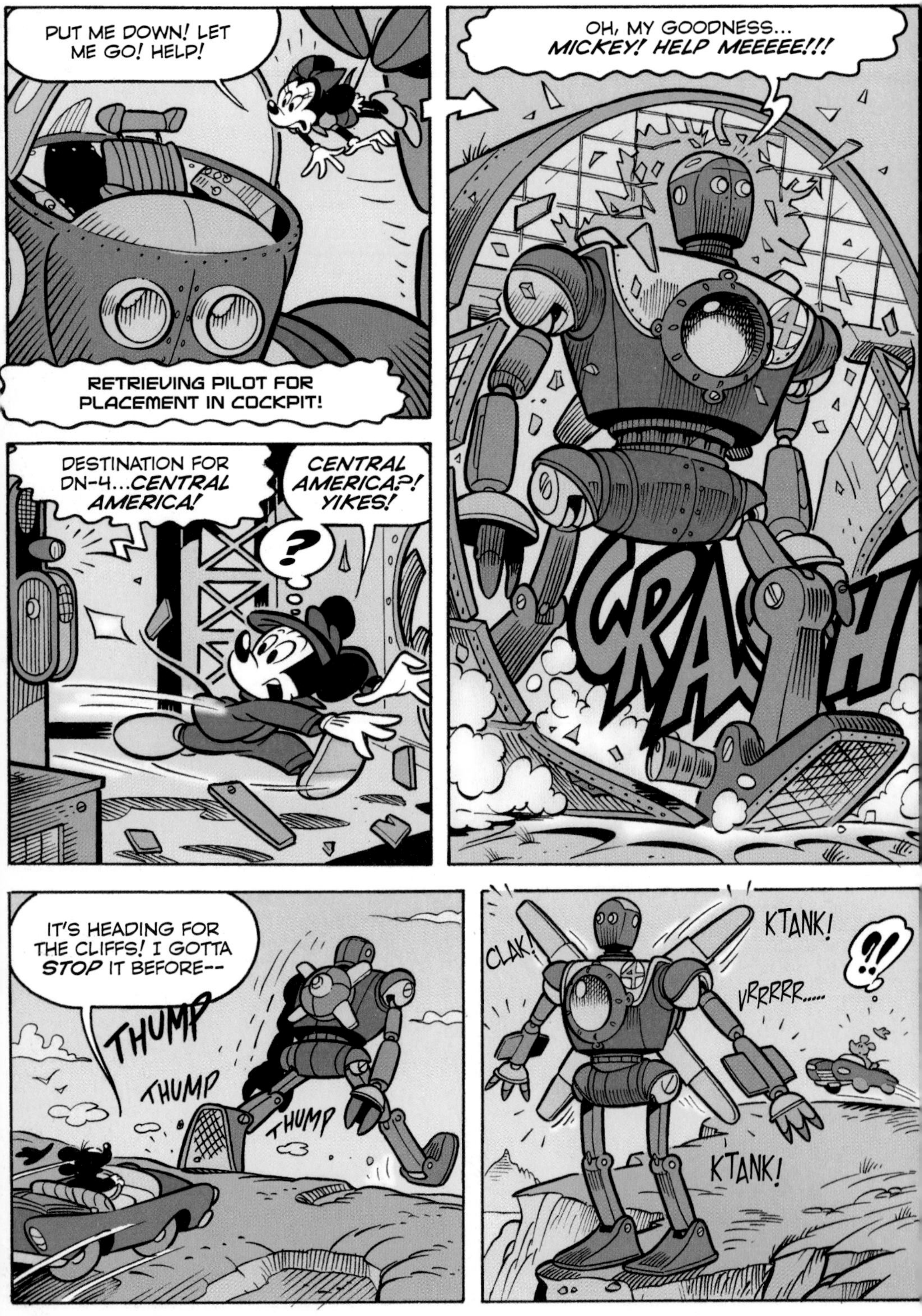
PUT ME DOWN! LET ME GO! HELP!
RETRIEVING PILOT FOR PLACEMENT IN COCKPIT!
OH, MY GOODNESS... MICKEY! HELP MEEEEE!!!
DESTINATION FOR DN-4...CENTRAL AMERICA!
CENTRAL AMERICA?! YIKES!
?
CRASH
IT'S HEADING FOR THE CLIFFS! I GOTTA STOP IT BEFORE--
THUMP
THUMP
THUMP
CLAK!
KTANK!
!!
VRRRRR.....
KTANK!

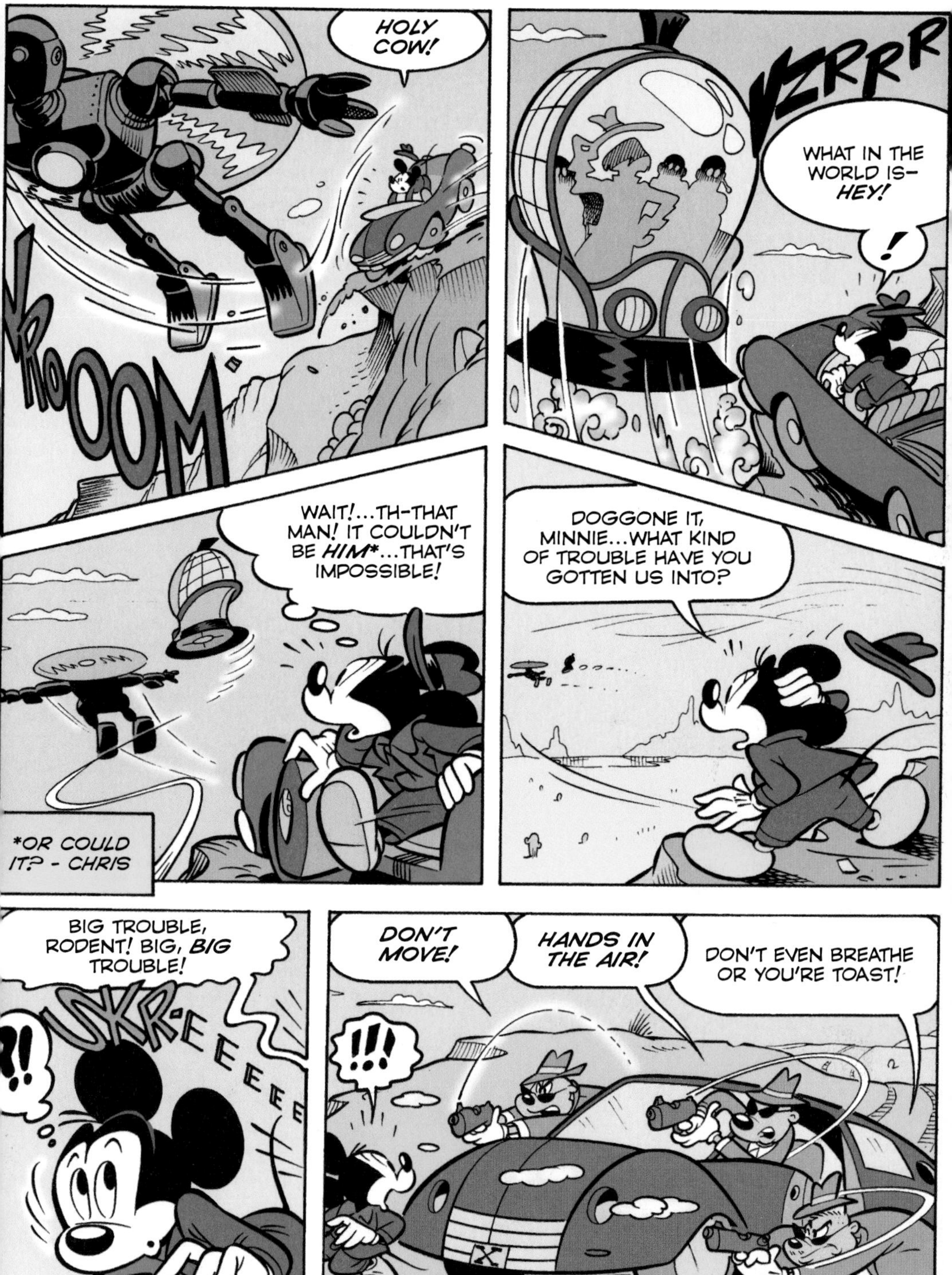
HOLY COW!
VROOOM
VZRRR
WHAT IN THE WORLD IS— HEY!
!
WAIT!...TH-THAT MAN! IT COULDN'T BE HIM*...THAT'S IMPOSSIBLE!
*OR COULD IT? - CHRIS
DOGGONE IT, MINNIE...WHAT KIND OF TROUBLE HAVE YOU GOTTEN US INTO?
BIG TROUBLE, RODENT! BIG, BIG TROUBLE!
SKR-EEEEEE
?!
DON'T MOVE!
HANDS IN THE AIR!
DON'T EVEN BREATHE OR YOU'RE TOAST!
!!!

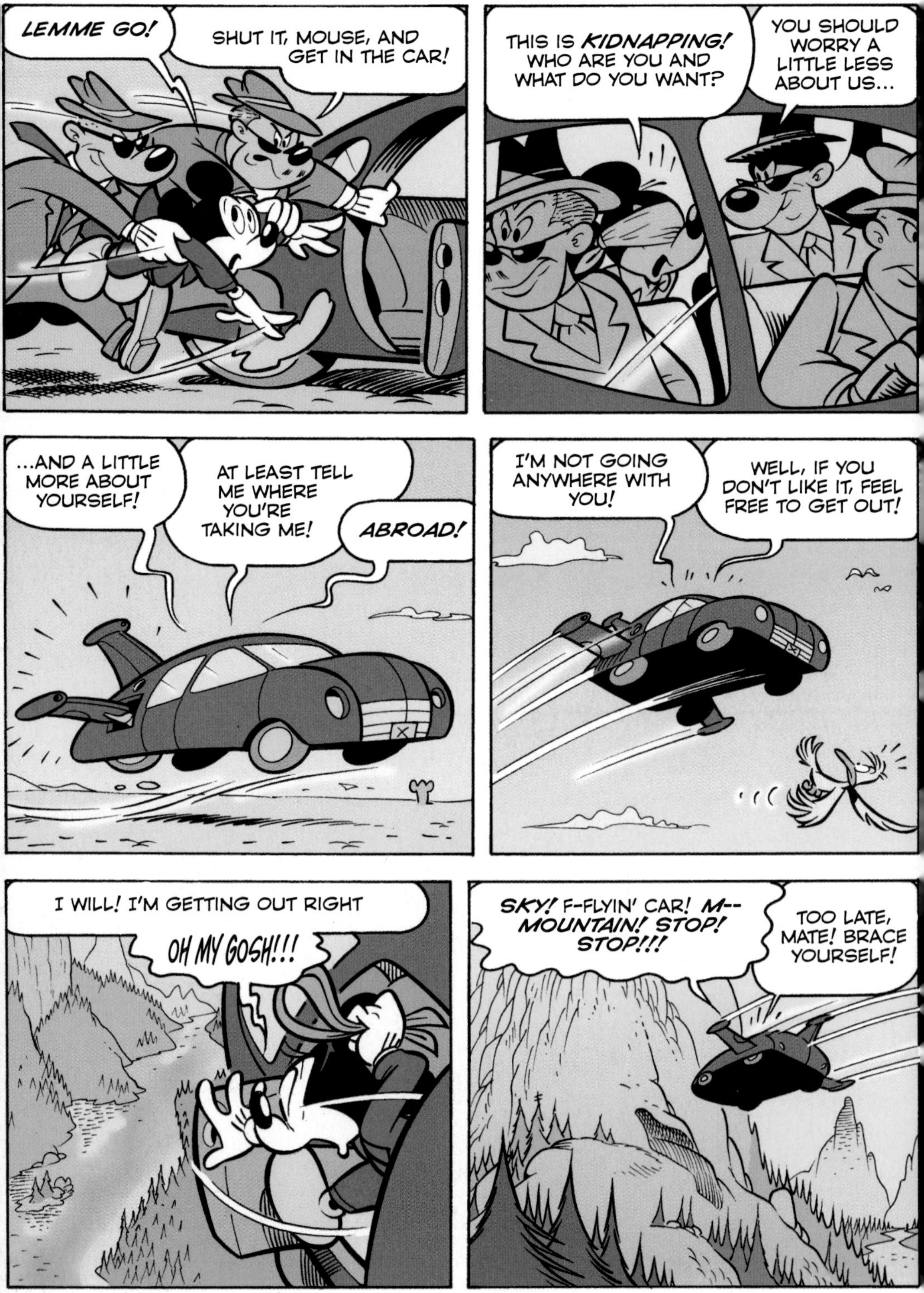
LEMME GO!
SHUT IT, MOUSE, AND GET IN THE CAR!
THIS IS KIDNAPPING! WHO ARE YOU AND WHAT DO YOU WANT?
YOU SHOULD WORRY A LITTLE LESS ABOUT US...
...AND A LITTLE MORE ABOUT YOURSELF!
AT LEAST TELL ME WHERE YOU'RE TAKING ME!
ABROAD!
I'M NOT GOING ANYWHERE WITH YOU!
WELL, IF YOU DON'T LIKE IT, FEEL FREE TO GET OUT!
I WILL! I'M GETTING OUT RIGHT
OH MY GOSH!!!
SKY! F-FLYIN' CAR! M--MOUNTAIN! STOP! STOP!!!
TOO LATE, MATE! BRACE YOURSELF!

Disney · PIXAR
WALL·E

A brand-new story that takes place before the hit film!
WALL•E finds himself isolated as more and more of
his companions shut down, until he finds a new friend
in the unlikeliest of places...and no, it's not Eve!

WALL•E: RECHARGE
DIAMOND CODE: JAN1100844
SC $9.99 ISBN 9781608865123
HC $24.99 ISBN 9781608865543

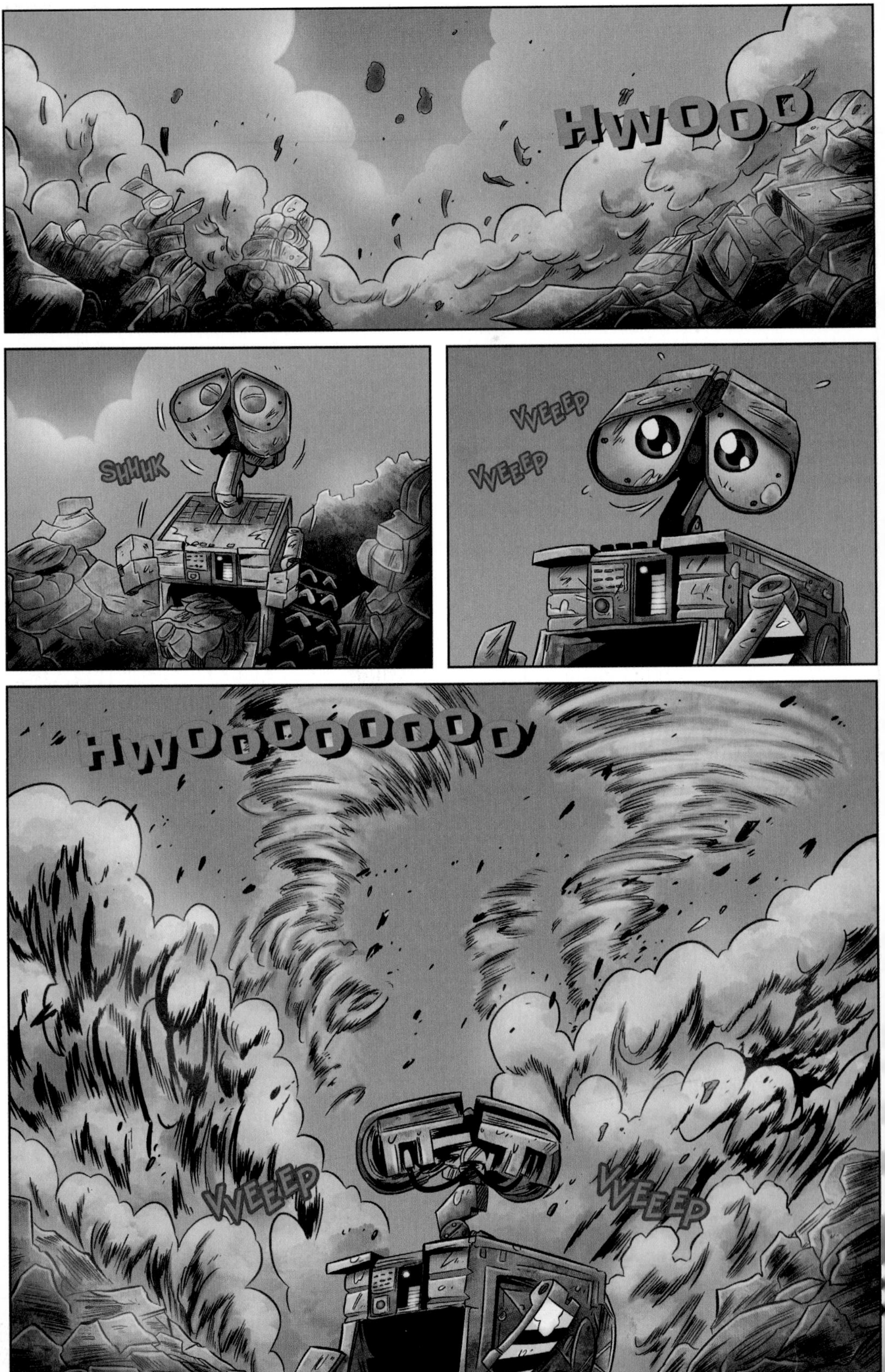
HWOOO
SHHHK
VVEEEP
VVEEEP
HWOOOOOOOO
VVEEEP
VVEEEP

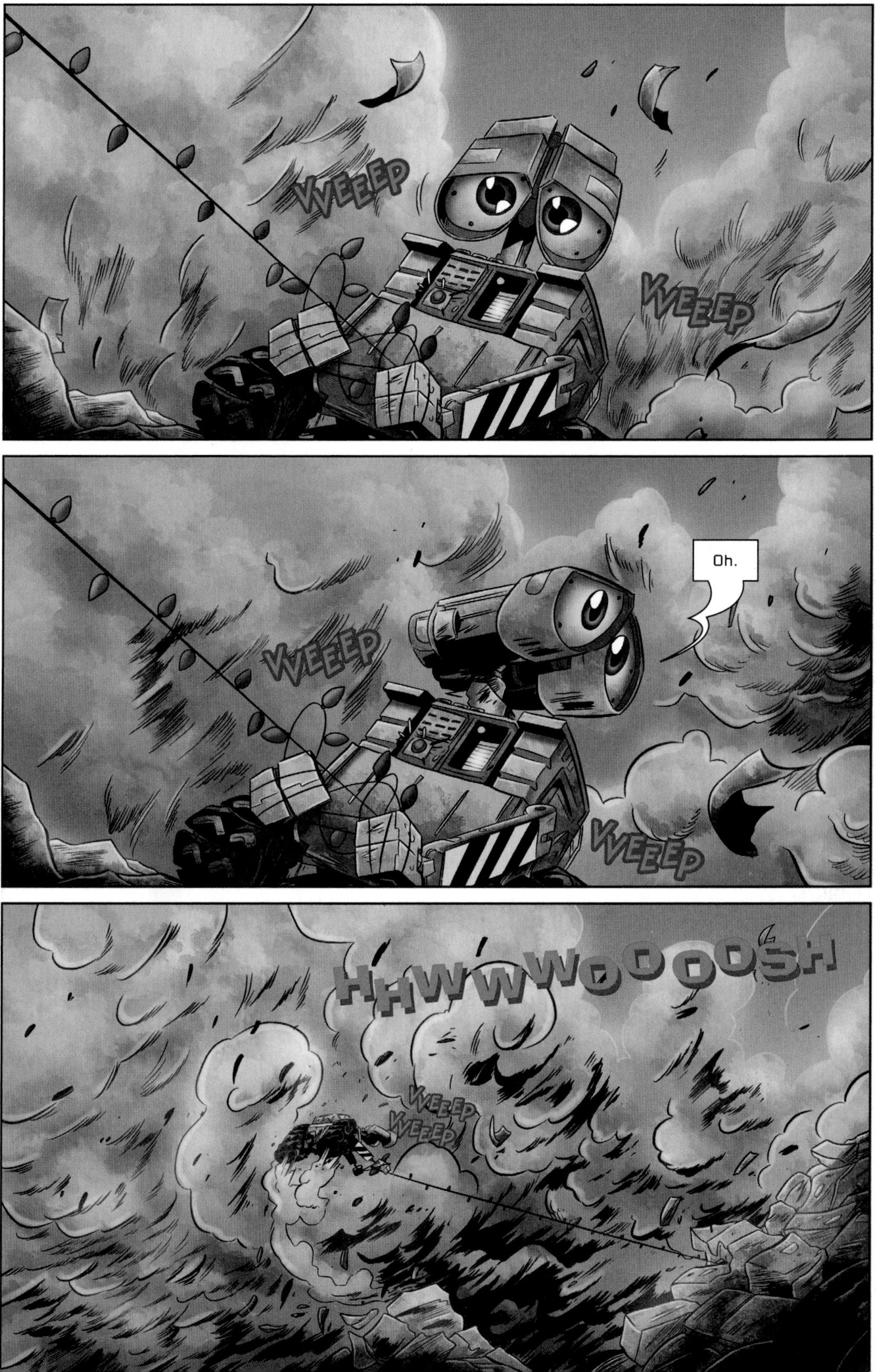
VVEEEP
VVEEEP
VVEEEP
Oh.
VVEEEP
HHWWWOOOOOSH
VVEEEP
VVEEEP

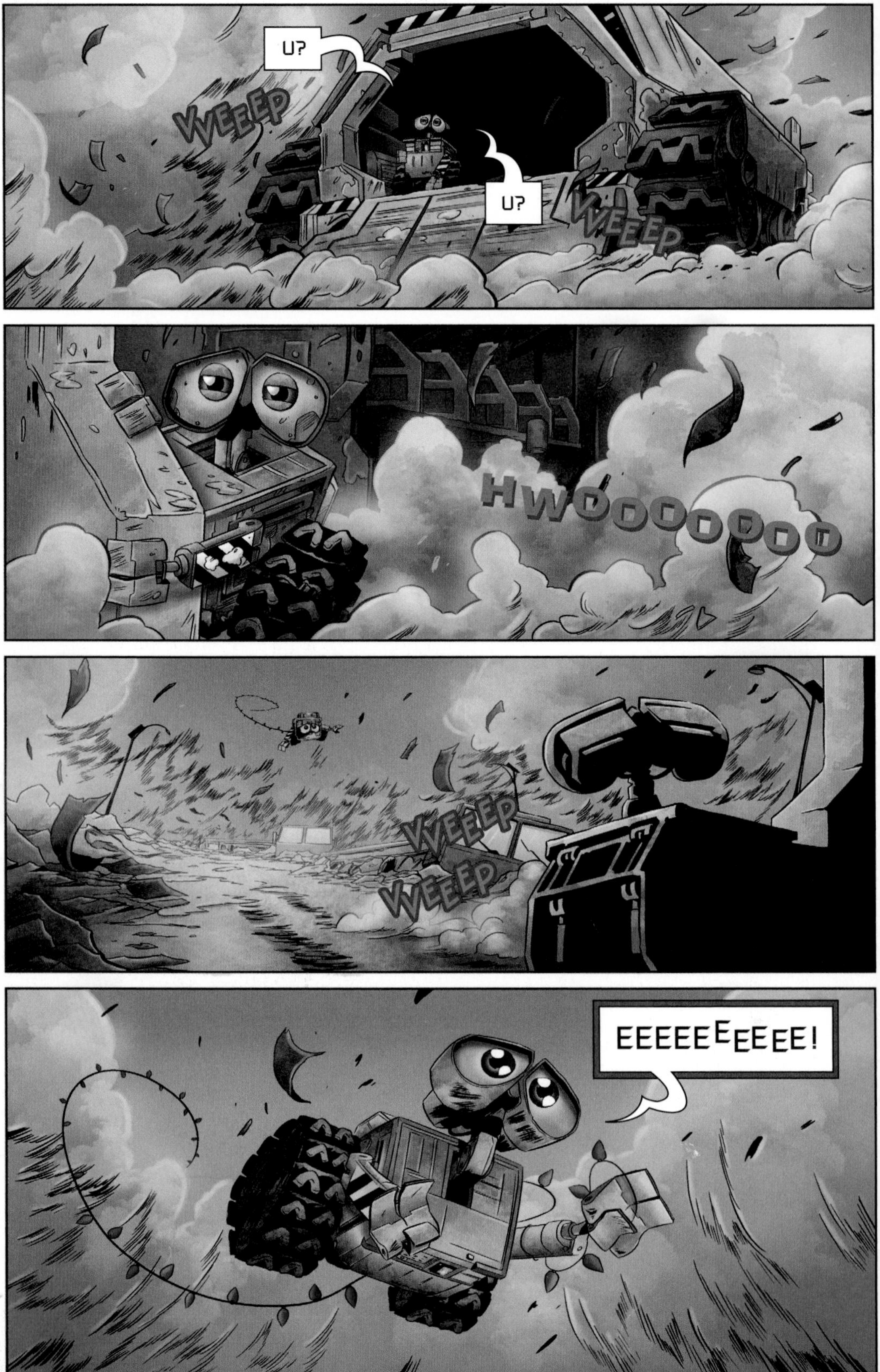
U?
VVEEEP
U?
VVEEEP
HWOOOOOOOO
VVEEEP
VVEEEP
EEEEEEEEEE!

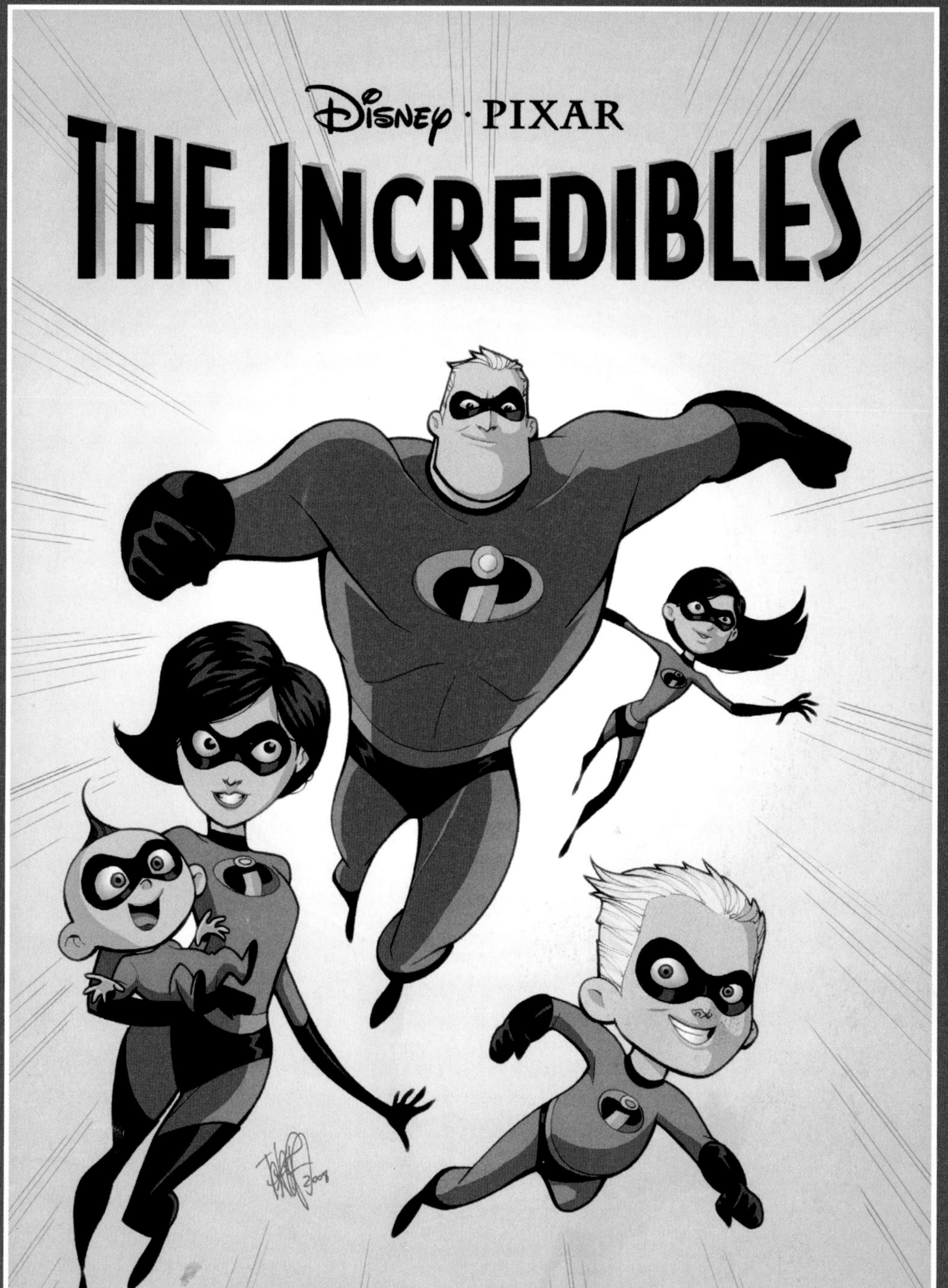
DISNEY · PIXAR
THE INCREDIBLES
FAMILY MATTERS

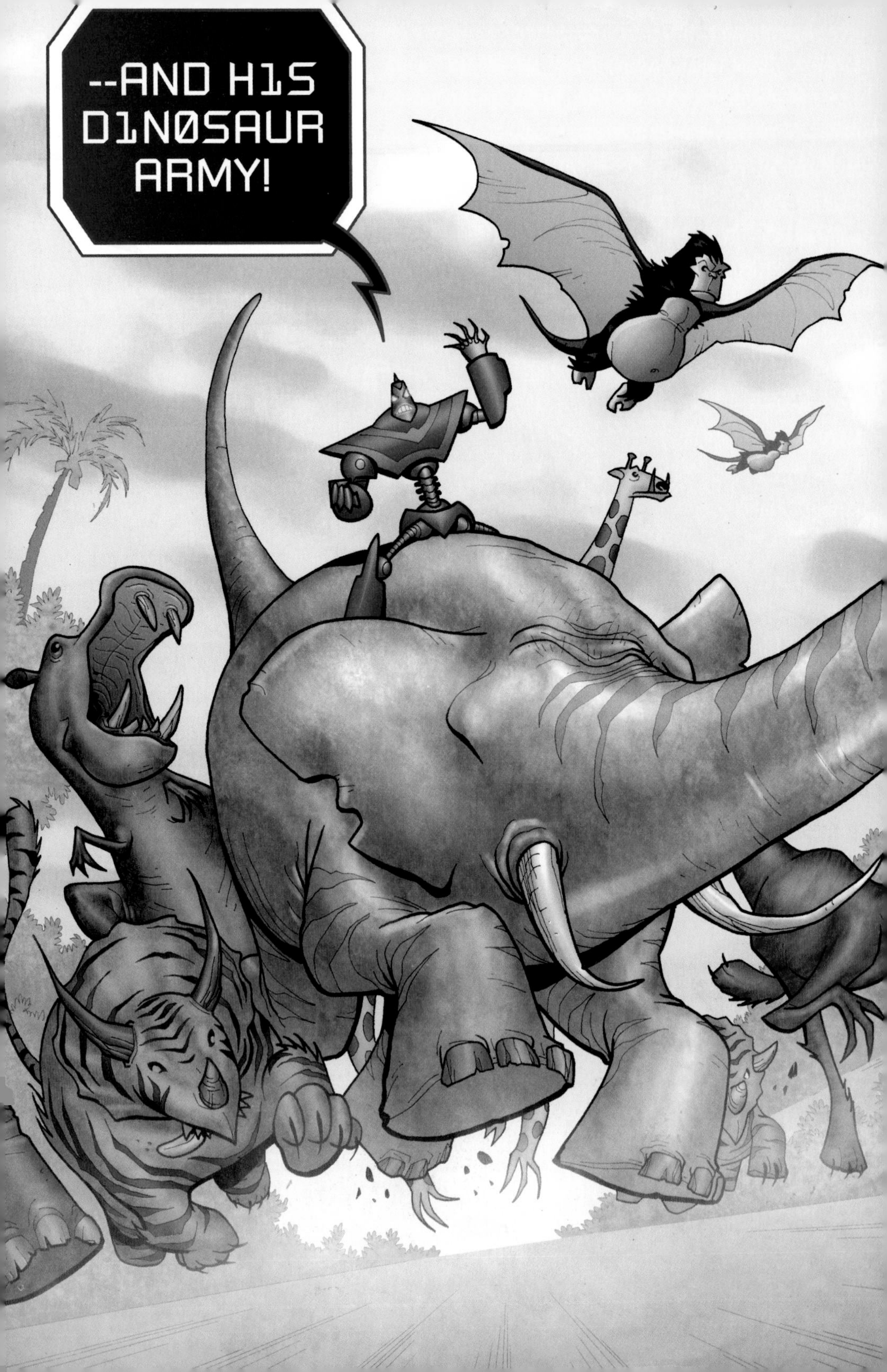
--AND H1S D1N0SAUR ARMY!

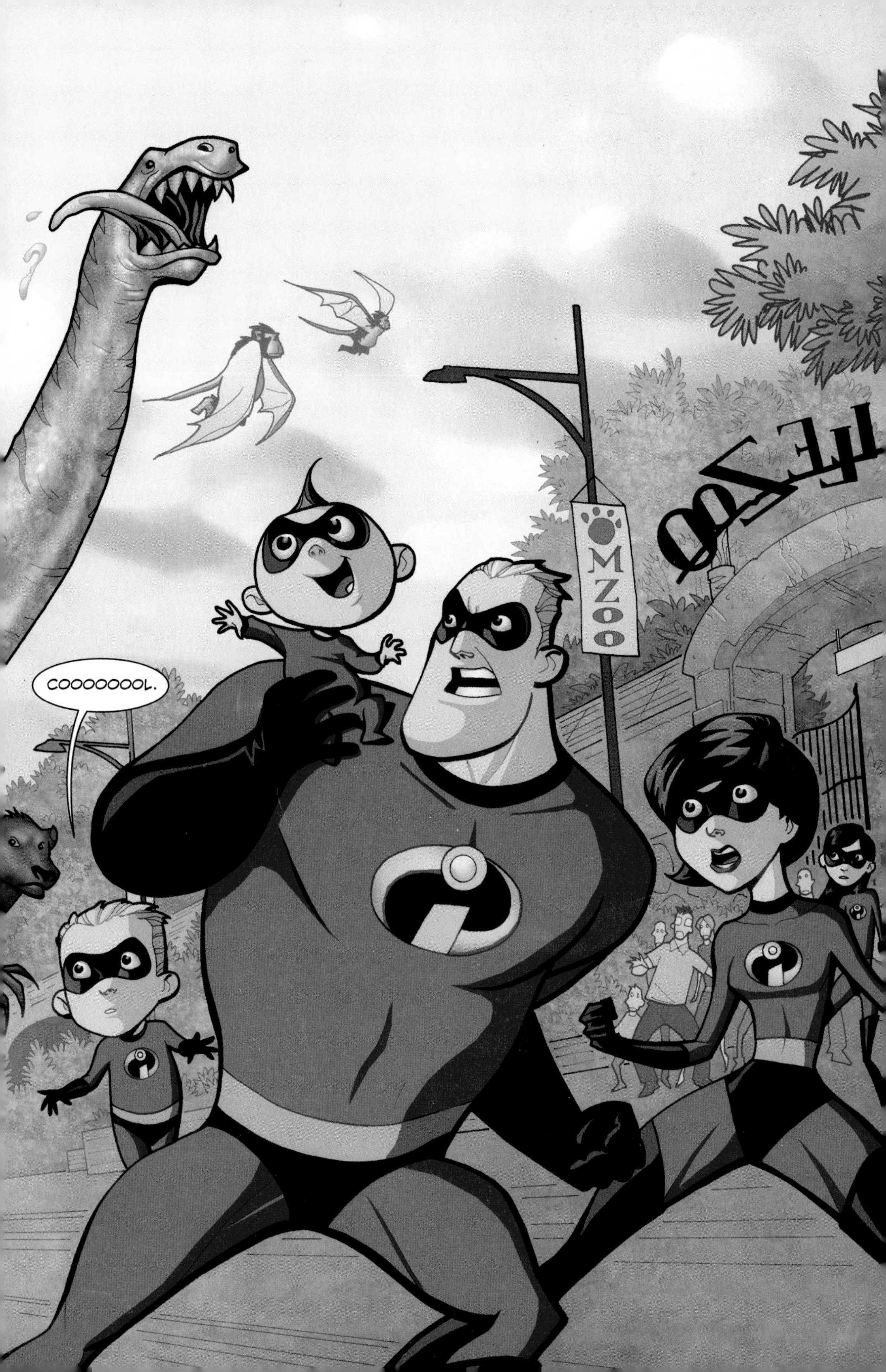
MZOO
COOOOOOOL.

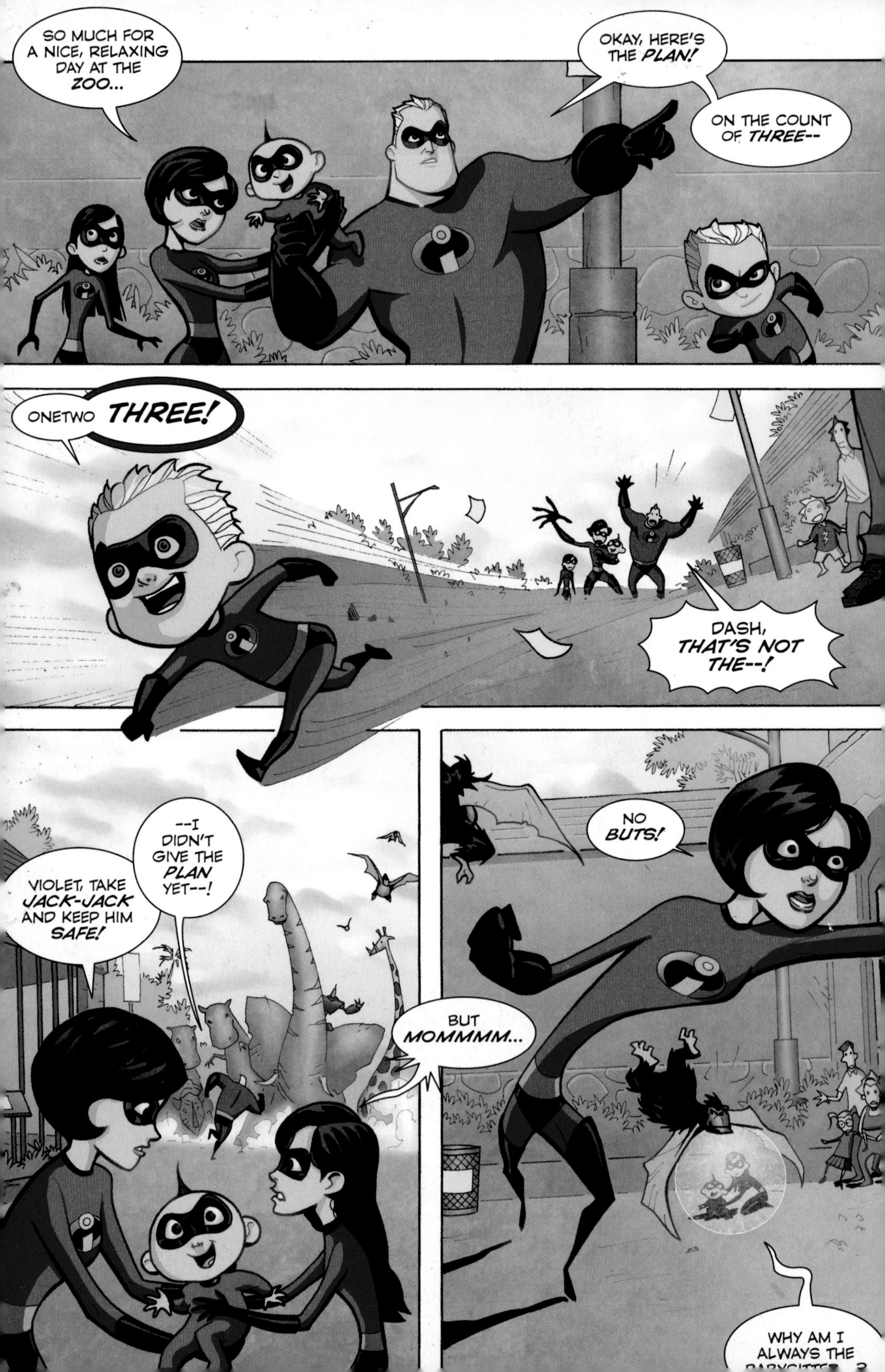
SO MUCH FOR A NICE, RELAXING DAY AT THE ZOO...
OKAY, HERE'S THE PLAN!
ON THE COUNT OF THREE--
ONETWO THREE!
DASH, THAT'S NOT THE--!
VIOLET, TAKE JACK-JACK AND KEEP HIM SAFE!
--I DIDN'T GIVE THE PLAN YET--!
BUT MOMMMM...
NO BUTS!
WHY AM I ALWAYS THE

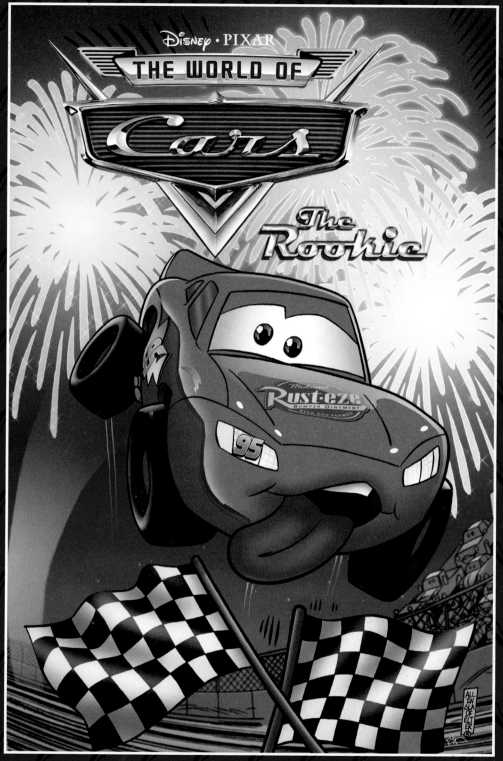

McQueen reveals his scrappy origins as "Bulldozer" McQueen—a local short track racer who dreams of the big time...

CARS: THE ROOKIE
Diamond Code: MAY090749
SC $9.99 ISBN 9781608865024
HC $24.99 ISBN 9781608865284

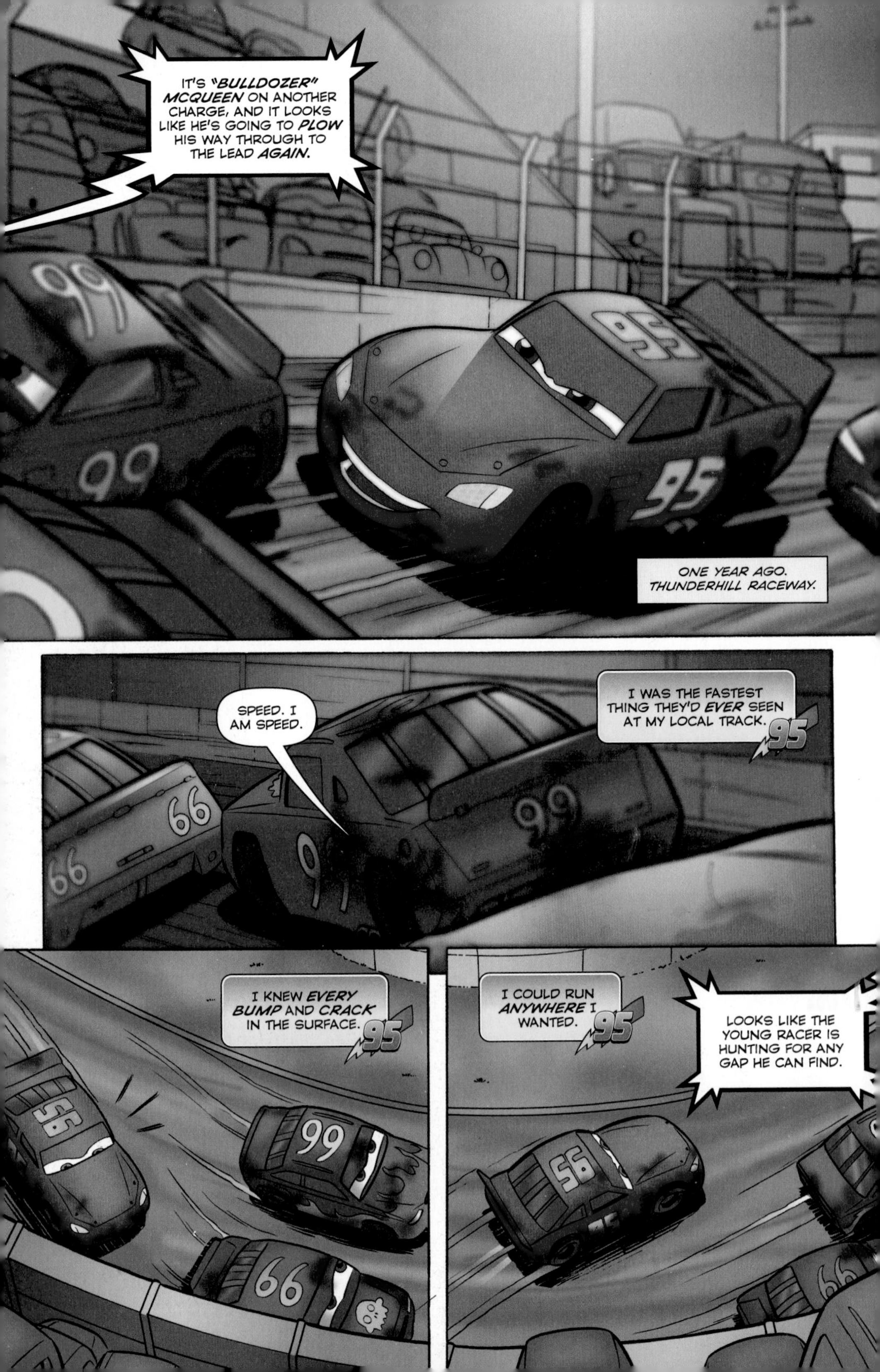
IT'S "BULLDOZER" MCQUEEN ON ANOTHER CHARGE, AND IT LOOKS LIKE HE'S GOING TO PLOW HIS WAY THROUGH TO THE LEAD AGAIN.
ONE YEAR AGO. THUNDERHILL RACEWAY.
SPEED. I AM SPEED.
I WAS THE FASTEST THING THEY'D EVER SEEN AT MY LOCAL TRACK.
I KNEW EVERY BUMP AND CRACK IN THE SURFACE.
I COULD RUN ANYWHERE I WANTED.
LOOKS LIKE THE YOUNG RACER IS HUNTING FOR ANY GAP HE CAN FIND.

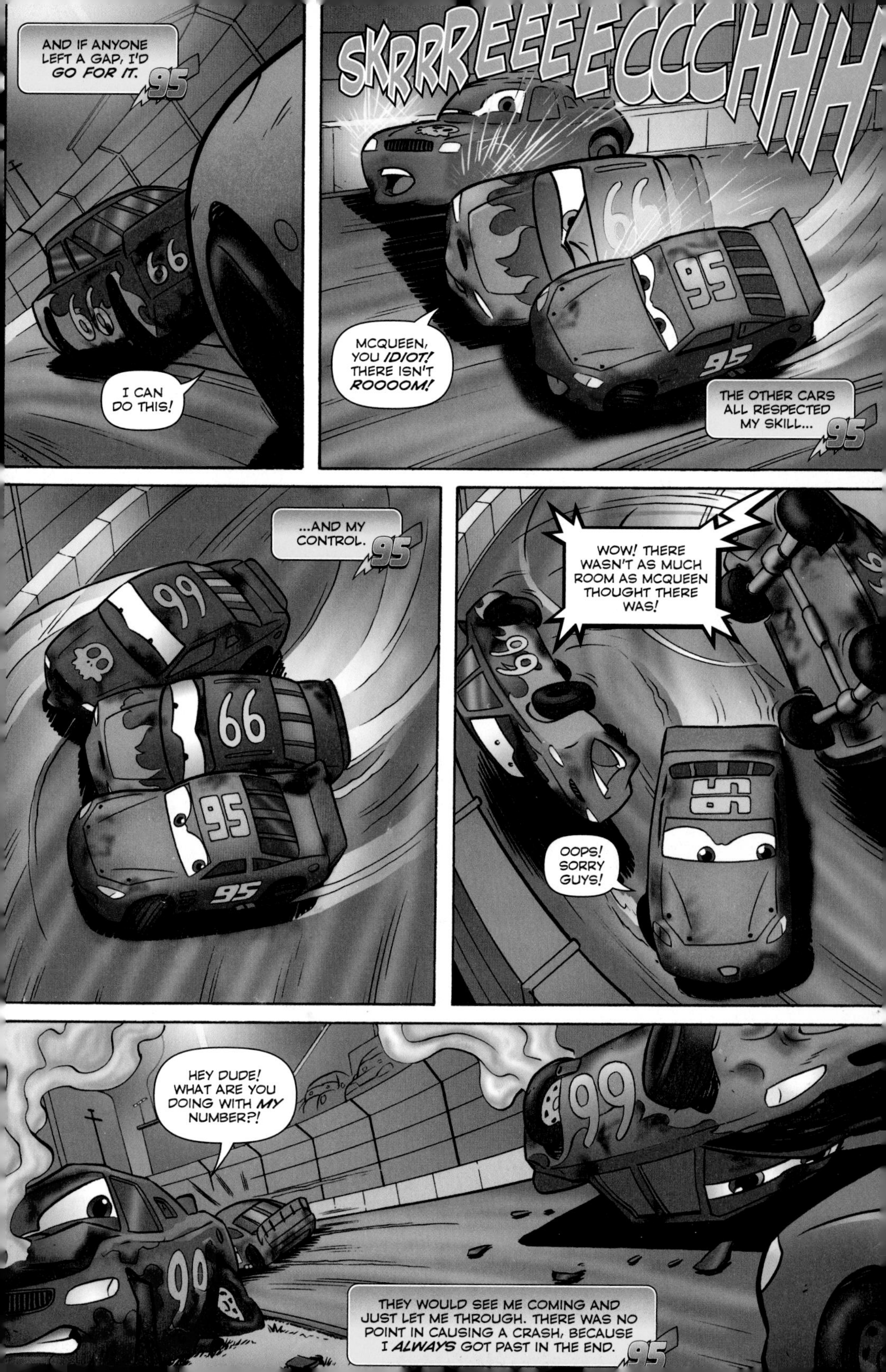

AND IF ANYONE LEFT A GAP, I'D GO FOR IT.
I CAN DO THIS!
SKRRREEEEECCCHHH
MCQUEEN, YOU IDIOT! THERE ISN'T ROOOOM!
THE OTHER CARS ALL RESPECTED MY SKILL...
...AND MY CONTROL.
WOW! THERE WASN'T AS MUCH ROOM AS MCQUEEN THOUGHT THERE WAS!
OOPS! SORRY GUYS!
HEY DUDE! WHAT ARE YOU DOING WITH MY NUMBER?!
THEY WOULD SEE ME COMING AND JUST LET ME THROUGH. THERE WAS NO POINT IN CAUSING A CRASH, BECAUSE I ALWAYS GOT PAST IN THE END.

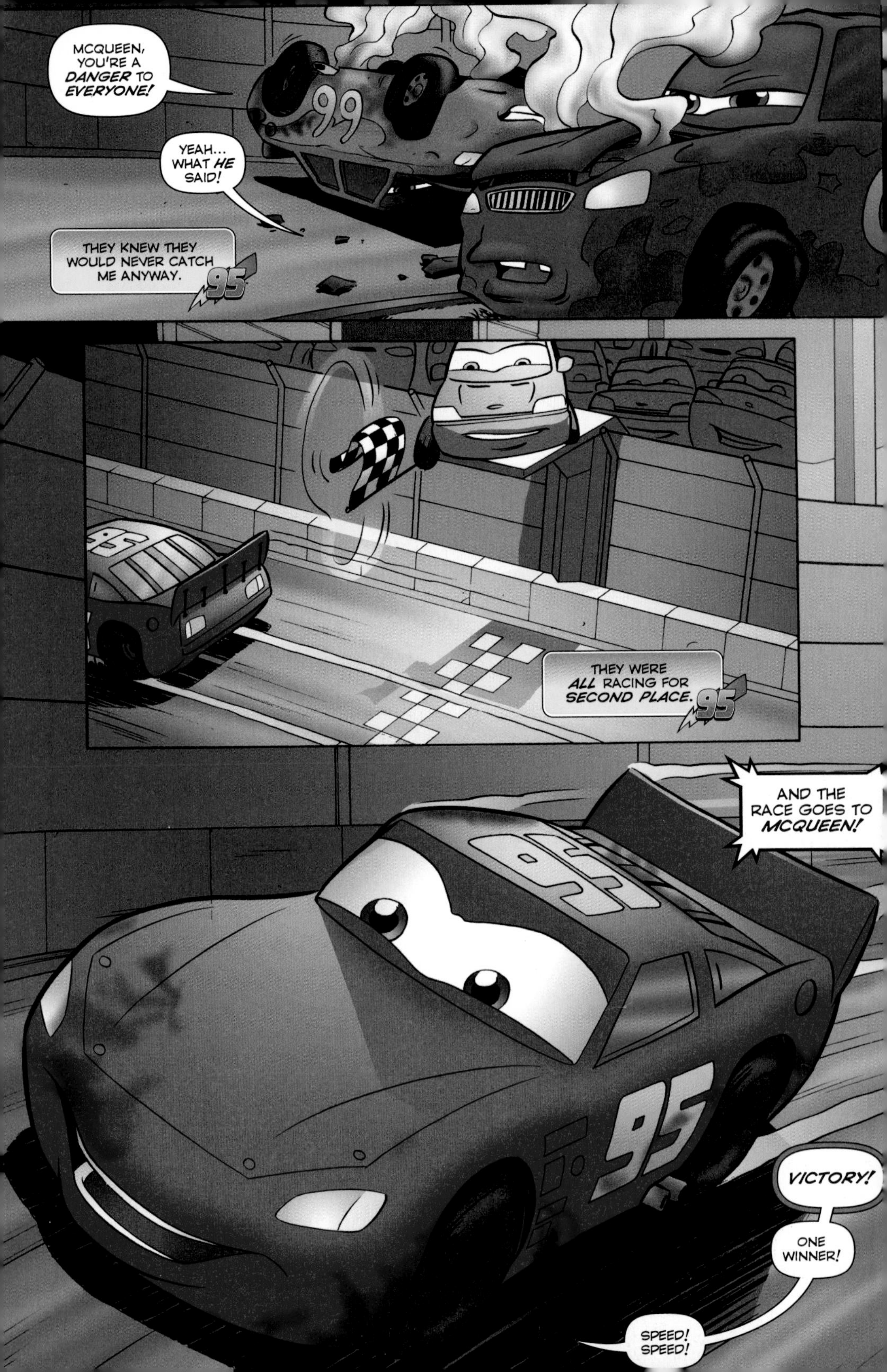
MCQUEEN, YOU'RE A DANGER TO EVERYONE!
YEAH... WHAT HE SAID!
THEY KNEW THEY WOULD NEVER CATCH ME ANYWAY.
THEY WERE ALL RACING FOR SECOND PLACE.
AND THE RACE GOES TO MCQUEEN!
VICTORY!
ONE WINNER!
SPEED! SPEED!

GRAPHIC NOVELS AVAILABLE NOW!

BOOM KIDS!

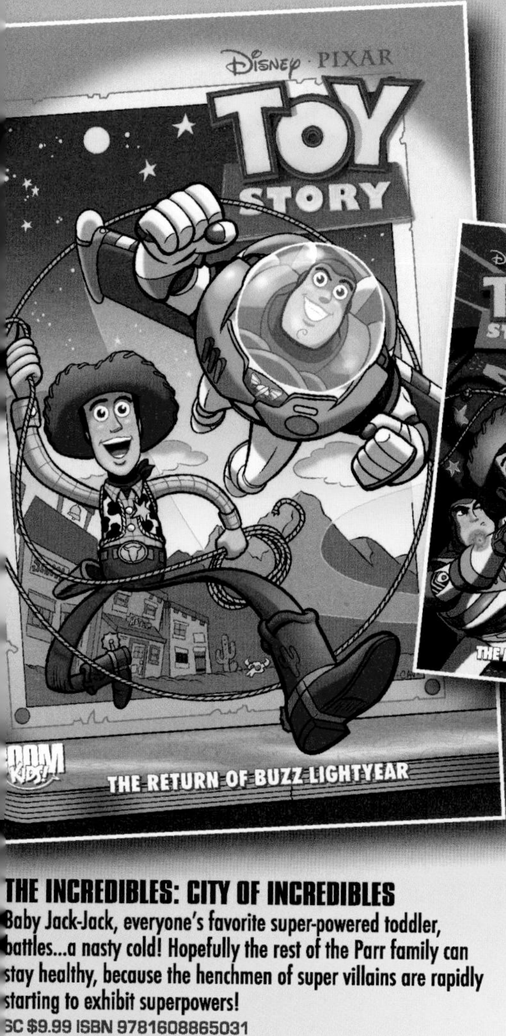

Disney · PIXAR
TOY STORY
BOOM KIDS!
THE RETURN OF BUZZ LIGHTYEAR

TOY STORY: THE RETURN OF BUZZ LIGHTYEAR

When Andy is given a surprise gift, no one is more surprised than the toys in his room...it's a second Buzz Lightyear! The stage is set for a Star Command showdown when only one Buzz can stay!

SC $9.99 ISBN 9781608865574
HC $24.99 ISBN 9781608865581

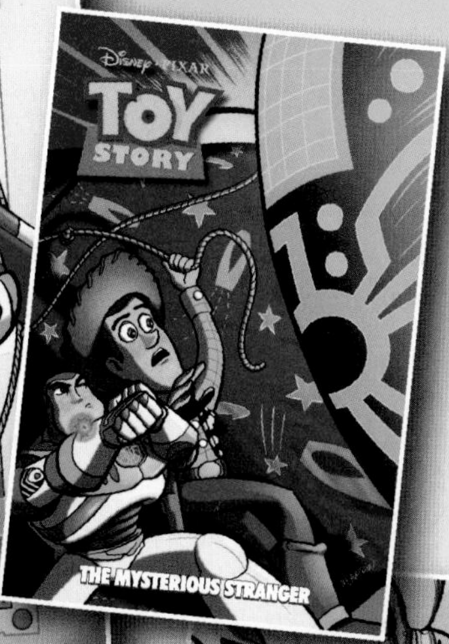

Disney · PIXAR
TOY STORY
THE MYSTERIOUS STRANGER

TOY STORY: THE MYSTERIOUS STRANGER

Andy has a new addition to his room—a circuit-laden egg. Is this new gizmo a friend or foe? This adventure kicks off the first of four self-contained stories featuring all your favorite characters from the TOY STORY movies – Woody, Buzz and the gang!

SC $9.99 ISBN 9781934506912
HC $24.99 ISBN 9781608865239

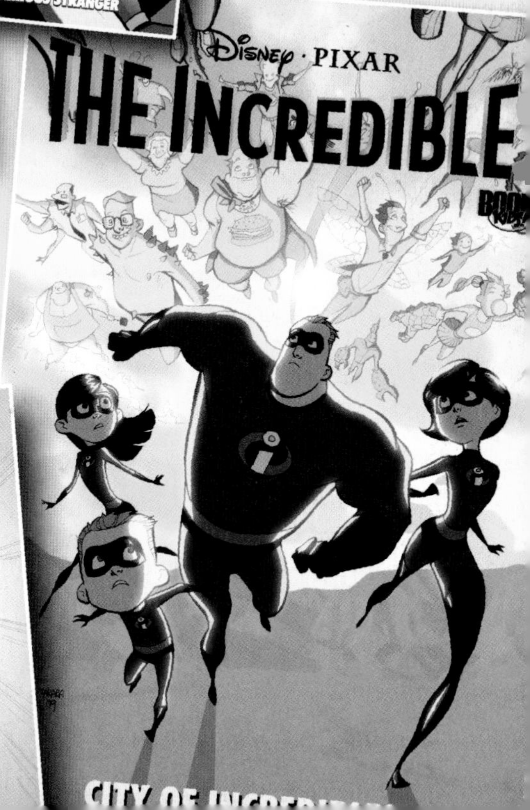

Disney · PIXAR
THE INCREDIBLE

THE INCREDIBLES: CITY OF INCREDIBLES

Baby Jack-Jack, everyone's favorite super-powered toddler, battles...a nasty cold! Hopefully the rest of the Parr family can stay healthy, because the henchmen of super villains are rapidly starting to exhibit superpowers!

SC $9.99 ISBN 9781608865031
HC $24.99 ISBN 9781608865291

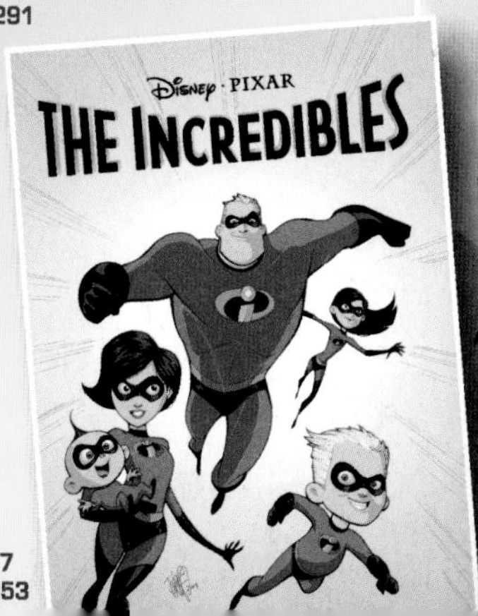

Disney · PIXAR
THE INCREDIBLES

THE INCREDIBLES: FAMILY MATTERS

Acclaimed scribe Mark Waid has written the perfect INCREDIBLES story! What happens when Mr. Incredible's super-abilities start to wane...and how long can he keep his powerlessness a secret from his wife and kids?

SC $9.99 ISBN 9781934506837
HC $24.99 ISBN 9781608865253

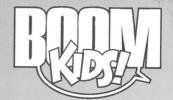

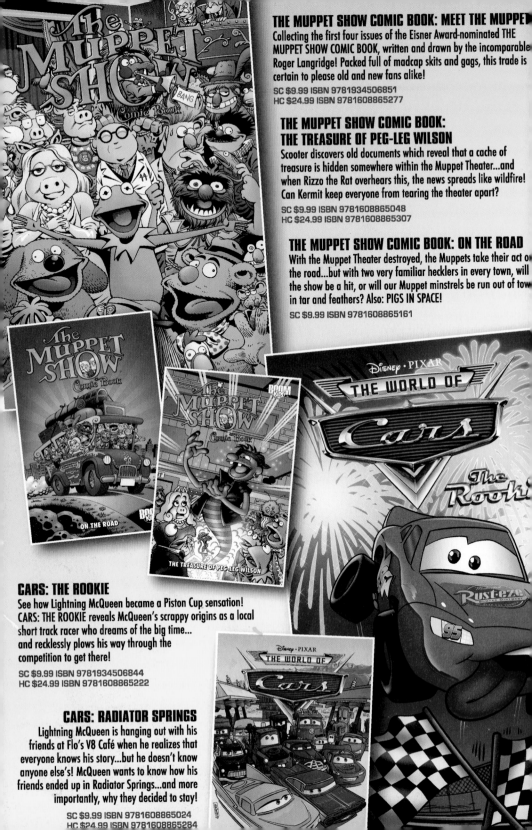

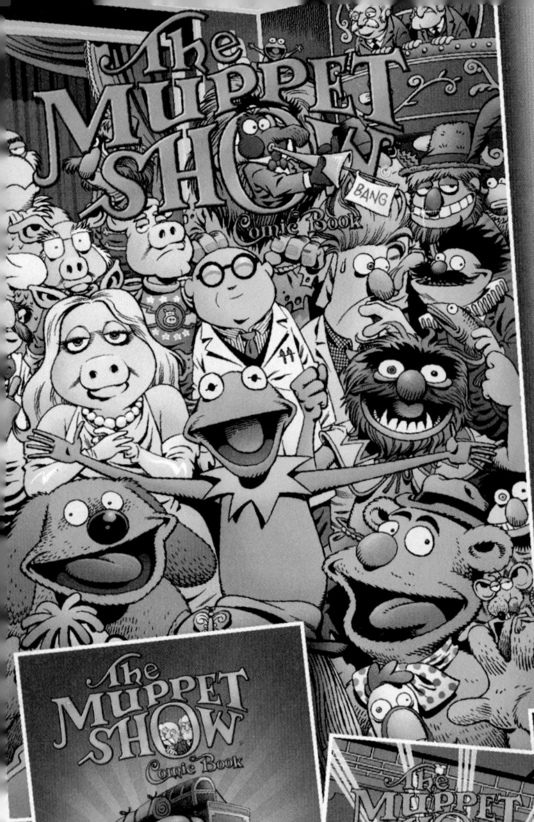
The Muppet Show
Comic Book
BANG

THE MUPPET SHOW COMIC BOOK: MEET THE MUPPET

Collecting the first four issues of the Eisner Award-nominated THE MUPPET SHOW COMIC BOOK, written and drawn by the incomparable Roger Langridge! Packed full of madcap skits and gags, this trade is certain to please old and new fans alike!

SC $9.99 ISBN 9781934506851
HC $24.99 ISBN 9781608865277

THE MUPPET SHOW COMIC BOOK: THE TREASURE OF PEG-LEG WILSON

Scooter discovers old documents which reveal that a cache of treasure is hidden somewhere within the Muppet Theater...and when Rizzo the Rat overhears this, the news spreads like wildfire! Can Kermit keep everyone from tearing the theater apart?

SC $9.99 ISBN 9781608865048
HC $24.99 ISBN 9781608865307

THE MUPPET SHOW COMIC BOOK: ON THE ROAD

With the Muppet Theater destroyed, the Muppets take their act o the road...but with two very familiar hecklers in every town, will the show be a hit, or will our Muppet minstrels be run out of tow in tar and feathers? Also: PIGS IN SPACE!

SC $9.99 ISBN 9781608865161

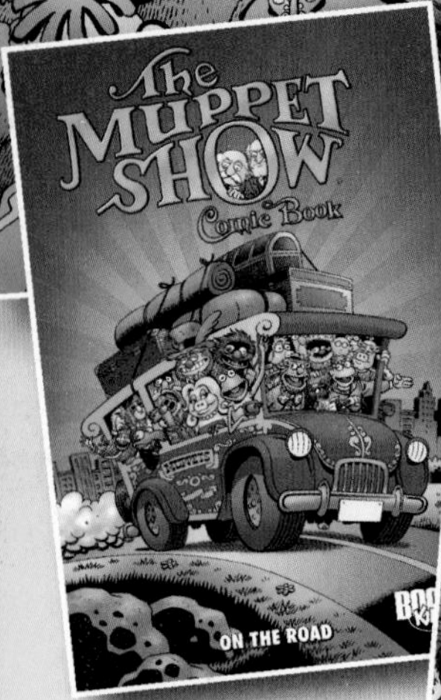
The Muppet Show
Comic Book
ON THE ROAD

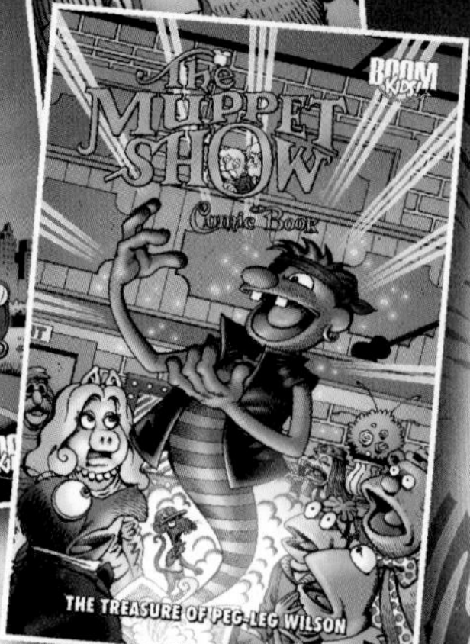
The Muppet Show
Comic Book
BOOM! Kids!
THE TREASURE OF PEG-LEG WILSON

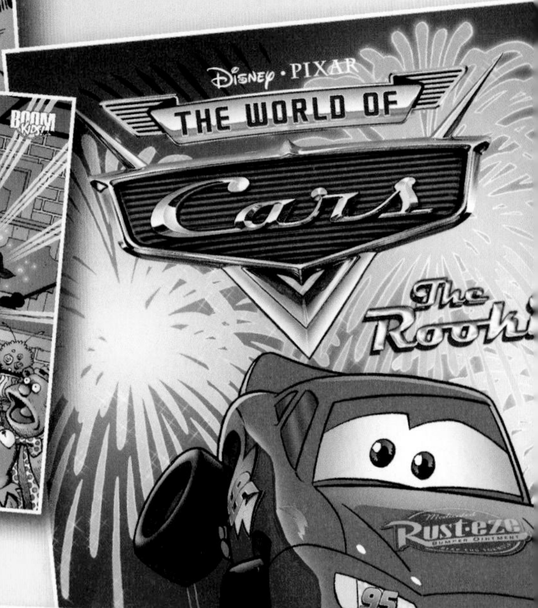
Disney • PIXAR
THE WORLD OF
Cars
Rust-eze
95

CARS: THE ROOKIE

See how Lightning McQueen became a Piston Cup sensation! CARS: THE ROOKIE reveals McQueen's scrappy origins as a local short track racer who dreams of the big time... and recklessly plows his way through the competition to get there!

SC $9.99 ISBN 9781934506844
HC $24.99 ISBN 9781608865222

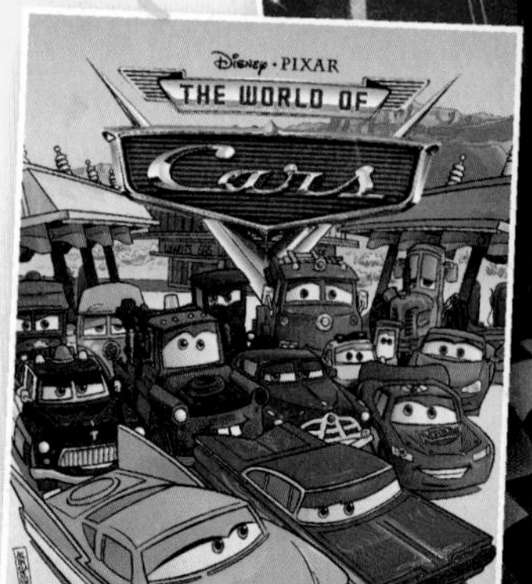
Disney • PIXAR
THE WORLD OF
Cars

CARS: RADIATOR SPRINGS

Lightning McQueen is hanging out with his friends at Flo's V8 Café when he realizes that everyone knows his story...but he doesn't know anyone else's! McQueen wants to know how his friends ended up in Radiator Springs...and more importantly, why they decided to stay!

SC $9.99 ISBN 9781608865024
HC $24.99 ISBN 9781608865284

WALL•E: RECHARGE

Before WALL•E becomes the hardworking robot we know and love, he lets the few remaining robots take care of the trash compacting while he collects interesting junk. But when these robots start breaking down, WALL•E must adjust his priorities...or else Earth is doomed!

SC $9.99 ISBN 9781608865123
HC $24.99 ISBN 9781608865543

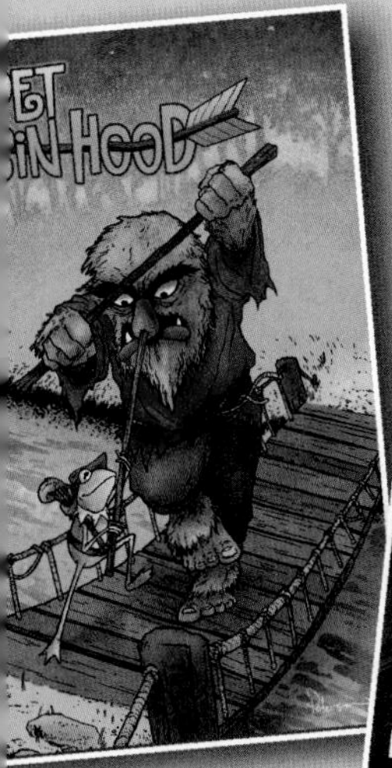

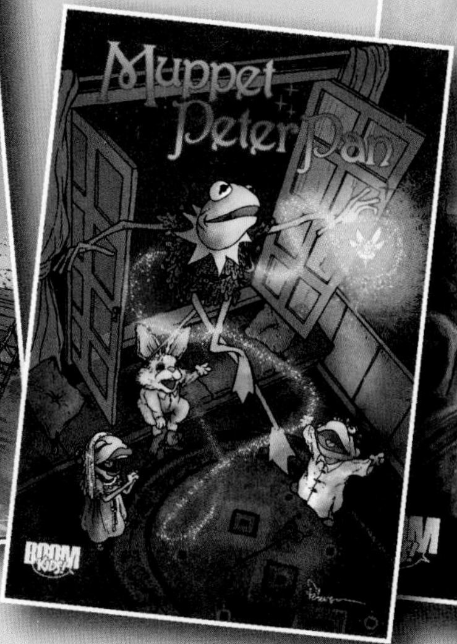
Muppet Peter Pan
BOOM KIDS!

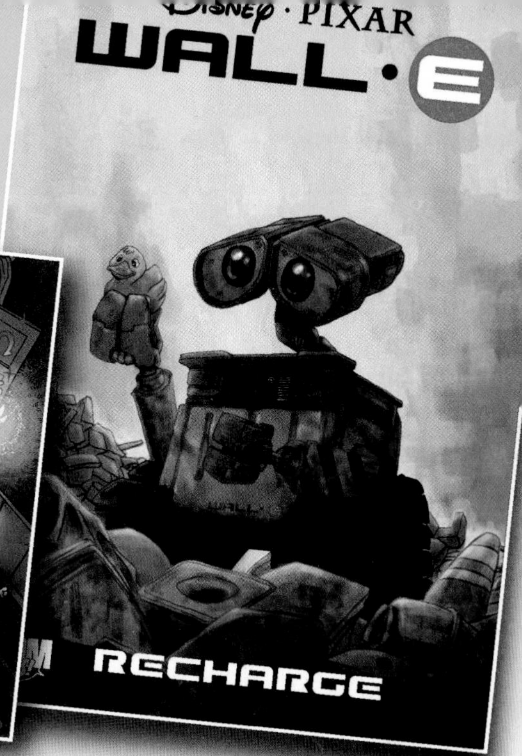
DISNEY · PIXAR
WALL·E
RECHARGE

UPPET ROBIN HOOD

e Muppets tell the Robin Hood legend for laughs, and it's the reader who will be merry! bin Hood (Kermit the Frog) joins with the Merry Men, Sherwood Forest's infamous gang of isfit outlaws, to take on the Sheriff of Nottingham (Sam the Eagle)!

 $9.99 ISBN 9781934506790
 $24.99 ISBN 9781608865260

MUPPET PETER PAN

When Peter Pan (Kermit) whisks Wendy (Janice) and her brothers to Neverswamp, the adventure begins! With Captain Hook (Gonzo) out for revenge for the loss of his hand, can even the magic of Piggytink (Miss Piggy) save Wendy and her brothers?

SC $9.99 ISBN 9781608865079
HC $24.99 ISBN 9781608865314

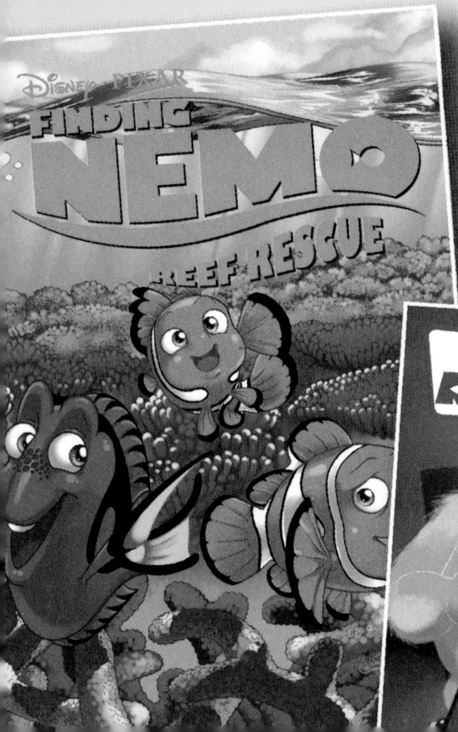
DISNEY · PIXAR
FINDING NEMO
REEF RESCUE

FINDING NEMO: REEF RESCUE

Nemo, Dory and Marlin have become local heroes, and are recruited to embark on an all-new adventure in this exciting collection! The reef is mysteriously dying and no one knows why. So Nemo and his friends must travel the great blue sea to save their home!

SC $9.99 ISBN 9781934506882
HC $24.99 ISBN 9781608865246

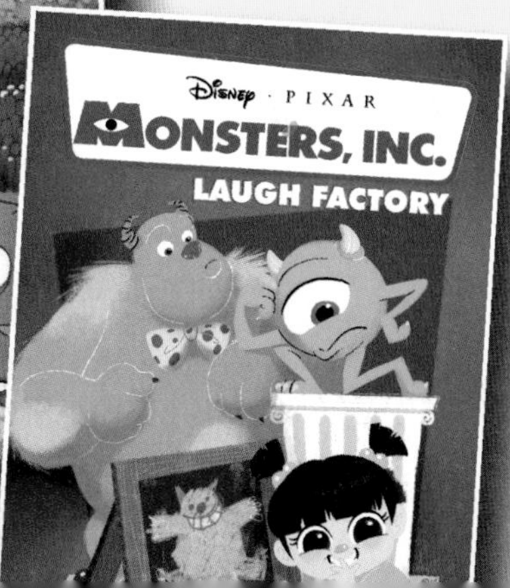
DISNEY · PIXAR
MONSTERS, INC.
LAUGH FACTORY

MONSTERS, INC.: LAUGH FACTORY

Someone is stealing comedy props from the other employees, making it difficult for them to harvest the laughter they need to power Monstropolis...and all evidence points to Sulley's best friend Mike Wazowski!

SC $9.99 ISBN 9781608865086

DISNEY'S HERO SQUAD: ULTRAHEROES VOL. 1: SAVE THE WORLD

It's an all-star cast of your favorite Disney characters, as you have never seen them before. Join Donald Duck, Goofy, Daisy, and even Mickey himself as they defend the fate of the planet as the one and only Ultraheroes!

SC $9.99 ISBN 9781608865437
HC $24.99 ISBN 9781608865529

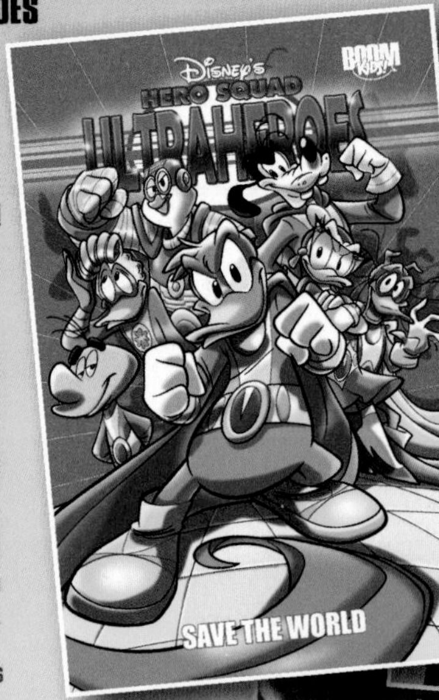
Disney's
HERO SQUAD
ULTRAHEROES
BOOM KIDS!
SAVE THE WORLD

UNCLE SCROOGE: THE HUNT FOR THE OLD NUMBER ONE

Join Donald Duck's favorite penny-pinching Uncle Scrooge as he, Donald himself and Huey, Dewey, and Louie embark on a globe-spanning trek to recover treasure and save Scrooge's "number one dime" from the treacherous Magica De Spell.

SC $9.99 ISBN 9781608865475
HC $24.99 ISBN 9781608865536

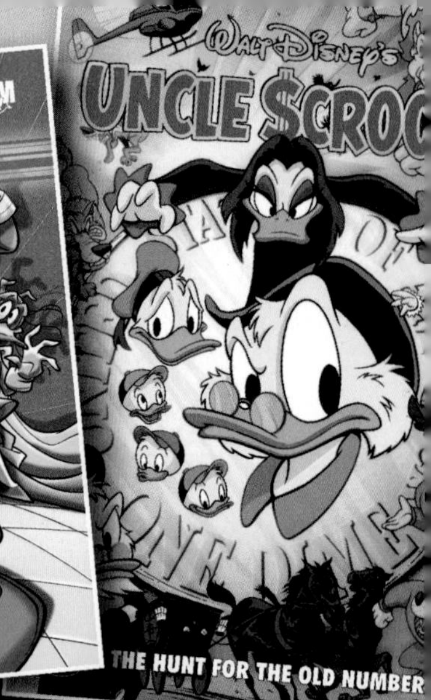
Walt Disney's
THE HUNT FOR THE OLD NUMBER

WIZARDS OF MICKEY VOL. 1: MOUSE MAGIC

Your favorite Disney characters star in this magical fantasy epic! Student of the great wizard Nereus, Mickey allies himself with Donald and team mate Goofy, in a quest to find a magical crown that will give him mastery over all spells!

SC $9.99 ISBN 9781608865413
HC $24.99 ISBN 9781608865505

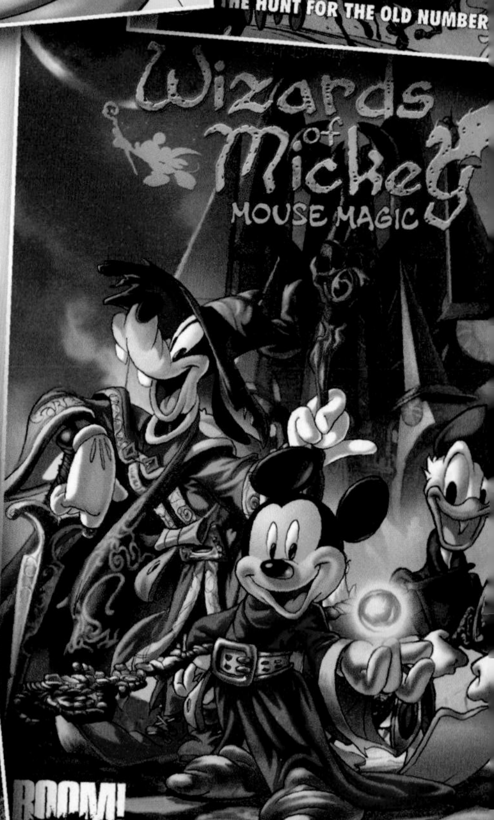
Wizards of Mickey
MOUSE MAGIC
BOOM! STUDIOS

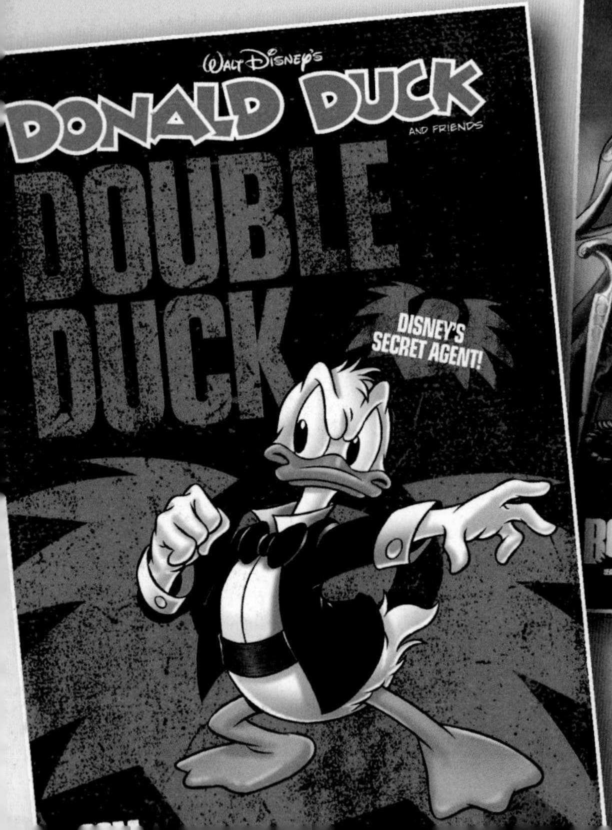
Walt Disney's
DONALD DUCK
AND FRIENDS
DOUBLE DUCK
DISNEY'S SECRET AGENT!

DONALD DUCK AND FRIENDS: DOUBLE DUCK VOL. 1

Donald Duck as a secret agent? Villainous fiends beware the world of super sleuthing and espionage will never b the same! This is Donald Duck like you've never seen hi

SC $9.99 ISBN 9781608865451

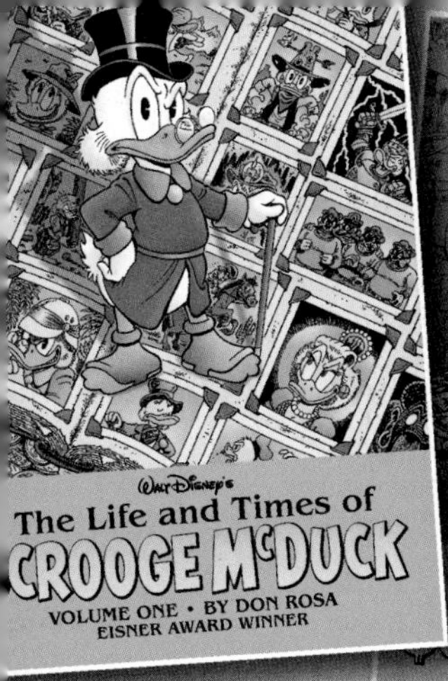
Walt Disney's
The Life and Times of
CROOGE McDUCK
VOLUME ONE • BY DON ROSA
EISNER AWARD WINNER

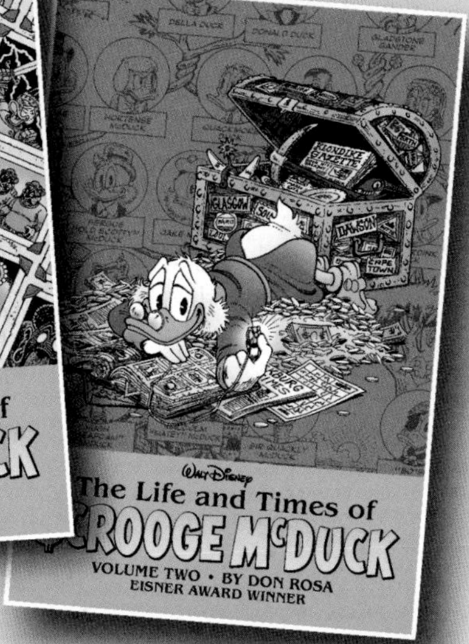
Walt Disney
The Life and Times of
CROOGE McDUCK
VOLUME TWO • BY DON ROSA
EISNER AWARD WINNER

THE LIFE AND TIMES OF SCROOGE McDUCK VOL. 1

BOOM Kids! proudly collects the first half of THE LIFE AND TIMES OF SCROOGE MCDUCK in a gorgeous hardcover collection – featuring smyth sewn binding, a gold-on-gold foil-stamped case wrap, and a bookmark ribbon! These stories, written and drawn by legendary cartoonist Don Rosa, chronicle Scrooge McDuck's fascinating life.

HC $24.99 ISBN 9781608865383

THE LIFE AND TIMES OF SCROOGE McDUCK VOL. 2

BOOM Kids! proudly presents volume two of THE LIFE AND TIMES OF SCROOGE MCDUCK in a gorgeous hardcover collection in a beautiful, deluxe package featuring smyth sewn binding and a foil-stamped case wrap! These stories, written and drawn by legendary cartoonist Don Rosa, chronicle Scrooge McDuck's fascinating life.

HC $24.99 ISBN 9781608865420

MICKEY MOUSE CLASSICS: MOUSE TAILS

See Mickey Mouse as he was meant to be seen! Solving mysteries, fighting off pirates, and generally saving the day! These classic stories omprise a "Greatest Hits" series for the mouse, including a story produced by seminal Disney creator Carl Barks!

HC $24.99 ISBN 9781608865390

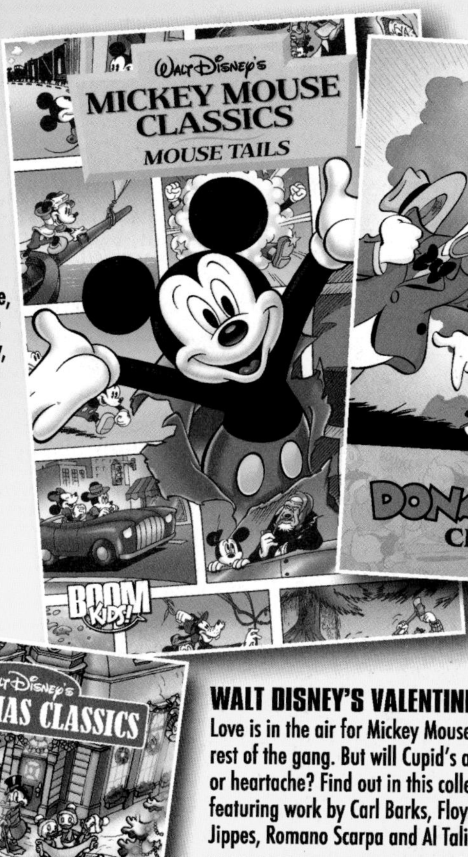
Walt Disney's
MICKEY MOUSE
CLASSICS
MOUSE TAILS
BOOM KIDS!

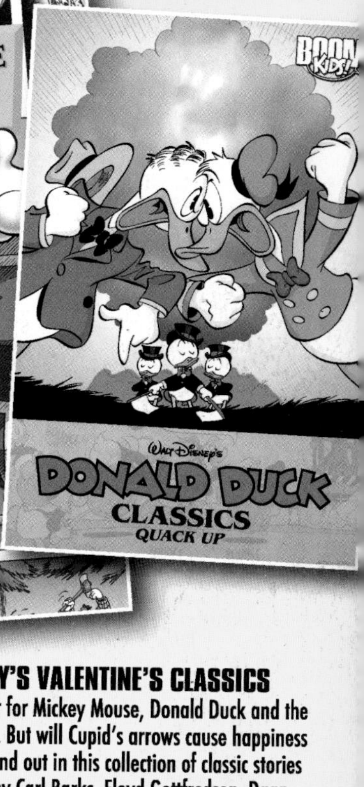
BOOM KIDS!
Walt Disney's
DONALD DUCK
CLASSICS
QUACK UP

ONALD DUCK CLASSICS: QUACK UP

hether it's finding gold, journeying to the Klondike, fighting ghosts, Donald will always have the help his much more prepared nephews – Huey, Dewey, d Louie – by his side. Featuring some of the best onald Duck stories Carl Barks ever produced!

C $24.99 ISBN 9781608865406

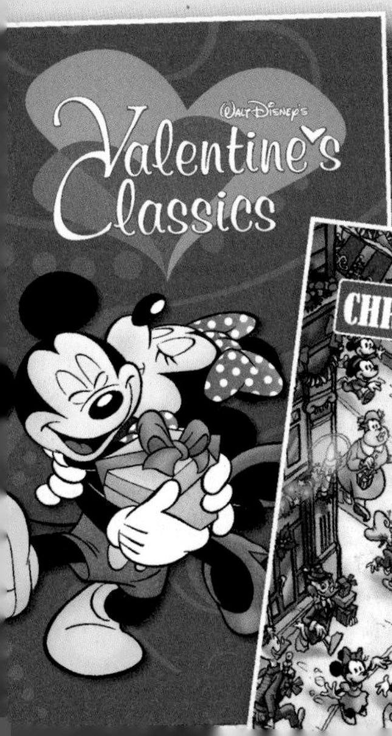
Walt Disney's
Valentine's
Classics

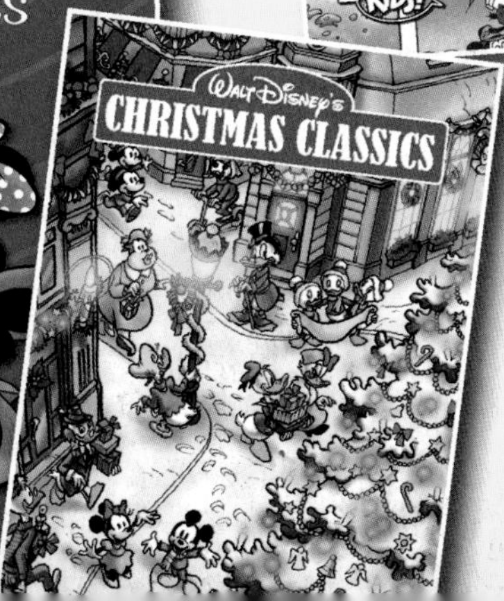
Walt Disney's
CHRISTMAS CLASSICS

WALT DISNEY'S VALENTINE'S CLASSICS

Love is in the air for Mickey Mouse, Donald Duck and the rest of the gang. But will Cupid's arrows cause happiness or heartache? Find out in this collection of classic stories featuring work by Carl Barks, Floyd Gottfredson, Daan Jippes, Romano Scarpa and Al Taliaferro.

HC $24.99 ISBN 9781608865499

WALT DISNEY'S CHRISTMAS CLASSICS

BOOM Kids! has raided the Disney publishing archives and searched every nook and cranny to find the best and the greatest Christmas stories from Disney's vast comic book publishing history for this "best of" compilation.

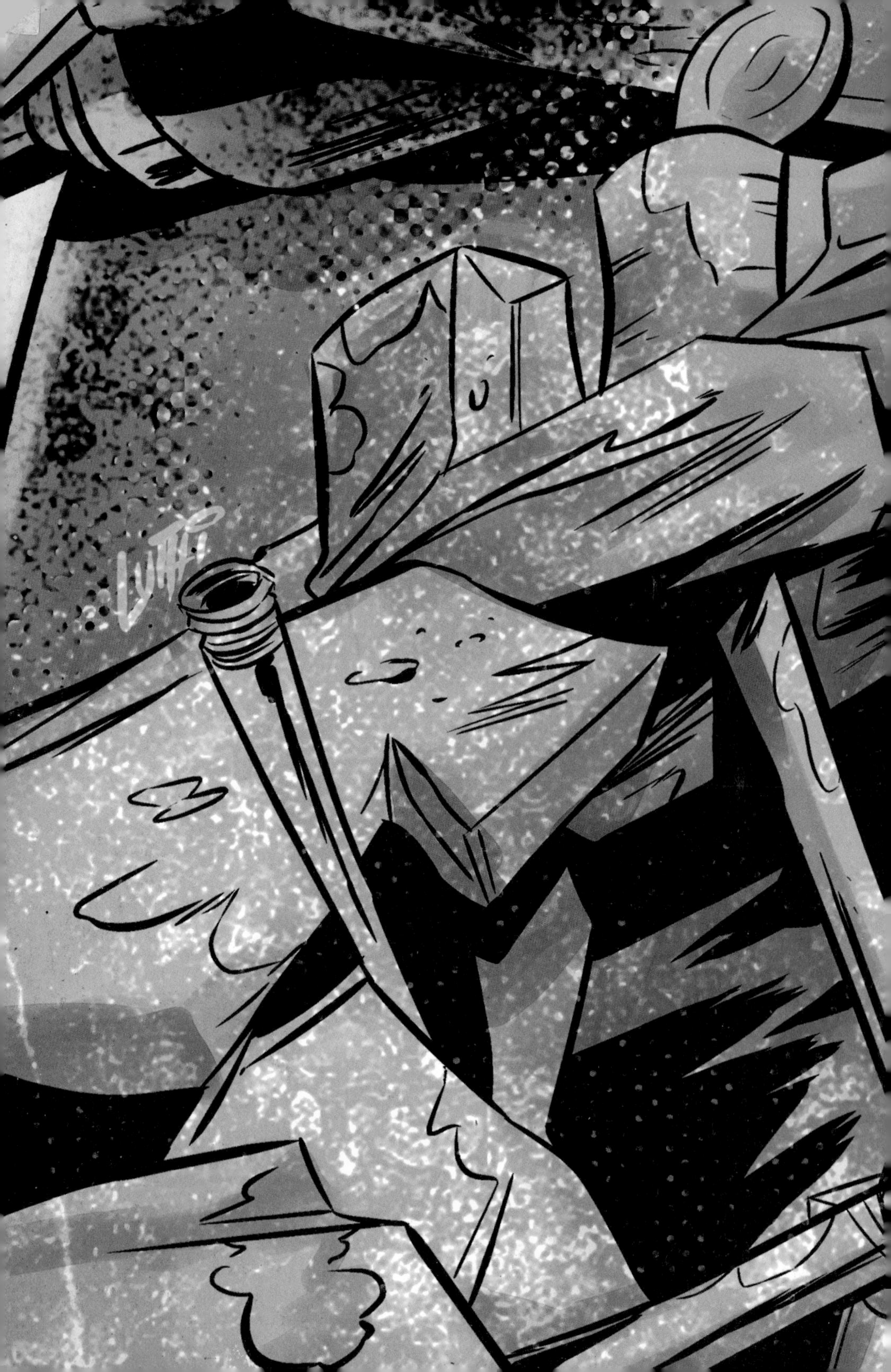